SINS OF
PROMETHEUS

BY:
ZACHARY
HILL

Published by White Feather Press. (www.whitefeatherpress.com)

ISBN 978-1-61808-083-7

Printed in the United States of America

Cover design created by Ron Bell of AdVision Design Group
(www.advisiondesigngroup.com)

White Feather Press

Reaffirming Faith in God, Family, and Country!

Here's a list of other great
White Feather Press Titles !

Uprising USA by George Hill

Uprising UK by George Hill

Uprising Italia by Zachary Hill

Blood and Tequila by Colin Webster

Blood on the Mississippi by Colin Webster

Available on amazon
and anywhere books are sold.

1

ALMA HAD SEEN A LOT IN HER SHORT EIGHTEEN YEARS OF LIFE. She had moved from Mexico to the U.S. with her mother when she was seven, got a new step dad at ten, began learning to shoot at eleven, entered professional shooting competitions at thirteen, saw the war start at age fifteen and watched the world end at seventeen.

It was a busy life.

It was about to get busier. Winter was ending and it was time to move out.

She woke up on what would be her last full day in what had been her stepfather's home. Her old familiar bed was warm, comfortable and smelt like everything she knew. Alma didn't want to get up and laid there while her alarm continued buzzing.

"Keep crying, you little turd and I'll smash you. Throw you right through the window. I'll do it too."

After a few restless minutes she threw the alarm clock against the wall and crawled out of bed. It shattered in a satisfying way. Good: because if it didn't she would have continued throwing it until it did shatter.

Alma walked through the silent house for the last time. Only the sound of her bare feet on the polished wooden floors echoed through the empty house.

She stopped in the living room in front of the window that nearly filled the wall and looked out at the graveyard of Las Vegas and its lone tower. For eleven months the house and the city had been painfully quiet. The sun hadn't cleared the mountains and the city was just a pink and purple jumble of shadows. There were no lights marking its presence anymore.

Vegas had been fun. She loved seeing shows with her family. She loved the lake and walking down the Strip. All of that was gone now.

She had to leave. She had to find her brother. She was in Vegas and Alex was a Marine in Virginia Beach. If anyone survived through all of this it would be him. He had to survive.

Her dreams told her so. For the past three months she had been having the same or similar dreams. In the dreams all her family were dead, but Alex was no where to be found. He wasn't with her and he wasn't with the corpses. He was somewhere else.

When 99.9% of the planet dies off in an artificially created super plague the odds that he lived were slim to say the least, but she had to try. There was no way he died and left her alone in all of this. No, he was out there somewhere.

After a year of waiting in a dead city she was ready. She would find Alex or she would die trying. She couldn't just sit on her butt doing nothing while expecting to be rescued.

When the plague first hit she and her stepfather, Derrick, hid out in their house and didn't leave. But then Derrick kept getting sicker and sicker. By the time he passed the hospitals were full of dead and dying people and the 911 dispatchers weren't answering anymore. She heard gunshots in the distance, cars racing by and alarms sounding all over the neighborhood. That lasted about two weeks and then everything went silent and stayed silent. She found that she missed the chaotic noise.

Three weeks from the start of the plague to the end. That was all it took. Three weeks and she was alone. She had no one. Only Alex.

She shook her head and walked to the kitchen. Her shelves were full of scavenged cans and she picked out a can of corned beef hash. She would have liked to have some eggs or bacon with it, but those hadn't lasted long. Now it was canned or nothing. Just one more side-effect of the plague.

The plague that the government unleashed on its enemies hit the civilians just as hard. It also hit the rest of the world as well. They had neglected to tell anyone about it until it was already across the oceans. Desperation made people do stupid things; stupid like going across the country after the end of the world kind of stupid.

China invaded California, almost all of South America invaded Texas, Arizona and New Mexico, and Russia leading the E.U. invaded the North East from Canada. It was very desperate.

Alma never really paid attention to the news until the war broke out. Some people on the news, sitting behind important looking desks, said America deserved what it got. Others wearing tacky suits and lots of jewelry said that it was going to be America's finest moment as they were about to be delivered by God.

Most of all she blamed the Chinese. After taking California they made a fall offensive into Nevada and bombed Las Vegas. One of their bombs hit the hospital where her mother had been working.

Bastards.

Her mother had survived draught in Sonora, cartel hit squads and corrupt Mexican army units. And she died because some Chinese pilot dropped a bomb on the hospital where she worked. If she and a Chinese man were the only ones left alive on the entire planet, she'd shoot him.

The Chinese were on their way here when the plague broke out. She remembered seeing the news on-line where the large red arrows representing the Chinese armies swooped right into Nevada, heading to Vegas.

All the news after that dealt mostly with the bodies stacking up into small mountains. She could still smell the stench of bodies wherever she went. Vegas always stank and she kept hoping that she'd get used to it. But the smell greeted her every morning.

After breakfast she went to the dinning room where everything she was taking with her was laid out for her to look over one last time. She couldn't afford to forget anything. She was justifiably paranoid about it. After all, if something happened she couldn't just dial 911.

On the table was everything she'd own for the foreseeable future. She had her poncho/tarp, hatchet, multi tool, survival knife, combat knife, crowbar, fire starter kit, matches, duct tape, twist ties, mess kit, water filter, first aid kit, wire saw, 550 cord, flashlight (the kind you shake), compass, personal hygiene kit, broken down MRE's, iPod, extra clothes and socks, AR-15 carbine with ACOG, twelve magazines and 300 rounds of ammo. Glock 34, 9mm, four mags and sixty rounds of ammo.

This was going to be a heavy pack, especially when she filled the built in camelback with water. But she was tough. If Alex could carry a pack around all day, so could she.

The guns and ammo, she could thank her step father for. It had been their way to bond. Though she never came to love him like a father, they had been buddies. He taught her all about competition shooting and she had been on her way to the top before things went south. A local gun company sponsored her and she wore their logo on her shirt whenever she competed.

She loved the thrill of the competition. She loved the rush of running and shooting, and especially of winning. She was always a competitive person and

Derrick said it would be good for her. She never understood why it would be good for her, but she loved it more than almost anything else.

The AR and Glock were her competition guns. She knew those weapons more than she knew her school work. She had been a straight 'C' student. She had never been good with English and that was always frustrating. Even now she still spoke with an accent and she hated to be reminded of it. Every time a store clerk or waiter asked her to repeat herself she wanted to tackle the person and strangle the life out of them.

She hadn't spoken to anyone in eleven months and right now she wouldn't mind if they hated her accent. It got boring talking to herself.

Books and movies kept her sane. Some of her friends had called her step father a "wacko survivalist" because he had installed solar panels on the house. Without electricity she would have gone nuts.

The world may have ended but she at least had her *Disturbed, Korn, 10 years* and *Flyleaf* to keep her company.

She ate her fill of the canned food that remained and watched the last movie she would watch in a very long time. She chose "*Tropic Thunder*" because she needed to laugh. She needed to laugh more and more lately.

Next she put on her best khaki cargo pants, lace up boots, Rob Zombie shirt, pistol belt, tactical vest, backpack, carbine and sunglasses. She tied her long hair (that kept getting longer because she was too lazy to cut it) in a pony tail, and put in the earbuds of her iPod.

The last thing she did was write a note and stuck it on the fridge. It was a note to Alex telling him where she was going.

Then she was out the door and clumsily got on her bicycle. It wasn't one of those wimp ten speeds that the people in spandex always rode. This was an off road bicycle. She would need it.

She looked back one last time at her home. It was a beautiful house. Her mother had picked it out. Now all she had of her was a photo in her wallet and the crucifix around her neck.

The morning streets of her old neighborhood felt like a graveyard. All the houses were silent and dark. Some had broken windows and open doors. She had already searched them all long ago. Their owners didn't mind anymore.

She'd make her way to the city, looting food as she went so she wouldn't use up her carry supply and then hit -15 and head North. From Utah she'd take 70 all the way to St. Louis and then take 64 to Virginia Beach.

Simple. No problem.

Right?

Okay, maybe not.

This plan was insane and she knew it. It would take a long time traveling through places she had never been. The world was changed now. She had no idea what to expect. There were sure to be survivors out there. Some would be friendly. Most would not. Whatever she found, she'd make sure to keep her mind sharp and her guns ready.

2

Alma, Las Vegas

ALMA SPENT THE FIRST NIGHT AWAY FROM THE HOUSE IN A HOTEL room on the strip. From her room on the fifth floor she saw a single light somewhere off in the city. She didn't need or want to find the source of the light. Someone else was still alive out there but she had no desire to find them. The casino's kitchen had some canned fruit that she scarfed down while lying in the bed and trying not to think of all the horrible things that could happen to her out on the road.

Was this the stupidest thing she had ever done? Probably.

She knew how to use a gun more than most people knew how to walk, but that didn't make her invincible. Alma imagined being tied up in some freak's shack while he looked through a book of cannibal recipes. There was also worse things that could happen to a young woman that was by herself.

Taking a life wasn't what bothered her though. She had never done it but knew she could. If someone got in her way, she'd kill them. It was as simple as that. She had no patience for idiots, weakness or obstacles. She had something to do and she was going to do it no matter what.

Eat bugs? Sure.

Sleep outside in the cold? Sure.

Trek across a desert? Why not?

Kill someone? No problem.

In the morning she made her way down to the lobby of the casino where she left her bike. The glass in the lobby was broken from the riots that happened when people realized that the world was ending. They came here for money as if that would save them. Idiots.

People were really stupid sometimes.

She walked her bike out into the street that was filled with garbage, dead cars and tumble weeds. The streets were clear in some areas but not in others. Crashed cars, a tipped over fire truck and the remains of a National Guard barricade were some of the clutter. If she had a car she wouldn't have been able to make it out. Trash and tumbleweeds were everywhere. Brown, scraggly grass was sticking up through cracks in the cement. A year with no people around made a big difference to the place.

Even if she did have a car she wouldn't have any fuel for it. The gas stations were the first places to run out. Before the news went out they kept showing the same footage of a gas station surrounded by honking cars. The ever-serious looking anchor always commented about it being the same all over the country.

She rode down one of the side streets running north, parallel to the Strip. If someone was alive they'd probably be watching the Strip and she didn't want to stop and chat.

Alma kept peddling until she was nearly out of the city. She came to a stop when she saw a new car lot. Many of the cars were still there.

"That's dumb, Alma. Even if one of those cars started, the roads out of the city are blocked," she said to herself.

"But what if it's a 4x4? We could go around the traffic jam. See? I'm going to go look."

She pulled up at the front door. It was locked but like all show rooms it was almost all glass. Her hatchet that was strapped to her pack broke the glass easily and she invited herself in. Her boots crunched on the broken glass and the wind from outside kicked up the layers of dust.

She found the office where the keys would be, in a metal box on the wall. Locked but her crowbar opened it up for her. The owners wouldn't mind.

She grabbed all the keys and went outside. The cars had been sitting there for a long time and she was no mechanic. If they didn't start for her then they simply weren't going to start.

Neither of her parents had been very good mechanics. Derrick was a banker and mother was a doctor. They didn't need to know how to fix things, they just paid others to do it.

She tried a big four wheeler truck. After finding the keys she tried to start it but no curse words seemed to work good enough. She tried a few other trucks but nothing, just dead engines.

When a truck failed to start she tossed the keys on the ground and spit on them. Next she tried the three SUV's they had. None of them worked. They were as dead as the rest of the city. A few choice four-letter-words escaped her lips as each car failed to start.

The thought of peddling her stupid bike all the way across country kept her trying more cars. Something had to work.

Then she tried an open topped jeep. She turned the key and the engine made a sick, gasping sound.

"Come on, baby!"

She turned the key and the engine made a few more wheezes. On the third try the engine sputtered to life. She ran over and threw her pack and bike in the back and then rolled out onto the street.

She never had a drivers license because the government limited them due to fuel shortages from the war. She checked the gas gauge and saw that she had half a tank. She had no idea how far that would get her at the best of times and the engine here was sputtering and acting sick, like it wanted to die at any moment.

She took the narrow, but clear, side streets out of the city and where the roads were crammed with dead cars she just took it to the dirt and drove along side the clogged I-15. It was slow but much, much faster than riding her bike. Miles and miles of rusting cars lined both the incoming and outgoing lanes. The plague had been faster than the traffic.

She saw that some of the cars were burned. Others had bodies, now mummified from being trapped in the heat of a car. She sped past without paying too much attention. She was concentrating on not running into some unseen ditch. The sight of dead bodies didn't effect her anymore. Now they were just part of the scenery.

After a few minutes, she was free of the mass of dead cars and back on the road. The open topped jeep felt great. It didn't sound great and kept threatening to die on her, but she was moving and that's what she cared about.

The wind blew her hair and heavy rock played from her headphones. It was good to be alive. Better alive than a mummy trapped in a car.

Alma breathed in the clean air now that she was away from the city. It felt better now that she was on the open road. She was free and ready for anything.

3

DRIVING IN THE SPUTTERING JEEP SHE PASSED A FEW TOWNS THAT were eerily silent. There were faded billboards and rusted road signs. The road had more cracks in it than it should have but the world hadn't fallen apart yet. The empty windows stared at her like eyes watching her every move.

The mountains were becoming taller and more jagged and she saw that she'd have to enter a canyon further ahead. A canyon was a great place to be ambushed. She knew she'd have to pass through here. If the jeep could make it she could make it through in no time and then the view would open back up. The worst would be over.

She slung the single-point sling of her AR and kept it ready to go. If she was about to get ambushed then she could at least make them pay for it. She wasn't about to be some weak, helpless victim. Screw that.

Alma wanted to gun it and tear through the canyon like a bat out of hell, but the faster she went, the less gas mileage she'd get and she was down to less than a quarter of a tank. If she couldn't find gas in St. George then she'd be peddling it from then on.

She kept her eyes scanning left and right like she was in a pop-up target course. Any sign of movement would get her full attention.

"*Venga aqui, putos*! I got something for you," she said, daring the imaginary attackers to come.

She turned down her iPod which was charging in the Jeep's cigarette lighter. Shame, it was "*Birthday Massacre*," one of her favorite groups. But listening for an ambush was a little more important than a good song.

About fifteen minutes into the long, narrow canyons with walls that claustrophobically towered over her, she saw a lone figure walking along the road. It looked like a man with a beard, backpack and scruffy clothes that looked filthy even from this distance. He had evidently heard her coming and was waving his arms. He didn't appear to be armed.

She wasn't going to trust in appearances. The nice guy down the block could be wearing people's skin in his basement at night. You never know.

She drove past him and stopped, turning off the engine to save gas. This was stupid. What if she couldn't get it started again? What if this guy was a creep?

But this creep was the first living human she had seen in eleven months. Her curiosity and desire to talk to someone other than herself made her stop.

She kept her carbine slung to her side and kept her hand on the butt of her pistol. He was still a good fifty yards away and she didn't want him to get much closer.

She turned around in her seat and saw that the man had stopped as well. He was holding his sunglasses in his hand and his eyes were wide. But it wasn't the wide eyes of surprise.

"Ca...can I get a ride?" The man called out.

"Who are you and where are you going?" She asked.

"I'm Robert. I'm just going I guess."

The man had a strange smile and a notably intense look in his eyes. He hadn't taken the end of the world very well.

"Stay right there, don't come any closer," she said.

He stopped and put his hands up.

"I won't hurt you. I just need a ride. Do you have any food? Any pot?"

"Pot? What would I be carrying pot around for?"

"You know, the world's gone to hell. Why not enjoy it, right?"

She had never smoked pot or even a cigarette for that matter, but she imagined that dulling her senses was the last thing she wanted to do at a time like this. As it was, she wasn't sure the senses she had were good enough.

"I don't have any drugs or alcohol," she said.

The man dropped his arms and looked frustrated.

"You have to have something! Pills? Medication? A smart, pretty girl like you has to know where some stuff is."

She didn't like the way he said 'pretty.'

"Sorry, don't have any."

"I got things to trade. Gold? How about some nice gold rings for a screw?"

"A what? Oh, hell no. You just back right off *puto* and don't come near me."

"Come on! Let's have some fun. Why not, right?"

This bum was strung out and definitely unwashed. Also, she wasn't a hooker. He seemed to not understand that part.

"I'm going to get back in my jeep and drive away," she said.

"Come on, gorgeous! We could make a great team! Think of the fun we could have!"

"*No gracias.*"

She backed away to her jeep and quickly got in. She turned the key and the engine just coughed.

"What's the matter? Can't start your car?" The man laughed.

Then she saw in her mirror that he had started walking towards her again. Yes, she had her gun, but now that she was faced with the actual chance of killing someone, she found that she didn't know if she could. He didn't have a weapon.

She tried the engine again and it just coughed and sputtered some more. She checked the mirror and saw that he was walking faster now.

"*Pinche coche!*" She swore.

She drew her pistol across her stomach with her left hand and got it ready while she continued to try the key with her right.

"Keep away," she said to him.

"I just want to talk," he said. His voice was getting closer.

He was definitely dangerous and she wanted nothing to do with him.

Then the jeep started. As soon as the engine wheezed to life the man broke out into a sprint towards her. She gunned the gas.

The man grabbed the door of the jeep and looked right at her. He had wild, blue eyes, yellow teeth and dirt all over his face. Underneath all of his disgusting filthiness he looked young.

"Don't go! Don't go!" He shouted as she picked up speed.

He tried to keep up but had to let go and fall back.

She watched him shrink away in the rear view mirror. After recovering from stumbling she saw that he was yelling something and was glad she couldn't hear it over the engine.

Her heart was racing and she kept looking back to make sure he was gone.

Alma's first contact with a survivor and it hadn't been a pleasant one. But she had lived and that was a good thing.

She calmed back down about the time the canyon opened up and she felt safer again. That had been stupid. Next time she wouldn't stop unless she knew it was safe and she needed something. Men couldn't be trusted. She knew she was pretty and knew that lonely guys would want one thing.

If Brad Pitt or Rob Zombie survived, then maybe she'd think about it.

4

Alma, Southern Utah, 1-15

SOUTHERN UTAH WAS REDDER THAN NEVADA. IT LOOKED MORE like some Martian landscape than the United States. That or an old Western. Maybe she should get a cowboy hat. They had cowboys in Utah, right?

Utah was full of Mormons. Did that mean there'd be less creepy men or more?

She was Catholic but she honestly never paid much attention to church stuff. The war started just after her quincenero and that had been the last time she had stepped foot in a church.

Her AR was from Utah. A company named 'Crusader Weaponry' custom built her gun just as she wanted it. Then with the permanent lubrication treatment she wouldn't have to worry about carrying gun oil everywhere she went. Not worrying about the quality of her weapon was one less hassle she had to deal with. The same guys also worked over her Glock to friction free perfection.

So, Utah couldn't be all bad.

Then her jeep shook, sputtered and died. She coasted to a stop and tried to start it again but no matter how she tried, it wouldn't start or even make a sound. Dead was dead.

The sun was going down and here was as good a place to spend the night as anywhere else. She dug through her bag and pulled out a black hoodie and scarf. It still got cold at night and now she was regretting considering a sleeping bag as a "luxury." First sporting goods store she came across she'd fix that problem.

She lay down in the backseat of the jeep and looked up at the stars. If one good thing came out of the end of the world it was that she could see the stars again. The lights of Vegas washed them out almost completely but now she could see them how they were meant to be seen.

Growing up in the old world she had never seen the Milky Way. Now she couldn't help but see the misty river roll across the sky. On her fourteenth birthday Derrick had bought her a telescope and she remembered going out on a freezing night to look at the stars. It was the first time she realized that stars are different colors. Strange how she had never noticed before then. Now she couldn't help but notice.

She was freezing but it wasn't so bad because she had a great view.

After a while of freezing she put on more layers of clothing and wrapped up in her rain poncho. It wasn't great but it was tolerable. She fell asleep and only woke up a few times during the night.

She also wasn't prepared for the absolute darkness night brought. It was dark and silent like death. When her side or arms fell asleep she rolled over and tried to go back to sleep while ignoring the dangers that existed out in the world.

In the morning, as the sky turned purple before the sunrise, she strapped on her pack and got on her bike.

"You got me here, little jeep. *Gracias*," she said with a curtsy she saw in a movie once.

Then she began peddling towards St. George. On the up hills she had to dismount and push her bike and on the down slopes she got a free ride. Riding with a pack was a pain in the butt, but it beat walking.

Shortly before noon she came to a sign that was hanging on by one screw. The wind beat it in an arhythmic pattern, like a crappy drummer. Once she got close enough she saw that it said "St. George 12 miles."

About an hour later she arrived at the outskirts of St. George. As she rode into the silent city she began to sort out her priorities.

1. Water. 2. Food. 3. Car with gas. 4. Sleeping bag.

She came to a gas station that didn't look too looted. Sugary snacks were scattered all over the floor and all the beer was gone. But soda and bottled water still remained. She drank down a whole bottle of water and threw a couple more in her pack. There was a can of Spam left on the shelf. Spam had a tab you just pulled and opened the can. Good thing because she had forgotten a can opener.

5. Can opener.

She would have killed for a coke, but sugar would only dehydrate her more. It was better to drink water and live, but not by much.

After leaving the convenience store her next assignment was to look for a grocery store and a sporting goods store.

She rode on and saw a grocery store with broken windows and weeds growing up through cracks in the parking lot. Almost everything in it was gone. But they did have a can opener at least and one can of peas. She hated peas. There were very few things she detested more than peas. Peas were up there with pedophiles and serial rapists.

But she'd do anything to survive so she ate the peas.

She left the grocery store feeling all healthy and crap, but not satisfied. She'd murder a small kitten for a good carne asada. She knew her uncle's recipe for it. All she needed was a cow.

Alma put her hand up to her brow to block the sun and looked over the dust covered city. The desert would reclaim this place soon enough. Without people the place was unlivable.

As she rode through the city she noticed signs of life. She saw crudely painted signs saying "this way to hell," "stay away" and "Abandon all hope, ye who enter here." She avoided those areas and rode on.

When she found a used car lot she hurried over and looted the keys. Then she went through them all, not caring what kind of vehicle.

None of them started. She would have been happy with the biggest piece of junk ever as long as it worked. But none of them did. It was just her and her bike for now.

She sighed and then mounted the bike again. The jeep must have been a fluke.

Alma didn't find a sporting goods place but she did find a Walmart. It had also been looted, but not very well. It was dark inside without the numerous lights all over and she broke out her rechargeable flashlight. She found a good, black sleeping bag and ate one of three cans of ravioli. The other two she tossed in her pack. She found bottled water, drank it and wandered to the book section.

One thing she had not thought to bring was something to read. She had never really read books before, but when the world was dead there was little else to do. She found that she actually really liked them.

She found a teen paranormal romance book about a witch that falls in love with a demon. Of course the demon looks like a hot teenage boy and not some horrible hell spawn.

The book was thrown into an outside pocket of her digi-camo backpack and she walked to the front of the store. By the checkout aisles there were small fridges with soda in them. It was all warm now because there was no power, but she grabbed a Mountain Dew. Dew was good warm or cold. Maybe dehydration was worth a good soda after all.

She gulped it down remembering the long lost flavor. It was a piece of the old world and it helped her remember. She remembered Derrick buying her the customary soda after a tournament. After a long day of competition shooting they'd sit in the parking lot of the convenience store and drink in silence.

She left the store and grabbed her bike from where it was leaning against the stone wall. In the distance she saw a thin, grey strand of smoke. It didn't look like an out of control fire like she had seen in Vegas. This looked deliberate and man made. Maybe someone was cooking something.

A part of her wanted to go find the source of the smoke and find out what the person knew. Was the rest of the world really as bad off as this? Did they know of any groups of survivors? Transportation?

But then she thought of all the negatives and changed her mind. She didn't want some psycho wearing her skin and telling his cannibal buddies how tender her back muscles were.

She would keep going.

Alma continued on I-15 heading north. It was all up hill going out of the city so she walked her bike. From the hill she could look down on St. George. In the middle was a large white church. It seemed strangely out of place. It had to be a Mormon thing. They seemed to like white.

When she finally got to the top she was relieved to finally get back on and start riding again. Walking was too slow. She felt the wind rush by her face and it felt good. It meant she was moving toward Alex.

She was so busy enjoying the wind that she almost didn't see the person walking along the side of the road. Alma immediately stopped the bike and raised her carbine with both hands. She looked through the x4 power ACOG to get a better view.

It was a woman. It was a tall, lanky, red headed woman. She had on a cowboy hat and was pushing a shopping cart full of food. She also had a long rifle on her back, a PSL, a poor man's Dragunov. It was basically an AK scaled up for a bigger round and stretched for accuracy. All she saw of the girl was her back and straight, red hair.

Alma lowered her carbine and thought for a moment. The girl had plenty of food, was armed, alone and most importantly, she was a girl. That meant no hungry eyes or wandering hands. She also wouldn't have any "stupid juice" or testosterone as some called it.

She wanted to speak to someone and learn something; anything. This was the best chance she'd get. She just hoped the girl wasn't a fiery as her hair and would start shooting at her before she even had a chance to speak.

Gathering the courage, she took a deep breath and rode fast to catch up to the red headed woman.

5

Alma, Southern Utah, I-15

THE RED HEAD WOMAN TURNED AND SAW ALMA COMING. IT WAS still too far away to get a look at her face, but she looked young. The woman immediately unslung her PSL and put the butt up to her shoulder, but kept the barrel pointed down. So, at least this woman wasn't trigger happy. Maybe she was curious like she was or desperate for company.

She hoped this girl was sane because she really didn't want to deal with another crazy person.

Alma could tell the red head was nervous because she kept fidgeting and adjusting her rifle while constantly looking to her sides.

Alma came to a stop about thirty feet away and held up her hands. Now she could get a good look at this chick. She was either late teens or early twenties, freckles and bright green eyes. She was tall and scrawny with a narrow but long nose and a large, flat mouth. She wore simple jeans and a faded gray T-shirt that she couldn't make out because the woman held the PSL in front of her.

The red head looked at her with wide eyes and she moved her mouth as if she were about to speak but kept stopping herself. It was fun to watch so many obvious emotions spread across this girl's face. Either she was out of practice (which was understandable) or she was the type to always show her emotions to the world.

"I ain't going to hurt you," Alma said loudly and clearly.

"Wh...who are you?" The girl asked in a quiet, shy voice, almost like she was afraid to hear herself speak.

"I'm Alma Attaway. I'm uh...I'm coming up from Vegas. What's your name?"

"Cassidy McCready."

"Where you from?"

"Just down the road."

Cassidy pointed with her thumb but quickly put her hand back on the rifle.

"I'm traveling alone. What about you?"

Cassidy thought about the question for a moment. Alma could see all the different responses playing through Cassidy's mind. She had to show this girl that she could be trusted so she admitted that she was alone. A smart person probably would have said that her whole gang was close behind.

Time to see if Cassidy would follow her example of honesty.

"Yeah, I'm alone," Cassidy said.

This was the first real person she had met in months. The crazy guy didn't count. This girl wouldn't try things with her and didn't look like a bandit. She would be safer if she traveled with this girl. Strength in numbers.

"Listen, let me put it to you straight," Alma said. "We're both young, reasonably attractive females and there's no more law. What do you think will happen if a gang comes by here?"

Cassidy looked down to the ground, obviously uncomfortable. Alma knew Cassidy had thought of it too.

"I'm a girl. You're a girl. We need a little girl power, right?" Alma said.

Cassidy looked up and squinted.

"How do I know you're not some weirdo?" Cassidy asked.

"Hey, I probably am, I could use years of therapy after all this, we all could. But I'm more likely to walk around in circles talking to myself than hurt you."

"Have you met any other survivors?"

"Just one psycho that thought I was a hooker."

The hint of a smile crossed her wide mouth and she scanned the area again. Good, she wasn't an idiot. She was staying observant incase this was all a distraction.

"You know how to use that weapon?" Alma asked.

"My dad used to take me hunting," Cassidy said.

Hunting animals and hunting people were very different things. Hunting was as different from fighting as target practice was. Its good to know but there are certain skills that had to be practiced like rapid reloads, tactical reloads, quick draw, fast target acquisition and a billion others.

"You going grocery shopping there?" Alma pointed to the grocery cart.

"Yeah."

"I had a nice place with solar power back in Vegas. Property value's gone down, but the neighbors kept quiet."

"Why would you leave that?" The big mouthed red head asked. She looked up from her feet and met her eyes for only a brief moment.

"Vegas was running out of water and I need to find my brother."

"He's alive?"

"Hell if I know. If he is then he's at Virginia Beach. That's where I'm heading."

"That's across the country."

"I noticed. Got a long way to go, right? You should come with."

"That's kind of far."

"It'll be fun! We'll talk about that later. Let's go to your place."

Cassidy hesitated. Had she pushed too hard? Getting Cassidy on her side was like fishing. If she started too strong the line would break. She waited for the reply while trying to figure out other arguments to use if she was rejected. She wasn't coming up with many. Cassidy had every right to be scared. This new world gave "Stranger Danger" a whole new list of meanings.

"Sure," Cassidy said.

She let out a sigh of relief got off her bike and walked alongside Cassidy.

"That's a fancy gun you got there. AR-15?" Cassidy asked.

"*Claro que si*! I used to shoot competition!"

"You any good?"

"The trophies said I was, but my stepdad kept saying I could do better. Matter of opinion, I guess."

"You came all the way from Las Vegas on a bike?"

"Well, no. I borrowed a jeep but it broke down just south of St. George."

"Oh."

They walked down I-15 for a mile or two until they came to a small dirt road. There was nothing all around but miles of desert, scraggly looking brush and rocks that she kept tripping over. Screw this hiking crap. It was hot and her feet hurt.

She followed Cassidy down the road for another hour before coming into view of a small ranch. There were dried up fields behind it and a stable that looked like it was ready to collapse.

"This your house?" Alma asked.

"Yes."

It was a single story, sprawling ranch house with boarded up windows and two dead cars out front. The house had a few brown trees beside it like the least promising oasis ever.

"We used to grow alfalfa for the nearby ranchers," Cassidy said. She pointed to the dried up fields.

Alma had no idea what alfalfa was or why ranchers would want it, but she nodded anyways.

When they got to the door Cassidy turned around.

"I...I wasn't expecting guests but whatever I have is yours," she said with a desperate smile. It was the first smile she'd seen from Cassidy, but it showed more uneasiness than happiness. The safety was still off on Cassidy's rifle.

"Thanks."

"Please, come in."

Cassidy opened the door and ushered her in.

The living room looked more like a warehouse full of everything that could ever possibly be useful. There were plastic tubs, buckets, boxes, and shelves of canned food, ammo, tools, parts and even books. It was like the neatest, most organized hoarder ever.

"I've been foraging for a while," Cassidy said, shifting her weight around and looking off to the sides like she was embarrassed.

"You're not about to run out of anything for a while, are you?"

"Well, sort of. The well out back is going dry."

"Always problems with the water. That's what happens when we live in a desert, Cass."

Cassidy gave a nervous, quick laugh.

"I got plenty of food," Cassidy said, quickly. "I got beans, carrots, peas, tomatoes, peaches, honey, anything you want, I got it."

"Awesome. I'm hungry!"

Cassidy smiled, unslung her PSL and leaned it against the wall. She kept the 1911 in the leather holster on her hip. Now that Alma could see Cassidy's T-shirt. It said "Zoso."

"Led Zeppelin! Right on!" Alma said.

Cassidy looked down at her shirt.

"I love them guys. Haven't heard them since everything happened. Haven't heard much at all. I like the Rolling Stones and the Eagles a lot, but also Guns and Roses, though I don't consider them Classic Rock at all. Same with Bon Jovi. I mean, just because he's old doesn't mean he's classic."

Once she got talking, it was like going down hill on a skateboard, it just kept going faster and faster. Maybe she could get along with this crazy girl.

Cassidy then hurried off towards what Alma assumed was the kitchen.

Alma set her pack down but kept her AR slung to her side and her hand near her pistol. Maybe Cassidy had a giant, deformed cousin that liked to keep cute girls for pets in the basement.

She followed Cassidy into the kitchen which was stocked full of canned food. She hadn't seen that much food since before the plague. The old floorboards creaked under her feet. The dark wood was stained from age and the whole house had this kind of Antique Road Show look to it.

"Cass, where'd you get so much food?" She could guess but now that Cass was talking she wanted to keep it going. She wanted this girl to trust her. She needed this girl. She needed someone to talk to and someone to watch her back.

She also wondered if she had gone a little crazy. It would be strange if she wasn't a little *loca* by now.

Now that she was here, she knew she couldn't leave without bringing this girl with her. The thought of hitting that road alone was too much now. She did good by herself, but now that she remembered what it was like to have someone, she needed it now more than ever.

"The other survivors looked in grocery stores. I looked in people's houses," Cass said.

"Houses?"

"You see, we Mormons like to keep a one year food storage. I got a few years worth here. I don't know how long it'll last though. Good for at least another few years you think?"

So, this was a Mormon. Not as weird as she thought they'd be, but still weird.

Cassidy fixed them up some chili and cooked on an old fashioned iron stove. She used dried brush for fuel which stank but burned real good. It took longer than a real stove, but this was something she'd have to get used to.

Once the chili was ready Cassidy took her to what used to be the TV room, but the TV wasn't there anymore, just a rack of hunting rifles. The whole house had an earthy, small, once was fashionable in the early '70's, feel to it. It even had fake wood walls.

Alma sank into the lime green easy chair and sighed. She hadn't been this comfortable since she left Vegas and all that riding made her legs and butt sore.

"Not, bad, huh?" Cassidy asked with a mouthful of chili.

Cass was smiling but the clasp on her leather holster was undone. Smart of her, but it showed that Alma still had a ways to go.

"So, Cass, have you heard any news about the outside world? I haven't heard a thing since they stopped broadcasting."

"No, nothing. I've been holed up here. No radio or anything."

Cassidy shook her head and kept her eyes on her food.

This felt strange to be sitting and talking like old times. She hadn't had a real conversation in so long.

"This was your family's house?" Alma asked.

Cassidy's smile faded away.

"Yeah, me, my parents and my five brothers and sisters."

"So, it's true. Mormons do have large families."

"I thought that was for Catholics."

Cassidy pointed to the crucifix hanging out from her shirt.

"I guess you guys got us beat," Alma said.

"What about you? Any siblings?"

"Got one brother. A Marine out in Virginia Beach. I'm going to find him."

"And you really think your brother's still alive?"

"He has to be."

Alma knew the chances were slim to nothing, but she had had that strange dream and it wouldn't leave her mind. She wasn't about to tell Cassidy that she was following a dream. She didn't want to seem crazy.

"I got some candles. If you want we can stay up and talk. I haven't talked to anyone in a long time," Cassidy said, stating the obvious.

Alma smiled and nodded and tried to act cool.

"Sure. Sounds fun."

6

Cassidy. Southern Utah. Ranch house.

CASSIDY TRIED TO EYE ALMA UP WITHOUT LOOKING LIKE SHE WAS staring. She looked like a good person. She wanted to believe she was. Beggars couldn't be choosers and Alma was definitely a beggar.

What she needed was a mutant power like Professor X, then she could read Alama's mind and find out if she was good or not. That would make life much simpler.

She had been praying and praying to find someone; someone that wasn't crazy or some other kind of horrible criminal. She needed people. She had been alone for so long that it was starting to hurt physically.

As long as she could remember, she had been ignored in school and hadn't met anyone she could call a friend. But she had always had her family. Science fiction, fantasy and comics had been her friends. One of her life dreams before the world ended was to go to comic-con. Now her dream was to survive.

All her life she had been surrounded by her wonderful, loving family. They were gone and their absence left a hole larger than she could have imagined. Her little brother would never grow up and get married. She'd never see them off to college or their missions. Their futures and potentials were all gone.

Maybe that was what hurt the most, their lost potential. They could have been anything. They could have played hilariously stupid games and they could have visited each other while watching their children play together.

The house had felt so empty but now Alma was here. Was that a normal Mexican name? Alma was a male prophet from the book of Mormon. Why name a girl after a man? No, Alma had one of those crosses around her neck, so she was Catholic.

Alma would have been considered pretty even before the End Times. Alma had long, gorgeous black hair, large, but well formed mouth and huge, brown eyes. She was thin but with the round hips and butt that most guys seemed to like. How'd she manage to be skinny but curvy at the same time? It wasn't fair. Whenever she looked in a mirror all she saw was skin and bone.

Alma was also really short. It didn't help that she was tall so when she stood by Alma, the difference was exaggerated.

At least she was skin and bone now. Before the End Times she had been kinda chubby. Chubby and homeschooled was not a good combination for dating.

Cassidy lit the candles. She hadn't bothered with them for months. It wasn't like there were any special occasions. Those had died along with her family. There was no point to celebrate when you didn't have someone to celebrate with.

It was hard to realize sometimes that everyone was dead. The graves of her family were out back and she'd go and talk to them sometimes and try to imagine that they heard her.

She knew what happened after death. Her family was in the spirit world awaiting resurrection. She just wished that she could see them sometimes or even feel them. But there was nothing. They were simply gone. Maybe the waiting list to visit living relatives as spirits was too long lately?

"Isn't this nice?" Cassidy asked.

"Yeah," Alma nodded.

Alma seemed to be enjoying the chili. No one had ever liked her cooking before. Maybe Alma was really hungry? Her mother had been like Tony Stark in the kitchen, able to make everything out of anything.

She had always wanted to be like Paul Atreides from "Dune" and be good at everything she tried. Paul could knife fight, put on a still-suit, ride a sandworm and fly ornithopters. He did it all. It seemed that she couldn't do anything right.

She looked over to the shelves of food. If she left, all that would go to waste. She couldn't just leave it. Her mother hated wasting anything. Maybe that was why she had been chubby.

"You grow up around here?" Alma asked.

"I was born in this house. Well, not literally. I even went to school here! I was home taught."

"I went to a private school. An all girls Catholic school. I had to wear white polo shirts. Totally lame."

Cross, Catholic school. Yup, she was Catholic.

"Does your name mean something?" She asked.

"Alma is Spanish for 'soul.' I never liked my name. In English it would be a hippie name."

Cassidy liked listening to Alma talk. It was warm, full of life and she liked the accent. She now wished she had an accent. Alma looked and even sounded cool. With her red hair she could probably pass for Irish. Rouge from X-Men had red hair and had a southern accent. She could do southern with a little practice.

Maybe a lot of practice.

Then Cassidy saw the earplugs dangling from Alma's shirt.

"What do you have there?" She pointed to the earbuds.

"An iPod. Hey, you wanna listen to some Led Zeppelin? I got them on here."

"You have batteries in there? I can listen?"

"Of course."

"Yes, please!"

Alma walked over and handed her the earbuds while she scrolled through the list of music. This was going to be awesome. She'd actually get to listen to music again. This was better than she had hoped for.

"Here we go," Alma said.

Then the sounds of Jimmy Page's electric guitar exploded in her ears. She had forgotten what real music sounded like. It was powerful and it was beautiful. Cassidy didn't realize how much she had missed it.

She let the sounds wash over her and through her. It was a piece of the world that was lost, a piece of joy and comfort. But this was one piece of the old world that they could hang on to for a little while longer. Not everything was lost.

Cassidy could feel her eyes water and tears run down her cheeks as the music's beauty overcame her.

When the song ended she removed the headphones and sat back with her eyes closed.

"Thank you for that," Cassidy said.

"*De nada.*"

"It's been too long."

"Go ahead, listen some more," Alma said.

"Really? Thank you."

She chose another Zeppelin song and closed her eyes. Then she listened to some Eagles, Kansas and Journey. Most of what Alma had was heavy metal stuff, but she did have a good selection of classic rock too.

She could have listened all night but it wouldn't be fair to use up all of Alma's battery. Energy was more precious than gold.

After listening to "Free Bird" she handed the iPod back to Alma.

"You love music, don't you?" Alma said it more as a statement.

"I do. I was learning guitar before everything ended."

"Really? I always wanted to learn. Well, I wanted to learn bass."

"Well, shoot, I can teach you to play bass. It's pretty simple, really."

"Now if we just had a bass."

"It'd have to be acoustic."

"I'd rather have electric."

"Not sure we really have a choice." Cassidy shrugged and put her empty bowl on the coffee table in front of her. Not sure why it was called a coffee table. Her family didn't drink coffee.

"True. Know any good guitar stores?" Alma asked.

"There's one that I know of."

"Maybe we should check it out sometime."

"We could tour the country with our new band. We can be like the Aqua Bats and play shows and fight monsters on the way," Cassidy said.

"I have no idea what you're talking about."

She let Alma sleep in what used to be her parents' room. Aside from cleaning it up she hadn't touched a thing. The bedroom was bigger, bigger closets and its own bathroom, but it just didn't feel right to move in.

In the morning she peeked in to check on Alma and make sure she was still there and not some hallucination that was a sign she had finally lost her mind. She kept her 1911 on her hip just in case Alma turned out to be a lunatic or thief, but she had a good feeling about her.

Alma was spread out, tangled in the sheets and mouth wide open. Apparently she wasn't a very elegant sleeper.

She decided to have breakfast ready. Too bad they didn't have bacon or eggs but she did have bacon Spam and powdered eggs. It would have to do.

She found herself saying that a lot, "It will have to do."

Alma finally stumbled in wearing nothing more than a long "System of a Down" T-shirt and yawning with that giant, toothy mouth of hers.

"Good morning," Cassidy said in her best 'cheerful voice' she could muster.

Alma muttered something and sat down on the stool by the kitchen island.

"I have bacon and eggs. Hungry?"

Alma's eyes shot open.

"Bacon and eggs?"

"Well...kind of, sort of. Try it!"

Cassidy served her up a plate and slid it over.

Alma inhaled it without pause. That probably meant she liked it. That had to be a good sign: Alma was the only person in the world to ever enjoy her cooking.

"Not bad," Alma said.

"Too bad we don't have any orange juice."

"What about water? You said you were running out of water or something?"

"The well out back is down to a trickle."

"Then what'll you do? It does no good to have all this food and no water. We're in a desert and summer's coming."

"I know, I know."

Cassidy had been wondering this for days even though she hated thinking about it. She didn't know what she was supposed to do.

"Come with me. I'm heading north and then east. Maybe we can find someplace nice, you know?"

Cassidy chewed her Spam and thought about it. This was her home. She had everything. Everything except water and companionship.

She was safe here and she had no idea what dangers were out there. But if she stayed she'd either dehydrate or go insane.

"Think it over, will ya? You have time. That's the one thing we do have plenty of," Alma said.

She didn't have much time to think it over. What would Malcom Reynolds from Firefly do at a time like this? Double down on where he was and try to find another well or go with the strange Mexican sharpshooter girl?

Maybe that wasn't the best example. Captain Malcom would go with the girl because she was pretty. Firefly had failed her for the first time.

7

Alma, Southern Utah, Cassidy's ranch house.

THE NEXT FEW DAYS WERE SPENT IN A LAZY, SUMMER VACATION kind of way. They ate, talked and rode their bicycles into town. They found nice acoustic guitars and basses and brought a few back to the house. They also raided the Barnes and Noble. Cassidy had been here and had already cleared out some of the history section and most of the science fiction and fantasy section. She suspected that the books that were left behind were ones Cass had already read.

She passed by the magazine shelves and saw the cover of a news mag that said "Super Flu: is this the big one?" That had been the last issue.

Alma filled her backpack with mysteries and thrillers. They found some bottled waters left in the café area and drank those on the way home. Cass was being unusually quiet. That was expected. She had a lot to think about and Alma was going to let her think in peace.

That evening they lounged out in the TV room as they read. It kind of sucked in a way. She'd read a book she liked but realized that the author would never write anymore. There were not going to be anymore books and what was out there was it.

"You think the government's holed up somewhere? Maybe they have a library and everything the world needs to start up again," Alma said.

"Maybe. If they're out there now, I'd imagine they'd cause more problems than fix em. But I'm sure the president and some rich generals are all hidden away in a fancy bunker somewhere."

"Probably with attractive interns."

"Gross."

They both laughed but the laughter sounded forced. They were both desperate for anything that wasn't completely horrible.

"What you going to do about that well, Cass?"

Cassidy put down her book and looked over to her.

"I've been thinking about that, Alma. What if we can find somewhere with lots of fresh water, wood, animals to hunt and where the winters or summers aren't so bad?"

"It just so happens, Cass, that I'm heading to Virginia. Heard it's a nice place. Low taxes."

"Virginia or Kentuky or wherever. Maybe we should look."

"You telling me that you're joining the band?"

"Yeah. I'll go. This place is dying."

Alma couldn't contain her smile. Her sense of relief relaxed every muscle in her body. Now she wouldn't have to hit the road alone. It wasn't just the company, though that was nice too. It was that there was safety in numbers and two armed people were safer than one.

"Awesome!"

"When do we leave? I've already said my goodbyes."

"We could leave tomorrow if you like."

"Let's spend all day getting ready and then head out the next morning."

"Thank you, Cass."

Cassidy shrugged.

"What else can I do? I can't stay here and I might as well leave with someone I trust."

"What about like?"

"I don't know about that yet," Cassidy said with a toothy smile.

"Aside from water there's going to be one thing you'll need to bring," Alma said.

"What's that?"

"Sunscreen. With your white skin you're going to burn, baby."

Cassidy winced.

"Oh, don't I know. I'll wear a large hat."

The next day they inventoried their backpacks and made lists of everything they cold think of. They ate and drank as much as they could to prepare for the long trip ahead of them. Once on the road they'd be back down to small rations. Alma wasn't looking forward to that. She was used to plentiful food.

One good thing about having a partner was that they could share the load. They only needed one of a lot of things so that freed up space and weight for water and food.

"Let's see your guns, chica," Alma said.

Cassidy brought out all her father's guns. Almost every one of them was a bolt action hunting rifle. The PSL was the only military rifle they had. The collection did have three different 1911's though.

"I guess you're stuck with the PSL for now," Alma said.

"I like the PSL! It was my fifteenth birthday present. He traded a shotgun for it and he never liked it, so I got it."

"Take all the pistols. It's always good to have spares and maybe we can trade them."

One good thing about the PSL was that they had eight, 440 round cans of ammo for it. Far more than they could carry.

The idea that their ammo would be limited by what they could carry worried her. She knew how fast a person could burn through ammo. But if they took bikes then there'd be no way to carry extra stuff, like in a wagon or something.

"Cass, should we walk but have a wagon with more stuff or travel lighter and faster on bikes?"

"I'd imagine that we'd be safer on bikes. We could get away from trouble."

"I suppose."

The thought of leaving all that ammo pained her.

Cass's collection did have some 5.56 and she packed a few more boxes in her backpack. With Cassidy taking some of the weight, she was able to carry more water.

By the end of the day both their packs were sitting next to the door, ready to go. Their rifles were leaned against the wall and their pistols were by their shoes.

"You ready for this, *chica*?" Alma asked.

"No, but I have to be. We can't grow by avoiding trials. We have to face our trials and work through them."

"Trials, eh? I don't plan to be arrested."

"No, I mean..."

"I was kidding, Cass. Yes, I know what you mean."

She'd been to church once or twice.

"I'll be praying everyday that we find your brother."

"I appreciate it but I don't think the Big Man upstairs is listening. Maybe he's got his phone on mute or something."

"How can you say that? He spared you from the destruction. He has a plan for you. If you're willing, he'll do great things through you."

"Great things? What's there to do? The world already ended."

"Maybe we can help bring it back."

"I'm not going to be some baby making machine."

"That's not what I meant."

"I just don't see what there is to do. The world got screwed. It can't really get any worse."

"You'll see. Heavenly Father has a plan for you. One day you'll look back and realize it."

So, this is what a Mormon was like. At least it wasn't about calling her a sinner and unbeliever. She would have preferred travelling alone to that garbage.

"Are all Mormons as optimistic as you?"

"Most, I think. At least, we're taught to be optimists."

"I guess that's better than being depressed all the time," Alma said with a shrug.

Cassidy just laughed that loud, honest laugh of hers.

That night she lay in bed and wondered if she had gone crazy. If they stayed here maybe they could dig another well? She didn't know anything about digging wells. It seemed that the whole southwest was drying up and she didn't have the skills or knowledge to live in a desert without all the modern conveniences.

She had to find a more hospitable place. There was no other way.

Then she heard footsteps in the hallway.

She reached for her Glock on the nightstand.

"Cass?"

She saw Cassidy's bright orange head peek in. She had her long hair put up in a bun.

"I can't sleep. I'm too nervous," Cass said.

"Well, you have to try. You'll need as much rest as you can get."

"I know. It's just that anything can happen out there."

"Don't think about it. We're two friends backpacking across the States. Besides, I'm good at what I do. I can protect you, right?"

"Yeah."

"Go...read the Bible or something. That always puts me to sleep."

Cassidy smiled briefly and retreated.

Alma put the Glock back on the nightstand and followed her own advice and went to sleep.

In the morning she put on her traveling clothes, laced up her boots and walked out into the kitchen. Cass was there cooking their final breakfast in the house. She couldn't help but have thoughts of a "last meal."

Neither of them spoke much. Despite all her bold talk, Alma had to admit that she was nervous as well. She'd be stupid not to be.

After they ate, they left their dishes right where they were and walked to the door.

Cass looked so nervous like she was about to cry.

Alma put her hand on Cass's shoulder.

"We're going to rock out there. We'll be fine."

"It would be kind of a waste to let us survive and then let us die on the road."

"Yes it would be. God isn't that lame."

She didn't believe in God, especially not after all of this, but Cass did.

They strapped on their packs and slung their weapons.

With just a simple nod they opened the door and didn't look back.

8

Alma, southern Utah, I-15

THE DAY WAS TURNING OUT TO BE UNSEASONABLY COOL; ONE LAST breath of winter. That was fine with Alma because it meant she wouldn't be using up so much water. They had only gone one day and already she was looking around for water.

They had about an hour left of sunlight and dark clouds were forming on the horizon.

Cassidy put her hand up to her brow and watched the storm approach as they walked.

"This doesn't look good," Cass said.

"We haven't seen a house or even a tree in hours."

Cass scrunched her mouth in her version of a frown and huffed.

This was not cool at all.

They kept walking and the storm kept growing bigger and darker. As the sun began to set, it caused the black storm to gain an angry red glow. Just what it needed: to look even more menacing. Occasionally the storm would flash from lighting somewhere inside it.

"*Que bueno*," she muttered.

She kept searching the land around them for houses or anything that could be used for a shelter and also for any signs of life. She didn't carry her weapons for the heck of it. There were survivors out there and many of them would be desperate. Desperate people did dumb things.

"What's that?" Cassidy asked.

Alma looked where she was pointing. There was something on the side of the road way ahead of them.

A rain drop hit the top of her head.

"I think we should hurry," Alma said.

They hopped on their bikes and peddled as the rain slowly started. As they rode and got closer Alma could see that it was a semi-truck sitting on the shoulder of the highway.

In the fading light she could see a wall of water pouring down and heading straight at them.

"Hurry!" Cassidy shouted.

They rode as fast as they could. She could hear the rain approaching from behind but didn't dare look back. It sounded like a tsunami rushing right for her.

They got to the semi truck just as the big, fat raindrops began to pour down. Alma opened the door (Thankfully it wasn't locked.) and jumped in while Cassidy climbed in the other side. They both slammed the doors at the same time. Aside from hair that was a little damp, they had made it.

The rain beat down on the windshield of the truck like a crazy death metal drummer.

"Listen to that!" Cassidy said.

"Drowning in a desert after surviving the end of the world. Yeah, that would have sucked."

It was dark inside the cab so Alma took out her flashlight and looked around. There were no keys or signs of the driver. A bobblehead of some wrestler stood on the dash. Behind her was a red curtain. Hoping there wasn't a dead body behind it she opened the curtain and flashed her light. It was a small living space with a tiny fridge and a bed.

"A bed! Would you look at that," Cassidy said.

"I call dibs."

"Wait, now hold on."

"I called it. Thems the rules."

"Wait a minute. We can share it."

Unlike Cassidy she hadn't grown up with a billion brothers. She had never had to share anything before, especially not a bed.

"Come on! It'll be fun. We can tell ghost stories."

"I thought you said it'd be fun."

Alma turned off her flashlight and leaned back in the passenger chair. There was just enough light now to see that the rain was turning the desert into one giant mud hole.

"You know how to hotwire a car?" Cassidy asked.

"Why? Because I'm Mexican?"

"What? No, no! I was just wondering because if this truck had gas maybe we could make it up to Provo or Salt Lake."

"Sorry, no can do."

"Eric, my oldest brother could. I guess you could say he was the black sheep of the family. Sometimes he would even skip out on church."

"No!" Alma said in mock astonishment.

"He sure did. He was a good guy though. He always thought of others first. When our daddy was dying he stayed by his side the whole time. I wonder why I was spared and not him."

"You weren't spared, you were just lucky to have some right combination of DNA or whatever. I don't know. Don't try to put so much meaning into it. Shit just happens."

"You don't need to swear."

"The whole world is dead, the cities are filled with bodies and we're two of the last people alive and you're worried about a little bad language?"

"Now more than ever. If we want to make it through all this, we need Heavenly Father's help."

"Seems more like a heavenly deadbeat dad to me. Maybe he's off drunk somewhere watching a football game."

Cassidy glared at her with her bright green eyes.

"Relax, Cass. Don't get so uptight."

"Don't make fun of God."

"I'll try not to."

"Do or do not, there is no try."

"Is that some Mormon saying?"

"Star Wars, Yoda."

"I'm assuming, you were a nerd, right?"

"A big one. Literally and metaphorically."

"You couldn't have been taller."

"Not taller. Since the plague I've lost fifty pounds."

"Not bad. You're a telephone pole now."

"Yup. I went to sci-fi and fantasy conventions. I usually went as a Sith."

"A what?"

"Like an evil Jedi."

"Right."

She still had no idea what she was talking about. She'd never seen Star Wars. Saw part of one where a CGI rabbit was running around talking like a Jamaican and turned it off.

"But now that I've lost all this weight, I bet I could go as Slave Leia."

Alma didn't want to know.

"When we get to Salt Lake or Provo maybe we can find a comic store and get you educated."

"Salt Lake? That's too far north. We're taking 70 east before we even get there."

"But we might find a vehicle there or other survivors."

"Pro tip: finding survivors might not be a good thing."

"But it might be."

"I don't know. If we could find a vehicle there..."

"There has to be."

Alma thought about it for a while. Cass was right. It was worth a detour.

They sat there in the cab, listening to the rain and watching the desert light up from the occasional flash of lighting. For a split second everything would be as bright as day.

"Were you and your brother close?" Cassidy asked.

"Yeah. It was one of those rare times where two people just clicked, ya know? It was like we've always known each other and were always friends. But when the war broke out he joined the Marines. He fought on the New York front against the E.U. but when the plague broke out he was on leave at Virginia Beach."

She loved boasting about her brother. It was her chance to tell the world how proud she was of him.

"I was filling out college applications. I would have been the first person in my family to go to college. What if your brother's heading west to find you?"

"Then we'll meet in the middle. I left a note in our house in case we didn't."

They fell silent and listened to the rain for a long time. This was strange. She was trapped in a broken down semi truck during a rain storm with a girl she barely knew, but it felt alright. This wasn't bad.

Things weren't all balloons and seashells, but it didn't all have to be horrible. She just had to look for these little moments and appreciate them.

"You ready to turn in?" Cassidy asked.

"Sure."

They crawled onto the bunk and tried to get comfortable. She had never shared a bed with anyone before and it felt awkward but Cassidy was out cold in what was possibly less than ten seconds. So, she was left wide awake and uncomfortable.

Still, it could have been worse. She could have been outside in that rain and thunder. Or she could have been alone.

Isn't this what parents were for? To keep their children out of situations like this? How could they leave her alone in this hell? She swore at them as she drifted into sleep.

9

Alma, Southern Utah, 1-15

ALMA WOKE WITH CASSIDY SNORING BESIDE HER. SHE LOOKED
out the window and saw that the rain was gone and the sun was
out. She sat up and stretched her arms out.

"Huh? What?" Cassidy mumbled.

Alma ignored her and crawled into the front seat. Now that it was light
she could search the truck better. All she found were fast food wrappers and
country CD's. Lame.

She was about to wake up Cassidy but then she saw how peaceful she
looked. No worries showed on her smooth brow.

That's why it was the perfect time.

"WAKE UP!" Alma shouted at the top of her lungs.

"What's going on?" Cassidy bolted up and scrambled for her pistol. Then
she stopped and looked at Alma. "What was that for?"

Alma had to stop laughing before she could answer.

"I'm sorry, I couldn't resist," Alma said.

"Well, next time try a little harder," Cass said with a hard glare.

"*Lo siento*. You have my permission to prank me anytime."

"I don't wanna prank you."

"Well, you should. A little revenge now and then never hurt anyone."

"Ok, Edmond Dantes."

"Huh?"

"Count of Monte Cristo? Most famous revenge story ever? Nothing?
Really?"

"I think my mom watched the movie once."

"I swear, if we find more books, I'm going to get you educated."

"What's the point?"

"So we don't forget where we came from. So we don't forget the past and make all the same old mistakes."

She had never heard anyone actually say why education was important. Usually they just said "so you can get into a good college."

Alma didn't want to admit defeat so she just shrugged and pretended she didn't care.

"Let's get going. We can't sit around here all day," Alma said.

They put their boots back on and strapped on their backpacks. Then they were back on the road heading north, riding on their bikes. The morning still had a bite of the cold rain in the air and now instead of a light rust color, the desert was a dark brown. She wondered what all the desert critters thought of the rain. Where did they go to hide?

"You know, the Mormon pioneers trekked across the country on foot over a hundred years ago."

"Yeah? So?"

"Maybe we could learn something from them?"

"I think maybe a boy scout handbook might do us better."

"That too. Two more reasons to head up to Provo."

"We're not going to Provo."

"There might be a car there."

"Okay, we're going to Provo."

The day got hotter as they went and they took a break around noon. They found a nice little rock formation for shade. They shared some MRE crackers with jalapeño cheese. She couldn't stand the MRE peanut butter. It's like the stuff just sucked all the moisture from her head.

Alma took out the map and looked it over.

"The next place we come to should be Cedar City. Looks small," Alma said.

"I've only driven through it."

"Let's get back on the road then."

Reluctantly they got back on their bikes and continued on. She wasn't going to admit it to Cassidy, but her butt was starting to hurt from sitting on that stupid seat all day.

Around five o'clock they came to the outskirts of Cedar City. It looked like a small, out of the way little place but then she noticed a Walmart. Alma tapped Cassidy on the shoulder and pointed over to it. Cass raised her eyebrows and nodded.

They rode to the Walmart, which was the second thing they came to right after a Home Depot. The front door of the Walmart had been shattered and they unholstered their side arms and entered to the sound of crunching glass. Empty shopping carts were scattered everywhere like they had been tossed around.

"You ever train with that thing?" Alma whispered and pointed to Cass's pistol.

"Daddy took me to the hills with some glass bottles a few times."

"So, that's a 'no' then. Make sure you know what's in front and behind what you're shooting at. Don't fire until you do know what you're shooting at. And don't shoot me. Oh, and take your safety off."

Cass looked down at her 1911 and thumbed the safety off.

"What about your safety?" Cass asked.

"Glocks don't have a safety."

"Really?"

"I'll tell you later. Focus on what we're doing."

They entered the store scanning for any sign of movement or recent activity. The place was a mess. People had definitely gone crazy here. They passed the empty deli on the right and went to the grocery area. Decayed meat filled the dead freezers along with dark stains that once were melted and rotted ice cream.

Then they came to the canned food isle. There were cans knocked everywhere.

"Jackpot," Cassidy said.

Then Alma thought she heard something.

"Sshh!"

She raised her competition Glock 9mm and listened. She heard it again, some shuffling sound a few aisles over. She turned to Cassidy and made a hand gesture that they'd go around and take a look.

Alma "cut the pie" like her step father had taught and turned the corner slowly in pie wedges so she had her gun pointing at whatever came into view.

It was definitely something moving around. She could hear a scraping sound almost like nails on cement.

She turned back to make sure Cassidy was following. To her credit, Cassidy looked calm and collected. She even held her pistol the right way. At least she wouldn't be totally useless.

Whoever was over there wasn't making the slightest attempt at being silent. They must not know they were there.

She got to the aisle and adjusted her grip one last time before turning the corner. In one fast and smooth motion she came around the corner with the Glock pointed chest high.

But there wasn't anybody there. No looter, no stumbling bum.

Instead what she saw was a wrinkly, long eared, short legged basset hound that was intently sniffing an ancient packet of tortillas.

"Awww! It's so cute!" Cassidy said from behind her.

She almost laughed at Cass's instantaneous transformation from badass to girlie girl, but she did have to admit, the basset was adorable.

"Here boy," Alma said. *"Venga aqui."*

It was a dang cute dog.

The basset looked up from its important sniffing and wagged its tail. The dog probably hadn't seen a live human in a year but he acted like it was the most normal thing ever. He trotted over and they both bent down to pet it. The dog seemed to soak up their attention and was perfectly okay with just sitting there being petted.

"What are you doing here boy? Looking for something to eat?" Cassidy asked.

They went to where they had the dog food and tore a bag open. The hungry dog instantly began eating away in loud, slobbery bites.

"Can we -" Cassidy started to say but Alma cut her off.

"No! We can't keep him. What are we supposed to do with a dog?"

"But look at him! He's so stinking cute! He'll starve if we don't help him."

"We'll starve if we do!"

"But this is a hunting dog. He can find us rabbits and prairie dogs."

"That's a hunting dog? What's he hunt? His dog bowl? Look at those little legs."

"Exactly. He's got short legs so the hunters could keep up. He could be useful."

Alma had serious doubts about this "dog" being useful. It looked too goofy to be useful.

"He could be a watch dog and guard us while we sleep," Cassidy said.

Cass had a point there. But was a little peace of mind while sleeping worth the food this beast would eat?

"Alma, please. I know you think this basset will be nothing but trouble and eat all our food, but this world's too short on happiness and this dog can bring happiness."

Alma looked down at the dog as it ate noisily and wagged its tail. She petted it on the hand and it looked up at her with those big, sad, brown eyes.

"*Maldita sea*! *Perrito estupido*! *Bueno*. He can come," Alma said.
Those were lady killer eyes and Alma was powerless against their charms.

10

<u>Alma, Cedar City, Utah</u>

AFTER PICKING UP EXTRA FOOD FOR THE DOG, (DEFINITELY THE goofiest dog she had ever seen) and a leash and muzzle, they walked out of the Walmart with full stomachs and some more bottled water.

Alma took out her map and found Cedar City.

"We can cut through on I-15 or take Main Street and see what this town has," Alma said.

"Let's see what it has."

"No more dogs, okay?"

"I know, I know."

They walked their bikes down Main Street. Most of the stores here looked like they had closed before things got too bad. They passed a dumptruck that had stopped in the middle of the street full of body sized plastic bags. They stayed clear of that. Even with being used to the smell of corpses that truck smelled.

Dead and dying trees lined almost every street and the red hills surrounding the town reminded them exactly where they were: in a freaking desert. With no irrigation this oasis was doomed.

There was no destruction here like she had seen in Vegas and St. George. It was like this town went to sleep and never woke up.

"A Dell Taco," Alma said, pointing to the "Mexican" fast food joint. "I could use a carne asada taco."

"Oh, don't talk about real food. I'm hungry."

"We just ate."

"I'm hungry for actual good food. Hot pizza, bacon cheese burger, chili dogs."

"Let's drop the subject then."

As they walked they didn't see anyplace even slightly useful until Cassidy spotted a library.

"Come on! They'll have Count of Monte Cristo there!" Cass said.

"Our packs are too heavy, Cass."

"But one book!"

"Alright."

As they approached the library she happened to look down and across the street. The hundreds of colored flags told her exactly what she'd find there.

"Cass, look. A car lot."

Cass's eyes lit up.

"See! If we get a car we can take all the books we want."

That wasn't the first thing that came to Alma's mind. She was thinking more about her feet and the time saved in finding Alex.

Cass ran in and grabbed the book just in case they couldn't find a car. She waited outside with the dog who was preoccupied in sniffing a random spot of dead grass.

"Hey, *perrito*, you smell us up something good, yeah? Find us a rabbit or something."

The basset hound looked up at her and waged its tail. She'd take that as a 'yes'.

When Cass came out they hurried over to the car lot. It was a dealership for new cars. She assumed that was a good thing.

She had to use the crowbar to get into the office where the keys were and she took half and Cass took half.

"Come on, boy. You're with me," Cass said and the smiling basset eagerly ran off with Cass, ears flopping as it lopped along.

They began testing the cars one by one. She wasn't a mechanic and had no idea why, she just knew that cars didn't like to sit around unused for long periods of time. Also, gas didn't like to store for a long time either.

Suddenly she heard a car alarm go off. She snapped around and saw Cassidy backing away from a honking car. If anyone was alive here, they'd hear and come running.

If the alarm was going off that meant the battery was still good. She ran over and looked for the key marked #43. It was a small SUV called an Enclave. She had never heard of it.

She found the key and quickly opened the door. She reached in, not an easy thing to do with her giant backpack and turned the key.

It started on the first go. It purred to life strong as any car before the end of the world.

She threw the doors open and tossed in her bag. Cassidy did the same and helped the basset into the backseat. It started barking which didn't help things.

When the alarm finally went off she heard shouting in the distance. Several male voices. She looked in the direction she heard the sound and saw three armed men running along the sidewalk toward them, about three blocks away. They looked dirty and scruffy. She did not want to wait around and find out if they were friendly or not.

"Get in!" Alma shouted.

They climbed in and as soon as Cassidy was in her seat Alma threw it into drive and began pulling out. Alex had taught her how to drive even though she never got a license.

"Maybe we should stop and at least see if they're friendly," Cassidy said.

Then shots began to ring out as they left the parking lot. The distant popping of gunfire killed any thoughts of being social. No bullet holes appeared in the windshield yet.

There looked to be three of them, all carrying rifles.

"That would be a 'no,' Cass."

Alma pressed down on the gas as far as it would go and the Enclave roared to life, slamming her back into the seat with the sudden acceleration.

Cassidy grabbed a hold of the door to keep from flying all over.

"Why are they shooting at us?" Cassidy asked.

"Want me to stop and ask?"

The men disappeared in her rear view mirror as she turned a corner.

She found I-15 again and was about to get on.

"No!" Cassidy said. "Let's go back for the books."

"Those guys are back there. What we can do is get on I-15 and head back to that Walmart and grab as much as we can carry."

"Alright."

She sounded disappointed that they were going after stuff they needed to live. Telephone Pole needed to get her priorities straight.

They filled the back of the SUV with every can they could find. She also grabbed a few Cokes and Mountain Dews and tossed Cass a Monster Energy drink as they got back in the car.

Soon they were heading north again on I-15. Out of curiosity, she tried the radio and found nothing but static.

"We got a car!" Cassidy said.

"I noticed. I happen to be driving it."

"We can get to Provo today!"

"And maybe sleep in a bed."

"They have a Cabllas up there and a Barnes and Noble and..."

"Yes, Cass, I get it. They have everything."

Cass looked in the backseat where the basset hound was just looking out the window with a big grin on its droopy face.

"Good boy," Cass said.

"What should we call him?"

"How about Caesar?"

"Caesar? Sure, why not."

"How you doing Caesar? You okay back there?"

Caesar just wagged his tail and continued to drool.

11

IT WAS CASSIDY'S TURN TO DRIVE SO ALMA SAT IN THE PASSENGER'S side with her feet up on the dash. She had her iPod plugged into the stereo so they were listening to great music the whole way. Now this was how to survive the apocalypse in comfort.

Rob Zombie's "Living Dead Girl" was blasting from the speakers and she was doing a soft, casual head banging to the beat.

"I always wanted to see him in concert," Alma said.

"I always wanted to see Creedence Clearwater Revival in concert. Of course, that wasn't really possible even before the world ended."

"I heard Artyrial Spray had just gotten back together. Rotten timing."

"If only Faith No More would have gotten back together."

A band Cass liked that was before 1974?

"I remember them! Angel Dust was such an underrated album."

"I know!"

That started them on a long conversation about under and over-rated bands.

The scenery here in Utah was kind of bland. She was so glad she didn't have to bike through this.

"Shame we had to leave our bikes," Alma said.

"Yeah, but maybe we'll find new ones in Provo."

"And gas. We're getting down to half a tank."

Alma looked in the back at Caesar. He was sprawled out on his back sleeping. He had been sleeping almost the entire time.

She had to admit, he was a dang cute dog. She reached back and scratched Caesar's belly which got no reaction from the basset.

"*Que guapa*! *Mi gordito precioso*!" She cooed to the dog.

"You warming up to him?" Cass asked.

"Maybe a little."

'A lot' was more like it.

They passed small towns and larger communities but they didn't stop. They drove through the graveyard of towns and tried to ignore the idea of how many people had lived there.

"If we find the gas and everything goes right, we could drive to Virginia in three days," Cass said.

"But everything won't be right. Roads might be blocked, gas will be hard to find, if not impossible, and there might be more people out there."

"And worse."

"Like what?"

"Well...."

"Just spit it out, *chica.*"

"Just before the radio fell silent, the guy, things were confused and crazy and they kept getting all kinds of contradictory reports and such..."

"Just say it already!"

"They said they had unconfirmed reports of a possible nuke in Denver."

"A nuke?"

The possibilities of that suddenly made her feel cold and she rolled up the window.

"Like I said, they were very confused and chaotic. It might not be true."

"Why would someone nuke a city that was already dying?"

"Spite."

"I remember the last news cast I saw on TV," Alma said. "It was one of the sound guys filling in for the anchor because the anchor was dead. There were only like five people there and they were down to rumors and guesses. I wondered what was the point? Why not just go have fun before you die?"

"I guess they felt they had a duty that was more important."

Duty. That was even more pointless. The only duty she had was to herself. In this world she couldn't afford to put other people's lives ahead of her own. It just couldn't work like that. She liked Cass but if it came down to it, she'd choose her own life over her new friend's.

It was a cruel, barbarous world, but it was what she was given.

"I wonder if the Pope is hiding in a bunker somewhere," Alma said after a long silence.

"Maybe. I'd rather have scientists in a bunker working on a cure."

"And cloning."

"Cloning?"

"Yeah, to fill the cities up again. Do you know how long it will take to repopulate?"

"No."

"Neither do I, but it'll be a while."

There was another long silence as the brown, boring scenery of Utah passed by.

"Maybe we can start a cow farm...or whatever you call it," Alma said.

"Cows? Lots of hamburgers."

"And we can get pigs."

"For bacon."

"And they eat garbage," Alma said.

"And goats."

"Chickens."

Alma raised her hand like she was in school or something. Alma humored her and pointed to her.

"I know how to raise animals," Cass said.

"Good, because I have no clue."

She'd never pictured herself as a farmer but then she'd never pictured herself as a plague survivor either.

"What do you think we'll find in Salt Lake?" Cass asked.

"Don't know. Never been there."

"It got attacked a few months before the outbreak. The Chinese did a major offensive into Northern Salt Lake. Destroyed Bountiful."

"Maybe we can find some army stuff. I wouldn't mind a bullet proof vest."

"I wouldn't mind a machine gun or a grenade launcher."

"Too heavy and the amount of ammo you'd need? Forget it."

She remembered how expensive ammo was. A day at the range could easily burn through a few hundred dollars of ammo and more. A chain fed machine gun? No way she was carrying that much ammo. Too heavy.

"A tank maybe?" Cass asked.

"Too much gas."

"You don't happen to know how to fly a helicopter or plane, do you?"

"No clue."

"I guess we're stuck with cars and bikes."

"Bikes? What if we get some badass motorcycles?"

"That would be cool! But where would we put Caesar?"

"Get a side car."

"Good idea!"

Caesar perked up and looked around before falling back asleep.

The sun was setting and the mountains were casting long shadows.

"We got about a half hour of sunlight left and about an hour before we reach Provo. Do we stop for the night or risk the headlights and keep going?" Cassidy asked.

What a strange situation to be in. Headlights were a danger? What next? "Don't wear your seatbelt!"

"I'd hate to stop for the night and not have it start in the morning," Alma said.

"Maybe I can drive without the headlights?"

"How's the moon tonight?"

"Have no idea."

"Let's see how we do without lights."

The sun went down and it eventually got too dark to see the road.

"We'll go with lights," Alma said.

"I don't know. I think if I drive slow enough I can see the road."

"Alright. If you think you can, do it."

They crept along at about 20mph. It was still faster than bicycles, but it still annoyed Alma how slow they were going.

An hour after sunset the moon rose above the mountains, lighting up the desert in a faint blue glow.

"That's much better!" Cass said.

They sped up to 35mph which made Alma feel much better.

Fifteen minutes or so later they came to the American Fork, the first town that blended into Provo. A few scattered cars lined the highway but not enough to block their way.

"What's our plan, Alma?"

"Let's find a big house with no bodies. More comfortable than a hotel and more stuff to take."

The fancy houses were up on the foothills of the mountains. Apparently people paid for the view. They exited I-15 and wound their way up the hills until they came to a swanky little neighborhood with large, three to four story houses that had enormous glass windows looking out over the valley.

The neighborhood was silent and still as the cemetery it was. They drove up to the entrance of a street and Cass parked the car.

"This is as good a place to check as any," Cass said.

Alma grabbed her AR and got out of the car. They left the sleeping Caesar in the car and they walked to the first house.

She looked over at Cass with her too long PSL. That wouldn't be very good for moving around inside a house. The PSL looked gigantic compared to Lanky Cassidy and Alma hoped Cass knew how to use it.

"Switch to your pistol when we get inside," Alma whispered.

Cass nodded.

The first door was locked. Alma remembered that a few houses on her street had been unlocked. Maybe the same was true here. So they went house by house, checking every door and window. On the fourth house they found a back door that was unlocked.

"I take right, you go left," Alma whispered before she opened the door.

Then she pushed the door open with her left hand while keeping her AR ready with her right. Inside was pitch black.

She really wished she had a flashlight on her gun. Being a competition gun, it had never needed one, but now she was regretting that. She took the flashlight out of her cargo pocket and held it under the barrel of her AR.

They began checking the house room by room. Except for dust, the house looked untouched. The living room had a giant flat screen TV that covered the wall. Shame. Now it was just garbage. The living room was open up to the third story. Ridiculously huge house. Paintings and an algae covered fish tank were the other decorations of the living room.

That made Alma think about what things really had value anymore. Fashion magazines, no. Yes, her iPod had value. It held songs that might not ever be played again. She couldn't let that music disappear.

They went up the giant, sweeping staircase to the second floor. The window that overlooked the valley came up both stories. There was a basement and an attic area as well. She had never been in a house this big before.

The basement had shelves full of food. It as a "two year food storage," Cass explained. Apparently it was a Mormon thing, but Alma didn't question it. She didn't care what it was as long as she got to eat.

The house was clear and no rotting bodies.

"I think we just found our new temporary headquarters," Alma said.

"I like it. Kinda small, but it'll do."

They parked the Enclave in the garage and unpacked only the essentials. The dog went around sniffing everything in sight while they brought up canned food and bottled water from the basement.

She ate some ravioli as she took her smelly boots off and stretched out on the couch. It was still very dark so they couldn't make a thorough search yet.

Alma wanted a bath very badly. Instead she ate and stretched her feet.

Cass walked over to the window with her can and looked out while she silently chewed.

"Hey, Alma?"

"Huh?"

"I think I see a light out there."

"What?"

Alma grunted, got up and walked to the giant window. In the dark valley, the single light was easy to see. It was north of them down in the middle of the messy, crowded city.

They got her binoculars and took a closer look. Whatever it was, it wasn't electric. It was a fire. A small, single fire down below.

"Someone's still alive," Cass said.

Again, Alma didn't consider that a good thing.

12

ALMA SAT IN THE KITCHEN AND LOOKED BACK INTO THE LIVING room. Caesar was sitting on the couch, still staring at her. She stared back but that didn't seem to intimidate the basset.

"It's rude to stare," Alma called out.

"Huh?" Cassidy asked, without looking up from the magazine she was reading.

"The dog. He's staring at me and he won't stop. Why's he staring at me?"

"He thinks you're cute?"

"Well, we both have huge noses."

"Come on. Your nose isn't...oh...yeah, it's kinda big."

"You're not helping."

Alma turned back around to her book: Count of Monte Cristo. Cass had been right. This was a good book. There had been a copy on these rich people's shelves. It was different and the language was old fashioned, but she felt sorry for the character. Fell in love and then got thrown in prison, even though, he was innocent. She hoped he gets revenge for all that.

She turned around one more time just to make sure. The droopy faced basset was still staring at her.

They had been there for two days, relaxing and eating. They had things to do but neither of them wanted to leave the comfort of the house to do them.

But, Alex was still out there. She knew he was alive and she was going to find him.

"We need to get moving," Alma said.

"Where to?"

"I was thinking, Cabela's."

"We could use a lot of stuff."

"And we can check out another gun store I saw a sign for. Also, the company that made my AR is north of here. Crusader Weaponry is in Murray. I want to check them out, maybe get you a decent gun."

"My PSL is plenty decent! Do you know how many deer I've shot with this?"

"But it's bulky, slow and heavy."

"Whatever. I like it."

"We'll find you a real gun."

"My daddy gave me this gun."

"There's no room for sentimentality, Cass. It's live or die. What's going to happen when there's no more canned food or bottled water to scavenge? Life is going to get a lot harder, honey."

Cassidy pouted but went back to reading her magazine. Apparently it was the last issue printed and ever would be printed.

After lunch they jumped in the SUV and headed back to I-15 to find this Cabela's. The narrow city streets were mostly clear except where a blockade had been set up or a car crash made things inconvenient.

"I wonder where that light was," Cassidy asked.

"Have no idea."

"But that means someone's still alive, probably more than one."

"If the virus had a lethality of 99.9% and Salt Lake had...say a million, how many people does that leave?"

"I suck at math. A few hundred?"

"I think it's around a thousand. But I guess I'd have to take all the surrounding cities into account because Salt Lake doesn't have a million people."

"Well, it's all one big spread out city anyway. A thousand people might be living here?"

"Yes, so we had better keep our eyes open. Got it?"

"*Intiendo*," Cass said in a horribly gringo accent.

Then they passed the gun store they had seen signs for. It was a big building with a big red sign over it.

"We passed the exit," Cass said.

"We'll come back for it now that we know where it is. Cabela's first."

When they took the off ramp for the Cabela's exit, they came to a bunch of piled up cars that made a roadblock of sorts.

"What the..." Alma said.

"Looks like someone's been here."

"One of our thousand guys, yeah?"

Alma got her AR ready. Cass was driving and Alma was on look out.

There was enough room to get by so they went around the sloppy roadblock and drove up to the enormous building on the hillside. It was like a mall but just one store. Tattered flags fluttered and the sign on the door said "closed."

The parking lot was empty except for two cars that looked like they hadn't moved in a long time. Grass was starting to grow up in the cracks of the parking lot and around the unmoving cars.

"How we doing this?" Cass asked.

"We go in and clear the place and once it's safe, we loot it."

"Sounds simple."

They pulled up to the far side of the store, keeping their car out of sight and then walked to the front doors. The glass doors were broken but someone had boarded them up again.

She glanced at Cass who had a serious look on her face.

Alma tested the door and found it locked. She went back to the car and grabbed her crow bar. It took both of them pushing on the bar to pry the door open. Once inside they moved off to the side where the customer service counter was. They ducked behind it while they waited for their eyes to adjust to the darkness. In the meantime they listened.

Once she felt she could see well enough she poked her head over the counter. In the middle of the store was a giant fake mountain covered in stuffed animals. There were racks of camouflage clothing and to the far left she saw the gun section.

She motioned with a nod of her head to the guns.

"I'll go look for food, you go for guns," Cass said.

"We shouldn't split up."

"There's nobody here and I'd rather get in and out than hang around."

She really didn't want to split up but maybe it would be better to just hurry and grab the stuff and go.

"Alright. You got five minutes and we're meeting back up right here. Got it?"

"Got it."

Alma hurried as fast as she could while still being quiet over to the gun section. It had almost been picked clean. There were a few old bolt actions, mostly Mosin Nagants, a few cases of ammo and some accessories. This place had been looted before everyone had died. That or the place was looted after everyone had died. Which meant there was a survivor around here that was sitting on a hoard of guns and ammo.

She grabbed a Turkish Mauser (it said so on the price tag) and the only box of 7.62x54r they had for Cass's PSL. There was nothing else of use to them. Everything had been picked clean.

Then she looked through the shelves of accessories and found a flashlight to go on her AR. She stuffed all the extra batteries they had in her empty cargo pocket and was about to head back to the meeting place when she heard a noise.

Alma froze in place.

It was voices. She heard the sound of two men talking. One was sort of laughing.

"Look what we got here! A cute little ginger!" A man said from across the store.

They had found Cass. She thumbed off the safety of her AR.

"Let's take her back to our place. We got lots of food, little girl. We give ya food and you give us something in return. Sound fair?"

"See, me and Nate here have been real lonely."

"Please, let me go," Cass said. Her voice was shaky.

"You alone little girl?"

"Yes. My family's dead."

Then she heard a third man.

"Guys, come on! Bring her and let's go!"

By the time she got to the front of the store, she saw four men taking Cassidy out to a large, four door, red pickup truck. They were all armed with AR's, AK's and a shotgun.

Alma silently swore as she watched them toss Cassidy into the backseat. If she fired now, there was a chance that she'd hit Cass as well. Also, four against one wasn't good odds. Getting herself killed wouldn't do anyone any good.

She made her way to the front door in time to see them drive away.

Alma unleashed a flood of cursing that wasn't in any particular language and ran for the Enclave. She jumped in and realized that Cass had the keys.

This went beyond cursing.

She climbed out and could hear the overly noisy sound of the big truck make its way further up the hill.

Alma stood there, suddenly feeling very tired and pissed off. What the hell was she supposed to do now? Going after Cassidy would be dangerous and there was the chance that she'd never even find her. There were four of them and they were heavily armed. Or she could go back to the house and continue to Virginia by herself.

It was a simple choice. Her philosophy was to look out for "number one" and not let emotions get her killed. Play it safe and don't take stupid risks. Getting to Alex was what mattered. Everything else was a distraction.

It was so easy.

Alma let out a long breath of the worst curse word she knew and began running after the large red truck.

13

Alma, Highland, Utah

ALMA RAN AS HARD AS SHE COULD. HER RIGHT ARM HELD HER AR in place as her left pumped as she ran. She had never run so fast in her life.

The road curved down and then back around so if she ran fast enough she wouldn't be able to catch the truck, but she could at least see where it was going.

There was a slight hill that made her efforts feel twice as painful but she ignored her muscles and ran up the entire hill. Her legs were screaming at her and her breaths were ragged gasps for air.

Once on top she saw the red truck at the distant intersection. It took a left and went east on Highland Highway. It quickly disappeared out of sight.

Alma took out her map and saw that there were several large neighborhoods in that direction. It was heading toward Alpine.

She took a second and weighed her options. There was nothing to do but go after them on foot. That gave them a huge head start and she tried to block all possibilities out of her mind.

So, she started jogging up Highland Highway. On the map it didn't look so long but on foot it might as well have been a hundred miles.

Eventually she saw a small neighborhood on the south side of the highway but the houses there were unimpressive. Far on the north side, where the foothills to the mountain were, she saw large mansions. She guessed that that was where they were. Why live in a small house when there were mansions for the taking?

She kept jogging. It felt like hours. It couldn't have been that long. There was no way she could run for hours. Each step brought a different thought about those men with Cass and she ran faster to block it out of her mind.

There was a grocery store on her right. She went in and grabbed one of the few bottled waters they had left, chugged it down and left the store. As she was leaving she saw something lying down near the side of the store.

A bicycle.

Without pausing she snatched up the bike and started riding. It was a girly, pink thing with tassels. She didn't care.

The closer she got to the rich, hillside community, the bigger it looked. This was taking too much time and it was only a guess to begin with.

An hour later she was staring up at a street full of giant, four story houses, one of which looked like an Italian villa and another looked like some fairy tale castle.

Street by street she began searching. All she had to do was glance down a street and see if the red truck was there or not.

She checked her watch and saw that it had already been an hour. Cassidy could already be...

Alma shook her head and peddled harder.

She didn't want to do this alone. She couldn't cross the country by herself. Also, she liked Cass. She was one of the few genuinely good people she had ever met which was even more important now. She wouldn't meet another like her.

As she got to the top of the hill she looked up and saw smoke coming from further down one of the streets. Instantly she rode toward that direction.

She came to the street and saw the red truck parked in front of the biggest house on the block.

Alma dropped the bike, shouldered her AR, crouched down and began sneaking toward the house. Her hands were shaking from exhaustion and she wondered if everyone could hear her loud gasps for breath.

As she got closer she could hear yelling and laughing. The fire was coming from the back yard where a group of six men were gathered around.

She crept around back and took a quick peek around the corner of the house. They were drinking and having a good time. It looked like they were throwing knives at a tree.

Then she saw Cassidy tied to a chair in the middle of the group with a gag in her mouth. They were petting her and whispering in her ear.

"No, no! The highest score gets to score!" One of the men said.

"That's not what I'm talking about. We should do it on one throw. We've been at this forever. Let's just decide who goes first with the girl and get it over with. I mean, we're all going to get a turn anyway."

Alma wanted to throw up but at the same time she breathed a sigh of relief. Cass was still alright. These animals were going to pay for even thinking about touching Cass.

But how was she going to do this? There were six of them here and all of them had holstered pistols and most of their rifles were in arm's reach. She tried to control her breathing just like she did right before a competition.

Competition.

She had to think of this like a competition. There were six targets and she had to be as accurate and as fast as she could. Putting it like that made it sound almost easy. She was used to shooting at targets much smaller than a plate so people sized targets shouldn't be a problem.

But these targets could shoot back. If she missed she wouldn't just loose points. She could end up dead or worse.

Also, these were people. She had always assumed that she'd have no problem killing and she didn't feel like she did now, but would she when it came time to pull the trigger? Also, two of them were standing right next to Cass. If she missed she could hit Cassidy.

"Forget this, I'm going first," one of the men said.

"Let go of her. You ain't taking her until we figure out who's first!"

"This is my house!"

"No, you saw it first, that's all."

"Well, I saw her first," another man said.

Now was her time. She put in her ear plugs and took ten slow, deep breaths to slow her heart rate like she always did.

She imagined the buzzer going off to start the match. All her training and practice came back to her. Her muscle's remembered what to do.

She swung out from behind the corner and simultaneously raised her AR in her perfect stance. Her feet were shoulder width apart, her body was crouched down to absorb recoil and she was squared to her targets. The arrow sight of her ACOG lined up perfectly on the first man's head and she squeezed the trigger in the smooth, unjerking way she had done countless times.

Before her mind even registered that she had hit her target, she was moving on to the next one. Just like in competition she fired, moved the sight to the next target and fired again.

It happened so quick that the men barely had time to turn around and register surprise.

Bam! Aim. Bam! Aim. Bam! Aim. Bam! Aim. Bam! Aim. Bam!

Six shots, six hits. All in less than two seconds.

As the bodies fell to the ground she lowered her AR and put it back on safe like she always did. Then she scanned the area for anymore targets. Her heart was pounding her ribs and her eyes registered bright red blood everywhere but her mind ignored it.

Cassidy was staring at her, wide eyed.

Calmly and still looking for signs of movement, she walked over to Cass and cut her ropes with her Cold Steel Tanto and trembling hands. She still couldn't believe she had just done that.

As soon as Cass was free she threw her arms around Alma and began sobbing in giant, shoulder heaving sobs. She patted Cass on the back and sat her down on the grass.

"There, there. You're okay now. I took care of them, see? You're safe," Alma whispered softly.

They stayed like that for a long while until Cass's sobs eventually died down. Cass wiped her eyes and nose and looked up at Alma.

"You found me. How?"

"I just did."

Cass looked around and noticed the dead bodies for the first time.

"How'd you do that?" Cass asked.

"I'm that good."

Cass gave a faint smile.

Alma helped her to her feet.

"Let's get out of here," Cass said.

"After we take their stuff. Consider it an Asshole tax."

Cass didn't complain about her cursing this time.

She searched the bodies and found the keys to the truck. Then she loaded all their guns, ammo and food (which was a lot) into the bed and drove back to Cabela's. Using a tube they found in the store they siphoned the gas from the truck into the Enclave and loaded the enclave with the loot from the evil men and what they had found in the store. Tents, first aid, coats, boots, pants and every other outdoor thing they could think of. They'd sort through it later.

Cass didn't talk on the drive back to the house. She sat curled up on the passenger seat, staring out the window without seeing anything.

She'd be okay. She was safe now. Alma wanted to thank a God she didn't believe in. She cared for Cass more than she would ever admit to her. She wasn't just a comrade or friend. She was family now.

14

Alma woke up to the sound of gut wrenching crying. She jumped out of bed and stumbled her way down the hall to Cassidy's room. Her dark form was sitting up with her knees tucked to her chin and crying. Alma rushed over and put an arm around her.

"What's wrong, Cass? Had a nightmare?"

Cass nodded.

"It was about my mom. She was captured by those...men," Cass said.

"Hey, I'm here. You're safe with me. No more going solo though."

"No."

Alma wasn't about to admit that she had also been having bad dreams. Every night it seemed. Her dreams were usually of her mother and step father lying in the living room in those gross, black plastic bags the government put bodies in before they ran out of body bags and people to do the work. She'd stand there, looking down at the grey faces of her family and talk to them. They'd talk back.

Her brother was never there. That was because he was alive somewhere.

"Cass, if bad dreams are all we have then we're lucky. We survived the entire planet dying off. It could be worse," Alma said.

"Are you okay?"

"Of course I'm okay."

"Yeah, but you shot six people today."

She had killed six people and that did worry her. She wasn't worried about them, they deserved to die. She was worried by the fact that it hadn't bothered her at all. It was her first time ever taking a life and she didn't feel a thing. It was as bothering to her as taking out the trash. Shouldn't she feel something? She had watched everyone she knew die, perhaps six scumbags more just wasn't a big deal?

"I'm fine, Cass. Those men deserved it."

They lay down and she kept her arm around Cass as the red head fell asleep.

In the morning she was greeted by a tail wagging Caesar. Caesar barked a few times until she took him outside to go potty and then filled his bowl.

When Cass came down the stairs, rubbing her eyes, Caesar barked some more and ran up to try to cuddle against her still moving legs. Cass almost tripped three times just getting to the kitchen counter.

"*Buenos dias*!" Cass said in her horrible gringa accent.

"*Buenos dias*. We need to plan what we're doing today. I say we hit that gun store we passed and go up to Murray."

"What's in Murray?"

"Crusader Weaponry. A guy named "Gundoc" made my AR custom just for me. I want to find his place and take his stuff."

"You're not a romantic, are you?"

"Romantic? I don't got time for all that love crap!"

"No, I mean, you're not sentimental or overly emotional."

"Sure I am. I love to let emotion cloud my reason and get me killed. Sounds wonderful."

"But after we finish playing around here you're going to want to head east, right?"

"That's right. We need more gas though. Unless we find some very well sealed containers, we ain't going to find much."

"We'll find what we can and go as far as we can. But I guess we better prepare to do some walking. Maybe a hand cart like the pioneers?"

"A what? Hey, I want to drive the whole way. I hate walking. Let's check every gas station from here to Salt Lake."

"Let's eat some breakfast and then head out."

"There's always time to eat."

"Right. This time we'll take Caesar. He can be our alarm."

She looked over to Caesar to see if he was prepared to save their lives. Caesar was passed out on the couch with his ears dangling down. Not very inspiring.

As the drove down the hill to I-15 she thought about other ways to haul their stuff around. Unless they were really good with finding supplies along the way, they wouldn't be able to carry enough food or water with them to take them all the way across the country. If they could find the gas and the car held out, sure, they could make it in a few days no problem, but she was going to prepare for the worst.

They stopped by one gas station. Without power they couldn't use the pumps but they tried to get into the underground tank. Again, the crowbar came in handy. However, the tank was bone dry.

Every station they came to was dry.

"This isn't looking good," Alma said.

"Looks like it might have to be a hand cart."

They got to the large gun store that was visible along the side of the highway. The sign said it had an indoor rifle range. She didn't like the indoor ranges. Too stuffy, crowded and too many rules.

The front door of the place was a heavy, metal door that was locked tight. The window had spider web cracks on it but it still held.

"I don't think my crowbar's getting through that," Alma said.

"Let me try."

Cassidy unslung her PSL and pulled out its magazine. Then she took out a magazine with a white dot on it.

"What's that?" Alma asked.

"I usually use soft point ammo, but I got a few rounds of those steel core penetrators. I guess its time to see how well it penetrates."

"Make sure you get that lock good," Alma said.

Cass put the barrel of her PSL up to the lock and made an exaggerated look of concentration. Alma covered her ears.

She fired and there were sparks and flying metal. There was a bullet sized hole in the lock. Alma tried the door and it still wouldn't open. It took three more rounds to blast the lock apart enough to get the door open.

Cass didn't want to use up the batteries of the flashlight on her AR so she pulled out her rechargeable one.

As she swept the room with her beam of light, glimpses of all kinds of guns perked her interest.

"Finally! We can get you a real gun," Alma said.

"I'm not giving up my PSL."

"Fine! Keep it. But you need another one in case we have to search more buildings."

That long barrel made going into buildings awkward to say the least.

"I suppose."

"We need something you can jump in and out of cars and clear rooms with. Something short but...Oh!"

Alma saw something that caught her eye. She crawled over the counter to the display wall and picked up a gun she had always been curious about.

"What's that?" Cass asked in wonder.

"It's Sig 556 Swat."

"It's looks awfully fancy. Do I need a college degree just to use it?"

"No, no. It's really simple. Easier to use than your big beast there."

She wanted and was definitely going to take it, but with it not being the most common gun, spare parts would be hard to come by. She wondered how useful it would actually be in the long run. Here, she could take apart any AR and use it's parts to fix something broken on her competition AR, but with the Sig 556, once it breaks, its gone.

She kept it. Maybe Cass would actually use it.

Since she was behind the counter she took one of the tactical range bags that were in display and filled it with two AR rifles, and the backpack, she filled with pistols of all kinds.

"Why so many pistols?" Cass asked.

"Currency."

A second backpack she filled to the top with ammo.

In the back room they found a mummified corpse that had locked itself in the small office. The hole in the back of the skull told what happened.

After loading the Enclave full of as many guns and as much ammo as they could, they continued on north towards Salt Lake.

At the Point of the Mountain, the narrow ridge that separated Utah and Salt Lake valleys, they got a good view of the sprawling cities. In the hazy distance she could see the tall buildings of downtown Salt Lake.

"You know where this place is?" Cass asked.

"I have the address and a road map."

I-15 was good and clear for most of the way. Some parts of the city looked burned from fires. She wondered if it was from appliances that were never unplugged or from the war.

"Hey, the front lines were just north of Salt Lake, right?" Alma asked.

"Yeah."

"We should find some cool gear there, maybe?"

"I suppose. I'd rather find where they keep their fuel."

"Good thinking."

If they didn't find any fuel, they'd have just enough gas to make it back to the house. This wasn't good. Cassidy's pioneer idea was starting to look more and more likely.

Alma turned up the music and tried not to think about hiking across the country.

She also didn't want to think about why Cassidy was quieter than usual. Cass had a lot more family to loose than she did.

They were driving through a cemetery full of buildings that held long dead corpses and that idea couldn't have been lost on Cass. She'd probably go crazy herself if she weren't fixed on the idea of finding Alex. She couldn't let her faith in him slip. If she lost that hope she was afraid of what would happen.

15

"WHAT'S YOUR FAVORITE MOVIE?" CASSIDY ASKED AS THEY drove north on I-15.

What does it matter? They'd never see those movies again. But, she sighed and answered the question anyways.

"The Ring, I guess."

"That super spooky one? I think mine is the King's Speech. It always cheers me up. No, I change mine to Lord of the Rings."

"Haven't seen them."

"You should."

She wasn't going to mention how unlikely that was going to be.

"Hey, there's the exit," Alma said.

They turned off the interstate and eventually found the right neighborhood. They found the house easily enough. Gundoc had given her dad the directions when they had met at Shot Show a year before the plague.

"It looks deserted," Cassidy said as they pulled into the driveway. The windows weren't broken and the door was closed. Those were good signs.

Alma got out of the car and readied her AR. Cassidy followed close behind.

She didn't want to try to break in and get shot if he was sill alive so she walked up to the front door and knocked.

"No one's home, Alma," Cass whispered.

Then a dog started barking from inside the house. It sounded huge, like a freaking wolf or something. Caesar then started barking from the SUV.

"Well, if someone is alive, they know we're here," Alma said.

The door swung open and she found herself looking down the barrel of a large AR-10.

"Um...hey, Gundoc? It's me, Alma Attaway. We met at Shot Show a few years ago. You built me this AR," she said in a rapid burst.

The AR-10 lowered just enough to see his face. Yup, it was Gundoc.

"Girl, don't you have any sense? You can't just go walking around here. This place isn't safe."

He motioned for them to hurry and get inside.

Once in, he closed and locked the door. A dog that weighed at least twice as much as she did walked up and began smelling her.

"There's a gang going around and you don't want them to find you," Gundoc said.

"What are you doing here?"

"I'm preparing to leave, that's what I'm doing. What are you doing here anyway?"

His face was a mix of anger and confusion, but there was more to it than that. This man had probably lost his family as well and no one came out of that unscarred.

"I came to see what I can get."

"Nothing, unless you got stuff to trade."

"What do you need?"

"I got plenty of guns but not enough ammo."

"Well, we happen to have ammo. I want spare parts for my AR and Cassidy here needs an upgrade from her PSL."

"PSL? Oh, yeah, I can do better than that. Come."

He led them through the house full of children's toys and photos of smiling blond kids and took them into the basement. Alma noticed the lack of any smiling blond children anywhere else.

In the basement where his workshop was, there were guns, parts of guns and accessories lying all over the place in somewhat organized groups.

The unshaven and slightly wild looking Gundoc walked over to a rack and took out the coolest AR-10 she had ever seen.

"This is called a *Broadsword*," Gundoc said with a wicked grin. "It can shoot half MOA at 200 yards and a quarter if you're trying. The optic switches between a red dot and a x4. Polygonal barreling, permanent Slipstream treatment, trigger job, foregrip, adjustable stock."

As he handed the Broadsword to Cass, Alma couldn't help but gawk at it. It was a work of art. She even liked the two-tone black and grey look.

"This is the finest rifle ever made. Shame the world ended before I could make more. Take it. Leave me some 5.56 ammo and you can have the spare parts for free. I'm leaving in a few days and can't take all this junk with me."

"Thank you," Alma said.

Gundoc just grunted.

After making the trade of some ammo for the Broadsword, spare parts and a Makarov pistol thrown in for kicks he basically shoved them back out the door. He didn't seem to appreciate the rarity of human beings in the world.

She wasn't a parent and couldn't possibly understand what it would be like to lose a child, let alone all of them. She didn't want to understand.

Both of them were silent as they left the front porch and walked back to their car.

They were back on I-15 heading north towards the front lines. The closer they got to Salt Lake, the more clear the damage to the city became. Skyscrapers had jagged holes in them. Some areas of the city were just blackened fields of rubble. There were marked off holes in the raised interstate where Chinese artillery had struck.

Alma thought back to the worst day of her life. A Chinese airstrike had hit her mother's hospital where she was working. Again, she was looking at evidence of their murder of civilians.

She was glad they were all dead.

"How you doing back there?" Alma asked Caesar.

Caesar raised his sad looking eyebrows but didn't respond.

"What's this?" Cass asked.

Alma faced back to the front where she saw something blocking the exit to downtown.

It was a makeshift barricade made from sheet metal and plywood but there was plenty of room to move past it. There was writing on it.

"Go to Temple Square," the sign said.

"Is this a trap?" Cassidy asked.

"I have no idea."

And she didn't. It could be survivors looking for other survivors or it could be that gang Gundoc had talked about.

"I think we should trust it," Cass said.

"No way."

"Look, see there, written in the corner? 'CTR,' it means Choose The Right. It's a Mormon thing. I got a good feeling about this."

"You got a good feeling about everything."

"Then my logic says that bad people wouldn't set up in Temple Square. They would have set up someplace where they had easy access to stuff they need."

"Let's hope you won't get a chance to test out your new rifle."

"You know, this thing's starting to grow on me. It's lighter and handier than my PSL."

"I'm not going to say I told you so, but...I told you so."

16

ALMA KEPT HER AR SHOULDERED AND READY TO GO AT A moment's notice. As they drove through the streets of Salt Lake City, they saw that the war had not been kind to the place. Holes in streets and buildings from enemy bombs were everywhere. Buildings had burned down and cars, and the occasional skeletal body, littered the street.

This was the first time she had seen so many bodies lying around. It seems that most people went home or somewhere comfortable to die. Maybe these people were homeless or were killed by the Chinese. Either way she hadn't seen it like this.

Alma had seen the piles of bodies wrapped in trash bags at collection points or in the back of garbage trucks, but these people look like they had just sat down and died where they were.

"Shame. Looks like this could have been a nice place," Alma said.

It was nothing like Vegas. There wasn't the lights and glamour, but it had its own charm, or at least it could have before the war and the plague.

The streets were wide and clean where there wasn't debris or brown grass starting to grow up in the cracks of the street and sidewalk. Some of the windows in the tall buildings were broken and dirt was everywhere. The city was falling apart.

"How long's it going to take before this whole place falls apart?" Alma asked.

"Depends. Depends if you mean 'not safe for living' or completely falls to plant covered rubble."

"Both."

"I have no idea on either one."

"I guess we'll find out."

"I hope we live that long."

"We will. Trust me."

"I wish I didn't have to see such times. I always imagined that I'd make it through the end of the world safe and with my family and that we'd be together when Jesus makes his Second Coming."

"You'll have me. That should count for something, right?"

"It does."

"But I don't think Jesus will be too happy to see me."

Cass managed a smile and tried to pretend she wasn't wiping her eyes.

Then Temple Square came into view as they rounded a corner. The tall, white temple towered over the rest of the square in a way the modern, glass buildings could never do. There was a wall around the place and the gates had busses and cars pulled up to block the entrance. Signs in English and Spanish were at the gates saying "We welcome anyone that comes in peace. We have food, water and medicine."

"Looks friendly," Cass said.

"Or it could be a trap. How could they have food and all that there?"

"We should at least try."

She didn't have a 'gut feeling' one way or another. Her instincts weren't telling her anything. All she had was her logic and it was telling her that it was 50/50. The question was: did the possible good outweigh the possible bad?

"Let's pull up, but keep your foot on the gas," Alma said.

Cass nodded and they slowly pulled up to the front gate. Four men with rifles appeared at the gate, peering over the bus that blocked the way. Two of them were smiling.

Alma didn't like people who smiled at her.

Cass rolled down her window and leaned out.

"Howdy," Cass called out.

Alma would have covered her face with her hand out of embarrassment but she had to keep an eye out for danger.

Howdy? Who says that?

"Hello there!" One of the men wearing an Army uniform said.

"What do you guys have going on here?" Cassidy asked.

"Next time I do the talking," Alma whispered.

"We have food, water, medicine and about fifty survivors. Where are you two heading?"

"East. My friend here is looking for her brother."

TMI, Cass: Too Much Information. She'd have to talk to her about that later.

"Might I suggest you rethink that? Denver, DC, and LA were nuked. I can't say what else might have been blown up. It's dangerous out there and that's a long distance to go. It's safe here."

"No thank you. We're set on our destination," Cass said.

Alma did have to admit that she was impressed by Cass's determination and loyalty. Someone else might have tried to convince her to give up her stupid plan.

"Alright, but don't say I didn't warn you," the uniformed man said.

"So, what's going on here?"

"We got gardens in here and the conference center roof. We have some of the military equipment left over from the war, though we could use more of it and we also have a surviving apostle."

"You guys got an apostle in there!? Awesome!" Cass said with a giant smile.

Alma leaned over to get into view of the man.

"Hey, you mentioned military equipment? Where's that at?" Alma asked.

"North of here. Can't miss it. It's all spread out all over the place. Looking for something in particular?"

"Fuel. We need fuel for our car," Alma said.

"We got the fuel in here. Brought it in before the Gang got it."

"Gang?"

"Yeah, we're not the only survivors out here. There's some bad apples that go around looting everything they can. Don't let them catch you. They're held up in a hotel south of here, the Grand American. We have a cannon here but no shells. Tell you what, you get us some 155mm shells and we'll give you some gas. Deal?"

"Deal," Cass said before Alma could respond.

17

"YOU KNOW WHAT TODAY IS?" ALMA ASKED.
"No."
She hadn't bothered with days of the week for a long time.
"It's May Day!"
"So?"
"So, we should celebrate."
"We are. We're driving into an old battlefield, picking up cannon shells and trading them for gas. Sounds like fun."
"Alma, where's your sense of celebration?"
"Give me something to celebrate. Cinco de Mayo, Halloween, July 4th, Christmas. Heck, a second cousin, twice removed, birthday party."
"Well, I'm going to celebrate."
"After we go back to Cabela's and get what we left."
"That's a yes."
"It's a maybe."
She didn't feel like celebrating. She was too worried about looking out for bad guys and keeping them safe.
That was what her brother had told her when he left to join the Marines. That he was going off "to keep people safe." Coming from him, she believed it. He was the first male she had ever known that actually put other people's happiness in front of his own.
Her birth father definitely didn't do that. He was a drunk that cared only about getting drunk. The night the police came to their door in Empalme and told them that he had died in a boating accident, she hadn't felt sad at all. Inside, she was glad he was gone. She was eight when that happened but even at that young age she knew she was glad he was dead.

They were heading toward the Salt Lake City International Airport where the soldier said an artillery battery was set up. Heading west she looked out her window and saw the Salt Lake spread out in front of her. She had grown up by the ocean and in comparison this lake (though really big) was just a dead, over sized mud puddle. It didn't have the life and light that the ocean had.

She wondered if she'd ever see the ocean again.

The stretch of road leading to the airport was flat and pretty empty which was a change from the usual clutter of central Utah.

The entrance to the airport had an open gate with two small tanks guarding the entrance. The gate was open and one of the tanks had an open hatch.

Cass slowly eased through the gate while Alma kept her AR up and ready.

They drove past the tanks and past some hangers that were filled with damaged army vehicles and helicopters. All kinds of stuff was lying around like a hurricane had come through. Tube canisters were scattered in front of the hanger and a crate full of rockets had tipped over.

She tried to think of a reason to take a rocket.

They stopped the car and got out. Alma walked over to the tank with the open hatch and stuck her head in. There was some water gathered on the floor but it looked safe. She crawled in and looked around. There were two M4's on a weapons rack and a whole chain of 7.62 ammo for Cass's "Broadsword." She took all that and carried it back to the car.

Cass didn't find anything they could use in the hanger, just spare parts for vehicles she didn't care about and rusty tools, so they continued on. Past the hanger, out on an unused airstrip were eight self propelled artillery cannons. She knew the term "self propelled" because her brother, Alex always used to watch the "Military Channel."

"Go get the car, I'll look around," Alma said.

"You said no splitting up," Cass said.

"Yes I did, sorry."

She mentally kicked herself for even suggesting it.

They both walked to the car and pulled up to the first gun. The hatch was stiff but unlocked. In the rear of the very cramped crew compartment she found a rack of shells. She opened it and tried to pull one of the shells out. It was about the size of a leg and made out of solid metal or something because it was heavy.

"Cass! I need your help!" Alma called out.

Cass crawled in with her and together they pulled out the painfully heavy, round shell and lifted it to the top of the turret. Then they, with some cursing on her part, got it to the ground and into the back of their SUV.

"What's that?" Cass asked.

Alma looked to the rear of the cannon and saw a hatch that looked like it could open to where they store the shells. They had to use the crowbar but they got it open and as she had guessed, it was an easier way to unload the cannon.

Cass helped get one onto Alma's shoulder and she hauled it to the truck. The thing was so heavy that it hurt, just holding it. She never imagined how something could be so dense. Getting it off her shoulder without dropping it on her foot was the hard part. They loaded up ten shells until they came to a shell that was larger than the others. It was white with a yellow strip.

"Should we get this one?" Cass asked.

"I got no idea what it is, but I guess so. Couldn't hurt, right?"

They loaded the extra large, white shell in with the others and kept looking around.

Then Alma heard something, barely on the edge of being audible. It was a truck engine. She looked around until she saw it. Coming on the highway from the west were two trucks.

Alma quickly got out her binoculars and took a look. Each truck had about four or five men in the rear, all armed.

"Cass, I think it's time we get out of here," Alma said.

"Ah, crud."

Cass ran over to the car and pulled out her Broadsword.

"I don't think fighting's going to help us, Cass. There's like, twelve of them and two of us."

"You worry too much. They're a good thousand yards away. I bet between the twelve of them none of them can shoot past 300 yards."

Cass leaned against the hood of the Enclave and steadied herself. She looked through her scope and began taking slow, deep breaths. While Cass was doing that, Alma jumped up onto one of the Paladin cannons and checked the machine gun. It had ammo, but when she opened it she saw a whole lot of rust. She tried to charge it but it moved only with a lot of effort. She took the bottle of Slipstream weapon lube from her cargo pocket and poured some on. After racking it a few more times she felt like it could work.

She swung the machine gun around just in time to see Cass fire her first shot.

The first truck was coming down the road to the front gate when Cass fired. From that distance she couldn't see if or where she hit but suddenly the truck swerved to the side and off the road. It tumbled to the side sending its passengers flying in all directions.

Cass adjusted aim to the second truck.

The second truck tore through the front gate at top speed. She saw muzzle flashes and heard bullets striking the cement near the Paladin. They were lousy shots.

Cass fired and this time it was close enough that Alma saw the windshield break into a large spider web pattern. The truck swerved and almost tipped over but it stayed upright and began going in a circle.

Alma squeezed the machine gun's trigger and opened up. The gun shook in her hands for a good ten round burst before it jammed up. Her bullets stitched up the side of the truck, hitting one or two of them in the back.

Cass fired again and she saw a red mist appear near one of the men's heads. The man toppled backwards into his companions.

One of the men, without a shirt and covered in tattoos jumped out with an AK-47 and actually fired from the hip. Alma almost wanted to laugh. What was he expecting to hit like that?

Alma was about to shoot him but Cass's round found him first and he fell down with blood spraying from the middle of his chest.

Now that the machine gun was unjammed, she opened up on the rest, spraying bullets all over. The gun thundered in her hands and the bullets tore a trench in the cement before meeting the truck and its occupants. Gore and shredded metal flew all over the place.

The fight was over and no one moved.

She looked down at Cass from the top of the turret. Cass was looking over her scope at the scene and wasn't smiling. Her red brows were bunched in the middle and her thin lips were pursed together.

"I guess your shooting's alright," Alma said.

Cass flipped the safety of her Broadsword back on and slung the rifle back over her shoulder.

"Let's get out of here," Cass said.

18

ALMA DIDN'T FEEL COMFORTABLE HERE. IT WASN'T THAT SHE WAS surrounded by people asking for news or that she was in the heart of the Mormon headquarters. It was that she was here, helping these people when she should be heading east to help her brother.

The more they delayed the more eager she was to get going.

The handful of children were gathered around Caesar who seemed to have an infinite capacity to soak up their attention. He didn't seem to mind getting manhandled by the kids at all. He just sat there, looking content as a dozen hands petted, patted and stroked him.

"At least someone's enjoying themselves," Alma muttered.

Cassidy was talking to a group of men that were leaders in her church. They were talking about gathering somewhere, and that if she came across any other Mormons, she was supposed to tell them where to gather.

It made sense. Why not concentrate what little you have left?

What had once been flower gardens were now vegetable gardens. They had a tunnel made out of cars, busses and junk that gave them a protected corridor to the Conference Center across the street. A building with gardens on top, huh? What will they think of next?

As good as this was, they were still living off of foraged food and foraging was made difficult by the Gang. That was why these people needed those artillery shells. A Paladin was parked right in the middle of Temple Square ready to go.

At least their Enclave now had a full gas tank. That was one good thing out of a crappy day.

"Come on Cass! Let's go do this," Alma said.

It was another fifteen minutes before Cassidy walked over with a large smile on her face.

"I just met an apostle!" Cass said.

"Great, but we got important things to do. You agreed to help them. They said they needed every gun they could get so here we are. Let's hurry and do this."

"They're finished loading it up. We'll be going soon."

"Soon" was another half hour. They had to pray first. Alma tried not to roll her eyes too hard.

Once they were off she felt much better. There was another truck full of armed men rolling with them.

It was slow going though. The Paladin didn't move as fast as she would have liked. The tracks tore up the already crumbling roads. The tall buildings loomed over them, blocking out the sun and the sound of the tank treads echoed through the empty city.

Alma couldn't help but notice the ruins of people's lives. On the side of the street was a store that sold heavy metal music and clothing. Over to her right was a "Hawaiian sandwich shop." These were the grave markers of the people that lived and worked here.

A few minutes later they came within sight of the giant hotel. It was just down the street. The tall, white building was away from the modern skyscrapers and looked like something from an old photograph with its attention to useless decoration and lack of glass covering everything. Cass said it was the fanciest hotel in the city. Alma believed it.

"If they haven't noticed us yet, they're about to," Cass said.

"Let's get this Jihad rolling, yo!"

The Paladin took aim. The large barrel of the cannon raised slightly and a few seconds later, fired.

The "BOOOM!" shattered glass on both sides of the street and kicked up a dust cloud around the cannon. Alma actually saw the shell sailing down the street and strike the second floor. A large, black dust cloud exploded out.

"Why the second floor?" Cass asked.

"Didn't you pay attention? Most of the bad guys are up high in the penthouse where they can see everything. They're cutting off their escape route."

"Oh."

The Paladin fired again and again, each time blowing a giant, smoking hole into the side of the building.

Then on the fifth round there was no explosion. Instead it was a white puff that looked like thick smoke.

"What was that? A dud?" Cass asked.

"I got no idea."

Smoke kept coming out from the hole and after a few minutes she saw flames.

"I guess it was some kind of incendiary round," Alma said.

A few minutes later and the first two floors were totally engulfed in flames as smoke rose up, covering the hotel like a rolling blanket.

Down the street a truck pulled up with more gang members in the back and fired at the Paladin. Their bullets were like throwing colored sprinkles against the Paladin's armor. Then the cannon fired one more time and the truck was blown high into the air, twirling to pieces.

"Did you see that?" Cass asked.

"Yeah, I'm right here, Cass. I saw it."

"Now that's how you celebrate May Day!"

They stayed and watched the burning hotel. In a way it was beautiful. She mustn't have been the only one to see it because they stayed there, staring at the dying building. The smoke twirled into hypnotic patterns and the flames glowed a gorgeous orange.

The other survivors surrounded the building and took care of anyone trying to leave. It was simple, brutal but effective.

Two hours later the building collapsed. It slowly tipped and then fell headlong into the street below, crushing the lower buildings beneath. A giant cloud of dust and smoke roared down the street toward them. The men in the Paladin ducked down into their hatches and she quickly rolled up her window.

The cloud enveloped them, spraying pebbles against their windshield.

Cass turned to her.

"Well?" Cass asked.

"Okay, okay. That was pretty cool."

"Glad you came?"

"Yes. I'm glad I rolled with you crazy Mormons."

To help the celebration she put on Kansas's "Wayward Son" and they sung it at the top of their lungs on their way back to the house. Caesar howled along with them.

19

ALEX WALKED INTO THE BARRACKS WHERE HIS TEAM WAS sleeping. Before the plague some had been civilians, some were military. Now they were all survivors.

Alex, though, was a Marine and always would be.

No one liked the barracks and he couldn't blame them. They had been staying in the swankiest houses they could until recently. But the barracks were right there at the base and that's where their work was. Besides, they were leaving soon.

They had a joke that the reason they were leaving was because they were sick of eating MRE's. That was probably half true. The rest of the truth was that they couldn't stay here. They needed to find someplace with a fresh water source, animals, land to grow crops and shelter. Good weather was a plus.

The old, wooden barracks were from WWII and had all the discomfort old barracks supplied. Trough toilets, creaking wood floors and peeling paint. In the summer they were too hot and in the winter were down right freezing.

There was Jennifer, a liberal college professor. Used to teach history. Maybe 38, 40? Despite looking and sounding like a total hippie, she was actually very practical and pragmatic. She realized that the world and its rules had changed. Kept a level head. She also knew about plants and making rope from hemp or whatever else she did.

Then there was Spencer. 26. He used to work at a fast food pizza place. Had been saving up for college. Probably would never have actually gone. Then got drafted into the army when the Chinese invaded. Metalhead, so at least he had good taste in music. Plays drums. Kind of lazy. Talks too much. Tries to help out, though.

Adam Green had sold fancy cell phones. Tall, muscular black guy. Age 35.

Didn't even have to go to the gym, and looked ripped. Not fair. Was going to be promoted to regional manager. Those plans had gone out the window along with the rest of the world. Serious guy but quiet. Kept to himself a lot. Did a lot of thinking.

Lastly there was Rebekah. She was twelve years old. Pale, porcelin skin, raven hair, dark eyes. Jewish. Had a large, warm smile and laughed a lot. Laughter kept everyone else sane. Not much good at anything but good to have on the team. Depression was a killer nowadays. How did she keep so blasted happy? Everyone she knew was dead. Maybe a great actor? Liked boy bands. Would have to correct that if she was going to travel with him.

He leaned against the door frame and watched all of their sleeping forms. They were good people. They weren't Marines for damn sure, but they were good people and that counted for a lot. Especially now. People were in short supply.

The sun was just coming up. If they didn't have so much to do today he'd let them sleep in. But vacation was over. Time to work.

Alex was about to wake them up but then he saw Rebekah sleeping peacefully. She had a look on her face that was completely free of worries. Her mouth was slightly open and looked like the child she really was. The end of the world made people grow up too fast. At least when she slept she could be a child again.

He let them sleep a little longer. Why wake her to a world full of problems any sooner than he had to?

Alex went to his locker and opened it up. The first thing he saw beside his small mirror was a picture of him and his sister Alma a few months before the war. They were at Lake Tahoe. They had life vests on and were sharing a jet ski. That had been an awesome summer.

They weren't genetically related but that didn't matter one bit. They were meant to be siblings. The rest was unimportant. He missed her more than anything. She was dead of course. The chances of her surviving were astronomical and he wasn't good with math. There was no point in holding out hope that she was still out there. He hoped she had gone peacefully.

He did think of her everyday though and imagined how she would be getting along in this messed up world. She was a smart girl and could definitely protect herself.

How would she have handled all of this? Her temper would keep her from getting killed or get her into worse trouble. Whatever she did, she would run right at it and never surrender.

Eventually, he got them up and they grumbled less than usual. They knew today was important. It was their last full day at Virginia Beach.

"Get up. I know you want to sleep all day," Alex said.

"Just a little longer?" Rebekah asked.

"No, we work first, relax later. You want to be loading up the Humvee at night?"

"Not really."

"Then we finish everything early, we relax for our last night."

"Barbeque on the beach does sound nice," Jennifer said between yawns.

"Not until we do what we have to do. Sooner we knock this out, sooner we can rest," Alex said.

"Ah, man! That's what my old sergeant used to say, but it was never true," Spencer said. "It was more like, sooner you do this, the sooner you'll get more work to do."

He ignored Spencer for now.

"Prepare now, because it'll save us a lot of trouble on the road."

"I know."

They got up and filed out of the barracks to the old Army mess hall where Jennifer and Adam cooked breakfast. Neither of them could be considered good cooks, but they were better than the rest which was kind of sad.

Once the breakfast of eggs and hand made bread was finished, they went to the garage where the Humvee was. Like all military bases it was a sprawling mess of random, deteriorating buildings, ugly in their utilitarianism. Most buildings didn't seem to have a purpose. Others were storage, barracks and machine shops. Roads had names of officers that no one cared about and the tiny non-denominational church sat at the end of the street. And, of course, there was a large open grass field for formations and "dog and pony shows" that only colonels and higher ranks actually liked.

The mechanics shop was a wide open bay that had all of their things spread out along the floor. Everyone was going to check, double check and then have their gear checked by him. They all had a different list of items they were to carry. Some tools they'd only need one of and sometimes they wanted redundancy. Then there was everyone's personal things: clothes, hygiene, etc.

Alex began checking everyone's things one by one while Jennifer organized the loading of the Humvee. They were taking cases of MRE's and bottled water.

They were also taking their weapons. They had had all winter to prepare for this new world and there had been a lot of ammo lying around. So he had taught them how to defend themselves using Army issue M4's.

Up on top of the Humvee was a .50 cal machine gun in case they ran into serious trouble.

"I hope we find gas in Richmond. I hate walking," Spencer said.

"A little walking never hurt anyone," Alex said.

"Walking won't be so bad. Virginia's really beautiful this time of year," Rebekah said.

"You want to walk and carry all this stuff? Be my guest," Spencer said and threw an oily towel at her.

Once he finished the first inspection he had Adam come and pack his things and he moved on to the next. A long while later everyone had their backpacks in the back of the Humvee.

While they were still loading food and their things into the Humvee, he went over and inspected his ride. His was a Kawasaki Ninja 650, all black and chrome. He was the scout that would go ahead and make sure the roads were passable and ferret out any trouble. He needed an appropriate scout vehicle and the Ninja was suitable.

If he had to be honest, it was because the bike was cool.

He had always wanted one and Alma would have killed to have one. Having the dangerous job had its perks.

By noon everything they needed was packed into the Humvee. Everyone gathered around him and he looked them over.

"You guys ready?" He asked.

"Ready!" They chorused back.

"Right then, let's get this barbeque going!"

They took their charcoal grill, food, blankets and paper plates down to the beach for one last night by the waves. Adam did the cooking because Jennifer didn't have much experience with meat. She used to be a vegetarian but that had changed.

Rebekah made the cool-aid. Adam and Spencer wanted beers but alcohol was a whole can of worms he didn't want to open. Getting drunk during a survival situation was the last thing they needed.

They sat down on their blankets and looked out at the grey ocean. It stretched on forever and the grey clouds above kept the weather cool.

"Look there," Jennifer said, pointing her skinny arm. "Dolphins."

Sure enough, dolphins were out jumping around in the waves. They were silver humming birds darting between the dark waves.

"Wow," Rebekah gasped with wide eyes.

"They're getting along just fine," Jennifer said.

"We will too, once we find a place to settle down," Rebekah said.

"We'll find it," Alex said.

The smell of cooking meat mixed with the salt in the air. The warm sand shifted beneath the blanket, conforming to his body. Did it get better than this? Of course it did, but this was as good as they could expect. To have more people would have been better. To have the world not end would have been nice too.

This was good, though. They could take up fishing but none of them knew how to fish. He had tried several times but never caught anything. Shame none of the Navy guys had survived.

His brief time in the Marines had all been on land, mostly in New York when the E.U. tried to take Manchester. The Marines didn't agree with the E.U. and the Marines were very persuasive.

They had kept a few stakes and hamburgers for a special occasion. Since they were leaving, they were eating all they could. Adam threatened to barbeque some Spam but Jennifer threatened to throw him into the ocean. Not much of a threat. He weighed at least twice as much as her. At least.

As he ate his second steak he closed his eyes and listened to the ocean and smelled the salt in the air. This was nice and he would miss it. He had grown up in the Nevada desert but he had really liked the ocean.

He wished Alma were here. She would have liked the ocean.

20

RICHMOND LOOKED LIKE A DUMP. EVEN BEFORE THE WORLD ended it had been a dump, now, like an aging Walmart customer, it just looked like the city stopped caring what it looked like.

He stopped his motorcycle and flipped up his visor. He was on the highway looking at the small clump of tall buildings, none of which could be called a "skyscraper." It wasn't that the place was run down due to abandonment. He was used to seeing that. But there were empty factories, boarded up buildings and vacant ruins that had been left long before the war. This was a city that had seen better days.

The Humvee pulled up to him and Adam leaned his head out.

"What's the plan?" Adam asked.

"Don't go downtown. There's nothing there," Jennifer said.

"Nothing there?" Alex asked.

"Yes, it's just a bunch of pawn shops, parking garages and boarded up businesses. Nothing to see. Go to Cary Street instead," Jennifer said.

"What's there?" He asked.

"Everything."

She gave him brief directions on how to get there and he took off ahead of them. If some gang had a roadblock set up then it would be much easier for his bike to get away than the Humvee. More dangerous for him.

But that was his job. He took care of these people. He had taken care of Alma and then left to take care of the country. He would probably regret that decision if he gave himself time to think about it.

He should have been there. Even if he couldn't have done anything, he should have been with her for her last moments. He hoped she wasn't angry at him for that.

He drove along the raised highway up to the city center. Richmond was on a hill overlooking the James River. No wonder the North had such a hard time capturing it during the Civil War: only one way to reach it.

Once in the city he was in a dark canyon of narrow, hilly streets with tall but old, decrepit buildings on either side. He didn't like it. Too many places for ambushes.

He passed by a large park filled with trees and garbage. Yellow emergency tents filled the spaces between trees and "FEMA" was written on each tent. Didn't look like they did much good.

Next they passed a building that looked like a mosque and then the main campus of Virginia Commonwealth University. As he drove by the overgrown commons building of VCU, he spotted a lone figure shuffling along, oblivious that he was there.

It looked like a friggin' zombie. An emaciated man with no shirt and ribs showing, was shuffling through the grassy field with a vacant stare on his face.

He unslung his M-14 from his back and looked at the shuffling, skeletal figure through his scope.

No, it wasn't a zombie, just a crackhead. The person looked so out of it that he might as well have been a zombie. He could have been driving a semi truck and the ghoul wouldn't have seen him.

That was as close to a zombie apocalypse as he'd get. He slung his rifle on his back and continued on. When he got to some big street lined with old fashioned looking apartment buildings that imitated antebellum southern architecture, he stopped and waited for the Humvee. There were more trees here and the place had an older, quieter feel to it. This was the part where people had actually lived.

A minute later the Humvee pulled up and Jennifer got out and stretched her legs.

"Cary Street is just one block over," Jennifer said.

"Hey, I've been here before!" Rebekah said. "There's a big synagogue just down that way."

"Richmond sucks," Spencer said, not bothering to get out.

"Take that back. I was born here," Adam said.

"Oh," Spencer said.

"Just kidding. I'm from Florida," Adam said.

Everyone laughed but Spencer.

"There's an art museum down that way," Jennifer said.

"Can't waste time or space," Alex said. He knew what she'd want to do.

"Shame. Maybe I'll come back for it later."

They continued on to Cary Street. It was apparently the artsy, bohemian side of town. All the stores there were weird, quirky or foreign. Figures that Jennifer would want to go there. Besides crappy art and three different Thai restaurants, what was here that was worth their attention?

They stopped in a small parking lot just off the main street behind some nerd hobby store. Some of the older wooden buildings had collapsing stair cases and sagging roofs and ivy and grass was growing everywhere.

It looked like everything here was built before the 20th century.

They turned off their engines and he listened for a few moments. Nothing, but birds and a dog far off somewhere.

"How we looking on gas?" He asked.

"We got maybe an hour left," Adam said.

"I haven't seen a lot of gas stations around," Spencer said.

"Let's look around on foot. Save gas. Split into buddy teams," Alex said.

Adam went with Spencer, Jennifer went with Rebekah and Alex went alone.

He cradled his M-14 in his arms as he kept to the side of the streets. Just because it was quiet didn't mean nobody was there.

Alex walked by some import store full of wooden African sculptures. Those would do no one any good now. He passed by several trendy restaurants and judging by the faded menus in the windows, they were also over priced. Seven dollars and sixty eight cents for a hotdog?

Then he came to a bike shop. Could be useful. If they ran out of gas, bikes would be better than walking.

Next door to the bike place was a guitar store in a brick building with a southern style porch. He wanted to learn guitar but he just didn't have room. If they could find gas he'd just toss a guitar into the back of the Humvee and call it good. He and Alma used to play some mean air guitar.

Best to wait on the gas situation.

He kept walking while looking into the windows of the stores for anything that could be useful.

Suddenly he came face to face with someone who was walking around the corner and not paying attention.

"Whoa!" He let out, slightly startled and took a step back and both hands went to his gun.

The girl looked up and jumped back like a frightened cat in a flash of smooth blackness.

She was a Chinese girl, maybe seventeen or eighteen or could be twenty five for all he knew. Hard to tell. She had earphones in and an iPod in her hand. She shouted something in Chinese while pulling out her earbuds and looked up at him. Her eyes went wide and she took a few more steps back.

"Hold on there, I'm not going to hurt you," he said calmly and with his "authority" voice.

She looked around as if she were about to take off running.

"I got four others with me. Two men, two women. We're just survivors like you. We're not here to hurt anyone. Just looking for gas," he said.

She kept her hands up by her chest and wouldn't look him in the eye.

"You...you army?" She asked with a thick Chinese accent.

"I'm a Marine. I'm here to help."

He took a moment to examine her a bit more closely. She wore all stylish, tight clothing in dark colors, big purse and black nerd glasses. Her hair was in a short ponytail and she didn't seem to have a weapon on her. That wasn't very smart.

"You're by yourself here?" He asked.

"Yeah."

"Come with me. Meet the others."

She smiled for a brief second.

"I thought I alone. No see anyone in months," she said. She stepped back and looked him up and down. Then her scowl turned into a faint smile with perfect, white teeth.

Holy mother of Moses, was she pretty.

"My name's Alex Attaway. What's your name?"

"Lisa Fang."

Fang? Awesome name there.

"Alright, Lisa Fang. Follow me and I'll introduce you to the others."

He took out his walkie-talkie and told the others to meet him at the Humvee.

As they walked back, he figured this was a good time to ask more questions.

"Where do you live?"

"Down Cary Street. Big house by river." She pointed the way.

"What are you doing walking around here?"

"Came to get music from store. Plan 9. Cool music store."

"Your place has electricity?"

"Sun power," she said.

Ah, solar powered.

"How's your food situation? Water?"

"Good, good. Canned."

She said "canned" with a slightly worried voice. His guess was that she had plenty of canned food but didn't know what to do once it ran out.

"We got plenty of food and water. We're going to go find a farm with usable equipment. Older the better."

"Farm? To grow food and animals?"

"That's right."

She made a face as if about to say something, but stopped herself.

As they walked side by side he noticed that she was quite a bit shorter than him and only came up to his chin. What was she doing going around here without a weapon? She sure couldn't take someone in a fist fight.

They reached the Humvee and the others were already gathered there.

"Oh good! It's another girl!" Rebekah said.

"I thought you'd want the opposite," Jennifer said.

Rebekah shrugged.

"I don't want a bunch of horny men around me that think 'they last man on Earth, me last woman. Make babies,'" Rebekah said.

Jennifer chuckled.

"Team, this is Lisa Fang, Lisa, this is my team."

"Hello, team," Lisa said with a shy wave.

Her eyes behind her glasses were perfectly calm. She made no expression to show fear or relief. If he were her, he'd have both.

A lone girl walking around a dangerous city with no form of protection? He hoped she would prove to have more common sense than that.

At least she was cute.

Very cute.

21

LISA HAD SET UP SHOP IN A MANSION IN THE SWANKY PART OF Cary Street where a bunch of mansions and old plantations were. It was near the river. It was a huge, old house from before the Civil War and had fire places and bedrooms for everyone. For water, Lisa hauled water from the river up the hill and filtered and boiled it. She had cleared out every house, grocery store and even the trendy organic foods store and her kitchen was filled with canned food.

But the problem was: what would she do once the canned food ran out? When they told her their plan, she seemed very excited about it. They were sitting in the living room of her giant mansion on furniture that was older than their grandparents. The chair he was sitting in had a straight back that went passed his head. It creaked every time he moved.

"I don't know farming, but I work hard," Lisa said.

"If you want to come with us, you're more than welcome," Alex said.

"Can I talk with you for a second?" Adam asked.

Adam took him into the other room and whispered.

"Alex, it's not safe to bring her with us," Adam said.

"Why's that?" Alex asked.

"She's Chinese for starters. They're the ones that started this war."

He didn't need to be reminded of that. It had been a Chinese bomb that had killed his stepmother.

"She used to work at an all you can eat buffet. Unless they trained waitresses as assassins, I think we're all right."

"That's not what I'm talking about. If we meet other survivors, some of them may not accept her as easily as we do. It could cause problems."

"Then we deal with it but we're not leaving her to rot here by herself."

"You think we should risk ourselves for her? She's not a part of our group."

"She's a survivor. As far as I'm concerned, our group is any living human that isn't trying to kill us."

"And if she does try?"

"What's she going to do? Strangle me with her headphones?"

"She's Chinese."

Adam said that like that explained everything.

"She's coming with us."

Adam looked him in the eyes for a moment before answering.

"Understood," Adam said, but he didn't seem convinced. "Also, we need to make sure she can defend herself. I want her to be an asset, not a liability."

"I thought she was already a trained assassin."

"Let's see what she can do."

"Of course. We'll make sure she doesn't shoot herself or someone else in the foot."

Adam folded his arms and leaned back against the wall.

"Now what do we do?"

"We need supplies."

"Right. Let's go to the local government and see what Richmond has to offer. Police stations, government facilities, national guard depots. Anyplace that might have gas or bullets."

Adam nodded and they went back to the living room.

Lisa was in a high backed chair cradling a small cup of tea in her hands. She watched them come back in with a slight worried expression that she quickly hid.

"We'll rest tonight and tomorrow we have to find gas," Alex said.

"I'll cook you dinner," Lisa said.

She hopped up and went to the kitchen with a small smile on her round lips.

"She seems eager to please," Spencer said.

"Well, she's been alone for a year and she's frightened about her future. We can help, so of course she's eager to please," Jennifer said.

"Maybe it's more than that," Adam said.

"What if we can't find gas?" Rebekah asked.

"I saw a bike shop. We'll ride bikes if we have to."

Rebekah grimaced. She must not have liked the idea of riding a bike instead of riding in the back of a Humvee. He couldn't blame her. He didn't like the idea either.

The house was big. He took the time to look the house over while Lisa was busy in the kitchen. Jennifer went in to help and talk to her.

The house looked more like a museum than a place to live in. But it had a little electricity due to the few solar panels up on the roof. So, at least they had lights at night.

Normally he'd be concerned with running lights at night, but there were enough trees to block the light from going to far. He didn't want unexpected guests.

The bedrooms looked like generically decorated guest rooms but then he came to what must have been Lisa's room. There were neatly stacked piles of clothes on the floor that were organized by types. There was a large stack of folded jeans, then T-shirts, then buttoned up shirts, etc. Apparently food wasn't the only thing she had been collecting. She had put up Chinese calendars like he was used to seeing in Chinese restaurants. She must have wanted a taste of home.

There were also duffle bags that looked full, probably more clothes. Most of the clothing was black or other dark colors. She seemed to like simple and dark. That certainly wasn't what she was wearing now. They must have caught her in a fun mood.

He didn't look any closer. Even at the end of the world people deserved some privacy.

Jennifer called up to him.

"Dinner's ready!" She said.

He made his way back down where everyone was gathered in the kitchen. Lisa was serving up everyone's plates. There were rice noodles, vegetables of all kinds and even some sort of meat which he didn't recognize.

It smelled wonderful and he didn't think it was just because he had been eating MRE's for the past few months.

"This looks wonderful," Rebekah said.

"Thank you," Lisa said.

They all sat down in the dining room at a giant wooden table with actual silverware. As everyone talked he noticed that Lisa stayed fairly quiet, only speaking if she was spoken to. She sat there, eating, smiling but she was definitely thinking of something because she was listening, but not to the conversations around her.

"Lisa, thank you for dinner," Alex said.

She snapped out of her own thoughts and adjusted her glasses as she looked at him.

"You welcome," she said.

He had to admit that he liked her smile.

He slept in a giant, old bed in a room that looked like it belonged in an old photo. The bed had too many pillows and most ended up on the floor. Alex wasn't used to a bed this soft and tossed and turned all night.

In the morning they left to find the local government building, but on the way there they found a police station. Inside looked like a mob had torn through the place. The square building had glass doors that had been smashed. The windows were all broken and some had smoke stains coming up from the gaping holes.

He kept his M4 up to his shoulder as he led the way through. They went through room by room checking for danger. He saw a records room, an armory, and even a shooting range. Once the building was cleared they split up into their assigned pairs. Lisa was now his unofficial partner and she followed him to the armory. The others were looking for where they might find fuel.

Maybe it might have made more sense to reassign new pairs and have Lisa go with someone else, but he'd abuse his authority just this once and make the call in his favor.

The armory had been locked but he grabbed the bolt cutters from the Humvee and let himself in. Inside there were only a few shotguns left, two M4's and a bunch of Glocks.

They had extra weapons in the Humvee, but waste not: want not. He handed her an M4 and grabbed all the ammo they had. Then he took Lisa down to the shooting range. The range was in the basement and had eight lanes with dividers between them. Normally you'd set your paper target on a cardboard silhouette and push a button to make the target move back to the desired distance but since there was no power he had to jump over the counter and do it manually.

Once the target was ready he began teaching Lisa the basics of gun safety. Basically, how not to shoot herself or him.

It reminded him of when Alma was first learning to shoot. Dad would show her the same way he was showing Lisa. At first it had just been him and his dad. It was their way to bond and when he first invited Alma he had been angry. It was their thing to do. He didn't want strangers intruding. He had still been upset by his father remarrying but now this strange girl was intruding on his time with Dad.

But Alma had proved to have a remarkable knack for shooting. They hit it off almost instantly.

Teaching Lisa reminded him of those lessons with Alma. He remembered when he first taught her to fire the AR. She had only fired handguns before that and thought the AR too heavy. He helped her hold it while he showed her how to operate it. But when he saw the grin she made after letting off her first magazine, he knew she was going to be great at it.

After teaching Lisa safety and the operation of the M4, he showed her how to load and clear and how to clear jams. After an hour of practice he began teaching her how to shoot. They wore earmuffs and protective glasses. She seemed to get the hang of it very quickly.

Either he had the good fortune to teach two natural talents or he was just that good of a teacher.

The others came in and they paused the lesson. Lisa stood there looking very natural with the M4 slung across her chest. She kept her finger off the trigger and he didn't have to remind her once.

"We found some National Guard armories and an Air Guard base just on the other side of Richmond. If we're going to find fuel, it's going to be there," Adam said.

"Right. We'll finish up here and then be on the way. Go to the armory and load up what you can."

"There's not much room in the Humvee," Adam said.

"Strap stuff on top if you have to."

They left except for Rebekah who wanted to watch Lisa's progress. Alex made her put in some trigger time as well. She wasn't exactly an expert and could use as much practice as she could get.

Afterwards, he tried to teach Lisa how to fight in a gun battle, but because they were in a cramped, indoor pistol range, he couldn't show her or let her try it properly. So, that lesson would have to wait.

Once finished they, along with Lisa's new M4, went back to the Humvee and took off to find this Guard armory. It was in a small town just outside of Richmond called "Blackstone" and it had a historical marker now overgrown with weeds that talked about some battle in the Civil War that took place there.

It didn't look promising. The armory was small and there were only two Humvees parked outside and a lot next door had some rusting 155mm, towed, howitzers. They searched the place and didn't find anything useful except an old box of MRE's and M-16 A2's which they didn't need or want. They did find a backpack for Lisa though. It was in digital camo pattern but she didn't mind.

"I guess they keep the good stuff somewhere else," Spencer said.

"Let's try the air base," Jennifer said.

The Air Guard base was just across the street (literally) from the guard armory and was considerably bigger. There were several hangers and one of them was open and showing an F-16 parked inside. The canopy was open and a rolling ladder stood beside it. This machine would never fly again. How long before people got to fly like before? How long would this Dark Age last?

Again they split into pairs and stayed in contact with battery powered walkie-talkies. It wasn't long before Jennifer and Rebekah reported a 50 gallon drum of gasoline.

Alex ran over as fast as he could. He crossed a runway that was growing cracks that would eventually make it useless. The others were gathered around smelling the drum. Adam had unscrewed a small lid and was smelling it.

"I think this is the good stuff," Spencer said.

It was.

The gas worked and soon they had a full tank and a little extra in smaller containers.

"Pay dirt, boss. Now what?" Adam asked.

"Unless there are any objections, I think we should head out in the morning," Alex said.

"Where to?" Rebekah asked.

"We'll discuss that once we get back to Lisa's house. Lisa, you still want to come with us?"

She quickly nodded.

"Alright. Let's get some maps and any information that we can and figure out where we're going. Jennifer feels that the Shenandoah Valley would be our best bet."

"I used to teach at Washington and Lee University, right there next to VMI. You'll have a hard time finding a better place. Green farmland, rivers, streams, trees," Jennifer said.

"Any objections or better ideas?" Alex asked.

No one objected.

22

ALMA WOKE UP IN HER ROOM IN THE LARGE HOUSE OVERLOOKING Utah Valley. She heard screaming. Without thinking she threw back her covers and ran out of her room.

It was Cassidy.

Alma ran to Cassidy's room and found her lying in bed screaming something about her mother. She was still asleep and having some kind of horrible nightmare.

"Leave her alone! Mom!" Cass shouted at the top of her lungs.

She grabbed Cass's shoulders and shook her awake. Cass blinked and looked around the dark room.

"What's going on?" Cass asked.

"You were having a nightmare and screaming out loud."

"I was?"

"Yes."

Cass was shaking and covered in sweat. Alma rubbed her head and tried to calm her down. By the sound of it, it was a very vivid dream. She had had her own share of horrible dreams since the world ended.

"I'm sorry," Cass said as she lay back down.

"Go back to sleep and try not to dream," Alma said.

"Okay."

Alma walked back to her room but stopped in her doorway. She knew she wouldn't get back to sleep. There was no point in trying. If she did manage to get to sleep, she'd just see the lifeless body of her father as it lay in the dirt waiting for her to finish digging the grave.

Seeing her father as an empty, lifeless shell had been more horrible than anything else about the plague. At her mother's funeral she couldn't stand looking at the body.

Alma wandered downstairs to the kitchen where they had all their maps laid out. They had planned what route they were taking and also alternate routes in case bridges or roads were out.

Alternate routes weren't their only concern though. They had enough gas to get halfway through Colorado. If they couldn't find gas then they'd be in trouble. Big trouble.

The gas situation worried her. She kept doing the math and it just wasn't adding up how she wanted it.

She spent the rest of the night checking and double checking all their equipment.

From Cabela's they got a small, backpack solar panel so they could recharge batteries for flashlights and her iPod. They also had water purifiers and even books on how to butcher and prepare wild game. She knew it would eventually come to that. She had added up how many calories they'd need per day and (once again) if they didn't find gas and had to walk, they'd probably go hungry.

She hoped Cass was as good as a hunter as she said she was.

Shortly after sunrise Cass wandered downstairs with eyes that were halfway closed. Her tall, lanky form stumbled around until it came to a rest at the kitchen table.

"*Buenos dias, chica*," Alma said.

Cass grunted something she didn't understand.

"Last meal in the house. What do you want? Might as well go all out because we can't take it all with us."

"I want everything. A little of everything," Cass mumbled.

"Then that's what you will have."

Alma made corn beef hash from a can, pancakes and bacon (spam) all on the living room fire place.

"If we ever find a pig, I'm shooting it because I want real bacon, not this canned crap," Cass said.

"And cows. I want carne asada."

"Hamburger."

"Hamburger with bacon."

"We'll never be able to go someplace and just order a hamburger anymore. Isn't that strange? If we want food, we'll have to make it ourselves."

"And clothes," Alma said.

"Oh, what are we going to do about clothes?"

"Collect what we can and learn how to make it."

"I'm not very good at sewing."

"Cass, I think we're both going to have to learn to do things we don't know how to do."

Cass looked down to her hands and began playing with her nails. She did that when she was thinking.

"This sucks," Cass said.

"Don't get blue on me now. We got a long way to go."

Cass nodded and went back to eating her fried Spam.

After a leisurely breakfast they packed the car while checking their lists and after triple checking that they had everything, they started the Enclave and pulled out of the driveway.

"Cass, tunes please."

"Roger."

Cassidy plugged in one of their iPods into the car's stereo and turned the volume up. They had extra iPods all loaded with as many songs as they could fit.

As they were pulling out of their neighborhood Alma saw a man with a large backpack walking up the road.

"Look!" Cass pointed out.

"I see it."

Cass leaned forward to get a closer look.

Alma recognized the figure. She had seen him before. He was the young, filthy hobo that thought she was a drug dealing hooker.

She sped up.

"What are you doing? Slow down and let's talk to him!" Cass said.

"No!" Alma said as they raced past the man.

She saw his face. It was him and he saw her. Her eyes met his and she saw the recognition in them. His filthy beard split as he shouted unheard insults at her. His bloodshot eyes were wide and spit was flying from his mouth.

She sped past the horrible man and down the street, away from what had been their temporary refuge.

The idea of that man finding them when they were relaxing and eating and not paying attention frightened her. She didn't want to image what would have happened. She hadn't been wearing her gun that morning.

She promised to never let her guard down that much again.

"Alma! Can you hear me? What're you doing?"

"That's not a good man, Cass. He's crazy."

Cass looked upset and looked back but she didn't argue.

"He must have seen the smoke from our chimney," Cass said.

"Maybe."

It couldn't have been an accident. The chances of stumbling on to the same man were pretty small.

She drove a little faster than normal until they were back on I-15 heading toward the road that would lead down Provo Canyon and head east.

Her brother was somewhere back east. He was alive and she was going to find him. Finally, she was going east. She had been going north which was necessary, but she felt that she was finally moving closer to him.

She leaned back in her comfortable seat and let the sounds of heavy rock fill her mind. She loved feeling the vibrations of the six strings and deep rumble of the bass and the pounding of the drums.

Cass put her feet up on the dash and adjusted her "cool" sunglasses. They were sleek, modern, all black ones that looked like something out of the Matrix. Alma had chosen a gold and brown pair of aviators. Now that they were both surviving the end of the world in style maybe they could enjoy it a little.

The ride up into Provo Canyon was the most beautiful thing she had seen in Utah so far. The jagged, rock walls of the canyons soared above her and she slowed down so she could get a better look.

"This isn't so bad," Cass said.

"No, it isn't."

This wasn't bad at all.

23

Alex, Richmond, Virginia

ALEX WAS UP BEFORE THE SUN LIKE HE USUALLY WAS. MAYBE IT was a Marine thing or maybe he just worried too much about the people he had to take care of. There were so many things that could go wrong. It wasn't like before the war where if something bad happened you could call the police, the firemen or the doctor. If something happened they had to take care of it themselves.

He walked out into dark hallway while holstering his Beretta M9. He slept with it within arms reach and never went anywhere without it. This world had far less people but the people that remained were far more desperate. Desperate people were dangerous. He didn't like dangerous people.

Alex went into the living room and immediately reached for his pistol when he saw someone standing in the shadows. But in the next instant he realized that it was Lisa. She was standing beside the window and looking out.

"I thought I was the only one up," he said.

She jumped a little and turned her head just enough to see him from the corner of her eye.

"You wake early," she said.

"Old habit. What about you?"

She shrugged.

"I never sleep much."

He saw her M4 leaned up against the wall. He prayed that she wouldn't have to use it. She deserved a life of peace.

"Have you been out there? Things can get rough," he said.

"I stay quiet. Nobody sees me."

"It's going to be dangerous out there. Make sure you stay calm and keep your head down."

"I will," she said with a faint smile.

"You going to miss this place?"

"It big and quiet. Too big. Too quiet. Not my home."

He walked to the window that looked out over the back yard and the river beyond.

"You fight in war?" She asked.

"Yes. New York."

"You hate Chinese?"

He thought for a moment. There were several ways he could answer that and several layers of sugar he could sprinkle on the answer.

"No."

He didn't hate the Chinese people but he did hate their leaders. They were the ones responsible for all of this.

"Why not? I think Adam hates Chinese."

"He'll be fine. Just give him time."

"Why you trust me?" She asked in a whisper.

That was a harder question: one he didn't have the answer to.

"You from Richmond?" He asked instead.

She looked at him for a moment before shaking her head.

"Dad got us over here. He pay mafia money and we work in buffet. Mom work there. Dad work there. Brothers work there. I work there too."

"I had my dad and a sister back in Las Vegas."

"No mom?"

"Killed in the war. A Chinese bomb hit the hospital she was working at."

Lisa looked down to the ground.

"Don't worry. I don't blame you."

She just nodded.

"Besides, I don't think any of that matters anymore. Do you?"

"Do they hate me for war?" She asked.

"Doesn't matter. We're all just people."

She put her hands in her jean pockets and wandered away from the window. She seemed to be looking around at nothing in particular.

"You still want to come with us? More the merrier."

She turned back to face him.

"Yes. I need to come with you. I can't stay here. Food run out. Need people around. Safe in numbers."

"Exactly. Just remember, if we run into trouble, don't hesitate. Keep down and if you see a bad guy, shoot him. Do not hesitate. Do not think about it. Got it?"

"Got it," she said with a sad smile and then turned away. "Now I make you breakfast."

He followed her into the kitchen where she pulled out cans of strange stuff and bags of rice. She began cooking up something that filled the whole room up with a delicious smell that made his mouth water. From the smell he could tell that it was going to be spicy. Also, her putting in a bucket of dried peppers gave him a clue.

"Is this really breakfast food?"

She shrugged.

"No, but it good."

He liked the way she thought.

After she finished the two of them sat down and ate until their bellies swelled. Neither of them needed to say anything. They both understood that sometimes you just had to close your mouth and enjoy.

She seemed content. He didn't know her well enough to read her expressions, but his best guess was that she was content. There was no food left and she didn't go back to the wood burning stove. She had made this feast just for them.

After everyone else got up and just had pancakes, they packed the Humvee and he mounted his bike. After triple checking that they had everything, they headed out across the James River on their way to Powhatan County. They passed through some toll booths which Alex couldn't help but flipping off. He hated tolls.

It was a humid spring day. Already the vegetation was starting to encroach on the roads. The few cars they passed were rusting and falling apart. How long would it take for their old civilization to be completely wiped away?

That was the problem though. They wouldn't be able to count on scavenging from the old world much longer. They had to become self sufficient if they wanted to survive.

The suburbs of Richmond and Chesterfield gave way to the small country towns of Powhatan. They'd pass old gas stations and older houses that looked like something from the Civil War.

The vines creeping up the sides of the old houses seemed natural, like it was becoming what it was supposed to be.

Eventually the forest grew thicker and they came to a faded sign that marked the end of Powhatan County.

"Eyes open everyone," he said into his walkie-talkie.

The Humvee pulled up behind him and he motioned for them to stay close. If he ran into trouble he didn't want to face it alone. These narrow forest roads with the thick trees were ideal for ambushes.

Now they were traveling through a dark tunnel of trees and he didn't like it one bit. He couldn't see far ahead or to the sides. He had his M4 slung across his back instead of his M-14. It was lighter and easier to maneuver while on his bike.

If he remembered his maps correctly they had another two hours before reaching the town of Buena Vista, the first town they'd come to in the Shenandoah Valley.

Once there they'd have another two hours of fuel to look around for a place to set up shop. It wasn't a bad plan.

Then he noticed something up ahead and slowed down. There were two burnt out cars in the middle of the road, completely blocking the way. It was obviously not an accident.

"Let's back up and try to turn around. We'll take an alternate route," he said into the walkie-talkie.

Just then gunshots rang out and he heard bullets slap on the pavement next to him.

He grabbed his handlebars and quickly turned around to get behind the Humvee. Adam leaned out of the passenger side window and began returning fire. Good man. He remembered his training. Jennifer began turning the Humvee around.

Once behind the turning Humvee, he saw where the muzzle flashes were coming from. He quickly grabbed his M4 and turned on the red dot sight. He placed the glowing red dot on where he thought the shooter was and fired a few rounds. The gun kicked in his hands and the smell of gunpowder filled his senses. The gunfire from the trees stopped.

This was all familiar. In the streets of some small town in New York he had killed his first man. The E.U. soldier with a French flag on his shoulder was running across the street for cover. Alex put the dot of his sight just in front of the running figure and fired. It had only taken a second or two and the man fell to the ground. It was the simplest thing. Pull trigger, man dies. It was his duty. But now he saw that scene in his mind over and over again.

He looked behind him and saw that three men with large hunting rifles were coming out of the woods. They were dressed head to toe in camouflage with black ski masks over their faces. They were sandwiched in.

"Go forward! We have to get through," he said.

Jennifer hit the gas and the Humvee shot forward. He quickly followed behind. He heard gunfire coming from the Humvee and when they passed by the first ambush spot he saw one dead man that didn't have a shirt on. Blood covered his neck and shoulders.

It wasn't his first dead body, but it was the first since the virus.

There were enough survivors out here to form a band of robbers. Interesting. Once he had time he'd have to think about that.

They sped down the old two-lane country highway as fast as they could. They were going great for a while but then he noticed smoke coming from the Humvee's engine.

Gradually the Humvee started slowing down.

Crap.

He couldn't show weakness now. They'd need someone to keep a level head even though he wanted to yell and smash things. His old self would have. But now he was in charge.

Eventually the Humvee came to a sputtering stop. Jennifer tried the engine again and it wouldn't start. Alex rode to the front and saw three bullet holes in the grill.

"Wonderful," he said.

They all got out and looked at the engine. They must have been using .308 or shotgun slugs or something like that because the inside of the engine was torn up.

"Now what do we do?" Rebekah asked. She kept glancing behind them.

"We grab what we can and set the rest on fire," he said.

They were somewhat prepared for this. Their packs were already prepared for such an occasion. He regretted leaving the extra stuff behind though. More than regret. It hurt. Especially the food. They'll be hunting sooner than they'd like.

They all had tactical gear on with magazine pouches and such so they were carrying as much ammo as they could, but he hated knowing that their ammo was finite.

Shouldering their backpacks he set off a thermal grenade in the Humvee and they began marching away. The Humvee erupted in flames and soon he heard the popping of the ammunition they were forced to leave behind.

"I guess we won't be getting there today," Spencer said.

"Probably not, Spence," Alex said.

"Stop crying," Lisa said. "We walk. It simple."

She was a tiny woman carrying a rifle and backpack that must have weighed as much as she did, but she didn't seem to mind at all. Maybe she was made out of tougher stuff than she appeared to be.

24

ALEX AND HIS SMALL GROUP OF SURVIVORS WALKED INTO A SMALL town called Buckingham or something. It was hard to tell because the sign was covered in vines. They had been walking all day and here was as good a place to stop.

"Alright, let's get into one of these houses and take a rest. Adam, Spencer, you two keep watch. I don't want a visit from any locals that might be around," Alex said.

It was a small town with one main road, a courthouse and some old, but large, houses. More than any other place he had seen the forest was reclaiming this place fast. Everything was covered with green. Saplings were sprouting out on the lawns and moss and ivy covered large parts of the houses. It was slipping back into wilderness.

They chose the first nice house they saw and found the door open.

"I'll check the kitchen," Jennifer said.

"Maybe they might have something Kosher," Rebekah said as she collapsed on the couch and put her feet up on a dust covered ottoman.

Adam pulled up a chair by the window and Spencer did likewise on the other side of the room. Lisa slipped off her pack and fell into a large, floral chair. They all looked completely beat. They had traveled fast and for several hours. If they continued this pace they wouldn't last long. His team just wasn't used to this kind of traveling.

The Marines loved running and marching. He was used to it but the others couldn't keep up. Lisa looked just as tired as anyone but he could tell that she was holding her pain in and was trying not to let it show. When she moved she winced and was far more still than she usually was.

"We'll rest here for the night. Get something to eat and stay off your feet.

Do a lot of stretches. I'm serious or you won't be able to walk in the morning," Alex said.

He saw them smile at the idea that they wouldn't have to walk anymore that day.

"Check your feet. Take care of them and they'll take care of you. I'll come by and check them myself."

He went and sat across from Lisa on the love seat.

"Shoes off. I want to see your feet," he said.

"I'm fine," Lisa said.

She looked at him with narrowed eyes and closed mouth. She didn't like taking orders. Who did?

"Please let me see them. This is no time to act tough."

She scrunched her face up in a look of annoyance and began removing her boots. As she said, her feet were fine. They were tiny feet. What was she? Size two?

"Good. Make sure to change socks," he said before moving on to Spencer.

One by one he checked everyone's feet. Some had blisters that they covered with Band-Aids they found in the house's bathroom. They had their own but they didn't want to waste their own supply.

Once it grew dark they didn't make any light. If those rednecks were still out there he didn't want to attract their attention.

Jennifer had managed to scrounge up some canned food from the neighbors' houses and they had a little feast. They couldn't carry it with them because they were loaded down as it was.

"You think we'll find a good farm in the Shenandoah?" Rebekah asked, as she ate her canned beans.

"Sure," Adam said. "I've been there many times. Used to live there. There's lots of good old farms. Should be plenty of animals left alive we can round up."

"Assuming no one's there already doing the same thing," Alex said.

"It's a big valley. Too big for what survivors could be there," Jennifer said. "But wherever we go, I'll need access to the Washington and Lee library. So many books we'll need!"

"Like what?" Spencer asked. He sounded skeptical.

"Everything! Math, history, science, farming, mechanics. You name it, we'll need it. There's so much we as individuals don't know that society does. We let those books go, we'll loose that much civilization. We can't afford to forget how a combustion engine works or who George Washington was and why Martin Luther King Jr. fought for equal rights. Those things are too valuable and they're only more precious now that they're in danger of being lost forever."

"Imagine that, Spencer, we don't have to figure it out on our own. Someone already done the work for us," Rebekah said in a teasing way.

"It's more than that. It's our history. It's who we are and where we came from," Jennifer said. She was sounding like the teacher she used to be.

"It will keep us alive," Lisa said. "Lots to learn."

She was fairly quiet most of the time and rarely spoke. Maybe she was starting to come out of her shell. She'd been silent all day and hadn't said a word. Maybe she just had a lot on her mind. They all did. It would be weird if she didn't.

When they laid out their sleeping bags he noticed Lisa put hers off to the side away from the others. She still didn't feel that she belonged.

"Who wants first watch?" Alex asked.

Rebekah raised her hand.

"I can't sleep yet anyway," she said.

"Alright. Go for an hour then wake the next person up," Alex said.

"I know," she said.

As they lay there they talked for a good while, mostly about good memories and future hopes. Spencer told a story from his basic training where someone accidentally sat on the Drill Sergeant's hat. The punishment lasted several days.

Lisa stayed quiet even though she was awake.

Eventually, they drifted off into sleep. He was awakened by Adam for his turn at watch.

"Who's already gone?" He asked as he rubbed his eyes.

"Everyone but you and the new girl," Adam said.

"Alright."

He checked his watch. 1:36am.

"She's a quiet one," Adam said.

"I noticed."

"Think maybe she's hiding something?"

"It couldn't possibly be because she doesn't trust a bunch of heavily armed strangers."

Adam grunted.

"Keep an eye on her or I will," Adam said.

"What are you expecting? For her to turn into a ninja and beat us all up?"

"Ninja's are Japanese."

"Yes, the whole thing's ridiculous, isn't it?"

Adam went back to sleep and he got up and went to the window. The light from the moon was coming in from the trees and he could see pretty far down the street. The old houses looked normal and peaceful at night, almost like a quiet neighborhood.

He didn't have a hard time staying awake. His mind had plenty to think about. Mostly he thought about Alma. He tried not to imagine her alone and dying in their house. Hoped she went peacefully in her bed while listening to her music. Maybe Dad had lived long enough to bury her. She deserved that at least.

He checked his ammo and counted it. He had 400 rounds for his M4, sixty for his M9, and he was packing his M-14 he kept tied to his pack. It only had 200 rounds of ammunition, mostly stored in his pack. It was heavy.

Adam carried a shotgun as well. Good for hunting. The others carried M4's and a few spare rifles. They all had thigh holsters with M9's except for Lisa who had a police Glock. They had many chances to get different guns, but these were common and they could all swap parts and he didn't have to teach them several different weapon systems. This kept it simple and manageable.

Though he would liked to have had an AK. He wouldn't have to worry about that thing breaking any time soon.

When it was time he woke up Lisa. She snapped away and quickly took in her surroundings. Good instincts.

"Your turn. Everyone's gone already so you wake up Rebekah in an hour."

"Okay."

Lisa got up and walked over to the chair.

"You okay?" He asked.

She shrugged.

"What's okay?" She asked.

"Good question."

"I be fine. Don't worry," she said with half closed, sleepy eyes.

"I'm here if you need anything."

She didn't respond.

25

"WHAT DO YOU MEAN YOU NEVER SEEN FIREFLY?" CASSIDY asked.

"I never saw it. Simple as that."

"How?"

"Because I never did. Had better things to do."

"But...I mean...how?"

"Because I'm not a nerd, I guess."

"It's not about being a nerd, though being a nerd is a compliment. It's about being an American!"

"I'm from Mexico."

"But you live in America. This is hard to believe."

"Is it really America anymore? All I see are empty, crumbling towns and abandoned gas stations."

They had passed Heber and gotten through the mountains about an hour ago. Now it was rocky hills, rugged canyons and blue reservoirs. There were also empty houses and dead, one street towns. The small towns were emptier than the cities. The convenience stores were completely empty. No water, no food, no gas. They had half a tank.

It was a wasteland and it all passed by as Alma looked out with her aviators on and headphones in. Breaking Benjamin and Shinedown played as the brown desert passed by in an endless slideshow.

They came to a small town called "Duchesne." It had one main street and a small, shallow river running through it.

Alma saw the crumbling ruin of a small, one room Catholic church. She thought of the small cement church she used to go to back in Empalme. She wondered how Empalme was. It was crumbling when she left and probably hadn't improved.

"Do you think they got DC?" Cass asked.

"Don't worry about it." Cass liked to worry.

They were only driving about 40mph because the roads were more potholes than road and it helped with miles per gallon.

"What's the next town?" Cassidy asked.

Alma checked the map.

"Roosevelt then...Vernal."

The desert here was pretty at least. When they didn't see signs of civilization it was actually easy to imagine that things were normal. It was actually greener than she thought it would be.

She looked in the backseat where Caesar was sprawled out without a care in the world. His giant ears covered most of his face.

"I envy him. I never could sleep in a car," Alma said.

"I could. My dad said I could sleep anywhere at anytime."

An hour later they reached Roosevelt. The main street (at least it had more than one street) was lined with old buildings that looked like stuff from old cowboy photos where the front of the building was taller than the actual building. Almost like a crappily modernized western town. Who were they trying to fool with that? She saw that the front windows of the pawn shop were smashed.

Dead cars filled the street and they had to squeeze in between a few places. They did come to a grocery store and they stopped to check it out but it had been picked clean.

"Maybe there are a few more survivors here?" Cass asked.

"Maybe. I'd keep that Broadsword of yours handy."

Cass held up the large and very sleek AR-10.

"I think I'll call it Dorothy," Cass said.

"Dorothy?"

"I heard you're supposed to give your gun a woman's name."

"That's if you're a guy."

"What'd you call yours?"

"My Glock is Treble and my AR is Bass."

"Good names."

"I thought so."

"The buildings here look worse than in Salt Lake," Alma said.

"Maybe they were built cheaper? The winters are harsher here. Weather can ruin buildings pretty quickly."

Out of all the places they had seen, this place looked the sorriest and most worn down.

"Well, Cass, looks like our time of easy meals is over."

They got back in the car and continued on. The roads were at least a little better so they sped up to 50mph. The rusted sign said the speed limit was 35. Alma flipped the sign off.

As they were leaving Roosevelt they went up a big hill with an elementary school that was decorated with Indian posters of eagles and wolves. They went down the hill and came to the "Ute Supermarket."

"Map says we're on the Ute Reservation," Alma said.

Ute or not, the grocery store was empty as well.

"Someone's been busy here," Cass said.

After letting Caesar go potty, they continued on to Vernal. Here the hills grew more rocky, taller and more like something from a western. It wasn't just pretty, it was stunning.

They were so busy looking at the gorgeous scenery that they almost didn't spot the road block ahead.

Two large pickup trucks were parked in the road, blocking both inbound and outbound lanes. Four men with rifles were on top of the trucks. Alma saw the glint of binoculars from one of them.

Cass slowed down and looked over to her.

"What do we do?"

"Four people is a lot for a roadblock. They have to have others somewhere else. Maybe they want to trade?"

"Or maybe they want young girls for breeding," Cass said and put a hand up to her throat.

"Would you like that?" Alma asked.

"Not funny."

Alma would have teased her further but they had to make a decision.

"Let's go see what they want. Keep your hand on the reverse in case we have to get out quickly."

As Cass drove closer Alma got her AR ready. She turned on her red-dot sight and put the stock to her shoulder while still keeping it pointed down.

They drew closer to the roadblock and one of the men stood up and raised his hand. He wore hunter camo and held a scoped AR-15.

"That's good enough right there," the man yelled out.

Alma stuck her head out the window. She didn't just see the four men on the trucks. She also noticed two snipers up in the hills.

"Hello there! What's going on?" Cass called out in her "we're all best friends" voice. Didn't she get it? Nobody was their friend out here.

"We're stopping anyone wanting to come in," the man said.

"We're just passing through. Got some things to trade," Alma said.

"Where you heading?"

"East. Heading through Vernal, to Denver and all the way to Virginia."

"Denver? Guess you hadn't heard."

"What?"

"It's gone. Nuked."

Cass cast a worried look to Alma and then faced the men again.

"Well, I guess we'll look for an alternate route."

"What you got to trade?"

"Different stuff."

At least she had the sense to not blather about everything they had.

"Alright, we'll escort you into town and go to the movie theater parking lot. Can't miss it. We have a market there."

"A market? How many survivors you have?" Alma asked.

"Two thousand."

"Thousand?"

They had to be lying. There couldn't be thousands of people gathered here.

"How? There were maybe a few hundred in Salt Lake!" Alma shouted out.

"We don't know. The plague sort of died out I guess. We lost a lot of our people, but we know we made it out better than most."

"I can't believe it!" Cass said.

"Did other towns survive?" Alma asked.

"Most of the Ute Tribe, Lapoint, Dinosaur Colorado."

They moved the trucks out of the way and they drove on to Vernal: population, two thousand.

26

Alma, Vernal, Utah

To Alma's surprise, Vernal was remarkably alive and kicking. There were more cars around than she would have guessed and also a lot of horses. Most people she saw were armed. Even their 'friendly escort' was well armed.

"You think they like Mexicans?" Alma asked.

"I see a lot of Latinos over there."

Cass pointed to a family that was walking in a large group and heading their same direction.

She let out a sigh of relief. She had never been out to the country and didn't know if these people were red necks or crazy or whatever.

"Relax, Alma, they ain't going to eat you," Cass said.

"I'll try not to look nervous."

They came to the old, run down movie theater where there were tables, tents and stall set up. There was even a booth selling fresh tamales. Cars and horses were parked off to the sides and people wandered around. It reminded her of a "*Tiangis*," a large, outdoor market they held on the weekends back in Mexico.

They pulled up and one of their escorts walked up to their door.

"Now, remember ladies, behave yourselves. No stealing, fighting, alchohol, drugs, prostitution or gambling. You have one hour and then we'll escort you to the other side of town so you can continue on your merry way. Understood?" The bearded man said.

They both nodded. Then their armed escort backed away but didn't leave.

"I guess they don't want anymore mouths to feed," Cass said.

"And they don't need breeders."

"Gross."

"Let's get started. What do we have to trade?"

"A few guns, some camping stuff. I don't want to give away our food."

They put the guns they were willing to part with in a duffle bag and walked out into the market. Cass pushed the button on the key ring and the doors locked. Alma held the leash for Caesar who trotted along without worries.

There were people with signs saying they needed work. Others had signs saying they needed other stuff like food, ammo, a pilot light, etc. Some tables sold what could only be described as junk. Others sold shoes and clothes and one table sold guns.

Then they saw a large white board listing what people had and what they wanted. Within a minute they had the name of someone who could trade food and medical supplies for guns and ammo.

Asking around got them pointed to a man in an Army uniform with a table full of MRE's. He was sitting there looking very displeased with everything.

"Jackpot," Alma said.

They walked up to the table and the man barely glanced at them.

"Greetings ladies. Are you here to do business or waste my time?"

"Business," Alma said.

"Let's see what you have," the soldier said.

She emptied the dufflebag out and laid the guns on the table. They had a few AR's, AK's, a CETME and some pistols. This wasn't all they had, but it was all they wanted to trade at the moment.

"If you're in the Army, why do you need guns?" Cass asked.

"We're the Vernal and Ute Militia. There isn't an Army anymore. We need all the guns we can get for our new recruits," the man said.

"Who would you fight? No one's left," Alma said.

"We heard Moab is still around as well as some small towns in Idaho, Wyoming and Colorado. We have oil wells here. People might come to take them from us."

"Can't be too cautious, yeah?" Alma said.

Then a large man with a shaven head and a goatee approached the table.

"Is that your 10mm 1911?" The large man asked.

"It is unless the militia here want it," Alma said.

The man looked to the soldier.

"I got dibs." The goatee man said.

"We don't need 10mm," the soldier said with a shrug.

"How much you want for that?" The goateed man asked.

"Food, water, gas, medical supplies," Alma said.

"I don't have gas."

"Know anyone that might?" Alma asked.

"Gas is for official business only, which is total BS. I had to ride a horse into town. I hate horses."

"What do you have?" Cass asked.

"Training. I can teach you how to use those...is that a Broadsword? Where did you get that?"

He pointed to Cass's fancy .308 AR10.

"Um, yeah, we got it from a guy named Gundoc," Cass said.

"Yes, I know Gundoc. I'm Mad Ogre, the firearms instructor for Crusader Weaponry."

"Small world," Alma said.

"Much smaller now," Mad Ogre said.

"You don't have food or water?"

"I got plenty of water. Now that we don't have to ask permission from the bureaucrats, we dug a well."

"Okay, training and some water and this 10mm is yours," Alma said.

"Deal."

They traded the other guns for several boxes of MRE's and shook hands with the militia soldier.

"We'll have to ask for more time. They only gave us an hour before they kick us out of town."

"I'll talk to them," Ogre said.

Mad Ogre walked over to their armed escort and had some very short words with them. When he walked back he told them that everything was alright and that they could stay until the training was done.

He took them and their guard to a large shooting range with pistol areas and even a 20–1000 yard target course.

Alma didn't need pistol training but Cass definitely did. It was like she had never really used one before. On the long range course however, Cass was brilliant and Alma looked like a noob.

But it wasn't just accuracy they learned, they learned to fight, to do quick draws, quick reloads and moving from cover to cover as a team. After four hours they were tired and very happy.

"That was pretty good," Cass said with a giant toothy smile. They were both sweating.

Alma had to admit that she felt much better about having Cass cover her back. They shook hands with the Mad Ogre and were promptly and a little rudely escorted out of town by their 'friendly escort.' They went through another road block, this one manned with militia in Humvees.

Then they were on their way again.

"Not the warmest welcome," Cass said.

"Warmer than I expected. They didn't rob us or attack us. I'd consider that very polite."

They drove through less scenic desert for another hour before pulling off the road near a stream.

"Might as well camp here for the night," Alma said.

"Got water. I could use a bath." She pointed to the stream.

"Yes you could."

"You don't smell like roses either."

Alma got out and stretched her back. She was a little sore from running and gunning at the training class. After grabbing the canteen of water that had its own filter and purifier, she went to the creek and filled it up.

"I think one of us should stand guard. Two hours on, two for sleep," Alma said.

"What? That sucks."

"Got to, *chica*. The world's a little more crowded than we thought."

"I know, I know."

She ate her MRE as she watched Caesar inelegantly walk to the stream and begin noisily drinking.

"He's kinda useless," Alma said as she chewed her cheese crackers.

"Who?"

"Caesar, that weird dog creature there."

"He's not useless!" Cass said too defensively.

"Oh yeah? What has he done? What can he do?"

As if fate was against her, Caesar looked up from his drinking and began barking. Then he took off, splashing across the creek.

They grabbed their guns and hurried to follow the goofy basset hound.

A baby deer leapt out of the bushes and began running.

Neither of them had to say anything. They both took aim and fired without pausing. The deer fell in mid stride and crashed to a halt. The two of them walked up to where the basset was sniffing the dead deer.

"We actually got it," Cass said.

"Of course we did. But now what do we do with it?"

"We got that book that tells us what to do."

They retrieved the book from the SUV and began following the instructions.

Skinning and cleaning the deer was the single most disgusting thing Alma had ever done. She was up to her elbows in blood and even then the deer looked like it had gone through a lawn mower when they were done with it.

"It's not pretty, but it's done," Cass said.

"We have to do this every time?" Alma asked.

"You bet! What's a matter? Don't got the stomach for it?"

As if this whole end of the world thing couldn't get worse. She suddenly really missed Wendy's and Five Guys.

27

Alex Attaway, Cumberland, Virginia

ALEX MOVED SLOWLY AROUND THE CORNER, KEEPING HIS GUN pointed at anything he might see. This was the fifth house he had searched and so far they had only found a few cans of food.

Lisa was right behind him with her M4. She moved very quietly and sometimes he had to look behind him just to make sure she was still there. She had her glasses, black baseball cap and hair in a ponytail.

She looked good in a tactical vest.

"This place is empty. We should go," Lisa said.

"Yeah, you're right."

They met back up with the others at their house and shared what they had found. It wasn't much.

"Alright, time to get a move on. We have a long way to go," Alex said.

"How far is it?" Spencer asked.

"About eighty miles," Jennifer said.

"About three days," Alex said.

"That long? We need to find a car, man," Spencer said.

"Sure, let's just go rent one," Adam said.

"That would be nice but I wouldn't hold your breath for a sports car. Like it or not, but we're walking," Alex said.

"Then we better get going," Adam said.

No one else said anything so they began walking down the road. Like the houses they passed, the roads were crumbling and falling apart. He wondered how long it would be before the roads were unusable.

"Drink water now. It's hot," Lisa said.

Alex tried not to act surprised by her unexpected show of leadership. Maybe she was more level headed than she first appeared to be. He sucked at first impressions.

The trees offered plenty of shade but the humidity had them drenched in sweat before noon.

"I don't like this heat," Lisa said quietly.

He slowed down a little so she could catch up to him.

"You don't like Virginia's lovely weather?"

"No. I come from town by ocean. Much better."

"Hey, I come from Las Vegas. It's hotter but much drier. You don't feel it nearly as much."

"Las Vegas?"

"Yeah."

"You there for...big attack, right?"

"Yes, I was there when China attacked."

Lisa looked to the ground and swallowed.

"Don't worry. I don't blame you. You're not in the Chinese Army."

She continued to avoid his gaze.

"Hey, the world's a different place now. All that's in the past," he said.

She made a brief and forced smile.

"Do you hate me?" She asked even quieter than before.

Not this crap. He had to nip this in the bud now.

"Lisa, look at me."

She glanced up and he saw her eyes above the rim of her black sunglasses.

"We don't hate you. I don't hate you. You're one of us. We're all in this together, okay?"

"Okay," she said and went back to looking at her feet.

It would probably take more than that to get through to her.

She slung her M4 to the side and grabbed her water bottle. He noticed how easily she moved the weapon and her pack around. This chick must have been hitting the gym a lot this past year and a half.

"Did you go to school?" He asked.

"John Tyler Community College. Part time. Worked at restaurant mostly."

"What did you study?"

"Criminal Forensics."

"Forensics? Really?"

"Yeah."

"That's pretty cool! You could be like that show, CSI!"

"I get to wear fancy suits and drive fancy car, get in gunfights," she said.

"Well, unfortunately the gunfight part has turned out to be true."

"I liked the...quiet of forensics. I know show was total crap."

"I was going to study law. Become a lawyer."

"You? A lawyer?"

"Hey, I wasn't always a Marine. I never even imagined myself as one. I always thought I'd end up being a lawyer. Even as a kid that's what I wanted to be. What six year old decides he wants to study law?"

"But you good at being a Marine."

He laughed.

"I don't know about that. I managed to live this long, so maybe I'm not totally awful at it."

"No, you are great, Alex. The people listen to you. They follow you and trust you. You are great man."

That took him aback. A great man? He wasn't great. He was barely 'alright,' maybe 'pretty good' on rare occasions.

"I think that's something we'll have to see down the road. If we don't make it to the valley and we don't find food and water, then you probably won't be so nice to me."

"We'll find what we need."

"You seem confident about that."

She shrugged.

"I got a feeling," she said.

They fell into silence for a while and only the steady beat of their footfalls accompanied them.

"Hey, if anyone starts to feel a blister forming or their feet start hurting, speak up. It's better to fix a problem before it becomes a big problem."

Rebekah was getting tired so they stopped for a quick and light lunch. Eating a lot when they still had so much walking to do wasn't a good idea. He just chewed on his MRE cheese crackers and wondered what Alma would be doing if she were still alive. She liked the jalapeño cheese from the MRE's.

He wished she were here. He could use her shooting skills right now. She would have out shot anyone in his platoon. Treble and Bass were the names of her competition guns. Her shotgun was called "Heavy Metal."

He didn't have a name for his gun. It needed a name. He always used to sing that song from Nacho Libre, the song about the nun, Encarnacion. It was a horrible name and not very catchy, but he christened his M4 "Encarnacion." Still needed a name for the M-14.

They were soon on the two-lane highway again. He needed to distract people from the discomfort of a long march.

"Anyone name their gun yet?" He asked aloud.

"Bertha," Adam said.

"Jezebel," Spencer said.

"Sweet Pea," Rebekah said.

"I don't think I'll do that," Jennifer said.

"Mulan," Lisa said.

"Come on now, Alex. What's yours?" Adam asked.

"Encarnacion."

He proceeded to tell the story of why, but they still thought it was a lame name.

"It's to remember my sister, guys," he said with a smile so they'd know he wasn't actually upset. Alma thought that was the funniest movie ever. She was always watching comedies.

"You never know, she could still be alive," Jennifer said.

"The odds aren't exactly in my favor," Alex said.

"There's always hope," Rebekah said.

"Not this time."

The others began talking about other things and he didn't notice Lisa walking up beside him.

"I know what you feel. I wonder about family in China. Maybe some of them still alive."

"I don't think either of us will ever find out. We'll never travel that far again. The world has ended and now we just have to find a quiet place to survive and build a new life. Maybe we should forget the old world."

"No, I don't think so. I think it good to remember ancestors. Also, we forget, we make same mistakes."

"I'm sure I'll make all new ones."

28

Alma, Western Colorado

SHE WOKE UP IN THE TENT AND ROLLED OVER TO HER BACK. CASS wasn't in her sleeping bag. Good. That meant she was still on watch. There were a lot of weirdos around and they couldn't afford to sleep without one of them keeping guard.

She crawled out and found Cass sitting by a small fire. She was cooking some of that deer meat they had butchered yesterday.

"Breakfast?" Alma asked.

"Yeah! Smells good, right?"

It kind of did. She crawled over and sat down on a rock next to Cass. She wiggled her toes in the warm sand. It felt good, almost like she was at a really weird beach.

As they ate their breakfast of deer meat, they looked over their map. They couldn't go through Denver but if they continued on Highway 40 they'd go north of Denver and bypass the radioactive area.

"Looks like the first town of any real size we'll come to is a place called 'Craig.' I hope our gas lasts that long," Cass said.

Alma looked back to the car.

"If not, we'll get Caesar to tow us."

After they ate they loaded up the car again and continued on. They had their music playing and Alma kept watch while Cass drove.

They drove for another four hours until they came to a sign that said "Craig 15 miles."

"Not far, yeah?" Alma said.

"Yeah, but our gas gauge is on Empty."

"Think we'll make it?"

As if to answer her question the car began to sputter and die.

"You got to be kidding me!" Alma shouted.

"No, no, no, no, no," Cass said repeatedly.

Despite their protests, the car came to a stop along the side of the road.

The two of them sat there in silence for a while. Then Cassidy looked over to her.

"I guess we're walking," Cass said.

"Yeah, I guess so."

Reluctantly Alma got out and went over to the rear hatch. She opened it and pulled out the wagon that was meant for heavy yard work they found at Home Depot. They put on their packs and filled the wagon with their food, ammo and weapons. Then they filled the other wagon. When they were both ready, they slowly began walking. Caesar was on a leash tied to Cass's wagon. He plodded on behind them like nothing was wrong.

"This sucks," Alma said.

"It doesn't help to complain. We still have a lot of blessings here."

"I'd rather have the car. Fifteen miles? How long is that going to take us?"

"Rest of the day, I imagine."

Suddenly the desert road looked a lot longer than it did before.

They walked on for an hour without talking and just looking as the hills as they slowly passed by.

"Think they still need breeders back in Vernal?" Cass asked.

Alma looked over to her and saw that toothy grin of hers.

"Maybe. We can go ask."

"You have some good birthing hips there, Alma. Maybe ten kids? Eleven?"

"Don't laugh. My great grandmother had twelve."

"Twelve? Wow!"

"Back in Mexico in those days, it wasn't rare. I'm not going to have twelve. No, sir!"

"Why not? This is your chance to make sure that countless descendants bare the name of Attaway. It could become the most common name on Earth if you have a lot of kids now."

"I don't think the benefits make it worth the pain."

"You lack vision," Cass said with a laugh.

"I'd rather have like a royal dynasty. We could rule our own country. A country ruled by queens instead of kings. Maybe women wouldn't kill off the world like the men did."

"Nah, whenever women are in power, they act identical to how the men act. Power is power. Gender doesn't really play into it."

"Then how would you suggest keeping this," Alma waved her hands around, "from happening again?"

"Understanding."

"You think if we just understood the Chinese they wouldn't have invaded?"

"No, it would take mutual understanding and trust on both sides over a long period of time."

"I don't see that happening."

"And that's what's wrong with the world. No one can trust anyone. Especially now. I'm afraid once civilization gets back on its feet it's going to look more like the Dark Ages than the 21st century."

"Can't argue with that."

After two hours they stopped and took a little break. Alma looked at their water supply and wasn't happy. It was enough for three, maybe four days at most.

And this desert was getting hot.

All the rest of the day they didn't see a single sign of civilization: not even a road sign.

They talked about school and what they had wanted to be when they grew up. Cass wanted to be a veterinarian for horses. Alma wanted to be a professional competition shooter with her own TV show.

"I wish we had some horses," Cass said.

"Never rode a horse before."

"I love horses. Maybe we can find some."

"If it gets me off my feet. I like it."

Around sunset they came to the edge of Craig Colorado. At first it was just a few small houses, but then the houses grew nicer. It was as good a place to camp out as any. They shouldered their weapons and began searching the houses. They found a few cans of food and found the nicest house in the area.

They slept on the top floor in dusty but very comfortable beds. Caesar slept in Cass's bed. It looked like a grandma lived here. Too much lace and pictures of flowers.

Alma couldn't sleep and looked out the window at the empty, dark street. The neighborhood looked torn up from neglect and it just didn't feel right. It shouldn't be this still and this quiet.

The world didn't feel right.

None of it did.

29

THE FIRST SIGN AHEAD OF THEM SAID "WELCOME TO AMHERST." The second sign said "Strangers will be shot."

"I could remark on the duality of mankind's nature, but I'll refrain," Jennifer said.

Rebekah walked up to the second sign and stretched her shoulders back. Her hands remained on her pistol belt.

Past the sign they could see a fire station, a fast food joint and a roundabout with flowers in the middle. Charming.

"Well, well. This is the only road that goes through the mountains here. If we don't go this way we'll have to go around and that'll take another...two days?" Rebekah said.

"It's already been four days," Adam said.

Lisa walked out in front of the group and tipped her glasses down to get a better look. Her brows knitted in the middle but she remained silent. He wondered what she was thinking. Sometimes she seemed remarkably open and talkative and sometimes she was as closed as a bank vault.

What made her tick?

"Is this some lone paranoid psycho or is it a group like we met a few days ago," Adam asked.

"Can we sneak around the town and get back on the road?" Rebekah asked.

Alex looked at his map. The map showed that last little town that led to the road through the mountain was called "Forks of Buffalo." The map showed that Amherst had a few roads around it that could help them navigate.

"Yeah, we'll go around," Alex said.

They got off the road and began circling around. They should come to a highway and then turn back west.

The forest wasn't so bad. It had more shade than the road and if he ignored everything else he could pretend he was hiking or hunting.

Their group came out at the highway and he went ahead to check the area out first. It looked empty each way. He waved for the others to come up while he kept watch.

They made it across the highway and made their way around Amherst. It added two hours to their travel but it was better to be safe. When they got back on the main road they hadn't got as far as they had hoped. In front of them was another sign warning strangers to not come to Amherst.

"I always thought the people here were supposed to be friendly," Rebekah said.

"I guess they had hard times," Jennifer said.

"Or bad people took over," Adam said.

"I don't care to find out," Alex said.

Then the sound of a truck reached their ears. They all looked in that direction, the direction of Amherst.

A truck full of armed men came from around the curve of the road. Six or seven men. They were spotted.

"Run," Alex ordered as calm as possible.

They ran back to the edge of the woods as shots rang out. Bullets hit the trees around them as they made it into the forest.

The truck came to a screeching halt and the men jumped out. Alex didn't try to get a close look. He was running and trying not to trip over a root or fallen branch.

"Why are they shooting at us?!" Rebekah asked.

A bullet struck a tree uncomfortably close to his head. He felt wood splinters hit his sunglasses.

These hillbillies would know the woods better than his little group. They'd track his friends even if they did manage to get away.

"We have to stop them," he called out.

Without waiting for their response he whirled around, got behind a thick tree and began firing. He hit one of them right off, looked like an arm or shoulder hit. He saw a spray of blood and the man with the bushy beard twisted to his right before falling down.

The others took cover behind trees and began firing back.

Bullets zipped by him and struck the tree he was hiding behind.

Alex looked back and saw his people taking cover and returning fire.

Good. None of them were freaking out.

He peeked around the tree, saw someone running for a small boulder. He snapped his M4 up, placed the floating, glowing, red dot on the man and fired. The man tumbled forward and landed on his face.

The man's buddies must not have liked that because several of them opened fire on his position. Alex motioned for his people to move around and flank them from the side while they were preoccupied with him.

A quick glance showed that there were five of the men left. They were dressed in hunting camo and had beards and wild looks on their faces. Whoever they were, they weren't just locals hard up on their luck. Highway bandits or something like that.

The bandits noticed his people moving around them and they shifted fire from him to them. They were throwing out shots as fast as they could. Decreased accuracy, but more chances of hitting. These were not trained men.

Alex popped back out and aimed his next shots at a group of three of them. But before he could pull the trigger one of them was hit right in the forehead. His hat flew off and the man next to him barely had time to register surprise before a bullet hit him in the head as well. It had taken about a second for it to all happen.

After seeing that, the remaining men turned tail and began running back to their truck.

Alex looked back to his group trying to figure out who had fired those shots. Either it was luck or one of his team was a better shot than any of them had realized.

"Follow them and take their truck!" Rebekah shouted out.

He had a split second to decide if the truck was worth the risk. One of their lives was not worth a truck, but then killing these men now might save lives down the road. It was simple math. He hated math.

"After them!" He shouted out.

They ran after the three men and got to the road just as the men were jumping in the truck.

Alex took aim at the head of the man that fumbling with the truck's keys. He breathed in and out and let the red dot rest on the man's temple. Slowly and smoothly he pulled the trigger.

The man's head jerked and blood flew all over the cabin. The man that had been right beside him also took the same bullet and both of them flopped over dead. The third man bolted out the door and ran for the other side of the road. He didn't have his AK.

Lisa came up beside him and raised her gun.

"He's unarmed," Alex said.

"So? He can get armed. He can go get friends and bring more bad men."

He didn't stop her. She took aim but before she could fire, Adam fired and shot the man between the shoulder blades.

As they approached the truck, Alex wondered if he should be pleased or bothered by his people's ability to kill. He also needed to know who shot those two men in the head.

"We got a truck again!" Rebekah said with a forced smile and a half hearted cheerleader pose.

Jennifer walked up and looked inside the cabin. Tears were welling up in her eyes. Probably the adrenaline dump. They had just survived an attack on their lives. Their stress levels were probably astronomical. Strangely, he felt alright. He was used to this and wished he wasn't.

"Why you cry?" Lisa asked.

"They were human beings."

"They were animals," Lisa said.

"I know, but I regret having to do what we did. It shouldn't have been necessary. None of this should. We caused all these problems," Jennifer said, waving her hands around.

"Taking a life isn't an easy thing. It shouldn't be. We're supposed to save it for when it's necessary, not when it is convenient. If we had let those men go, they'd continue to prey on the weak. There's no judges or courts. We're it. We're now the law." Alex said.

This got him a firm nod from a steel faced Lisa.

Rebekah was trying to act as steel faced but she was also on the point of tears. He would have to talk to her, but in private.

They pulled the bodies from the truck and did their best to clean off the blood. The truck started up with a roar and they were on their way again, heading up into the Blue Ridge Mountains. On the other side was Buena Vista, Lexington and the rest of the Shenandoah valley where hopefully they'd find their new home.

30

Alma, western Colorado

Alma hated jogging or walking up hills. She hated mountains even more. They had been walking uphill all day. The Rocky Mountains were huge. She had never seen mountains this big before and they hadn't even gotten to the actual mountains yet. The grey, snow capped mountains were still in front of them and had been all day.

"I don't think I'm a big fan of mountain hiking," Cassidy said. She removed her straw cowboy hat and wiped her brow.

"It can't be that bad, we only have another week or so walking through treacherous mountain passes."

Cass groaned but she kept marching on.

"If Vernal survived, how many other towns you think made it?" Cass asked after an hour of silence.

Alma was too out of breath to answer so she sat down on the side of the road and took out one of her water bottles.

"I don't know. America's full of small towns. Heck, most of the Dakotas are probably still there. And the islands and New Hampshire. No one ever goes there," Alma said.

"Maybe Alaska made it?"

"Maybe."

"I've been thinking, maybe we can find one of these towns and settle down."

"After we find my brother."

"Oh, of course. But we'll have to show that we're useful and not just two dumb teenagers."

"We are useful. You're smart and we can both shoot."

"I was thinking that we might need something more. Maybe we can find a book on how to be electricians. Maybe that'd let us in."

"We got time. We have to make it all the way to Virginia first."

"I know. I was just thinking."

She was probably right. They needed to learn more if they wanted to survive.

Once they were rested they continued on walking. The roads here were in better shape than most of Utah and weren't crumbling before their eyes.

"I think I hate Colorado," Alma said.

"It wouldn't be so bad if we had a car."

"Find me gas and we'll walk back and grab our car."

"Yeah, right. These small towns don't have anything."

"Didn't have much before the war."

Cassidy started coughing. Alma didn't think much of it, but she kept coughing. She also didn't look too good.

"You alright?" Alma asked.

"Yeah, fine. Just feel a little tired."

"Okay, but if you start getting sick, tell me."

"Will do."

A simple cold wasn't so simple anymore. There was no more medicine to prevent a cold from turning into a deadly fever.

They marched all the rest of the day, walking for an hour and resting for fifteen minutes. Alma kept her eye on Cass and by the time they stopped to make camp, Cass wasn't looking so good.

They used their fire starter kit to make a nice fire and set up their two-woman tent.

"Hey, we're taking tomorrow off," Alma said.

"Good. I think I can use a break."

Cass lay down beside the fire while she poured two cans of beans into their pot.

"Okay, Alma, I think I'm coming down with something."

"You think? Pretty darn obvious, Telephone Pole."

"Yeah, yeah. My mom always got after me about that. She had to force me to stay home from school or church."

"I thought you were home schooled."

"Not during elementary."

"So, you've always been stubborn."

"Pretty much."

Cass draped her arm over her eyes and a few minutes later she was snoring.

She woke up long enough to eat some beans but then went right back to sleep.

Alma wasn't going to show it in front of Cass, but she was worried.

Her mom was a nurse but whatever talent that required wasn't passed down. Maybe it skipped a generation. Her mom, despite working with traditional medicine, always liked natural remedies best.

Now Alma wished she had paid more attention.

But then, maybe this was just a small cold and she was worrying about nothing.

As Cass slept Alma sat there looking up at the stars. The air was so clear here and the mountains, now that they were finally getting near them, were very beautiful, even at night.

She was glad to have lived to see this. Perhaps she still had some things she still had to do in life. Was it fate? She had never really believed in fate before and didn't really believe it now, but for the first time she was wondering.

Maybe she was kidding herself with all this. Maybe she had gone crazy. Chasing after a brother that was, more than likely, dead. Cass had a point. It would make more sense to find a good town and settle down. They had a much better chance of surviving in a community. On their own they were vulnerable to anything. One mistake could cost them their lives.

But then she couldn't stop thinking about Alex. She knew he was alive somewhere and she was going to find him no matter what and no matter how long it took.

She looked at Cass who was sleeping by the campfire. She was an orange lump she could barely see between the flickering flames and the glowing sparks. Until she found Alex, this was her family now. Even if she did miraculously find him, she would always be family.

"Sleep well, *Hermana*."

31

As Alex drove through the narrow, winding mountain roads of Virginia, he looked around the cramped truck at his people. They were his clan now and yet one of them had shot two men in the head in less than a second. Alma was capable of something like that, but from watching her he knew that it took years of training to accomplish something like that.

Someone either got really, really lucky or someone was better at fighting than they let on. The latter was a disturbing thought.

Or it could have been two people. That was possible. Just fortuitously timed shots and aimed shots.

Except in his experience, luck was seldom a good thing.

The sunlight flickered through the trees as they drove around the curving bends. If he had been on his motorcycle this would have been a fun road to speed down. He hated having to leave it with the Humvee.

Eventually they reached the summit and there was an opening in the trees. He slowed to a stop to get a better look. The valley lay open in front of them. He could see rolling hills, a blue river and green land until it disappeared into the haze of the distance.

Already he could tell that he liked this place.

"You picked a good spot, Jennifer," Spencer said.

"I did, didn't I?" Jennifer said.

"It's so pretty," Rebekah said. "Like a promised land."

Lisa remained silent.

The slope down was steep and all he had to do was coast. By the time they reached the bottom he had to keep his foot on the breaks just to maintain control.

The first building they saw was a plain but large looking house on the right and then they saw a tourist info place. Was there really that much to learn about this town that it required a whole building?

The road curved and soon he was passing by old, run down garages, small apartments and eventually a four way intersection with a Hardee's that had broken windows and a collapsed roof. Back west in Vegas, Hardee's was called "Carls Jr." He had no idea why.

"Alright, which way?" Alex asked.

"Main Street seems to be to the left," Adam said. He didn't look up from the map.

He took a left and went down what passed for a main street. There was a closed down grocery store that had been empty since before the war and then they came to the smallest, saddest looking movie theater he had seen.

"Look up there," Rebekah said.

He looked where she was pointing and saw that on a hill was a giant, red and white building with towers and arches. It looked very old, like something from the turn of the century and had Russian looking union domes.

"What's that supposed to be?" Alex asked.

"It's Southern Virginia University," Jennifer said.

"Sounds like as good a place as any to spend the night," he said.

"I'd like to see their library," Jennifer said.

"I bet their cafeteria has cans of food," Adam said.

They drove up the long driveway to the front yard of the giant red building. It sure didn't look like any school he had ever seen. It looked more like a crazy mansion mixed with a hotel.

They parked their truck in front of the main entrance that had a large porch like an old plantation house, complete with rocking chairs.

"Looks cozy so far," Rebekah said.

Lisa went to the door first and tested the knob. Unlocked. Her sunglassed eyes looked to him and nodded. She opened the door and Alex entered first. Inside was dark but the windows let in more than enough light to see. The main lobby had some dusty old antique furniture and a large fireplace. There were pamphlets about the school, paintings of people that used to be important and a large tapestry that was too faded to really tell what it was. The carpeted wooden floor creaked with every step.

The bottom floor was offices, meeting rooms, a ballroom with a sagging wooden floor and the cafeteria. The kitchen had lots of canned food, mostly beans, macaroni salad and flour.

"I could make a cake with this," Rebekah said.

"I thought you didn't know how to cook," Alex said.

"I don't. Cake is the only thing my mom ever taught me to make."

"I could make dinner with this," Lisa said.

"Please do, fangs," Alex said.

"Fangs?"

Lisa raised an eyebrow.

"Yeah, because you're vicious. You have fangs."

"I'm not mean," Lisa said.

"It's a joke."

Rebekah began working on her cake, Lisa started cooking up something that smelled good and Adam and Jennifer went off to scout the area out some more. The place had several buildings and there was a lot to search.

As they worked in the kitchen he and Spencer went and brought all the stuff in from the truck and began to lay all their supplies out for inventory. They picked up two AK-47's, a Ruger Mini-14 with a scope, a large .357 revolver and a plain Jane FAL. They also had some canned food, some knives, some camping gear and detailed maps of the area.

"Maybe Lisa will want an AK. You know, remind her of back home," Spencer said.

"Chinese don't use AK's anymore and she wasn't in the army."

"So she says," Spencer said.

"You can't go around blaming every Chinese person because our governments had a war. Common people don't get asked what they want."

"Maybe you should ask her who she wanted to win."

"It doesn't matter."

"It matters to me."

"Whatever she says won't change anything."

"Maybe it's for my own peace of mind. They destroyed my life. I'd at least like to know if she supported it."

"Let it go. Maybe she was a Democrat. Maybe she liked Pepsi instead of Coke. Maybe she was Team Edward. It doesn't matter because all of that is gone."

"Maybe you're not thinking straight," Spencer said and grabbed his crotch.

"I'd do the same for anyone. We're short on humans if you haven't noticed."

"I want you to find out what she says."

"I'm not going to ask."

"Ask her."

"No."

"Maybe I will, then and I won't be so nice about it."

"You touch her or even annoy her and you'll have to deal with me. Understood?"

"Fearless leader's love sick. How cute."

Spencer walked out of the dinning room and Alex was glad to see him go. It was a headache he didn't want to deal with.

The food was ready before Adam and Jennifer came back. He called them on the walkie-talkie and they took a few moments to respond.

"Food's ready," Alex said.

"We'll be there in a few. Just want to check this place out first," Adam said.

Lisa came out holding a giant bowl of...he didn't know what, but it smelled good. There was rice and vegetables all mixed up. His mouth began watering.

"Lisa, if for no other reason, we'd keep you on just because of your cooking," Rebekah said.

"I like cooking," she said with a shy smile.

They were halfway finished with the meal before Adam and Jennifer came back.

"The library's pretty unimpressive, but it's something. I'm sure we can find books that could help us settle into a new life," Jennifer said.

"Excellent. We'll look at that tomorrow. For now, sit and eat."

They sat around one of the cafeteria's tables and talked and relaxed. It felt almost normal. Even Spencer was smiling.

"We made it to the valley," Alex said. "I say we take tomorrow off and just relax here and see what we can find."

"I like that idea," Spencer said.

"My feet like that idea," Adam said.

"Then the day after we'll look around and see if we can find a nice place to settle down in," Jennifer said.

"We have to stick together. Farming is a group effort," Adam said.

"Agreed," Alex said. "We need fresh water, land, animals, and hopefully equipment that doesn't require gas."

"Tall order," Rebekah said.

"We have time to look." That was the one thing they did have lots of.

32

L ISA REQUESTED THE TOWER BEDROOM FOR HER TEMPORARY home. She claimed she wanted it for the view, which in all fairness was partially true. The view was indeed stunning.

But the main reason she wanted the tower was because it gave her privacy. And right now she needed privacy so she could use her Sat-Phone. She kept it in her purse where no one would really look.

She hung up the phone and put it back in the false bottom of her purse. She kept her Makarov in there as well. She was always armed, but didn't want to appear to be armed.

When she saw Alex walking along the street and his friends further back, she had to hide her AK-47 in the alley before making her "accidental" encounter with him. It was probably still there. Shame.

She hadn't been able to call Bejing in several days and she had to give her report. A lot had happened in the past few days. Also, it would feel good to speak Mandarin again. She hated pretending to speak English badly. That had been her cover for so long that she automatically did it with these people she had never met. Now she was stuck with it.

She was stuck with them as well. No one could have predicted that the Americans would unleash a doomsday virus. She thought the days of Mutually Assured Destruction were over. Now she was trapped here in a devastated world and in a country that wasn't her own.

Things could be worse, not much but it was possible. She found a group of survivors she could trust. Which was more than she had hoped for. They needed help indeed, but she needed them as well. Without them she wouldn't be able to survive. She knew nothing about farming and most Americans' distrust of the Chinese wouldn't help either.

She was stuck and she had to make the best of it.

But, this was a beautiful place and there were worse places to survive the end of the world.

"Hey, Fangs! Breakfast is ready!" Adam called up.

"Be there in minute!" She called back down in her stupid fake accent.

She had been training for cultural infiltration since she was thirteen. This had been a mission she was born for. Now none of it mattered. For five years she had trained to be an agent in America, now it was all pointless.

She was pointless. She would survive, but what was the point of survival without a purpose?

She was a tool that no longer had a function.

The only thing she could do was continue to play along and hope she wasn't discovered. Some of them were warming up to her, even Adam. But for some reason Alex didn't mind at all that she was from China. Most Americans did. Her country had killed his stepmother. He should have been angry.

Unless he was hiding it, but he seemed too occupied to lie about such things. Unlike her.

She walked down the spiraling staircase and found the others gathered in the cafeteria. There were no lights but there were plenty of windows that let in the morning sun.

Whatever they were eating didn't smell good at all.

"What is this?" She asked as she took her seat next to Alex.

She trusted Alex.

When did that start? She couldn't tell when, only that she did.

"Spam and instant eggs. It's good," Alex said.

"Is it?"

She had her doubts and her first forkful confirmed her suspicions. She must have made a face because Adam commented on it.

"See? She don't like it either," Adam said.

"I'm glad it's not kosher because I wouldn't want to eat it. I'll stick to my eggs," Rebekah said.

"After breakfast let's search around the University here and then we'll search the town," Alex said. He was always business first and fun second which was how it should be. She respected him for that. He wasn't like the other Americans who were so wrapped up in their selfish desires that they couldn't be bothered to sacrifice for the whole.

"I don't think we'll find much," Spencer said.

Spencer was a prime example. All his life he had just smoked pot and played music. Even now, after military training he continued to do what he wanted.

She wasn't impressed with him.

"We're not just looking for supplies, we're looking for things that can help us down the road, antique farm equipment, seeds, tools, I don't know what else, but anything," Alex said.

"I'll be in the library," Jennifer said.

"Good, look up books about farming. None of us are farmers and without some kind of knowledge, we're going to starve," Alex said.

After breakfast she slung her American M4 and followed Alex around the school. As part of her preparation she had been well trained on the M4 and all its variations. She knew more about this weapon than all of them except for Alex.

It was a small school. There were a few dorm buildings, a three story brick building where classes had been held, a small office building in an old rickety house and down the ways a bit was an art studio filled with students' art.

It was a shame but art wouldn't be useful for a long time, not until society rose above the level of survival. She didn't know how long that would be. She never understood art. Never had time for it. Too busy training. Still, sometimes a very pretty painting would make her stop and examine it.

Her government education covered a lot of topics and much had been expected of her, but some things just weren't on the schedule. Surviving the end of civilization wasn't on the agenda.

She missed China and knew she'd never see it again. She'd never see the Yellow River. Most beautiful place on Earth.

"Ready to hit the town?" He asked.

"Sure," she said.

They walked down a narrow, crumbling stone staircase down the hill and into the town. Some of the houses looked pieced together from other bits of houses. Others looked old and some looked old and nice.

Rural America wasn't what she had thought it would be like. It wasn't what she had seen on TV. She had expected sweeping prairies, cowboy hats and country music. This place was just like the rest of America except smaller, poorer and older.

She scanned the buildings for signs of movement or occupation. Somebody might have survived here. Perhaps the survivors went elsewhere?

Main Street had several shops with glass windows, all covered in dust and cobwebs on the inside. No bodies.

Then she heard something moving between two old stores, a pizza place and an ice cream parlor. She spun around and raised her M4. There was nothing in the alleyway except an old cat scrounging around for food.

"A cat," she said.

"We could eat it," he said.

"Too loud. Waste ammo," she said.

They needed something like a .22, a smaller caliber for smaller creatures. She began to think of recipes for cat. Fried cat was good.

"Just kidding. I'm not that hungry yet."

Growing up in the state orphanage made her used to eating anything. The food was never enough and some days they'd go hungry. So, they hunted whatever they could.

They found an antique hardware store on their main street that had old non-motorized farm equipment.

"Jackpot," Alex said.

They looked around the store while he took notes on a small notebook. Carrying around a notebook was a good idea. She'd have to remember that.

"You have family back in China?" Alex asked as he checked out a dusty plow.

"Yeah," she said. She didn't but her cover identity did.

"I'm sorry."

"It okay. You no end world."

"How long you been in America?"

"Five year."

"I bet you miss China."

"I do," she said truthfully.

"I miss Las Vegas but I know that if I went back, it wouldn't be the same. I don't think I'd want to see it without power or people."

She couldn't imagine an empty Beijing, but nearly empty it was. Perhaps it would be best if she didn't have to see it like that. She wouldn't want to see it slowly die and crumble. She wondered if her commanders were surviving in a bunker somewhere. They had to have had a plan to escape. They were too good to just die in a plague.

"This my home now," Lisa said. Again, truthfully.

Through all her lies the truth came out whenever it could. She hid her lies behind simple honesty.

"My home as well."

After taking inventory of the old, used farm equipment, they continued down Main Street looking for anything else of interest. There wasn't, so they started searching homes. They did that for a few hours and found a few cans of food, some hunting rifles and shotguns and some ammo. She had slung on her back a Ruger 10-22, a semi-auto .22 that would be great for small game.

With a suppressor it would make a great assassination tool. A .22 often didn't have the power to penetrate the skull on the way out and sometimes ended up bouncing around the cranial cavity. Very messy.

They walked past that alleyway and she saw the same cat. They had to make their more durable supplies last so any fresh food had to be taken advantage of.

"Alex, hold on," she said.

She took aim down the low magnification scope on the .22 and put the simple crosshairs between the cat's large, green eyes.

"Pretty kitty," she said before squeezing the trigger.

33

Alma, Colorado

ALMA LOOKED AT THE MAP AND JUDGED THE DISTANCE ONE MORE time. She looked back in the tent where Cass was sleeping. It was well past noon and she didn't look any better. Hayden Colorado wasn't too far away, about ten miles. If they could get there they could find a comfortable place for Cass to rest up.

But then looking back at Cass it didn't look like she could make it two miles, let alone ten. So, they were stuck right where they were.

She recharged one of their iPods with their portable solar panels and listened to the other. There wasn't much else to do.

An hour later Cass woke up and came over to sit across from her around the fire.

"Sorry about all this," Cass said.

"You're sick. It happens."

"Yeah, but the timing could have been better."

There was no good time anymore to be sick. She remembered her mom telling her about how in the olden days people were always dying of simple stuff like colds and pulled teeth.

"You feeling any better?"

"Not really."

"There's a town a few miles up the road. When you feel like you can make it that far, let me know. Maybe we can find medicine or at least a more comfortable place to rest."

"Sounds good."

The rest of the day Alma listened to her iPod and Cass read a book while resting in the tent. The days were getting warmer and she had her hair up in a bun to get it off of her neck and shoulders.

At night, Cass listened to Alma ramble about nothing in particular. Alma felt like talking and it didn't matter if Cass answered back or not. She just needed someone to listen to her.

She had hated being alone. She hated it worse than she realized.

In the morning Cass claimed she was well enough to travel but she didn't look any better.

They started off and fell into the pattern of walking for fifteen minutes and then resting for five.

Slowly they made their way towards the town of Hayden. An hour or so before sunset, they came to a roadblock. Four armed men were standing behind the old cars.

"Trouble?" Cass asked.

"Just in case, stay back here and cover me with your Broadsword."

She hadn't counted on the place being occupied. That proved that Vernal wasn't the only surviving town.

"Alright," she said half coughing.

Alma took a deep breath and walked closer to the barricade. It was made from highway signs, plywood, sheet metal and ruined cars. One of the cars looked alright and she wondered why it was there but then saw it was a Prius. Halfway there one of the men called out.

"Hold on right there!" He said.

Alma stopped.

"We're just passing through," Alma said.

"Where you heading?" The bearded man asked. He was wearing a jean jacket and an NRA ball cap.

"Virginia."

The man whistled.

"That's a long way to go."

"You a member of the NRA?" She asked.

"I was."

"I won my division at the last NRA competition. Three gun."

"You don't say!" He sounded genuinely impressed.

"I do say."

"You that Attaway girl?"

"Alma Attaway."

"I'll be darned. Read about you on Facebook. Who's your red head friend with the AR-10?"

"That's Cassidy. I picked her up in Utah."

"You all come in from Utah? Anyone left there?"

"Vernal, just across the boarder is still alive. There's a few survivors in Temple Square in Salt Lake."

The four men looked at each other and talked quietly.

"How intent are you on going to Virginia?" The man finally asked. He leaned over the barricade and slung his rifle. The other guard did the same. She felt her muscles relax slightly.

"Why ask?"

"Well, we kind of have a situation and we could use your help."

"What kind of situation?"

"It's kind of...you see...there's a FEMA camp about fifteen miles east of us. They have a few refugees, but not many. Mostly it's a few government types that think they still have power. They want to move in and take us over."

"So, tell them no."

"We have, but they got more guns. They got themselves a few national guard fellows with a small tank."

"That's not good. You want me to help fight these FEMA guys?"

"If you do, you can stay here as long as you like and we'll even hook you up with supplies for your trip. I know it's a rotten thing to ask a girl your age to fight, but it's a hell of a world now and we need all the help we can get."

"Hold on."

She walked back to Cass.

"What you think, *Chica*?" Alma asked.

"Fight? I don't want to kill nobody! The world's got few enough people as it is."

"But we can use the supplies. Besides, you need to rest. They didn't say anything about you fighting, just me."

"You think I'll let you go out there and fight alone? We don't split up, remember?"

"Okay, how about I agree if they let us have some medicine."

Cass wrinkled her brows as she thought.

"I still don't like it. There's got to be some way to talk to these FEMA folks."

"We'll see. But in the meantime we agree and if we have to, we'll fight."

"So, we're mercenaries now?"

"We're whatever we have to be to survive, Cass."

"There's no point in surviving if we have to live like animals."

"Think of it like a cause. We're helping these people fight oppression."

"Do you really care?"

"Does it matter? We need medicine and supplies or we die."

Cass put her hands on her hips and kicked a stone with her boot.

"Fine."

"*Bueno*."

She adjusted her hat to look professional and walked back to the barricade.

34

Any farming equipment, food, tool, weapon, or anything else useful they found in Buena Vista, they stored in the gym of Southern Virginia University. They had a small mountain of stuff.

"Excellent! Now that we successfully raided Buena Vista, it's time to move on to Lexington and then we have to find a new home," Alex said.

"We're looking for a new home. That's pretty exciting. House shopping!" Rebekah said.

"We need to look for certain things," Jennifer said. "We need a source of fresh water, plenty of open land, a big and sturdy enough house, can be lived in without electricity...that means we'll need a stove or something so it'll probably be an older house."

"Look for farm houses with chimneys," Adam said.

"Or solar panels," Spencer said.

"Open ground all around. See enemy coming," Lisa said.

"That's a good point. There are some remote spots out here. There may be survivors. We have to keep an eye out. No one relax today. Eyes open. Stay alert," Alex said.

They piled into the truck with everyone in the back. Lisa took shotgun and he drove.

They left BV and drove to Lexington. On the way there they noticed several houses that were potential candidates. Large farm houses with rolling fields. They'd stop by on the way back. They even saw a few scattered cows here and there. At least a few had survived. He had been worried that they wouldn't find any. Now if they could find a bull they'd be set for a long time.

Lexington was a very old town that was attacked during the Civil War. VMI was there and Robert E. Lee went to teach there after the war. VMI was a cool fortress looking place but it didn't offer what they needed. They need a place they could stay in the long run and make a living: a farm.

On the way into Lexington they passed a Taco Bell with broken windows and a fancy bed and breakfast place. Downtown Lexington looked like something from an old photo from the Civil War. Narrow roads went up and down steep hills with old houses, brick churches and quirky store fronts filled their view. It was actually a very nice looking town.

"Lots of church steeples," Lisa said quietly.

"People were a bit more religious back then," he said.

"And Washington and Lee University has a great library," Jennifer said. "Drop me and Rebekah off there and we'll find useful books we'll need."

"Will do."

"We'll check out VMI," Adam called from the back.

After dropping their teams off and checking their radio comms, he turned to Lisa.

"Want to check out Main Street?"

"I don't think we find much there," she said.

"It's worth a look. I saw a Stonewall museum back there. Maybe they'll have something useful. Look for antique stores. Older the better."

They parked the truck in a parking lot beside an old, large, brick church. Across the road was an Italian pizza joint.

"I could go for some pizza," he said.

"Pizza is good," she agreed with a serious nod of the head.

She seemed to have a hard time telling when he was joking or not.

With their rifles ready they began walking around the historic center of Lexington. Many of the shops were quirky artsy places but some were actually very interesting. He saw a Scottish store that sold kilts, a very old book store, art galleries and a hippie store. Not surprisingly the hippie store didn't really have anything useful in it, not unless they wanted to sit around and smoke hookahs. He had been hoping for a book on how to make soap or something else. That would be something useful.

But then they came across an antique store that looked more like something from a hoarder's garage. He used his Army bayonet to pry the door open and looked inside. There were piles of old junk.

"Look," she said and pointed to an old, glass lantern.

"Useful."

They found old saws, axes, two plows, farming tools and a small hoard of other possibly useful things. They even found a yoke for oxen.

"Not bad," Lisa said.

"You know anything about farming from back home?"

"No, lived in small city. City girl. Look around valley for survivors? Find farmer?"

"We'll do that once we find a new home."

"Home," Lisa said so softly that he barely heard her.

Sounded like she was missing home. He couldn't blame her. She was stuck here in this country with a bunch of strangers. Who could blame her if she felt a little down?

"Lisa, are you going to be okay? I mean...is this a place you could call home?"

She thought for a moment before answering.

"I think so. It's not home, but maybe it could be."

"We're all we have. We've all lost our families and everything else we cared about. Lisa, you're now my family and I will do anything I can to help you. If there's anything you need, tell me. Understand?"

She nodded with watery eyes and quickly looked away so he wouldn't see her face.

"I don't know what else to do. I have no where to go. No friends. No family."

"You have us. We all have to trust in each other."

This only brought a darker, more pensive expression to her face. He decided to drop it in case he made it worse.

They went to the W&L library and found Jennifer and Rebekah with a pile of books.

"We found gold here," Jennifer said. "Books on simple farming techniques and books on how to live in the nineteenth century! I learned how you really make butter. Fascinating stuff."

"This book says we'll need salt," Rebekah said.

"That might be a problem," Alex said.

"No, we can get it from the roots of a Hickory tree, beets, carrots, chickens, ducks and meat," Rebekah said.

"But will that be enough?" Alex asked.

"It should be."

That wasn't as reassuring as he had been hoping for.

Adam and Spencer returned a short time later.

"We found a bunch of .22 target rifles and crates and crates of ammo. Great for target practice and varmint hunting," Spencer said.

"Varmint?" Rebekah asked.

"You know, squirrels, raccoons, possums. I hope you like possum because we're going to be eating a lot of it soon."

Rebekah made a 'yuck' face.

Rebekah probably also thought Spencer was joking. He wasn't.

Lisa stood off to the side with her stone, unreadable expression.

35

THEY DROVE ALL THROUGH THE COUNTRYSIDE AROUND LEXINGTON and Buena Vista, taking notes and marking potential houses on a map. To his relief they had found several promising prospects.

"This might actually work," Spencer said from the back of the truck.

"Well, we need to make a decision soon because we're running out of gas. We need to choose and then use the last of our fuel to haul all the supplies we found to the house," Alex said.

"We need horses," Lisa said.

"Agreed. Horses for transportation, cows, sheep, goats, chickens, rabbits. Anything and everything we can find. We don't have the gas for that so we'll be wandering the countryside for the perceivable future," Alex said.

This got a groan from Rebekah.

"I'm not touching any pigs," Rebekah said.

They drove for a while and came upon a Walmart. The windows were smashed and the place was completely cleaned out of anything useful.

"Someone's been here. Survivors," Adam said.

"Why do you say that?" Spencer asked.

"The time it took to move all this. The plague happened too fast for systematic looting like this. It had to be done after the plague ended," Adam said.

Alex had to agree. This wasn't ransacked by a frightened mob. This place was thoroughly cleaned out.

"Should we try to find them?" Rebekah asked.

"With luck they're far from here," Alex said.

"What do you mean, with luck?"

"If they're nearby then they'll be competing for the same resources. If they're far enough away we can trade and barter like friends," Alex said.

"And if not?" Lisa asked.

"Ever hear of the Hatfields and the McCoys?"

"No."

"You should read up on it."

In the Walmart parking lot, next to a Lowe's which hadn't been cleared out, they gathered around the tail gate of the truck and looked at the map. Lisa had taken pictures of all the houses and their lands with her camera and they compared the photos to the dots on the map.

"Okay, we have to look at the house, its structure, size, defensibility, livability, and condition. We need to look at the land, how it can be farmed, grazed, source of water, trees, etc. We need to look at everything," Alex said.

One by one they went through all the different houses, each one had something wrong with it. None of them fit what they needed.

"Are we being too picky?" Jennifer asked.

"No, these aren't wants, they're necessities," Alex said.

"What's out that way? Have we checked out there?" Rebekah asked. She pointed past the Walmart towards the river below the hill.

"No, but we might as well," Adam said.

"Alright. We'll go around there and take a look, but after that, we're heading back to BV, picking a house, loading up the stuff and heading out. Understood?" Alex said.

They agreed.

They drove out past the Walmart and the countryside opened up before them. There were enormous fields of plowed land and down below was the river that snaked its way across the map.

This was more like it. Finally they found an area that looked like what they needed. Up ahead of them was a series of large, warehouse looking buildings. As they got closer they saw a relatively new looking sign that said it was a horse farm. The place had giant fields and, to his disbelief, he saw horses grazing in the fields.

"No way," Spencer said, echoing Alex's own thoughts.

They were fenced in but with plenty of room to roam around and graze. They weren't going anywhere for now.

"We found transportation," Adam said.

"They're so beautiful," Rebekah said.

They continued on across the river and in a round bend they found a farm which was more like a complex. It had work sheds, silos, barns, storage sheds, a cabin and a large, two story farmhouse with chimneys.

"What do you guys think?" Alex asked.

Adam read off their check list and this place fit all their criteria. The river was right there, plenty of open land but not too far from the woods, defensible, and the house was old enough to have what they needed.

They got out of the truck and walked toward the house. He noticed that Lisa kept her M4 shouldered and was scanning the area for trouble. She had a good head on those shoulders and would have made a great Marine. Completely wasted as a waitress at a buffet.

They called out but of course no one answered. The front door was unlocked and they walked right in. The place had a few modern touches like a flat screen TV with surround sound, but there were also antiques scattered around. In the upstairs master bedroom he found a closet full of guns, mostly hunting rifles but it had a few workable military surplus: an M1 Garand, M1 carbine and a beat up, but serviceable, SKS. The kitchen, which was a strange mix of old fashioned and modern, had an isle and all the modern appliances, but also had a stone chimney with an iron stove. It also had plenty of canned food. And in the basement they even found bottles of wine. Out in the yard there were goats wandering around.

"Perfect," Jennifer said.

"Home," Lisa whispered.

No discussion was necessary. He could see on everyone's faces that they liked this place. They quickly drove back to BV, loaded up the truck. Which required Adam and Spencer to sit out on top as they drove very slowly back to their new home. It was a nice evening out and they didn't complain. They were too excited about a new home to complain.

Whoever had raided Walmart left a lot of the home and garden section alone, so they picked out bed sheets, pillows, blankets and anything else they wanted to make their new home more comfortable. He noticed that Lisa took black sheets and pillow cases. She was a strange girl.

Before nightfall, Adam and Jennifer, the only two with experience with horses, went and rounded up all the horses and fed them apples from a nearby tree to get them back into the huge barn. Seven horses in all.

Alex knew that this was far luckier than he had any right to expect.

As the sun set they all gathered on the front porch of their new home. There was even a rocking chair and a porch swing. He took the rocking chair and Jennifer and Rebekah took the swing. Lisa leaned against the wall beside him with her arms folded. Adam sat on the steps and Spencer leaned back against the rails.

"Welcome to our new home," Alex said. "We made it and I know you all know how lucky we were to find this place. Beyond lucky. In honor of our Jewish sister who pointed the way to this place, I propose we call this farm, "Promised Land.""

Rebekah gave a huge and bright smile. They all agreed.

"For dinner," he continued, "I say we celebrate tonight. We should take every chance to celebrate that we can get and this is a very good reason to do so."

They all agreed to this.

Jennifer, Adam and Lisa cooked the meal, producing a feast out of nothing. They broke open a bottle of the basement wine and passed it along. There was no law anymore so there was no drinking age and Rebekah had a few sips as well.

He noticed that Lisa didn't drink.

They sat on the porch in the cooling air of a Virginia spring night. The crickets were out and gnats buzzed around and the humidity felt a bit more tolerable. They'd have a lot of work to do tomorrow, but for now, they were celebrating their new home.

Adam loosened up and told jokes, something he surprisingly had a knack for. Spencer played on an acoustic guitar they found in Lexington and Lisa even smiled a little.

The evening wore on and they talked like old friends and family. They were united into a...clan? Tribe? Future city state? Whatever it was, it was home.

When he finally got too tired, he made it up to his new room, the former master bedroom with a view overlooking the river and threw on his new Captain America blanket and went to sleep a very happy man.

36

ALMA LAID PRONE ON THE TOP OF THE HILL LOOKING OUT OVER the small valley and the FEMA camp below. With her binoculars she could see a small tent city but there weren't many people around.

The town sent them out to take a look at what they were up against. It wasn't looking good. There were a lot of armed men along the edges of the tent city.

"FEMA set up the camp, but the plague killed most everyone," the local man said.

He wore old Army BDU's and had a .338 Lapua rifle for reaching out long distances.

She continued to look and saw the sleek, shark-like profile of a Stryker armored vehicle, four Humvees and a few Deuce and a halfs, the big transport trucks. She had no idea what "Deuce and a half" meant. The Stryker was a problem. It was armored and had a machine gun on top.

"Looks like they have a few National Guard guys with them," Alma said.

"They also have some contractors with them," their guide said.

"Like, construction workers?" Cassidy asked.

"No, like professional mercenaries," the man said.

"Oh."

Cassidy was feeling better now but her head was still swimming from the pills she had to take.

"How many civilians down there?" Alma asked.

"Maybe thirty. Fifteen FEMA men and woman, ten contractors and seventeen National Guard," the man said.

"How many guys do you have?" Cass asked.

"About fifty armed men and woman. We could probably get more," the man said.

"So, you outnumber them. What's the problem?" Alma asked.

"They've been here for a while and the whole time they've been telling us to submit to their authority. Lately, they've been trying to move in and "confiscate" supplies from people they find outside of town."

"They're bandits," Cass said.

"They haven't harmed anyone yet, but it is a problem. They keep thinking they can take us over. I don't see why they don't find someplace else and start their own town."

"Have you tried talking to them?" Alma asked.

"Of course, but their leader, a Mr. Newman, refuses to discuss anything except our total capitulation."

"Nice word," Cass said.

"I've been looking for an excuse to use it."

"Doesn't he know the world's ended?" Alma asked.

"The government's gone. I don't know if he's crazy or if he's a scam artist."

The man took off his hat and ran his fingers through his shaggy hair. It seemed most of the people in town were growing their hair out. Too busy to get hair cuts.

"Well, I guess you got two more on your side. We'll do what we can to help," Alma said.

They walked back to Hayden and found the Mayor.

"What do you think?" The Mayor asked.

She was a woman with long blonde hair tied into a bun. She wore hunting clothes and was surrounded by three of her sons, all decked out in camouflage and AK-47's. She was standing by the hood of a truck and looking at a map with several other men.

"They're a problem," Alma said.

"I know that. I was hoping fresh eyes might see a solution," the Mayor said.

"I say we move in at night and take them out before they become a larger problem," one of the men beside the map said.

"And how many of our people will get killed during that? They have machine guns and that APC. What are we supposed to do against that?" The Mayor asked.

The man fell silent.

"Cass here is a remarkable sniper. I'm sure you can find a use for her. I'm a good fighter as well, but I'm a bit more up close," Alma said.

"We appreciate it. If you help us we will reward you. Give you some supplies for your trip to Virginia," the Mayor said.

"Thank you," Alma said.

For now they put them up in a room in the hotel. Alma put her solar panel in the window to recharge her iPod and Cass laid on the bed for a nap. She still wasn't looking good at all.

Cass slept the entire rest of the day and so did Caesar. Those two had more similarities by the day.

At the risk of leaving Cass alone, she went outside and tracked down the hospital. After running around trying to find her, she finally found the doctor.

"What is it? I'm incredibly busy," the woman in a white coat said.

"My friend is sick. Some kind of bad flu or something. They gave her some decongestants. Not sure how helpful that would be."

"Symptoms?"

"She's tired, pale, weak and coughs a lot."

Without looking, the doctor...or whatever she was, reached in a drawer and took out a small bottle. She tossed it to Alma.

"What's this?" Alma asked.

"Oregano oil."

"You mean snake oil."

The doctor looked at her for the first time.

"Listen, girl, that stuff will knock out any infection your friend might have. It's all natural and there won't be any side effects. If it don't work then you can come back and yell at me all you want. It's really strong. Use a drop or two at a time in some food. Now get out of here."

Alma walked out and examined the small bottle as she went. It didn't look like much and Alma was convinced that she'd be back to yell at the doctor.

Cass hadn't woken up during her absence and still lay on her back, sprawled out all over the bed.

She opened a can of ravioli and put in two drops of the oil. She really didn't see how two tiny drops were supposed to do anything.

Then she woke Cass up and made her eat even though she didn't want to.

"How long was I out?" Cass asked between bites.

"Almost all day. Its five."

"Wow."

"How you feeling?"

"The same."

"Well, that stuff should make you better."

"It tastes like oregano."

"Oh, well, that was added for flavor."

"They added too much. I can barely taste the food."

"Sorry. Just eat it."

"You really want to help these people out?" Cass asked.

"I really want the supplies they've offered."

Suddenly there was a frantic knock on their door.

"Come in!" Alma shouted.

A teenage boy wearing a cap with a picture of a fish and a hook on it ran into the room, completely out of breath.

"The FEMA guys are moving in with everything they have," he managed to get out between breaths. "They're going to attack!" The boy said.

"Where are they?"

"Coming down the road."

Alma grabbed her equipment vest, belt, gun and ammo. Cassidy grabbed her Broadsword and followed.

37

ALMA FOLLOWED THE TOWNSPEOPLE TO THE BARRICADE THAT was made out of sand bags and pickup trucks that would never move under their own power again.

All the town's fighters were here including one woman in Army ACU's and an M4. Some were cops and others were veterans. Most were just normal people.

They all began setting up position and readying their weapons. Their unofficial officers were giving orders and trying to keep order. She went up to the Mayor who stood there with a scoped AR15.

"Mayor, where do you want us?" She asked.

"Wherever you think you can do the most good."

"Right."

She turned back to Cassidy.

"Cass, let's go up on that hill there so you can get into a good position. I'll spot for you."

"Alright," Cass said with a worried look on her face.

"What's wrong?"

"We're going to be in a battle?"

"Looks like it, *chica*."

"Alma, I don't want to die here."

"Then don't. Look, I got your back, right? I won't let you get hurt. Besides, they're blocking the road and won't let us through unless we give them our supplies. I don't know about you, but I want to eat. If we want to go on through to Virginia, then we have to deal with these guys."

"Deal? You mean kill."

"I mean whatever it takes."

She patted Cass's cheek and led her up the hill to a good position in a clump of trees. This was the narrow end of the small valley and the FEMA people were coming down the road toward them. They'd get bottle necked here at the entrance. The battle would have been over before it began except FEMA had a National Guard APC. Where'd they get gas for that thing anyway?

A few minutes later the APC followed by three Humvees and some men with guns came within shouting distance of the barricade.

"Okay, Cass, this is it. Don't fire yet."

The FEMA army came to a stop and a Humvee drove out halfway and halted. A man came out holding a white flag. He was wearing a white shirt and tie. Maybe he thought that it made him look like he was more in charge. What douche wears a tie during the apocalypse?

"Cass, aim for that man's heart, okay?"

"Okay."

Alma looked through her ACOG which only had a x4 power scope. The Mayor drove out and got out to talk to the FEMA man. They talked and then they yelled. Finally the Mayor got back in her truck and drove back. The man also drove back to his line.

"Looks like it's going to be a fight," Alma said.

"This is ridiculous! Why? There's plenty of land around! Haven't enough people died already?"

"I guess not. There's always going to be someone that wants what you have. When the shooting starts, find that man and shoot him."

"If he's the one causing all of this, I will."

Then the Stryker began to roll forward. The machine gun on top began moving and a second later it opened fire. The town people all ducked down as bullets tore through the sandbags.

Cass breathed calmly and took aim. Alma knew not to bother her and let her do her thing.

She fired. Her bullet hit the machine gun and it stopped firing. Some cheers rose from the barricade.

"Not bad, Cass. Not bad at all."

"I have my moments," Cass said.

The people behind the barricade opened fire and the battle started. The Humvees moved up and the machine guns on top began roaring out the staccato sound of automatic fire.

Alma took aim and fired. The un-uniformed man in the Humvee's turret jerked back and went limp.

Ignoring the sight of the dead man she fired at the driver but missed by a few inches.

A bullet hit the tree beside her and she ducked down. Cass did as well.

"I guess they know where we are," Cass said.

"Let's find a new position," Alma said.

They crawled down the hill and went over to the other side and took up a new position behind a boulder.

"Okay, Cass, do your magic."

Cass began picking targets and firing at a slow, but steady pace. The concussion from each gunshot rattled her teeth and the shinning pieces of brass flew away like falling stars.

At this distance Alma's targets were just small shapes moving around. She fired and hoped she hit something.

Then the FEMA troops began pulling back. They ran away and the vehicles that could move turned around and began to speed off.

The Humvee with the leader pulled into view and the leader stood up in the turret to give one parting glare at the town.

"Cass," Alma said and it was the only thing she had to say. Cass knew what to do.

She watched Cass take aim. She could see her focus and concentration in the tightness of her jaw and the half closed look in her eyes. Her back rose and fell and stayed still.

Then Cass fired. A single shot and a single spent casing flew out to the side.

The man's chest exploded and his tie went flying into the air.

Alma slapped Cass on the shoulder.

"Good job, Cassidy!"

Cass looked down to the ground as she put her weapon on 'safe.' She didn't look happy and it wasn't just the sickness.

"I hate this," Cass said.

"I know."

She did too. She still saw the faces of those men that kidnapped Cass. She couldn't stop thinking about it. In a better world she wouldn't have to do this, but this was far from a good world.

They just had to get used to it.

They marched back to the barricade where people were laughing and cheering. She found the man that had led them to the FEMA camp.

"How'd we do?" Alma asked.

"Pretty dang good. We only lost a few."

"Only?" Cass asked with a sour expression.

Alma didn't have time to debate the morality of all this. She had to find her brother and these FEMA douche bags were in the way. It was as simple as that. Morality was for people that could afford it.

The Mayor stood up on the back of a pickup truck and began giving some speech that Alma didn't care about. This wasn't her town.

"What about those refugees at the FEMA camp?" Cass asked.

Alma tried not to think of it and tried to block it out of her mind, but no matter how hard she tried the thought of the innocent people at the FEMA camp kept coming back.

She didn't want to care, but she did.

After what had to be a stirring speech, Alma led Cass over to the Mayor.

"We saw you take out the Stryker's gun. We owe you a great deal for that," the Mayor said.

"You can start by answer me this: what happens to them?" Cass said.

"Them?"

"The people in the FEMA camp."

"If they're too stupid to leave and find a home then they deserve to be there. There are plenty of places to go."

"Maybe they're scared and confused. Maybe they want somewhere where there's people and some civilization left," Cass said.

Despite her sickness Cass was a ball of fury.

The Mayor thought for a while.

"Very well. Why don't we send you two along with a delegation to go make peace with them. We have plenty of space here and they can help us farm," the Mayor said.

The people at the FEMA camp were as Cassidy described. They were confused and scared. They wanted a safe place to live and the FEMA man had promised them that. Now that he was out of the equation they were much easier to talk to.

Alma and Cass guarded the five men of Hayden's delegation as they talked.

Alma saw a Guardsman standing beside a white FEMA SUV and walked over to him.

"Hey, that thing got gas?" Alma asked.

"A full tank," the man said numbly.

"Got anymore gas lying around?"

He pointed to several 50 gallon drums.

Alma looked back to Cass and knew that Cass probably wasn't thinking the same thing.

38

LISA PULLED AT THE GOAT AND IT WOULDN'T BUDGE. IT DIDN'T look that big but it was strong for its size. She had underestimated it.

How had she gone from one of China's top military training programs to pulling goats into a barn?

They had spent all week searching the countryside for animals and already they had a bunch of cows, chickens, goats, two donkeys, horses and some pigs that Rebekah won't touch.

The hippie professor, Jennifer, was gathering seeds of all kinds and trying to figure out how to farm.

She wiped her brow and sat on a tree stump with the rope still in her hand.

"Listen, goat. I'll make you a deal. Go in the pen with me and I promise I won't eat you," she said in Mandarin.

Apparently the goat only spoke English because it didn't budge.

Her trainers would shake their heads in shame if they could have seen her right then.

"That's it goat. It's me or you," she said in English.

She grabbed the goat by the horns and pulled with everything she had. The goat resisted and pushed its legs out front, but she finally won and yanked the goat into the barn and closed the sliding door.

This was her life now. As strange and surreal as it was, this was it.

Somehow she had been in the less than 1% that had survived the world ending plague and now she was helping these Americans build a new life. She hadn't even looked at her sat-phone in days. There was nothing it could do for her.

There was no more mission. No more duty. No more Chinese Government.

No more American Government. To continue on would be absurd.

She was no longer an operative. She was now just Lisa Fang, survivor and farmer.

Alex walked out onto the porch talking to Adam about something while gesturing out at the woods. Alex always had a plan. He had the imagination and the drive to get things done.

She respected him. He was a capable man and would have gone far if the world hadn't ended.

Lisa wondered if he expected her to be his...mate. She wasn't sure what to call it anymore. She was his age and physically fit. If he didn't already, he would probably end up wanting her or claiming her for his own.

She had trained how to gather intel, how to not be seen, how to fight with her hands, knives and guns. She knew how to kill, but she had never learned about relationships. It hadn't been important.

What was expected of her? Did the same rules even apply now? She was hopelessly ignorant on the subject and didn't know what to think.

Her teachers had told her that when she was confused, go back to the beginning, and start with what she knew.

She knew he was respectable. He was a good leader. He looked out for the people below him before he thought of himself. He had a smile that made her want to smile.

This was ridiculous. She didn't have time to worry about this. She knew nothing of the subject so she should just avoid anything to do with it.

Besides, she'd never be able to tell him who she really was. He was completely trusting and honest with her but she could never return that honesty. As long as she lived, she would have to wear this mask and pretend to be someone she was not.

What would they do if they did find out? They didn't mind that she was Chinese, but if they found out that she was an operative working for the Chinese Government, they'd blame her for the war. She would go from friend to enemy.

She didn't know if she could take that. These people, as strange as they were, were all she had. Without them she'd be alone in a world that she no longer understood. Perhaps living a lie was better than being completely alone.

Lisa swore in Mandarin and walked over to where Alex and Adam were talking.

"All the goats in the barn," she said.

"Good. Spencer and Rebekah are still out checking out farms. Jennifer is in the garden," Alex said.

"What else can I do?" She asked.

"I don't know, what else can you do?" He asked with that crooked grin.

That took her back for a second.

"I can... try to hook up solar panels to house," Lisa said.

"Do you know anything about that stuff? I thought we'd need an electrician. It seems kind of a waste to have them and not be able to use them," Alex said.

"I will try."

"Be my guest," he said.

She knew computers and security systems. The same basic principles would still apply.

She walked into the living room where the solar panels they had found in Lexington were. Someone had ordered them for their house and had never gotten around to putting them on. Whoever it was hadn't left the instruction manual.

Unlike all the others here, she hadn't lost anyone she cared about. She had had no one. Being an orphan had certain advantages after all. When she didn't care about anyone, she had no one to lose.

Despite all her training and better judgment, she was beginning to like these people.

Lisa spread all the components out on the living room floor and took a quick inventory. That done, she began to trace the flow of electricity from panels to the end. Then she got up and began searching for a place to connect the panels' cords through the converter and into the house.

She entered the kitchen and found Rebekah dicing up some fresh apples they found in a nearby farm.

"Hi," Rebekah said.

"Hello."

"Whatcha doing?"

"Looking for power."

"You a politician now?"

"No, connect solar panels to house."

"Really? You think you can get that to work?"

Lisa nodded.

"That would be wonderful!" Rebekah said while clapping her hands.

Lisa left Rebekah and the kitchen and searched the laundry room, the dinning room and then went upstairs.

Alex's door was open. For a military man he was rather messy. He had all his weapons laid out in a row on the floor. Five M4's, two longer civilian AR15's, four hunting rifles with scopes, a FAL, 2 M14's, an Enfield, two Mosin Nagants, an AK47, pistols and revolvers of various kinds, knives and even a pair of brass knuckles. The strangest one was an FNH 2000 they had found in a big house in Lexington. It was a $2000 gun. Only in America could someone afford something like that. It was a shameful and wasteful display of personal wealth and pride.

She wanted it.

But, unfortunately, there was no way to connect solar panels in his room.

Rebekah's room was filled with stuff she had looted from Lexington. She knew how to ride a horse and had filled its saddle bags and her backpack full of art supplies, some books and clothes.

No power there either.

It wasn't until she got up to the attic that she found it. All the innards of the house were exposed up there and what she searched for was lain bare in front of her. There was a small round window near it.

Lisa opened the window and looked out. It was an easy reach to the roof so if she could get someone up there, they could pass up the panels and connect them with no problems.

It was dangerous but she managed to climb out onto the roof. The view was spectacular and well worth it. She was above the trees and could see for miles around. She traced the flow of the curving river and saw the top of the VMI castle.

Lisa sat down and took a few moments to soak in the beauty of it all. She had never really taken the time to appreciate beautiful things like this. She was always in a rush, training and doing missions and working, that she had never taken a moment to really look at beauty. She had, in the back of her mind, convinced herself that one day she'd take a brake and allow herself to be a human, but it probably never would have happened.

Then she spotted something that didn't fit. She stood up and put her hand to her brow to block the sun.

Far off, rising above the trees, was a faint line of gray smoke, as if from a controlled fire.

39

THEY HAD FOLLOWED HIGHWAY 40 AND THEN GOT ONTO 34 TO go around Denver. They didn't want to drive through a radioactive, pile of rubble. Once 34 got to 76, then to 80 and then they cut down to 70, which they'd follow all the way east. Bypassing Denver had made a simple way into a pain in the butt.

But now they were cruising through Kansas on their way to Virginia in a straight and easy to follow line. She was back on the road to finding Alex and she was excited. They had a car and some stolen fuel. Enough to make it to Virginia.

Though she was in a rush, she only drove 60mph to keep from burning through the fuel too fast.

"I still can't believe they let us take all that gas," Cass said.

"Yeah, they were nice," Alma said.

She felt a little guilty for lying to Cass about stealing the fuel, but what Cass didn't know wouldn't upset her. The town had been nice enough to let them take the FEMA SUV, but they only allowed her to take whatever fuel happened to be in the tank.

That wasn't enough. So during the night she placed some extra gas cans in the back of the FEMA truck and went back to the hotel to wake up Cassidy.

They left before anyone else was awake.

Cass would probably demand they go back and return the stolen gas.

Cass always tried to do what was 'right.' Even Alma found herself swearing less. But what Cass didn't realize was that right and wrong were different now. Survival was now the priority and right and wrong were secondary. But Cass seemed to think that a survival situation made it even more important to do what was right.

"I've never been on a road trip before," Cass said.

"Well, it's an American tradition."

"I think Caesar's happy to not have to walk across the Great Plains."

Caesar was passed out on the back seat with his head resting (and drooling) on Alma's backpack.

"I wouldn't want to walk across Kansas. We've been driving for hours and all we've seen are dead and dried corn fields."

The place was a wasteland. Winds were constantly picking up dust devils and some were large enough to worry her. This place had been America's breadbasket and now it was just a patch of dried up dirt. There was no one left to feed and no one left to farm. It was all gone. If anything showed the death of this country, it was Kansas.

"How long does this go?" Cass asked.

Cass was fiddling with the map and trying to judge distances.

"Eighty three point two miles."

"Really?"

"No, I have no freaking idea, Cass."

"There's no food, no people. There's nothing here. How did people live here?"

"They ate a lot of corn."

They turned the music up and Alma sped up a little. She was growing very tired of this place. She couldn't wait for Cass's turn to drive so she could get back to the Count of Monte Cristo. The Count was at a dinner party at some creepy old mansion in the country with his enemies and had no idea what he had planned. It was going to be good, whatever it was.

By nightfall they were on the outskirts of Kansas City. Again they had to detour around the city to avoid the highways that were packed full of cars.

"I'll take over," Cass said after a while.

Alma didn't argue. She had been driving all day and into the night. It was time to rest only now it was too dark to read.

Cass took over and Alma tried to go to sleep. Cass put in her earphones so her music wouldn't disturb her.

She must have dozed off pretty quickly because she didn't remember falling asleep. She sat up and rubbed her eyes. It was still dark and Cass was driving. She stretched out and sat up. Her mouth felt gross so she opened her half-full bottle of Dew to get the taste out. Nothing like warm, flat Dew in the Morning.

Outside was darkness and the small section of cracked road illuminated by the truck's harsh headlights. It was like traveling through space and she wondered if Cass was thinking about one of her nerdy sci-fi books.

"Where are we?" Alma asked.

"Almost to St. Louis," Cass said too loudly. Her headphones were still in.

Cass looked sleepy. Healthy, but sleepy. That oregano oil must have done the trick! Now she couldn't go beat up the doctor.

"I'll take over."

"Good, with the headlights and all it's starting to look like warp speed and that's not good."

Alma had called it. Nerd reference: check.

Cass curled up in the passenger seat and Alma drove.

She put her iPod on her heaviest play list to keep her awake. When she came to a convenience store she stopped and grabbed some Amps and Monsters that were lying on the floor. She downed the Monster and slowly sipped the Amp as she drove.

Getting around St. Louis was even harder than Colorado. The first bridge over the Mississippi they came to had been demolished by a stray barge. The barge was on its side and pieces of the bridge jutted out from the water.

She passed by some flooded neighborhoods along the river until she came to a small, two lane bridge. All of this she saw in the harsh headlights of the FEMA truck.

Everything felt like a dream. Her head was swimming from lack of sleep and the caffeine. Nothing felt real, like she was playing a video game of herself.

She looked in the backseat and Caesar was awake for once.

"*Que pasa, perrito*? You hungry?"

Caesar whined a bit.

"No? Need potty?"

Caesar's ears perked up.

She stopped and took Ceasar out on his leash. If he didn't have the leash Caesar would wander off with his nose leading the way. Apparently, sniffing was a basset hound's chief occupation aside from sleeping.

Once Caesar finished she petted him and helped him back into the rear seat. The cab was a four door deal and most of their stuff was on the floor boards of the rear and in the bed.

Maybe because it was dark, but Alma didn't see a single sign of life anywhere. The houses looked abandoned. The stores were empty and the old barns they passed were crumbling.

"What do you think Alex is doing now?" Alma asked Caesar. "Maybe he's looting a grocery store for food or sleeping in the largest bed in a mansion. You think he found other people? I hope so. He'd be safer and less lonely with others."

She turned back to check Caesar's reaction. He just continued to stare at her.

"You don't stare at Cass like that. What about me makes you stare? You like Mexicans? Don't like Mexicans? Like my hair? I admit it does need to be washed. I'm starting to look like a cavewoman."

They were just past Louisville when the sun started to rise. She hadn't realized it, but she had been going about 80mph almost the whole night.

Cass woke up and they stopped to have breakfast. They were on the side of the road with only a few scattered houses in the distance and some gnarled looking trees. The sun was up in that weird light of early morning.

The sun was up, but it still didn't feel like day and Alma felt weird from driving all night with little sleep: like a zombie.

"Where are we? Cass asked.

"Between Louisville and Lexington Kentucky."

"We're almost there, Alma."

"Almost. We should be in Virginia around noon."

"Then another four hours to Virginia Beach, right?"

"Correct."

"You know…" Cass started to say in her 'worried' tone.

"I know! I know this is crazy. But I have to look for him."

She tossed her empty can into the grass and licked the spoon clean.

"And if we don't find him?" Cass asked.

"I'm not going to think about that."

"And how long will this take? When should we start looking for someplace to settle down?"

"I said we'll think about that after. End of subject."

Cass looked like she wanted to say more but she kept her lips sealed and after breakfast they were on their way.

Cass had a very valid point though. What were they going to do? She'd keep her eyes open as they traveled for any place to settle down.

Kentucky was a beautiful place with thick, dark green grass.

"If he's not in Virginia Beach," Cass began. Alma shot her a dirty glare but Cass continued. "If he's not there, we have to assume he hasn't gone relatively far. So, we can put out flyers in places we know people will see them. We can find other survivors that might be able to steer us in the right direction."

"Milk cartons."

"Kind of."

If she prayed she'd be praying that he was still in Virginia Beach. If he left then there'd be no way to find him. He could literally be anywhere and how long and far could she possibly search before giving up? She was getting closer.

40

ALEX LOOKED THROUGH HIS BINOS AT THE SMOKE RISING UP IN the distance. They were all standing on the roof to get a look.

"Yup, it's a fire," Alex said.

"Should we go check it out?" Adam asked.

"We have to. It could be other survivors," Jennifer said.

"That might not be good thing," Lisa said.

"We have to be careful," Alex said.

"It's worth the risk," Jennifer said.

"Right, let's saddle up. We'll take the truck and the last of the gas," he said.

They grabbed their gear, strapped on their side arms, slung their rifles and piled into the truck. Spencer and Rebekah stayed to guard the farm.

Alex had a map and marked roughly where he thought the smoke was coming from.

They passed the Walmart and drove further on into the country. The hills here were clear of trees but covered in boulders too big for the farmers to move. They passed large, fancy houses that all looked too modern and delicate. Having a house made half of glass had been cool, but now it was too impractical to heat and if the glass broke there'd be no replacements.

That was what could be called a "paradigm shift."

Eventually they saw the smoke ahead. Down the road was what looked like a truck stop, but it was on fire. A truck was parked out in front of the blaze and men were gathered around in a circle yelling and waving guns around. It looked like they were kicking something on the ground. They looked like they were smiling and laughing.

"What's this?" Adam asked from the backseat.

"Eyes open everyone," Alex said.

As they drew closer the five men turned and saw them coming. They all faced their approaching truck. All of them were armed.

They pulled up at 50 yards or so and Alex could see two figures lying on the ground by their feet. Instantly he knew he wasn't going to be exchanging pleasantries.

"Where the hell did you all come from?" One of the men in an old military uniform called out. It was out of date BDU's with patches on it that definitely weren't US Army.

"We were driving by and saw the smoke," Alex said.

"This don't concern you. We're just taking care of some business."

"I can see that. What did these people do?"

The para-military men looked at each other as if they weren't sure what to say.

"They stole from us," one of them finally said and the others quickly nodded.

Really.

"They stole from us and tried to run off. This is our land and our laws. We deal with it as we like," the leader man said. "We give them everything they need and they show nothing but ingratitude. We try to take care of them and they stab us in the back."

Then one of the figures moved. It was a man with a bald head, glasses and beard. He was dressed fairly nice and in his arms he held a little girl, maybe eight years old.

"Very slowly, take your weapons off of safe," Alex whispered to the others and then turned back to the five men. He knew a bad situation when he smelled it.

He had to find a way to deescalate this situation. He didn't want violence. Not because he didn't want to kill them, but he couldn't risk one of his people being killed.

"We'll take them off your hands. We could use some workers. We're heading to DC to see what we can salvage," Alex said.

"DC? You dumb? They nuked DC. All you'll find there is radiation poisoning," the lead man said. He had on sunglasses and a balding, round head.

"You sure? I haven't heard that," Alex said. He knew DC was gone.

"Yeah, we're pretty damn sure."

"Well, Richmond's still there. We can go there and see what we can find."

"These people are our problem. We'll deal with them like we deal with all thieves."

"I'll take man on far left," Lisa whispered.

"We can't just shoot them," Jennifer said.

"They're going to kill those people," Alex said.

"We shouldn't risk our lives for strangers," Adam said.

"They bad men with guns. We should kill them now or they be problem later," Lisa said.

Lisa at first had seemed like a typical, airheaded girl, but lately she had been showing a stone cold and calculating side to her. She was like a small, Chinese Terminator.

He was inclined to agree with her. These men were only going to be problems at a time that they couldn't afford problems.

"I'll take the leader," Alex whispered.

"Far right," Adam said.

Second to right," Jennifer said. "But I do object to this. What if they have friends? What if they really are thieves?"

"They looked like they were enjoying it," Adam said.

"That's a little girl there. I don't care if they did steal something. You don't kill children. When I say fire, take out your target. Do not hesitate or one of us may get hurt. Understand?" Alex said.

They all nodded and he turned back to the militia men. He saw the man on the ground, huddled over the girl to protect her.

"We'll trade you for them," Alex said.

"What do you got?" Asked the man.

"We have lots of bullets. Fire!"

With that, him and his crew snapped their rifles up and fired. A burst of gunfire erupted in the air with smoke, concussion and noise. Jennifer was probably the slowest and Lisa was probably the fastest, second only to him.

Three of the men went down in sprays of blood without even realizing what had happened. One of them instantly began raising his rifle and the other stumbled backward and began fumbling with his AK.

Alex sprung the red dot of his sight to the quick reaction man and fired another two shots. One bullet hit the man in the chest and the second hit him in the head, right between the eyes and he fell backward. Adam then shot the fumbling man.

Before the brass had even hit the ground Alex was running for the man and girl.

The man was bloody but not too badly beaten. He looked Indian and was dressed in a dirty suit with no tie. The girl looked up with dirty tears running down her cheeks.

"It's okay, we won't hurt you. Why were they doing that to you?" Alex asked.

"We tried to run away," the man said in an Indian accent. "They kept us like slaves."

"Well, you're safe now. We'll discuss it back home."

After they piled the bodies in the truck, they put the man and girl, who looked related, into the truck and Adam and Jennifer took the captured vehicle and they headed home. On the way, they stripped the bodies of anything useful and threw them into the river so anyone who came looking for them wouldn't know where they were killed.

Then they sat the man and girl in the living room for a long chat.

41

Alex, Promised Land, Virginia

ALEX LOOKED AT THE TWO PEOPLE THEY HAD RESCUED. THE middle aged Indian man and an Indian girl that looked maybe nine or ten now that he got a better look, appeared to be related.

"You her father?" He asked.

"Uncle. I was taking care of her while her parents were back visiting India when the plague hit," the man said.

The girl was still crying and staring down at the floor.

"What's your name?" Alex asked.

"Ranbir and this is Rehka."

"Glad to meet you. Now tell me who those men were and why they were attacking you."

"Some of them were in a militia or something. Called themselves the Appalachian Hunt Club."

"Innocent sounding name," Jennifer said from somewhere behind him.

"They were anti-government criminals. But then a colonel from the national guard and a few surviving soldiers moves in and takes them over. Now they do what he says. He is a tyrant that makes everyone do what he wants," Ranbir said.

"How many people are we talking about?" Alex asked.

The Hunt Club were in the deep woods when the plague happened so all twenty six of them survived. But they have about four ex-soldiers, counting the colonel, and about thirty survivors. He has them farming like peasants. They took all our belongings and said it was for security. We have nothing left."

"It's alright. You're with friends now," Alex said. Then he turned to Rebekah. "Rebekah, could you get these two something to eat?"

He then motioned for the others to follow him and he led them outside.

"What do you think?" Alex asked.

"Twenty five armed men? We can't handle that many," Adam said.

"There's only six of us and some of our fighting skills are lacking," Jennifer said.

"I know. But we have to do something. We need to find out where they live, maybe get some of those refugees to our side," Alex said.

After Ranbir and Rehka finished eating, he sat down with Ranbir in the living room. Lisa and Adam were with him.

"Where do these guys live?" He asked.

"They live just outside of Stuanton," Ranbir said. "They have a farm. Lots of land. Animals, fields. They often send groups out to scavenge what they can. They guard us but not always. They said we couldn't have religion anymore, that it caused disunity. They wanted to take Rehka away from me. Many don't want to stay but are too afraid.. Some are looking for a way out and some are too scared to even think about leaving. They're slaves but they're safe."

"Some would sacrifice liberty for safety," Alex said.

"I think it best if they don't know we here," Lisa said.

"I agree. Let's not alert them to our presence. However, we do need to scout them out. I'm going and I need a volunteer," Alex said.

Lisa's hand went up. Maybe it was the cool, emotionless way she fought or the fact that her accuracy was starting to get spooky good, but he didn't question her ability anymore.

"Alright. Me and Lisa will go check this place out. The rest of you, use the .22's to do some training. Not just target but shoot, move and communicate."

"We don't have any gas left. There's some in the truck we captured. It will get you there but I don't think it'll get you back," Adam said.

"That leaves the horses then," Alex said.

"Ride horses?" Lisa asked. She adjusted her glasses and cleared her throat. He was as uncomfortable with the idea as she was, but he couldn't show that. They had had a few lessons but neither of them could be called 'experienced' riders.

The two of them packed backpacks with supplies and got Ranbir to show them on a map where the farm was.

"It's there, away from main road. They have guards. Be careful," Ranbir said.

"We will."

With that, he saddled up and watched Lisa saddle up as well. She was still a learner and wasn't great with horses, but she was a quick learner.

Then they took off toward Staunton. They wouldn't get there until nightfall but he had brought two pairs of night vision goggles with him. Hopefully that would give them an advantage.

"Remember, Lisa. This is a recon mission. Don't engage unless you're fired upon," he said.

"I know. But we should take opportunity to kill some if we can do in secret."

He didn't know if he loved the way she thought or was disturbed by it. He thought about it as they continued riding at an even pace. It couldn't be called fast, but it wasn't walking either.

"You've been quiet lately," he said.

"I have?"

"Yes."

"I'm thinking."

"About what?"

"Home. Future."

"Do you not see a future with us?"

She turned her head and looked at him with those impenetrable sunglasses of hers.

"I do, but I wonder if others do."

"Others? They all like you. You're part of the family now."

She shrugged.

"Look, Lisa, we're all in this together. We need each other but for that to work, we need to trust each other. They trust you. Do you trust us?"

She thought for a while before answering. He hated it when women took a long time to think. It usually meant something bad.

"Most of the time," she said.

They continued at a steady pace down the road. It was much slower than he would have liked. After all, he was used to cars and trucks. This was something that was going to take some getting used to.

"You fought in New York? You fought Russians? EU?"

"I did."

"Do you hate them?"

"Hate them? No. I was pissed that they'd invade us for nothing more than greed. They saw the head lion was sick so they pounced. I hate their reasoning and I hate the politicians that steered them into it, but I don't hate the people."

"And the Chinese?"

"We already discussed this. Why ask?"

"We met many violent, angry men. This is normal."

"No, they're just the loudest. Don't judge us by the actions of a few bandits."

"And if you do find Chinese soldier? What then?"

"As long as he doesn't try to kill us and he's honest with us, there shouldn't be a problem."

"Honest. Yes."

His words seemed to have the opposite effect he'd intended. Now she seemed gloomier than usual.

"If something's wrong, Lisa, I wish you'd just -"

She interrupted him before he could finish.

"That man and niece lived. Maybe family connection? Maybe your sister is alive?"

"No, I don't think so. She was a step sister. Not related by blood."

"Still, she could be."

"I almost hope not. I don't think I'd like her surviving all this by herself. Maybe it would be mercy if she had died."

She turned to him.

"Don't think like that. You might have someone out there. You should hope so. You might see each other one day."

"I don't see that as a possibility."

"I will never get back to China. I have no one and I know it."

"You have us. The world is different now. We have to accept the changes."

"And you should accept hope."

He noticed that she brought the FS2000 this time. It was slung across her chest.

"You found the FS, I see," Alex said.

She looked down to it as if noticing it for the first time.

"Oh, Yes. I saw it and liked it. Very handy."

"That it is. You ever shoot guns before all this?"

"Yes, my uncle took me shooting twice at gun club in Beijing. It was fun."

"You're a natural. You should have been a Marine."

She smiled a brief and humorless smile. He could never tell what was going through her head. Reading her was like reading Chinese.

Towards nightfall they found the road the farm was on and then began riding in the woods to avoid being seen. They put on their NVG's and once they reached the end of the woods, they dismounted.

In front of them were fields with white, wooden fences around them. On the far end, maybe half a mile away, was a large farmhouse and a barn. The barn door was open and light was poring out. The house had a wrap around porch with two stories and a tower.

"We need to get closer," he said.

She nodded in agreement and the two of them began running in a crouch toward the blindside of the barn. There was a guard with a rifle on the front porch of the house. All the lights in the house had what looked like lantern lights.

The barn looked more like a barracks. As he got closer he saw cots laid out in rows and people hanging around in groups, talking but no laughter.

"Survivors," he said.

"Two guards around house. Third over in fields."

She pointed off in the distance and saw a man walking in a wide circle around the property. He hadn't seen the patrol. Lisa had good eyes, even with glasses.

"Let's take a look at what they have."

They snuck around the farm while sticking to the shadows. They had a natural gas well and a bunch of machinery that looked like it was in the middle of construction. They had a small pond, a creek nearby, some outlying buildings, some more vehicles and several large drums of that was probably fuel.

There was also a tree with a body hanging from it.

Lisa looked up at it without expression.

"Animals," he muttered.

He checked to make sure the safety was off on his M4.

42

Alma, Petersburg, Virginia

ALMA WATCHED THE SMALL, HISTORICAL HOUSES AND TRUCK stops pass by her window. Virginia was thicker with trees than anywhere else she had ever seen. Historical markers seemed almost as common as McDonalds. More than anywhere else she had seen Petersburg was being overrun with grass, weeds and ivy. Some of the roofs on the older, more beautiful buildings were sagging. Without people to take care of them the past year and a half, it had been harsh.

"This looks like it could have been a really pretty place," Cass said.

It was Cass's turn to drive and Alma had her feet propped up on the dash with the window open. Cass had on her straw cowboy hat and sunglasses on. She actually looked kind of cool.

"I always read about Virginia in history," Cass continued. "My daddy loved Civil War history and would always tell us stories about it. Here in Petersburg was a huge battle. Nearby should be the Battle of the Crater. The North dug a tunnel under the Rebel lines and placed a bunch of dynamite. Then they blew it up and the explosion was so big that instead of charging in while the Confederates were all stunned and confused, they gawked and awed and stood where they were."

"Cool guys don't look at explosions."

"Guess the Yankees weren't cool."

"Do you think we're going to remember all that?"

"What do you mean?"

"I mean, how much do you think we're going to forget. Are we going to forget how to make engines, guns, gas, plastic? How much have we lost? I guess nuclear power is out the window."

"I don't know, but I don't want to lose any history. That's more important than plastic, at least in the long run."

"Will there be a United States again?"

"I doubt it. There may be countries that try to be, but it won't be the same."

"George Washington was born here, right?"

"Further north I think. Thomas Jefferson's house might be around here somewhere."

They drove past Petersburg and the scenery just became more walls of trees. It was strange not seeing the sky except as a small sliver above her. The closer they got to Virginia Beach the more anxious she felt. She was getting closer to finding out the truth.

She also started to wonder if she wanted to know the truth. Could she take finding his body?

Too soon it seemed she saw a sign that said "Virginia Beach 20 miles."

She sat up and couldn't think of anything else but Alex for the remainder of the distance. Alma did have enough sense left to get out her more detailed map of Virginia Beach they had gotten from a rest stop and she traced the path to the different military bases.

"If Alex was on leave, where do you think he'd be?" Alma asked.

"Barracks. They wouldn't put them anywhere fancy I imagine."

"We'll start with the different barracks and then work our way to places he might be. Keep an eye open for any sign of life," Alma said.

As the city grew and the buildings began to be closer together with more fast food joints and convenient stores, (things civilization was judged by) they'd stop, get their bearings, loot for soda or snacks and keep going. Everywhere they looked they found nothing but death. Like most places the streets were mercifully free of bodies.

Alma sipped a warm Vanilla Coke as she kept her eyes peeled for anything out of the ordinary.

"Think they'd be by the beach? Maybe they fish a lot?" Cass said.

"Worth a try."

Her stomach grew uneasy as they approached the closed fence of a military base. It said "National Guard Armory and Training Facility."

"National Guard? That won't work. Your brother was a Marine, right?"

"Yeah, but it won't hurt to check it out. If he's alive he'll be with other survivors. Branch of service won't matter."

The place was empty and falling apart. She pointed to a cluster of two story buildings that looked like barracks. Each was marked with a letter and they were all identical.

They stopped the truck and got out. With weapons ready they entered the first building. The stench almost knocked her back. She covered her mouth with her Rob Zombie shirt and backed away. The building was filled with bodies in uniform.

Cass looked at her and then tied a red bandana around her mouth and went in. Without saying anything Alma knew that Cass would be checking the name tags of all the bodies in uniform.

Alma waited outside, unable to think of anything else. What if? What if?

It was a while before Cass came out. She carried a backpack with her.

"They're all Army," she said, which was a kind way of saying that her brother wasn't a rotted corpse.

"What you got there?" Alma asked.

"More supplies. MRE's, knives, medical kit, AR mags and a few other odds and ends."

She wished they could respect the dead, especially dead soldiers, but Cass and she were alive and needed the stuff.

In the same way they checked all the barracks. Whatever Cass found she threw into the back of the truck without talking. Neither of them talked.

They spent a good three hours searching the National Guard base. A lot of it was offices, a church, and a one screen movie theater, but they also had an armory and they threw in every bit of ammo, every M16, M4 and M9 they could fit into the back of the truck. They left the SAW's and 240's. Belt fed machine guns would eat up all their ammo for too little gain.

Alma was about to leave but then she saw something that caught her eye. It was a crate full of grenades for the M204 grenade launchers. She loaded the crate and a few of the M4's equipped with under-barrel grenade launchers into the truck.

"You think we'll really need that?" Cass asked.

"There's no such thing as overkill."

"Well, if you're hunting there is."

"There is no hunting like the hunting of a man," Alma said.

"Hemmingway! Alma, I'm impressed. You actually read one of the books I gave you."

"That and Heart of Darkness, thank you very much."

"There's hope for you yet, Alma Attaway."

It was getting dark so they set up some of the cots in a clean (free of bodies) building. Cass ran around and played with Caesar who needed to get out and stretch his stumpy little legs more than he did.

Alma watched the two of them playing. Each of them had the biggest smiles she had ever seen. She didn't know basset hounds could smile.

She knew that this was all foolishness. She knew her brother was dead and that they'd been chasing a ghost the whole time. She'd known it since before she left Vegas. If it weren't for this small, nagging part of her mind she would have given up long ago.

She couldn't live with herself if she gave up or she'd be wondering about Alex the rest of her life. This was the only way she'd ever find peace. Maybe it was because she had gone crazy. It was possible. She did feel out of balance. Her emotions were all over the place and she was ready to burst into tears at any moment.

A little while later Cass came up to her.

"Hey, I saw a sign saying that there's a beach just down that path over there. Want to go?"

"Sure."

She had been looking forward to seeing the beach. She followed Cass and Caesar down a little road through the woods until it came out to a sandy beach with a table and benches. It was sunset so the ocean was dark. The small, whitecap waves crashed gently into the shore, more like friendly shoves.

It was beautiful. Even if she never found her brother, she was glad she came. The ocean spread out in a painfully long distance. It was so vast that she had trouble taking it all in.

She finally got to see the ocean.

"It's pretty, isn't it," Cass said in a huge understatement.

"Let's sleep on the beach tonight," Alma said.

Cass smiled a large, toothy smile.

"I'll get the blankets," Cass said. She ran off with Caesar on her heels.

43

Alma, Virginia Beach, Virginia

THEY SLEPT UNDER THE STARS ON THE BEACH. THEY HAD CARRIED their cots to the beach because as beautiful as it was, she didn't want to be covered in sand and crabs when she woke up in the morning.

The sound of the waves was far more soothing than Alma would have guessed. She needed soothing right now. It was hard to relax when all she could think about was that she was so close to finding out if Alex was alive.

If he was alive, would he even still be here or would he have left? She doubted that he would have left a note or any kind of sign. He wasn't crazy enough to think that she was crazy enough to come across a dead continent to find him.

He was the only family she had left and she had to know the truth, no matter how hard it was.

Alma woke up as the sun was just starting to turn the sky purple. Somehow Caesar had crawled up on her cot and was sleeping by her feet. He sensed her stir and looked up at her with his curious, sad eyes.

As the sun rose the sky grew more brilliant and beautiful.

"Cass! Wake up! You don't want to miss this," Alma said.

Cass woke up and reached for her 1911. But then she froze when she saw the coming sunrise.

The sunrise over an ocean was something she had not known she was missing, but now that she saw it, she knew she hadn't known what beauty was. Reds, yellows and oranges sparkled off the water, reflecting the sky back at itself with enhanced beauty.

They sat there, watching it until long after it was over and the sky and the ocean were both a crystal blue.

"I'm glad I came with you," Cass said.

"Me too," Alma said.

They left the cots there and walked back to where their truck was. Before leaving Alma and Cass both found pairs of ACU pants and boots that fit them.

"It's not 5th avenue, but it'll do," Alma said.

"These are actually kinda comfortable."

Alma drove this time and Cass had Caesar in her lap. Caesar seemed thrilled that he got to sit up front with the humans. He had his head near the window and his tongue hanging out. He would occasionally lean back and lick Cass on the face which would make Cass squeal in fake protesting.

They went to the Navy base next, where Alex would most likely have been when the plague hit. The place was much larger and much newer looking than the beat up old Guard base.

They searched building by building until they came across the barracks. She grew sick when they found it full of decayed, mummified bodies. This time she searched along with Cass. They found where the Marines had been staying and began searching through the name tags.

After two hours they finally came to the end.

"He's not here," Cass said.

"No, he's not," she said and let out a long sigh.

They found a map of the facilities and spent the rest of the morning searching but they found nothing.

The only place left was a small army base. It was called a depot, whatever that meant.

It was easy to find and near the beach. Like the National Guard place, this was just as run down and old looking. The first thing she noticed was a large hanger full of tools, dismantled Humvees and vehicle parts. She pulled up outside it and got out.

There was a trash can full of empty MRE packaging and dirty rags near the entrance and Cass walked over to take a look.

"Someone's been here fairly recently," Cass said.

Alma nodded but didn't comment. She didn't want to get her hopes up just yet.

Next they searched the barracks. One of the buildings had piles of books, magazines, filled trash cans and didn't have dust everywhere. Someone had definitely been here recently.

"Survivors," Cass said.

"Well, these idiots didn't leave a note or anything."

"They probably thought anyone that would come looking for them wouldn't have their best interest at heart."

Caesar sniffed around. She wished she had something of Alex's to let him get the sent, but she didn't know if basset hounds even did that.

Just to be sure they searched the rest of the small facility. The armory was missing a lot so whoever these survivors were, they took the weapons with them.

But there was nothing else and no sign of who these people were.

"We didn't find him, so there's still hope," Cass said.

There was, but it was also just as likely that Alex had crawled off somewhere else to die. If he had gone into the city then there would be no finding him. They couldn't search an entire city for one corpse.

If he was dead then she would never find him now and she'd always wonder what happened to him. Now she realized that as horrible as it would have been, it would have been merciful to find his body instead of wondering for the rest of her life.

Was he really alive? What were the odds that it had been him that was here? Did he fix up a Humvee and drive out of here?

She led Cass and Caesar back to the mechanic's and looked around. There was an empty fuel drum and no other sign of gas anywhere.

"How far can a Humvee go on a full tank?" Alma asked.

"I don't know. I don't imagine it to be very fuel efficient."

"So, if they left here, they couldn't have gone too far. Where would you go if you were looking for a safe place to settle down?"

"Umm...well...historically, people looked for fertile river valleys."

"Would that still be what people need?"

"If you're looking to stay for the long haul, you'll need farming, which means a river. Valleys protect against the worst weather. So, look for a valley with a river and lots of farm land. That isn't much to go by. They could be looking at a whole different set of priorities. What if they want...I don't know, a power source or a factory or something?"

Alma closed her eyes and tried to imagine what Alex would want. Then she took out the four different maps of Virginia she had and laid them all out on a folding table. Cass came over and stood beside her.

"There's a lot of rivers in Virginia," Cass said.

"That doesn't help our cause. We don't have a lot of gas left so we need to narrow our choices down."

"I don't think he'd want to be by the coast. Too many hurricanes."

"Okay, so, away from the coast. In the center of Virginia is Richmond. Just driving through I could tell that place was a dump. I don't think they'd be there or all the suburbs either."

"Would he want to be someplace remote and hidden?" Cass asked.

"Would he need to be? I think he would want to find other survivors. I don't think he'd be too hidden."

"I'll look at the topographical map, you look at the others with all the cities and towns and stuff."

Alma stared and stared at the map but nothing logical or rational came to mind. It just looked like a bunch of useless dots on a map.

Then she grabbed the topographical map which showed a satellite view of the state and her own map and went to a window. She overlaid them and began studying. The James River was good but it had too many cities and towns, including Richmond.

If they took a Humvee, they'd drive west, away from the coast and the crowded part of the state. So no eastern or Northern Virgina and no central. That left the western part of the state which looked like a mountain range.

Then she saw it.

"Shenandoah," Alma read aloud.

"It's a valley with a river on it. It also looks like the best place to be. Away from all the dying cities."

"They could have gone to Pennsylvania or north Carolina," Alma said.

"They could have, but we don't have the fuel to check all those places."

"We got enough to get there?"

"Probably."

"I wish I had Google Maps or something so I could se what these places looked like."

"Think of it like this, Alma, if we don't find him there, it would be a good place for us to settle down. We need to think about our future too."

"Caesar, what do you think? You're just as clueless as me, huh?"

44

THEY RODE BACK INTO THE FARM IN THE EARLY MORNING. ADAM was out chopping wood, Spencer was feeding the cows and Rebekah was feeding the chickens. They all dropped what they were doing and rushed over.

"What did you find?" Adam asked.

"They're there, alright. There's a lot of them and they got a bunch of survivors in a barn like slave labor. They had hung someone," Alex said.

"I'm hungry," Lisa said.

"Agreed. Let's do the debriefing in the kitchen."

They went to the kitchen where Jennifer made them some eggs and spam. At least the eggs were fresh and "organic" though the spam was nothing of the kind.

As they ate he told them everything they saw.

"What are we supposed to do?" Adam asked. "There's too many of them."

"Me and Lisa discussed this on our way back. We need to win some of those civilians over to our side. And if it ever comes to blows then we do what any other outgunned force would do, we launch hit and run attacks, ambushes, sneak in at night and kill them in their sleep."

Jennifer covered her mouth and shook her head.

"We can't let it come to that," she said.

"I hope it doesn't, Jennifer, but this world doesn't run on good intentions. Our first defense is to make sure that it doesn't come to a fight. We don't want a war with our neighbors, but at the same time, many of those civilians need our help. They're trapped there like slaves and don't have anywhere else to go. Do you see the dilemma here?"

"How long before they find us?" Rebekah asked.

"At best, until winter. But once we start burning wood all day long for heat, they'll see the smoke from our chimney. But if they're looking they'll see our cooking smoke sooner than that."

"There has to be a way to hide our smoke," Spencer said.

"If you can figure out a way, please do."

"If it comes to a fight, you have to shoot to kill them. No hesitation," Lisa said.

This quieted the others up.

"Let me assure you that these are bad men," Ranbir said. "If they find us, they will demand things that we can't afford to give them and then they will take the rest."

"So, they're like militia freaks, right?" Rebekah asked.

"Some of them. Their leader isn't. He ran for State Senate under a Democrat ticket. He runs the place like a commune almost."

"Right Wing militia communists? That doesn't make sense," Adam said.

"They're not about politics or ideas. They're about their own personal power and nothing else. Tyrants don't rule for ideas, they use ideas to rule over others," Ranbir said.

"This new world's turning very quickly into the old one," Jennifer said.

"Because people are people and now they don't have laws and society to keep them in check."

He wished Alma were here. That girl could run a gun better than he ever could. She was a child prodigy with it. Of course, she trained twice as much. That probably had something to do with it. While he had been out on dates with girls, she was on the range practicing her technique. She never had many friends because of her dedication. Dad used to say that she was overly competitive but that it was a good thing when she wanted to be a professional.

He missed that little runt.

The first time he met her was at the airport and he couldn't help but wonder at how scrawny she had looked. She was a small, frail thing but the intense, almost angry look in her eyes warned him not to underestimate her.

"Alex?" Lisa asked.

"Huh?"

"Something wrong?"

"No."

"You had funny look on face."

"Just remembering."

She nodded like she understood. Most likely she understood all too well.

If anyone felt lonely and out of place, it was her.

After he finished eating he went up to his room and went to bed.

When he woke up it was still light outside and he still felt painfully tired, but he needed to get back to a somewhat normal sleep schedule. So, he got up and wandered outside. Jennifer was on the porch sewing a rip in some pants.

"Where's everyone else?" He asked with a yawn.

"Adam and Spencer took two horses and are out foraging for whatever they can find."

"I hope they bring back more of those apples."

"You haven't been throwing the seeds away, have you?"

"No, way."

"Good. I'm going to plant them and one day we'll have an apple orchard."

"For now we'll have to make due with what we find."

"We have enough canned food for this winter, but I'm thinking about the next one. I've been reading up on canning and preserving. Next time you're in town, look for any glass jar and lids you can."

"Will do. Where's are new recruits?"

"They're working in the garden. Since they're vegetarian I figured they wouldn't want to work with the animals too much."

Adam and Spencer returned later that evening and Lisa didn't come down until dinner time. She was yawning and rubbing her eyes. She was wearing Iron Man pajamas that they had found in Lexington and a black tank top that looked rather...nice on her.

They had dinner out on the porch because the weather was so nice. As they ate Spencer picked up the guitar and played Hotel California.

Alex sat back and listened to the melancholy chords of the song. He knew what the song was about, but at that moment the song was about finding a home and he knew how fortunate they were to have found one. Perhaps he could relax, just a little this night.

He began singing along and when it got to the guitar solo at the end he performed a little air guitar. Everyone laughed, even Lisa who hid her laugh behind her hand.

It was a very pleasant, happy evening and Alex had to admit that he was enjoying the simplicity. This was what life used to be like. He wondered if it wasn't a better way than before.

But then he thought of all the technology. If someone broke a leg or got sick, they didn't have any hi-tech hospitals to go to. They'd have to fix it themselves.

However, right now everyone was laughing and smiling. Even Lisa was smiling and she had a wonderful smile. Now that she didn't have her sunglasses on, he saw that her eyes were as brilliant and beautiful as they were dark. Her black hair was somewhat messier than usual and loose strands hung around her face.

When Spencer began playing "Tribute" by Tenacious D, everyone, even Lisa, sang along.

He stayed up with Adam and Spencer, talking late into the night. They talked about movies, about family and anything else that came up.

"So, tell me something more about this sister of yours," Spencer said.

"I've told you about her already."

"Yeah, but you're always mentioning her. Tell me something I don't know."

"Well, she gets angry very easily but she doesn't really mean it. It's like when a bird ruffles up their feathers to make themselves look big."

"I had two sisters," Adam said.

"What were they like?"

"Mean as rattlesnakes, but I loved them."

"I had two older brothers," Spencer said. "They always teased me about wanting to be a musician. They said I should get a real man's job. They were in construction. They shut up when I joined the Army."

"You should have gotten a real man's job and joined the Marines," Alex said.

All three of them bust out laughing.

45

<u>Lisa, Promised Land, Virginia</u>

LISA AWOKE IN THE MORNING STILL FEELING TIRED. BUT SHE WAS used to that. During her training backing China, she would have to operate with two hours of sleep each night for a week or more. This was nothing.

She stretched and began doing her pushups and sit-ups. She loved pushups. They worked so many muscles and she didn't need a fancy gym to do them in. She loved how exercising cleared her mind and right now she needed a clear mind.

She still hadn't made any sense of her new life and this new world but last night was the first time that she had felt at home. These were her people now and this was her home. She was no longer Chinese, she was...whatever they were now. A Virginian? Promise Landian?

Lisa dressed in some cargo pants and a Lynard Skynard shirt that she had found in the laundry and walked down to the kitchen. Rebekah was there boiling eggs.

"Good morning!" Rebekah said with the kind of genuine smile that had her eyes closed and showed all teeth.

"Good morning. Boiling eggs?"

"Yup! Adam and Spencer are preparing for another patrol. That's what they call it. But it's just them going out and looking for food and stuff."

"I see."

She grabbed a raw egg, cracked it open and slurped it up.

"Ewww!" Rebekah said.

"Not ewww. Its how we did it in China."

"Really?"

"Yes. We also bite off heads of chickens and eat them."

The look of horror on Rebekah's face was priceless.

"I'm just joking," Lisa finally said.

"I hope so. Dang, I thought you were a good cook."

"I am good cook."

She had learned to cook for herself long ago. No one else would do it and she liked eating good food, so she learned. It was a small pleasure in a mostly pleasureless life.

She walked outside and found Alex standing on the porch leaning against a post and staring out at the farm.

"Alex?" She said.

"Huh?"

"Is this place going to be like old world and men get to go out and have fun and women stay home cooking and cleaning? If so, I tell you now that I not have that."

Alex smiled.

"Actually, I was thinking of having Adam become our official cook. But right now it's dangerous to patrol and I don't want to risk Jennifer or Rebekah. Besides, they're my two lousiest shots and Rebekah's too young. Are you saying you want to go out on patrol?"

"I do, but not today. Too busy."

He chuckled.

She stood beside him and tried to see what he saw. The place was indeed beautiful. They were fortunate to have found it. She didn't believe in God, Buddha or anything, but if there was some deity out there, he created this place for them.

Lisa was about to tell him what she was thinking but at the last second she closed her mouth. Why was she reluctant to tell him? She trusted him and they had a sufficient camaraderie. Was she nervous about appearing to be a fool? Would he laugh at her small thoughts?

Not knowing the answers she grabbed all the solar panels, tools and parts and went up to the attic. It took a lot of work to get the panels up on the roof, but she managed. They weren't small panels and together should provide 800 watts of power. Once there, she looked over everything and planned it out in her head. She always tried to plan out before acting. That's why training was so important. It made her plan out a battle before it took place.

She was supposed to drill the panels in place but since she didn't have a power drill, she had to use a hammer and nails. After finding the support beams of the roof, she hammered the panels in place and began connecting the cables. Then she swung back in through the attic window and began connecting it to the converter which connected to the house's power. The converter could also store power so they'd have some at night. Not a bad system and they had back up panels and converters in the barn, just in case.

Once finished, she flipped on the attic light and to her surprise, it came on. She couldn't help but smile. She didn't realize how much she had missed electricity. She had brought power back to the house.

She didn't think it would actually work.

Lisa turned the light off and hurried downstairs. Rebekah was still in the kitchen reading a book about raising animals. She walked to the light switch and cleared her throat. When Rebekah looked up she flipped the light on.

The look on Rebekah's face was worth any trouble she had gone through. It made her happy just to see Rebekah that happy.

"Lisa! How'd you do it?"

"Solar panels. I hooked them up."

Rebekah ran over and through her arms around her neck in a tight embrace. Despite being much younger they were almost the same height.

"Now we can use the stove and the washing machine and the air conditioning and..."

"Yes, yes. We have power. Don't tell anyone. Keep it secret. Okay?"

"Secret?"

"Yes, I want to surprise them tonight."

Rebekah smiled and nodded.

This was her home now so it was time she did her best to make it a home she wanted to live in. It was also time she got to know the others. Their unity would be the only thing that would get them through the hard times.

She spent the day feeding the horses, getting water from the river and boiling it and feeding the cows. Jennifer did the milking. Good, because she didn't want to touch those udders.

When dusk came around, something that she had never really paid attention to before, they gathered on the porch to relax before dinner. Dusk had been the time between day and night and nothing else. Now it was a time to end their work and relax. As the sunlight grew dimmer Alex reached for the lantern.

"Hold on," Lisa said and stood up.

"What's up?" Alex asked.

She then flipped the porch light on and everyone gasped. Adam began clapping and laughing in that baritone voice of his and Jennifer began crying.

"Lisa, how did you manage this?" Alex asked.

"I hooked up solar panels."

Suddenly she was surrounded by people giving her hugs, rubbing her head and patting her on the back.

She had now earned her place here. She was one of them and belonged.

They had dinner while Spencer played the guitar under the bright, electric porch light. She only knew a few of the songs, but the songs she did, she tried to sing along. One thing she had liked about America was the music. No where else had music that was so energetic and full of life.

After everyone had gone to bed she took her sat-phone and went out into the woods. There was nothing the phone could do for her. It was a connection to a place that she no longer belonged to.

She took out her folding army shovel and dug a small hole. Carefully she placed the sat-phone in the hole and covered it with dirt. She stood over the spot of earth and thought about her new life. Her new life had no room for undivided loyalties.

With that done, she returned to the house and laid down in her bed.

There were strange sounds coming from Jennifer's room. At first she didn't know what it was but then quickly realized that it was her making love. She had heard it before. During training a male and female student had gone off to an empty room to have sex and it had been her turn for guard duty. She stumbled upon them. She had been too embarrassed to even report them.

Now she heard the same sounds. She tried to listen and hear who the partner was. For some reason the thought of it being Alex turned her stomach in anger. No matter how hard she tried, she couldn't tell so she silently crept to Alex's room and cracked the door open. He was sleeping quietly in his bed.

She let out a breath and she felt her body relax. Then she walked back to her room, confused about why she was so worked up about the thought.

46

"**A**LRIGHT, LISA. YOU READY FOR PATROL?"
Lisa checked the safety on her FS2000 and gave a quick nod. He checked his M14 and slung it over his back.

"Let's ride," he said.

He had always wanted to say that.

They mounted the horses and headed out. They were off to search Lexington some more. They had a detailed map of the city and were checking it section by section in a methodical and orderly manner. There was no telling what house held something vitally important. It had been a random house that had the solar panels. Maybe someone had medical supplies or a book on how to survive the end of the world.

The ride into Lexington wasn't long and they passed by VMI and Washington and Lee University.

"Maybe we can set up defense in VMI? It's on hill, like castle. Place to retreat to?" Lisa said.

"That's not a bad idea. We'll send a team tomorrow."

"I'll go with team."

"You were wasted as a waitress, Lisa. You have a mind for this sort of thing."

She just shrugged.

"Are all you Chinese this hard core?"

"I'm not Chinese now. I'm Virginian."

"I guess you're right about that. We all are. Heck, I'll never see Las Vegas again and now I'm not sure I'd want to. It would just be a ghost version of what once was."

He looked over to her to judge her reaction but she was her normal statue self. He wondered if beneath all that she was utterly unimpressed with him.

She never gave any signs of one way or another so she could completely hate him or admire him with equal probability.

Then they heard the sound of a truck in the distance. They both froze in place. Before they could pinpoint it the truck came screeching around a corner. There looked to be four men in it: two in the front and two in the bed.

The men saw them.

"Let's go!" He shouted.

They yanked the reigns of the horses into a side street as the truck began turning towards them.

One of the buildings in the side street had an open door. It was the only place to hide. There were probably more but he didn't have time to think, only react.

"Let's hide the horses in there and take position elsewhere," he said.

She nodded.

They stashed their horses in the rear of the old dress shop and ran across the street to an Italian restaurant. The tables were covered in dust and most of the front was glass with a waist-high wall that would offer concealment but not cover. Bullets would go right through most things in this place.

"Guard the front, I'll check the back," he said.

He didn't want to be trapped in a building with no exit. Fortunately the place did have a back door that led to an alley. The storage had boxes of rotted flour but the 2-liters of soda looked good. Even now he was assessing what he could scavenge.

"They coming," she called out.

He ran up to the front and hid behind some boxes.

The truck pulled to a screeching stop at the side street where they had left the horses.

"Check the buildings!" One of them yelled.

"They will find the horses," Lisa whispered.

"I know."

"We can't let them have them. We need them."

"I know."

She raised her rifle and reluctantly he did as well. They couldn't out run them on horses and they couldn't hide with horses, but at the same time they couldn't give the horses up. They were too valuable.

He placed the cross hairs of his scope on one of them and began to slow his breathing.

"I take right, you take left," he began. "Three, two...One!"

They both fired at the same time, shattering the store front windows and both shots hit. Both men with down with holes punched right between the shoulder blades (his) and the other struck the back of the man's head. (Lisa.)

The two remaining men instantly ducked behind their truck. He couldn't get a clear shot. One of the men poked out long enough to let loose with a burst from his AK. The bullets tore through what was left of the glass and the wood around them. The air was suddenly filled with dust, gun smoke and flying splinters. Alex couldn't see what the other man was doing.

Then a small cylinder flew threw the air, thrown from the man behind the truck. It burst into purple smoke and within moments he couldn't see anything past the window.

Suddenly one of the men leapt into the window and tried to grab Lisa. She blocked his arms with her FS and, without hesitation, Spartan kicked the man right in the gonads with all her strength. The man crumpled over and Lisa booted him in the face for good measure. His nose crunched and blood gushed out, covering his face and shirt.

The sound of the truck peeling out alerted him back to the purple cloud in front of them. He ran out but could only see the dark form of the truck taking off at top speed.

"Damn it!" He shouted.

When he went back inside Lisa had the man handcuffed to an exposed pipe.

"What we do with him?" Lisa asked.

"You got a Chinese whore with you? They destroyed our country and you're working with them?" The handcuffed man said.

"You from the Hunt Club or whatever it is you call yourselves?" Alex asked.

"I ain't talking to you traitors."

Lisa motioned with a jerk of her head to speak outside. They walked out into the street and she began whispering.

"One escaped. He tell others. They come looking for us," Lisa said.

"Believe me, I know."

"What we do with him? He no tell us anything."

"We can use him for a hostage."

"He eat food. They might not care."

"True, but they might."

"This going to be war, no matter what. Those men come and try to kill us. They no talk. No negotiate. They come to take us and everything we have.

What you think they do to me when find me?"

He could imagine the answer. He saw what the Russians did to civilians they found. He wasn't going to let that happen to her.

"I say we kill him now."

"Hold on. This isn't a battle. Executing someone is very different than in a battle. Heck, it's bad enough in battle. It's ten times worse when they're not fighting back."

"I do it," Lisa said.

"No, I've done it before. I'll do it." He didn't want to stain her hands.

Lisa was right. These men would be out for blood no matter what. There might as well be one less of them.

He pulled out his M9.

"You just going to kill me? My friends are coming for me and when they see me dead they'll kill every single one of you!" The man spat at them.

"We're trying to build a new world here: one that's better than the old. But you guys are trying to make it into the Dark Ages again. We saw your farm. You use those survivors as peasants and you're the lords."

"Why not? The ones that work hard are in charge of the ones that work less. Simple as that," the man said.

"Shut up," Lisa said.

"You shut up, China whore! You love long time?"

She kicked him right in the mouth. Her black combat boots knocked at least one tooth because he saw the bloody, white thing fly across the room and hit an intact part of the window. Lisa's face was still completely unreadable.

Alex tried several times to get him to talk, to give him a reason to spare his life, but all he got were insults and threats.

He motioned for Lisa to stand back. She did and he took aim. He lined up the sights on his face and fired without hesitation. As soon as he saw red splash against the wall he turned away.

It wasn't his first execution, but it was his first that he wasn't ordered to do.

"Let's get our horses and get out of here."

They grabbed the man's AK .357 revolver and the other two men's things and mounted up. They rode quickly back home and immediately gathered a meeting.

He left out the execution part.

The group came to a general consensus: They were screwed.

47

Alma, Buena Vista, Virginia

ALMA DID HAVE TO ADMIT, EVEN THROUGH HER FOUL MOOD, that this place was gorgeous. The hills and the trees just kept getting prettier and prettier. Now she knew why some people liked the country more. They weren't crazy, they just liked peace and beauty. Even if she didn't find Alex, she knew she could live here.

She had to have Cassidy drive because she was too upset to drive correctly. Cass hadn't appreciated the tight mountainous turns while going seventy miles an hour. Inside her heart and mind were fighting a battle. Her heart insisted that Alex was alive and her mind told her that it was an impossible dream.

"You know what I read once?" Alma asked.

"What?"

"Dreams are like rainbows: only idiots chase them."

"That's funny."

"Am I an idiot?"

"Absolutely not."

"*Mira*, we both know my brother is dead. This search is a waste of our time and resources. We need to just find a place to settle down and wait out the apocalypse."

"Well, we're coasting on fumes here so once we hit this valley, we aren't going anywhere unless we're walking."

"Maybe that's for the best. It'll force me to give up this *tonteria*."

"I'm not sure what a tonteria is, but you got to have faith, Alma."

"Faith? Faith doesn't change facts. Alex is dead and I'm chasing a ghost."

"I'm not giving up. If your brother's alive, we'll find him."

"Why do you care?"

"Because you do."

Alma went back to looking out the window. Cass was an idiot as well.

The truck ran out of gas near the top of the mountain. They pushed it up the rest of the way which wasn't very far and the incline was barely noticeable. Then they coasted the rest of the way down.

By coasting they were able to pick up a lot of speed and by the time they reached Buena Vista Cass had to keep her foot hard on the brakes just to stay in control.

They passed some crappy looking apartments, a run down auto shop and a church with a sign saying "Prepare to meet God."

The truck finally came to a stop at an intersection with a Hardees and an All A Dollar on the corner.

"Last stop, Buena Vista. End of the line," Cass said.

"Why is there a town with a Spanish name in the middle of Virginia?"

"I don't know. Maybe named after the Battle of Buena Vista?"

"What's that?"

"A big battle in the war with Mexico."

"What's that freaking huge red building on top of the hill?"

"Don't know. It'll be dark soon, it's probably as good a place to rest as any."

"What do we do about the truck?"

Reluctantly they used the wagons to haul everything from the truck and up to the huge red building. It took three trips up and down the hill.

It turned out the place was Southern Virginia University. There were dorm rooms in the red main building and they found a room in the tower to sleep in for the night. They let Caesar run around the grassy fields and Alma fixed them dinner: she opened the cans of cold chili for them.

She took out her map again.

"This town is too small and cramped. They'd need more open space for farming," Alma said.

"We can check out Lexington tomorrow. There's bound to be some bicycles in town. We'll take those to Lexington and wherever else. If we don't find Alex or anyone else, we can look for a place to live."

"The valley is huge so we'll just follow the river."

"Good idea. Maybe we can find a canoe instead?"

"I don't like boats."

They slept in the tower and in the morning she was greeted with a beautiful view of the town. This place had its own kind of charm. The narrow side valley the town was nestled in stretched out with the river running along a hill. The town looked nice, but it wasn't what she was looking for. Still, this tower would make a good watch tower.

Cassidy was already up. She was reading pamphlets about the school.

"Alma! This is a Mormon college!"

"So?"

"The apostle told me to look for a gathering of Mormons to put my stake down."

"What the hell does that mean?"

"This is a place where Mormons gathered. We're on the right track! I'm going to live somewhere near here."

"We know that already."

"Yeah, but now, I know, I know it."

"If you say so."

She tried to brush it off but even she felt guided or pushed along. Maybe she should go to mass again if there ever is another mass.

They put Caesar in a room with plenty of food and water for three days. They planned on being back on the second.

They left and began their search of the town. On Main Street they came across a bike shop. Simple enough. They got their weapons and backpacks and left the other stuff in the tower of the school and began biking along the river. Soon they lost track of the main road. Most of the time it was off road.

It was slow going and when the river met up with the road again they took the road. It was a long bike ride. When they paused for lunch she took out her map and a tourist map of Lexington they found.

"Look, the river goes right by VMI. We need to check that place out," Alma said.

"Good idea. It would be a place where survivors would have gone, even if temporarily."

The idea of a castle appealed to her. It was safety and permanent, two things people would want nowadays.

Occasionally they'd see a house and go over and investigate. All the houses were empty of life though some still had bodies: dried husks, dark stains and a lingering stench.

Would God let them come all this way just to meet with disappointment and failure? Absolutely He would. He let the billions die of a stupid plague. He'd have no problem with one Mexican girl not finding her brother. It wasn't even a blip on His cruel-O' Meter.

Sometime around three, they saw VMI up on a hill. They had to push their bikes up the slope of the river to the street. There was a football field to their left and then a really steep hill and a winding road that led up to it.

From the hill she saw a music store a little further down the road. If they were going to settle here she'd have to loot a guitar or five.

The steep road went past a stone church and a castle looking building and came out to a large open, green field with a statue of some Civil War dude.

They put their bikes in the church while they looked around on foot. She had her trusty competition AR and Cass had her larger Broadsword.

"Should we call out?" Cass asked.

"Let's look around. I'd rather be the one to see them first."

They walked in through the open gate of the castle building and saw that it was a bunch of rooms circling a wide courtyard. It had four levels with balconies going all the way around. The courtyard was grass with cement paths radiating out from the center like the spokes of a bicycle tire.

Some of the rooms still had left over things from students but there weren't many bodies. They moved up to the second floor where all the rooms faced out into the courtyard. The first room looked ransacked. Old uniforms were thrown about and the bed was toppled on its side. Nothing useful here.

Then Alma heard something. She put her finger to her lips to tell Cass to stay silent.

The sound was coming from the courtyard and it sounded like horses. Then she heard the faint sound of talking.

"Someone's here. Stay down," Alma whispered.

Carefully she peeked out from the over the ledge and saw three people on horses with a fourth pack horse. It was loaded with heavy looking bags.

One of the people was a large black man with sideburns and a military M4. The other was a young, skinny white guy with spiky brown hair. He didn't look nearly as professional as the other two. The third was a small Chinese woman with sunglasses and a grim business face. She carried an FS2000 close to her chest and she looked like she knew what she was doing.

The Chinese girl seemed to be the boss and was motioning to the others and saying something she couldn't hear. All three of them looked to have military training of some kind.

"What do we do?" Cass asked.

"We have to risk it. We got to make contact."

Cass took a deep breath and nodded.

They both stood up and put their hands in the air.

Instantly the Chinese woman had her gun trained on them and the other two quickly followed. The girl was fast. Competition fast.

"Don't shoot! We're not here to fight!" Alma called down.

"Put your guns on the ground and come down slowly!" The Chinese girl called out in a high, but forceful voice. She was someone who was used to giving orders.

After leaving their guns (something she hated doing) they walked down the stairs with their hands up and the woman stood watch while the two men came over and patted them down.

"They're clean." The large black man said in a low voice.

"What you doing here?" The Chinese girl asked in an unfriendly tone.

Alma looked to Cass and shrugged. It was worth a try, right?

"This is a long shot, but hell with it."

"Don't swear," Cass whispered.

"You wouldn't happen to know an Alex Attaway, would you?"

She watched as the eyes of all three of the people went wide.

48

Alma, Lexington, Virginia

ALMA WATCHED AS THE SURPRISED CHINESE WOMAN LOWERED her weapon slightly.

Her heart was pounding away like machine gun rocking on full auto.

"Who are you?" The Chinese woman asked.

"My name's Alma." She paused to swallow. "I'm looking for my brother. His name is Alex Attaway. He's about five eleven, shaved head, Marine, really nice guy."

The woman looked to her two companions and they looked even more shocked than she did.

The scary looking Chinese cleared her throat.

"You have ID?" The woman asked.

Alma pulled out her hand which she noticed was now trembling. She could read their reactions. They knew something. What they knew would either destroy her or give her joy like she had never had before. Either way, she was more nervous than she ever remembered being.

The woman looked at her ID and up to her again.

"Alma Attaway," the woman said in that thick, choppy, Chinese accent of hers.

"I can't believe this. This is crazy," the young man said.

"Please, if you know anything about my brother, tell me," Alma said, almost to the point of tears.

The woman slung her FS2000 down by her side and took a step forward.

"Alma Attaway, you brother is alive and well. We take you to him."

Just like that she felt an immense weight lift off her chest and she began to cry. Cass quickly put her lanky arm around her shoulder.

"I told you. You just gotta have faith," Cass said.

"This is impossible. Are you sure?" Alma asked.

"Yes. Your brother's told us many times about his awesome little sister," the young white guy said. "Like the time you borrowed his mountain bike and crashed it into a fire hydrant two blocks down."

"Wait...Aren't you supposed to be in Vegas?" The black man asked.

"I knew he was in Virginia Beach so I traveled all the way here from Vegas. When I didn't find his body there, I thought about where he might have headed. Cassidy here suggested that we look for a river valley with lots of farms. So we came to the Shenandoah and started looking along the river."

The black man laughed.

"Well, damn, girl. You are your brother's sister, aren't you? Come on, let's go. We got a reunion that I don't want to miss."

"He's going to freak out," the white guy said.

They introduced themselves and she learned their names. Lisa, Spencer and Adam.

They grabbed their weapons and collected their bikes. Then they headed out, going to meet with Alex.

She was so excited she found it hard to breathe. She had almost given up hope. But just like that, she had stumbled upon Alex's companions. This was crazy. She was dreaming or something.

"Were you all at a small army depot in Virginia Beach?" Cass asked.

"We were. You guys went there?" Adam asked.

"We sure did. We looked all over the different military bases and didn't find hide nor hair of Alex. So, we figured he was still alive."

"I still can't believe you found us. The odds are...impossible," Spencer said.

"I knew the odds but I felt he was alive. So I had to come looking," Alma said.

"Utterly amazing," Adam said. "Why would you even think he was alive?"

"I just knew."

"We thought you were..." Spencer started to say but stopped himself.

"What's my brother doing here? You guys have a farm?" Alma asked.

"We found ourselves a nice little place. Plenty of room for everyone. We got cows, sheep, goats, chickens and we're trying to grow crops," Adam said.

"Your brother's going to freak when he sees you. Freak might be too small a word," Spencer said.

The Chinese woman was strangely silent and would occasionally glare at them from behind her sunglasses. What was this chick's deal?

"Lisa, how'd you meet my brother?" Alma asked. If Lisa had a problem with them, she wanted to nip it in the bud.

"They found me in Richmond," Lisa said. "I worked at restaurant."

"Now she's one of the best shots we have," Spencer said.

"She's better than you anyway," Adam said.

"We heard you're a fair shot," Spencer said.

"My brother tell you that? I'm good, but not as good as he says. Won a few awards," Alma said.

They continued down the road and eventually took a smaller sideroad in view of a Walmart and crossed over the river. This ride was taking forever. How far were they? From the bridge she could see a beautiful house with fields and pastures around it. The river ran close by.

"That's it," Adam said. "We named it Promised Land."

"It's beautiful."

They rode up to the house and a middle aged woman stood up from the porch and greeted them. There was a machine shop and two people working in a garden.

"My, my. Who are our guests?" The woman asked.

"Jen, this is Cassidy and this is Alma. Alma Attaway," Adam said, over pronouncing her name.

"Alma Attaway?"

Jen looked over to her with a face that told Alma she understood exactly who she was.

"Impossible," Jen said.

"Everyone keeps saying that. Am I the only one that believed it?" Cass said.

Probably.

"I'll go get him," Jen said.

"No, where is he?" Alma said.

"He's up in his room cleaning weapons."

Alma dropped her backpack on the ground and handed her AR to Cass.

"Upstairs on the right," Adam said.

She marched into the house but as she got to the base of the stairs her knees grew weak. This couldn't be happening. Her brother, the man who she loved more than anyone else was right up the stairs.

Slowly she gripped the handrail and pulled herself up.

She suddenly became aware of how filthy and raggedy she must look. She tried to straighten out her hair and clothes but knew it was a hopeless battle. After weeks without a bath, there was only so much she could do.

Once at the top of the stairs she saw a door that was slightly open. She crept up to it and peered in.

The familiar sight of Alex's back as he cleaned weapons filled her vision. He always had to sit on the floor when he cleaned his guns. Alma had picked up that habit as well. After all, he had taught her.

He looked perfect, like a vision of what she had always remembered. He was strong, healthy and in one piece. She stood there in the doorway watching him for who knows how long. Just seeing him was more than she had actually hoped for.

She wanted to say something cute like "you shouldn't have your back to the door," but all that came out was a sob and the word "Alex."

Alex stopped what he was doing and turned his head. Then he saw her and their eyes made contact.

Alex

Alex heard a familiar voice say his name. It was almost a sob. The voice was so familiar but he couldn't place it.

He turned around and there, standing in the doorway was Alma. He stared at her but knew it had to be a hallucination. Maybe he had fallen asleep and this was a dream.

It couldn't be.

It was definitely Alma alright. She was a little older and she looked dirty like she hadn't bathed in several weeks. Her raven black hair was in a messy ponytail and she wore his old Rob Zombie shirt he got from their first concert together.

She was crying and standing there, smiling at him.

As soon as he realized that it was real and not some dream he instantly bolted up and ran over to her. He threw his arms around her and pulled her into his shoulder for a tight embrace. Her skinny arms wrapped around his waist and she buried her face in his chest.

They stayed like that for a long while. She continued to cry, something he had never seen her do, and held each other.

"How?" He finally managed to get out through a tight throat.

"I came looking for you. I knew you were alive."

"You came all the way from Vegas?"

"I found a jeep and I drove north to Utah. I found a crazy girl named Cass and we drove up to Salt Lake and then went east. We fought with FEMA and we had to go around Denver because Denver was nuked so we couldn't go there. We drove through Kansas and oh, we stole this truck and gas to get here. We went straight to Virginia Beach but you weren't there. I almost gave up but Cass was like "you got to have faith!" So we kept going *y no se que paso' aya, pero* we kept going *y buscemos* on *un mapa y* figured you'd be on a river and Cass said something about ancient civilizations on *rios, no se. Pero fuimos* to VMI and we saw Lisa *y los otros* and they took us here."

It seemed that she had said all that in one breath. He understood maybe half of it. She only broke into Spanish on accident when she was extremely emotional. Usually the emotion was anger.

He pulled away and looked at her face. She was covered in tear streaked dirt, but it was her and more beautiful and wonderful than ever.

"Let's go get you something to eat and then you can explain it all in a more coherent manner."

She rubbed his head and then slapped him playfully on the cheek.

"Be nice to me. I just drove across the apocalypse to find you."

49

Alex, Promised Land, Virginia

Alex took Alma down to the kitchen and found everyone gathered in a group surrounding a tall, skinny red headed girl that was wearing a straw cowboy hat. The group turned when they noticed him and Alma.

They all flooded into the kitchen and stood around as they got food for Alma and the red head.

He held his hand out to the freckled girl.

"Hi, I'm Alex, Alma's brother," he said.

"I gathered that. I'm Cassidy. I told her she needed faith and looky here. You're alive," the girl said with a toothy but infectious smile.

"It's good to meet you Cassidy. Thanks for taking care of my sister."

"It was my pleasure. At least she does have good taste in music," Cassidy said.

"Thanks to me," he said.

"Yes, he taught me the love of a Heavy Metal," Alma said.

"So, you guys drove all the way from Vegas on a one in a million chance that he was alive? How did you expect to even find him?" Jennifer asked.

"We tried not to think about it," Alma said.

"We went on blind faith," Cassidy said.

"You guys are crazy," Spencer said.

"We're crazy, but we were right," Cassidy said.

They all helped make a big pot of chili and they sat down on the porch (their unofficial meeting place) and ate and talked.

They went step by step from leaving Vegas, going up through Utah, through Colorado and driving across country. It took a while and the whole time Alex found himself staring at Alma. He still found it hard to believe that she was sitting there, bowl in hand and smiling. This was surreal. He had long assumed her to be dead.

It was like waking up from a dream only to find parts of the dream were still real.

Her smile was huge and just how he remembered her.

"What's that rifle you got there?" He asked Cassidy.

"Broadsword. Made by the same guy who made Alma's gun," Cassidy said.

"What? You met Gundoc from Crusader Weaponry?"

"Yeah. We traded ammo for this. I have to say that this rifle is only the most awesomest rifle I've ever shot," Cassidy said.

She handed it over for him to look at. It was lighter than he would have thought. Everything on it was top of the line. It would make a great competition gun and a battle rifle.

"If I thought about it, I would have gotten you one," Alma said.

"We have a whole pile of M4's and M16's," he said.

"We have a small arsenal as well, but we had to leave it in Buena Vista where we ran out of gas," Alma said.

"We'll go get it tomorrow," he said.

"We also got some food and other supplies. And if you got fuel we got a working car," Alma said.

"Cars we have. Fuel we do not," Jennifer said.

"We have horses though," Alex said.

"Horses? You, Alex?" Alma asked with look of surprise mixed with disgust.

"Yeah, you know, like cowboys? I'm sure you've heard of them," Cassidy said.

"I wasn't born in a barn like you," Alma said.

"Oh, this is going to be great. Alma will have to learn how to ride! Maybe we can get you a cowboy hat as well," Cassidy said.

"Adam, Spencer, take a cart and go to Buena Vista to get their stuff," Alex said.

They told them where to find their stash and Alma told them to bring a big cart.

"So, this is the famous Alma Attaway," Rebekah said.

"What have you been telling them?" Alma demanded, faking being angry. She was always like this, joking about everything.

"Nothing but the truth," he insisted.

"Oh, sure. You probably still blame me for those missing concert tickets."

"They went somewhere."

"Is it true that you're the best shot in Nevada?" Rebekah asked.

"Well, I'm the best female shooter of my age class," Alma said. "So, yeah, I guess I am. Now that I'm in Virginia I'm the best shot in Virginia as well."

Yup, surreal was a good word for this.

"So, you got a nice farm here, Bro. Anything else going on? Any neighbors? Other survivors?" Alma asked.

"Well, yes. There's another group of survivors. They're not good neighbors."

He told them everything they knew about them and everything that has happened.

"So, it's a shooting war now and I bet they're going to come looking for us," Alma said.

"That's a pretty accurate statement," Jennifer said. "They don't know where exactly we live, but we're not hard to find. And when they find us, they'll bring more guns and more men."

"Good thing we showed up. Well, not good for us," Cassidy said.

"Let's not talk about that right now," Alex said.

After they ate and talked for a few hours Cassidy insisted on a bath and they split up to all go do their own thing. He took Alma up to his room so he could continue cleaning the guns while they talked.

"Who's the angry little Chinese woman?" Alma asked.

"That's Lisa Fang. We found her in Richmond where she had been working at a Chinese buffet."

"Sure."

Just a waitress? Right.

"She's become very good with a gun and I trust her."

"She doesn't seem to like me much."

"She doesn't like any stranger much."

She picked up his M14 that was leaning against the wall by his bed.

"You always wanted one of these," Alma said.

"Got it free from the Marine Corp."

"Very nice. So, besides shooting things, what needs to be done around here?"

"Farming. Finding fuel. One of the books said we can find natural gas in the area, maybe rig a truck to run on that, but none of us know how."

She was staring at him with a funny grin on her face.

"What?" He asked.

"I knew you were alive. Well, I didn't know, know, but I knew."

"Because you're crazy."

She shrugged.

"Maybe I am. I came to look for you and here you are, leader of a group with a nice farm."

"It could be worse. It could be much worse. You said you found a few surviving towns. I wonder if there are other towns around."

"I would assume so."

"I guess we should find you and Cassidy a room. There's one in the guest house."

"You guys have a guest house?"

"Sure do."

"I was hoping I could have a room in this house, with you."

"I'll see if someone's willing to trade."

"Thank you, Bro."

"Why can't I ever say 'no' to you?"

"Because you love me."

"No, maybe I'm just scared of you."

"Even better."

50

LISA WATCHED AS ADAM AND SPENCER CAME BACK WITH A CART loaded with supplies and weapons. Also, sitting on top of the pile was the most ridiculous looking dog she had ever seen. It was short and chubby with loose folds of skin that made it look perpetually sad and huge ears that dragged on the ground.

"Oh! Look at the cute puppy!" Rebekah exclaimed while clapping her hands.

It was one more mouth to feed and it wouldn't contribute anything.

Lisa walked over to the cart and began looking through it. Camping gear, canned food, portable solar panel, ammunition and assorted fire arms.

They would need all the guns and ammo they could get. She knew the Hunt Club would be coming after them. If only they had more bodies to hold the guns.

The "dog" hopped down from the cart and began sniffing her feet.

"Back away, mutt," she said in Mandarin.

She had to speak to Alex about the situation with the Hunt Club. If they messed up, they'd be wiped out by superior numbers. She'd been thinking about this almost constantly. Something had to be done and done soon. If they were made to go on the defensive, they'd lose the initiative and be forced to react instead of dictating the conditions of the fight. They had to attack.

Lisa found Alex in his room cleaning off his body armor. She had a vest like that as well and she figured that she'd need to start wearing it soon. Alma was there too. She was cleaning a rifle: an FAL by the looks of it.

"Alex, we need to set up security," Lisa said.

"What do you suggest?" He asked, looking up from his armor. He had that smile on his face that came so naturally and had a way of easing her fears when all logic and reason told her to be very fearful.

Every gesture and expression she did was controlled and calculated. She wondered if she had any honest expressions or if everything she was, was just a role to play. Was there a real Lisa under her mask? Even her name was fake. It was Ling, not Lisa.

"I think not using lights at night. Someone keep watch and everyone keep weapon on them, even Ranbir and Rehka," Lisa said.

"They don't know how to fight."

"Then they learn."

"I sense you have more to tell me."

Damn. He was perceptive. That gave her a shot of momentary fear. How perceptive was he? Did he suspect her?

She shifted her weight before realizing and she took control of herself again.

"Now we have two more fighters, we need more organization. I assume you team up with sister?"

"No, I'll stay with Cass if you don't mind," Alma said.

"Me and you will continue as a team," Alex said.

She felt a wave of relief wash over her.

"Adam and Spencer team," she said.

And as backup we have Jennifer and Rebekah but I don't want them to fight unless it's absolutely necessary," Alex said.

It probably would be.

"They protect house. We keep big guns up here. Sniper rifles. Look out over road. Shoot bad guys that come this way," Lisa said.

"Alright. Sounds good," he said.

"Also..." she began to say.

"Yeah?"

She took a deep breath. This was the important part and she mentally swore to herself that she was forced to use this fake, crappy bad English.

"Also, we need organization here. You leader. Who second in command? Who does what?" Lisa said.

"She wants you to form a government," Alma said.

"Isn't that a bit premature? How it is now seems to be working."

"But once we get more survivors here," Lisa said.

"You mean the people from the Hunt Club's camp."

"Them too."

"You've been thinking about this."

Lisa nodded.

"She probably has a plan," Alma said.

"You got a plan?" Alex asked.

"Jail break," Lisa said.

"What, break the prisoners out? Sneak them out or run and gun?" Alma asked.

"Both. Sneak and gun. Go in quiet. Shoot with silencers as many as we can. Spring prisoners."

"Sounds dangerous," Alex said.

"Less dangerous than other plans. Kill them before they get chance to kill us."

Alex rubbed his chin and thought about it for a while.

"We need to start on that right away," he finally said. "The longer we wait the more time they have to prepare. You up for a run through the countryside, Lisa?"

She was. She was very ready. She loved working and she also liked spending time with him. It was irrational and didn't make sense, but she knew she enjoyed her time with Alex.

"We go now. Get there by dark. We need people," Lisa said.

"Me and Cass are up for it," Alma said.

Lisa tried to hide her annoyance. When she was around, Alex paid a great deal of attention to Alma. It made sense. A sister thought dead, shows up out of nowhere, happy reunion. But she still disliked it.

"Alma, do you know how to ride a horse?" Alex asked.

"Of course not."

"Then you can't come. We'll be riding hard and fast."

"What? I'm the best shooter you have!"

"Then you're perfect for staying here and guarding the farm until you learn to ride."

Alma glared at him but he was unmoved.

Lisa had to stifle a smile.

"We leave in a half hour," Alex said. "I'll go get Spencer and Adam. They'll be our backup. They can travel a distance behind us and stay in the woods while we sneak onto the farm."

She could agree to this.

Lisa went to her room which she had decorated with red lanterns and began strapping on her vest, thigh holster, loaded magazines and her backpack.

Which gun to bring? She had her Beretta PX4 9mm on her thigh and a makarov in her boot as a backup. That was good for now. But which rifle? Alex seemed to switch between his M-14 and his M4. She wasn't overly fond of the M4, maybe because it was the weapon of the American military. She knew that was a silly notion now. She was technically an American now. The rules and the world were different.

She grabbed her SF2000 and slung it across her chest. It wasn't the best weapon but it was more compact than an M4 and fully ambidextrous. It was also set up with a red dot sight for close quarters fighting.

Next she filled her camelback using a water filtration pump. She didn't have time to boil water so she pumped the water from the river, through the pump's filters and into her camelback. Simple.

Once she was ready, she saddled hers and Alex's horses and got them ready to go. She made sure her first aid kit was fully stocked and Alex came out of the house by the time she had finished checking her red dot sight's battery.

"We're ready to go?" He asked, somewhat surprised.

"Yes," she said.

"Dang, you even saddled my horse. Thanks."

She liked it when he praised her.

Spencer and Adam were out soon and saddled their horses.

Once ready, they mounted up and rode out. Alma was on the porch with her arms folded and her face scrunched up in a hideous scowl. She was a very pretty girl except when she made such faces.

"I think your sister is angry," Lisa said when they had ridden a safe distance away.

"Alma likes to act angrier than she really is. It's her way of looking tough. She is tough but for some reason she thinks she needs to look tougher."

"You're tough."

"Sometimes."

"You need to not act humble. It doesn't help."

"You really think I should step up and be king, huh?"

"Not king, but something."

"I don't want to be a dictator."

"Too bad. These tough times. Need tough leader. You can be tough leader."

"Assuming I do this and form a chain of command and duties and such, I'm going to have it a democracy or something similar. It's not worth surviving if you can't be free."

That was a strange notion. Americans always put their own welfare above that of the state or society. That always seemed selfish and petty to her. It was better to sacrifice one's own life for the good of the whole.

"I don't understand you," Lisa said. "Is not better to give self for good of whole group? Is not better to take charge and direct with strong ideas?"

"No, not at the cost of the others' liberty. The group is strengthened when each individual is allowed to reach to height of their abilities instead of being pushed down into what they're told they should be."

"But what you do when group has different ideas?"

"We vote and majority wins."

"And when no time for vote?"

"Then whoever's in charge will have to make a decision."

"I see. Just what I say."

"Well, not exactly what you were talking about."

So, at least he understood that he'd have to make quick and hard decisions. She could accept that. If there was anyone she could trust to lead this group, it was him.

"So, Lisa, what's your favorite and least favorite thing about America?" Alex asked once they crossed the bridge.

That was a random question from nowhere. She wasn't sure how to respond.

She liked some of the food, but for the most part it was bland, pre-processed instant crap. She liked real food. She did like the music.

"Favorite thing: music. I like all kinds, no country or rap or screaming. Least favorite thing: Greed and materialism. Everyone so occupied about buying new things."

"You don't have to worry about that one anymore."

"Guess not."

"Favorite movie?"

What was with all these questions?

She hadn't had time to watch a lot of movies but as part of her training she was shown the most culturally relevant movies so she had to pick from the ten she'd actually seen.

"Matrix."

She had really liked that one. They had to use Chinese fighting to win and she thought it ironic in an American movie. Also, it was just an amazing story. But then, she did have a very small sampling to choose from and hoped he didn't laugh at her choice.

"I love that flick! Great choice."

She couldn't help but smile.

"You?"

"Heat, Inception or maybe Gladiator. Hard to choose."

She'd never heard of any of those but she nodded like she had.

51

Caesar, Promised Land, Virginia

CAESAR WOKE UP TO THE SOUND OF HUMANS TALKING. NONE OF them said "treat," "potty," or "walk" so he closed his eyes again.

Then he smelled Alma and Cassidy come down the stairs and he opened his eyes. They were talking to the adult male and female. They smelled of black powder and oil of the metal long things they carried. Those things made a lot of noise and hurt his ears.

He watched as the new man and woman got on horses and left with two other adult males. Alma and Cassidy went back upstairs. By the smell, he could tell that Alma was angry.

Caesar stretched out and yawned. He had slept enough for now so he got up and walked outside. This new green place had many new smells to discover. He had to find out what they were.

He wandered down the steps and into the large open space in front of the house. Something smelled interesting so he followed his nose. There were so many other things to smell but he decided to follow this one for now.

The smell led into the woods. It wasn't a rabbit. It wasn't squirrel. Those were fun to chase. Hadn't caught one yet, but he'd keep trying.

No...it smelled like a human. Yup, definitely a human, but not one he'd smelled before. Wasn't a human that lived in this house. That much was certain or the scent would have been everywhere.

He padded along, following the smell. Whoever this human was has been walking around the edge of the woods. Been here for a while.

Maybe this human had a treat?

He hurried along, his short legs carrying him through the woods.

Then he came upon the human. It was a female, a young one. She smelled different, more covered in earth and less healthy. He could smell that she wasn't as healthy as the others.

"Hey there, puppy," the young female said. He knew that "puppy" was what some humans called him.

He padded up to the young female and she began petting him which he liked. He liked it a lot. Eventually he lay down and she rubbed his belly which he really liked even more.

She spoke to him some more but he didn't understand. It didn't matter as long as he was getting his belly rubbed.

For some reason he smelled a little fear on her. Sickness and fear. Maybe she was hurt?

He licked her hand and she laughed.

Caesar stayed there for a while enjoying the attention.

Eventually though, he got hungry and she didn't have any food. So he licked her face a little and trotted back to the house. Alma and Cassidy were sitting on the porch and he walked up to them, wagging his tail.

Maybe they wanted to know about the other young female? They gave him treats so maybe they would give the female treats as well.

So he barked.

"What's the matter?" Cassidy asked as she rubbed his head.

He barked some more and then hurried down the stairs.

"You found something?" Alma asked.

"Maybe he found a rabbit?"

That made them follow him.

He led them back into the woods to the sick, scared female. Maybe he'd get a treat for this? That thought made him trot a little faster.

Then they came to the clearing where the young female was and Alma and Cassidy stopped. The young, sick female began to smell more of fear. Her eyes grew wide and she looked like she was about to flee but Caesar trotted up to her and barked to tell Alma and Cassidy that it was alright. The female was safe and probably needed a treat.

"Good boy, Caesar. Good boy," Alma said.

He knew what "Good boy" meant. It meant he was going to get lots of attention and probably a treat.

52

Alex

IT WAS LATE AT NIGHT AND ALL HE COULD HEAR WAS THE SOUND OF the wind through the trees. It was a hot, humid, Virginian night. Sometimes it felt as if the temperature didn't go down with the sun at all. Back in Nevada, once that sun went down, so did the temp. But Virginia was its own special kind of uncomfortable.

He could see the barn where the civilians were. There was one dim lamp on inside and the house where the armed men lived had all but one light out as well.

They had been watching for a while and he thought they found who the leader of the civilians was. At least he hoped his guess was right. Everyone kept going up to him to talk and he seemed to be the center of attention.

The people in the barn had been herded in there like cattle and one of the men was beaten up.

"I see two guards walking around house," Lisa said.

"I see them. As soon as they go back around the house, we'll move in."

"Maybe it better if I go alone."

One was sneakier than two, but then he couldn't keep an eye on her. He wasn't about to let her get hurt. Better him than her.

"Maybe, but I'm coming."

Once the guards were out of sight, he stood up and began sprinting across the field to the nearest tree. He heard Lisa's footfalls close behind him. She was fast.

Once at the tree, he stopped and scanned the area. No movement or any signs that they had been seen. He looked back and nodded to her. She nodded back.

Then they made the final sprint to the barn. He ran across the open field as fast as he could while still keeping an eye out. He only carried his weapon and ammo and left everything else back with the horses.

All he could hear were his own footfalls and his heavy breathing.

He came to a stop at the side of the barn, out of sight of the open door. He looked to Lisa, who was right behind him, to make sure she was ready. She gave him a quick nod.

Alex peeked around the corner and spotted the man he was looking for. He appeared to be their unofficial leader and he slept near the doorway. He looked like a truck driver to him. He was large, but not fat and had a beard. Though, with the lack of razors and running water beards would probably grow in popularity. He scavenged the best razors and shaved out of habit. That probably wouldn't last once winter hit.

There were about twenty army cots set up and eighteen looked to be filled with sleeping people.

He moved in as silently as he could and crouched down next to the cot. He covered the man's mouth while Lisa shook him awake.

The man began to struggle but then looked him in the eye and stopped.

"Please don't make a sound. We're here to help you, not hurt you," Alex whispered.

The man nodded and he removed his hand.

"Who are you?" The man asked.

"We have a farm not too far from here. We've had run-ins with your bosses," Alex said.

"They're not my boss, they're our masters."

"We've noticed. We came here to offer you our help. If you come with us we can give you your freedom back."

"Can you protect us from them?"

"If enough of you come with us, we can."

"Doesn't sound very safe."

"You'd give up your liberty for security?"

"Hell, no. I'm in, but how can you get us out?"

"We'll come back tomorrow night. Have your people ready by then."

"I don't know if I can get all of them, but I'll try."

"Please do. We'll be back."

With that, he and Lisa quickly left the barn and ran back to the woods.

"How'd it go?" Adam asked.

"We told him to be ready for us tomorrow night," Alex said.

"I hope the Hunt Club won't also be ready," Spencer said.

"What's our plan, then?" Adam asked.

"We go back home and use the last of our fuel for a truck that can fit all of them."

"That's a lot of fuel."

"We don't have a choice. We can't walk them back home, the Hunt Club freaks will find us before we got five miles."

It was a long night but they rode back home and caught a few hours of sleep. He hated working while tired but after being in the Marines he was used to it. This was all familiar to him and wondered if it would ever stop being familiar.

He woke up with that painful, tired feeling behind his eyes and woke everyone else up. This time Alma and Cass were coming with him. If things went bad he'd need every shooter he had. They had an old flatbed that would fit everyone. It had belonged to a nearby farm and had been used for hauling hay or something similar. Now it would haul survivors.

He wished he had an APC or another platoon of grunts, but he had to work with what he had.

Jennifer came up to him saying something about the dog finding something but he shooed her away with a promise to deal with it later. She looked pissed and he'd probably pay for that later.

Alma walked up wearing his favorite 'Avengers' shirt. She always considered his stuff to be hers but not the other way around.

"How many civilians?" Alma asked.

"Around eighteen or so," he said.

She looked to the flatbed and shook her head.

"I know. It's not an ideal situation," he said.

"We need a distraction or something," Alma said.

"Got any ideas?"

"We get their attention. Me and Cass can go make some noise and have them come after us. Maybe set up a light that they'd go investigate. It's night time so a light will be visible."

"Hurry and think of something that won't put you in danger. We don't have a lot of time."

"I'm on it."

"And don't get yourself killed. I just got my sister back. I ain't losing her now."

"You won't," she said with a warm smile and patted him on the cheek.

She ran off to talk to Cassidy.

Lisa walked up to him carrying an M4 with an IR laser and suppressor.

"No FS2000 today?" He asked.

She patted the laser.

"We go in with NVG's. We can see in the dark, they can't. We take out electricity and we have advantage. We kill them in the dark. Quick. Quiet."

Now he had a choice. He could go with Alma's plan of distraction or Lisa's plan of cold, calculated violence.

Having Alma and Cassidy cause a distraction put them in danger but if planned to outright murder his enemies, he risked losing something else.

Lisa's eyes held no hesitation and he wondered where her inner steel came from. Had the end of the world changed this waitress or had she always been like this?

He didn't know the answer, but the woman she was now was amazing. She was strong and helped him far more than she could know. He needed a woman like that by his side.

He meant that politically.

Didn't he?

All he knew was that he wanted her with him at all times.

53

<u>Alex</u>

ALEX DIDN'T KNOW WHICH PLAN TO CHOOSE. DID HE GO WITH Alma's idea of a distraction which could put her in serious danger or did he go with Lisa's plan which could put him in a place he did not want to be.

The debate was a farce though. He already knew which plan he was going with, he just didn't want to admit it. But the fact was, he'd do anything and sacrifice anything, even a part of his humanity to keep Alma safe.

Lisa was standing by the truck Adam was trying to fix. She had her arms folded and the M4 slung across her back. She stood there as still as a statue.

"Lisa," he called out.

She looked up at him with her dark sunglasses. What happened to her normal glasses? Maybe those were just for reading?

"We'll go with your plan," he said.

She nodded.

"We need to leave soon," she said.

"I know. I'll go gather the troops."

He went over to where Alma and Cassidy were looking at a bunch of flares and fishing wire.

"Hey, we have a change of plan," he said.

Alma looked up and squinted.

"No more diversion?"

"Afraid not. These guys are dangerous and we can't allow them to continue to threaten us."

Alma put the flare down and put her hands on her hips.

"What you talking about *hermano*?"

"We're cutting their power and then going in with NVG's. We'll try to hit them while they're sleeping and take out the awake ones before they know what hit them."

"Wait, we're going to kill them all in their sleep?" Cassidy asked.

"What would you have us do? Call them out at noon and see who draws first? Or should we let them live so they can come murder us in our sleep? As long as they're out there we'll have to keep watching our backs. We need them gone."

"I understand, I'm just...I don't know," Alma said.

"I understand fighting them, but killing them in their sleep?" Cassidy said.

"This is war, not some game of honor. We have to kill them before they kill us. It's as simple as that. Come on. Time to gear up. Grab your stuff and meet by the truck."

He couldn't tell if Alma was upset or saddened. Whatever it was, he hated that look coming from her. It was like he had disappointed her.

Alex walked up to his room and looked through his arsenal. If he was entering the farmhouse he wouldn't want his M14, though he would have liked the extra power. He could put the PAC II IR laser on anything with a rail, but it was already on the army issue M4, so he grabbed that, his 1911, his IBA body armor and his NVG's.

Adam and Spencer were already there in their full kit of body armor, weapons and NVG's. They were trained by the military so he didn't have to worry about them.

He went back inside to find something to eat and carry with him for later. But when he walked in he saw an unfamiliar girl sitting at the kitchen table eating an apple. She looked about a year younger than Rebekah and had bright blond hair in two long braids. She had a blanket around her shoulders and looked kind of pale.

The girl looked up and gave a shy wave.

Alex stopped in his tracks.

"Who are you?" He asked

"I'm Kierra."

"Um...hi, Kierra. Where did you come from?"

Then Jennifer walked into the room carrying a small basket of eggs.

"I tried to tell you earlier but you were too busy doing manly things to listen. Caesar found her in the woods. As our leader you should really take more of an interest in what goes on around here."

"Yeah, but...I mean..."

They just found a strange girl in the woods and no one told him? Of course, she had tried to tell him and maybe it was his own fault which just made him feel more foolish.

"Kierra, this is Alex, our thoughtless leader," Jennifer said.

"I hope you like it here, Kierra," he said with what he hoped was a winning smile.

"I do already!" Kierra said with a giant smile that was missing a tooth.

He grabbed a can of Spam and hurried outside before his embarrassment and confusion grew worse.

Lisa came out of the house behind him. She had all her gear on and was ready. She always looked ready to kill someone. He found that strangely attractive.

This was a bad time to think about that sort of thing. He had been telling himself that for a while now: that it wasn't a good time for distractions. In this world he doubted that it ever would be a good time.

So, for the first time, he let himself be distracted and really looked at Lisa Fang. She was beautiful. It was like watching a lion, mesmerizing to look at but it came with the knowledge that she could tear him apart with little effort.

She had small, round but tight lips that seldom smiled. She had eyes that were dark as shadow but felt like ice. It was that brillian,t but cold, intellect behind her eyes though that intrigued him. He never knew what was going on behind her mask.

Whatever she was, she hadn't been made to be a waitress at a cheap Chinese buffet. He trusted her opinions and he trusted her. That much he did know of her. He respected her for everything she had done since joining up with them.

Damn, she was gorgeous.

He looked away and pretended to inspect one of his magazine pouches before he was accused of staring.

If she was a distraction, she was a very pleasant distraction.

He wondered how soft those lips were.

"We're ready, *hermano*!" Alma called from the yard.

He looked over and saw everyone had gathered together.

Why did he feel that everyone was suddenly looking at him like he was the biggest fool? No, they didn't know what he was thinking. He had to get his mind back in the game and stop acting like a blundering high schooler. What was he going to do? Pass her a note asking if she liked him?

"Alright, people. We know who the enemy is. We know that they don't mean to become friends with us. We're at a critical point in history and no, I don't say that lightly. We really have a chance here to make a new beginning. But we can't do that if we're under constant threat of people who just want to dominate us. I hate to say this, but it's us or them and it's as simple as that.

"If we let them live, we'll be looking over our shoulder everyday. We couldn't work in our fields or gardens without setting guards. They could sneak in here and murder us in our sleep. I won't allow that.

"They have civilian refugees that need our help. Our priority is helping them get out safely and onto our truck. Adam, Spencer, you're in charge of helping them. Alma, Cassidy, you're going to cut the power and take out any exterior guards. Me and Lisa will go into the house and take out who we find in there."

"Let me go!" Rebekah called out.

"Not this time. You're too young and too valuable to risk."

"I can shoot."

"But I'm trying to make a world where you won't have to. Besides, I don't want that on your conscious. When we get back, I'll train you further and then we'll see."

"We can't show mercy. I know we like to think we're wearing the white hats around here, but let's face facts. We can't afford to let one of them live," Alma said.

He hadn't thought she liked this idea and didn't know why she was suddenly supporting it now.

"Alma's right," he said. "We go in there and we take out every single one of them. If we let one live, he will come at us for revenge and he'll strike when we're least expecting it. I'd rather them die than any one of you."

With that they loaded up in the truck and headed out toward Staunton and the enemy's farm.

54

Alma didn't like this plan but she understood it. Survival wasn't a question of liking something. When a life was on the line it was about doing what had to be done and these assholes had to be taken care of.

Perhaps this wasn't heroic but if it got rid of these guys without one of their own group dying then it was worth it. They couldn't afford to lose anyone.

Alma looked over to Cassidy. All of these men's lives weren't worth Cassidy's life. Her own life wasn't worth Cassidy's.

In spite of everything Cass still maintained her innocence and goodness. That was a trick Alma knew she'd never be able to learn.

"I see one," Cass said in her plain, simple voice. All Alma could see was Cass's mouth. The NVG's covered the rest.

Cass was looking over her Broadsword at the field in front of the enemy's farm house. There were two armed men walking the perimeter.

"Hold off, Cass. Let's wait for orders."

Cass nodded.

Alma got on the walkie-talkie.

"*Hermano*, what's the word?"

"We're still getting into position," Alex whispered back.

She couldn't see them but she knew he was out there sneaking up to the farm house. Him and that Lisa *chica* had silencers on their M4's.

Lisa was kind of a *bruja*. Alma didn't see what Alex saw in her. She was mean and that seemed to be the only emotion she had. Even though this was a last man on Earth kind of situation, she hoped Alex would go for someone else. Maybe Cassidy would make a good match?

These NVG's were great though. The entire farm looked as bright as if it were high noon, except everything was green. She could see everything. She could even tell that one of the men they were watching was carrying an FAL, a badass battle rifle.

But a FAL wasn't as badass as Cass's Broadsword.

"We're in position," Alex whispered over the walkie-talkie.

Somewhere Alex and that Spencer guy were watching the guard by the barn, ready to cut the power. Alma couldn't see the entrance to the barn from this side of the house. But she could see the collection of vehicles, a machine shop and the chicken coup.

These guys had a lot of stuff. They'd be able to roll up on Promised Land and wipe them all out with little trouble. She just prayed that the other bad guys were inside the house sleeping.

"Team Zulu's ready," Adam said.

"Team Power Puff is ready," Alma said.

"Cut power then give us two minutes then start," Alex said.

Then the radio was silent.

A few seconds later and the porch light went out as did the one light on the top floor.

With her NVG's she saw Alex and the *Bruja* sprint across the field and make it to the front of the house without being spotted. The two guards they were watching were too busy smoking and joking.

The only problem was that Cass had to look through her ACOG with NVG's and that made it awkward and with precision shooting, awkward wasn't good for accuracy.

"You ready for this Cass?" Alma asked.

Cass breathed out in a slow, even way and nodded.

"Yeah, I'm ready."

"You can do it, *chica*."

"Just be ready to get the second guy in case I can't."

"Will do."

She had always thought that having a Night Vision setting on a civilian red dot sight was a little pointless, but now she was glad to have it. She could look through her NVG's to see the target but still use the red dot without it blinding her.

But it was awkward with trying to get the weird headset in the right position with a cheek weld and everything.

Suddenly she heard gunshots inside the house and the two men they were watching whipped around and began running for the house.

Alex!

"Take them!" Alma said.

Cass fired. The flash lit up the grass in front of them and sent a small shockwave over the grass like a pebble dropped into a pond.

Miss.

"Dang!" Cass said as she lined up another shot.

Even in a stressful situation like this Cass wouldn't swear.

Alma fired and missed. She swore.

Cass fired again and this time one of the men went down. The other man stopped and got down to the ground. There was no way he could see where they were.

Alma aimed and fired. Missed. All she could think about was Alex getting hurt and was dying inside the house. She didn't travel the country just to see him die now.

She could see in the dark but she couldn't hit. Maybe it was her own nerves. She fired again. It was too far away and in the NVG's her red dot was just too freaking big.

"I got him," Alma said.

She fired and the man's head jerked back and he went still. Finally.

"Awesome! Let's go!" Cass said.

She picked herself up and began running to the house.

Suddenly a man came out from behind one of the parked trucks. He was looking around frantically and holding a mini-14. The man saw her and scrambled to get his gun up and ready. He had to drop his porno magazine first.

Before Alma had time to even stop and raise her rifle, a bullet struck the man in the side of the head. His head opened up like pumpkin on Halloween and green stuff (everything in the NVG's was green) went flying everywhere. Alma looked back and saw Cassidy crouching down in the grass with her rifle up and ready. Cass gave her a thumbs up.

Hardcore, *Chica*. She'd have to thank her later.

Alma continued running to the house. When she got to the door she met Alex and Lisa walking out. Alex was holding a cloth to his arm.

"You alright?" Alma asked, almost out of breath.

"Yeah, just a scratch," Alex said.

Alma slapped his hand away and looked at the wound. It wasn't bad at all.

"Did you get them all?" Alma asked.

"Yeah, we got them," Alex said.

Lisa nodded and Alma noticed she had blood splatter on her face.

Then they heard gunshots coming from the other side of the barn. That was where Adam and Spencer were.

They all began running to where the gunfire came from. There were a few more shots including one that sounded like a handgun.

The people in the barn were now up and huddled together, sitting, crouched and lying on the ground. They ran past them and to the field between the barn and the woods.

There was a dead body there of one of the guards. He had two holes in his chest. They ran passed and saw Adam coming out of the woods. He had his eyes closed and his teeth showing as if in pain.

"Spencer's dead," Adam said so plainly and calmly that it was as if he was telling them there were no clean socks.

They all stopped.

"What happened?" Alex asked.

"The second guy ran for it. We fired at him but he made it to the woods. We followed and we exchanged fire. We hit him and he went down. So we approached but he wasn't dead. He had a pistol we didn't see."

Adam stopped there and took a deep breath to keep in control.

Alma looked to her brother and saw the pain on his face. She knew that he felt responsible and that he was going to blame himself for this.

"Alex..." Alma started to say.

"Let's go check on the refugees," Alex said without looking at her or anyone.

55

SPENCER WAS DEAD? SHE HAD LOST MEN IN THE FIELD BEFORE, but there had always been more than enough replacements. But Spencer wasn't replaceable. None of them were.

Then she saw the look in Alex's eyes. He was barely keeping his emotions in check. To him, Spencer wasn't just an asset: a tool to be used. He had been a friend and family.

She knew that American officers often formed emotional bonds with the men under their command. When she was still in training back in China they'd teach her how every kill she performed would weaken American resolve. Every American casualty served to end their desire to win the war.

She had thought the Americans foolish to put so much emotion in a soldier's death but now she felt horrible for ever thinking that. Now she saw it as they saw it. Now she thought as Americans do.

Spencer had not been a disposable asset.

And Alex was suffering for it. He blamed himself.

What did people do in a situation like this? Shouldn't she show her remorse or try to comfort him? Isn't that what normal people did?

Normal people? Was she so abnormal?

"I...I'm sorry, Alex," she said.

Alex looked away.

"We have work to do. Let's go," Alex said.

To see him struggling so hard to maintain control and think of the mission made her chest hurt worse than a bullet wound. At that moment she would have done anything to ease his pain.

She followed him back across the field to the barn. Alma approached the refugee leader and began talking. As she did that Lisa went over to Cassidy.

"Let's secure the parameter," Lisa said.

Cass nodded and the two of them began walking around the farm to make sure there weren't anymore surprises.

"Spencer's dead," Cass said as if she couldn't believe it.

"I know."

"Did you get all the guys in the house?"

She remembered as they walked into the house, crouched low and guns at the ready. There were about ten men sleeping in the living room, sprawled out wherever they could. That was easy. Silencers weren't silent and as soon as they started shooting, people began waking up. But ten targets split between two people at that range was only a matter of seconds. Those men hadn't had time to register what was going on.

Then they went upstairs to where the presumably more privileged men slept. One by one they went through each room. They caught one man getting his pants on. It was in the last room where they encountered a man with a flashlight. He had been awake. The flashlight blinded them but as Lisa had been trained, she fired in his direction as soon as she saw the blinding light while simultaneously dropping to the floor. Only this time she had pulled Alex down along with her.

She had thought of him first. That certainly wasn't in her training.

The man had gotten a few shots off and grazed Alex but one of her bullets had luckily found its target. The man went down with a wound to the stomach and as soon as the flashlight hit the floor and no longer blinded her, she finished him off with a bullet to the forehead.

"Yes, we got them all," Lisa said.

"How come you don't like Alma?"

That question took her off guard and in an increasingly more common situation, she didn't quite know what to say.

"Alma is a good shot," Lisa said.

"That's not what I mean and you know it. Are you jealous?"

"Jealous?"

Why would Cassidy think that? Where would she have gotten such a ridiculous notion?

"You're jealous, aren't you? I can see it. Don't be. She's his sister and only family member left. She came back from the dead to see him. I think she's earned a little time with her brother. Don't you?"

"I...I, um...I don't think like that."

Were these Americans mind readers? Was she such a lousy agent that everyone could read like a neon sign? What else did they see in her?

Cassidy smiled.

"Oh, who you trying to fool, me or yourself?"

Lisa didn't respond. She had no idea what to say. She didn't want to admit it, but Cassidy was right. She did have certain protective urges toward Alex that she didn't quite understand.

Fortunately, the red headed girl didn't ask anymore questions. She was unnerved enough and being unnerved was unfamiliar territory.

They did their sweep and came back to the barn. It was decided that the people would sleep here tonight and in the morning they'd discuss what they wanted to do. They were all free to make their own choices but Alex had offered them a place to stay where they'd be free and equal.

Even as Alex talked in his disciplined and professional way, she could hear the strain in his voice. Maybe he should have been immune to the loss of one man after the death of the entire world, but Lisa knew that Alex would take the loss even harder for the same reason.

Alex gathered his people into a huddle.

"We have a lot to do." Alex said. "We need to secure the weapons, ammo and food and take an inventory. We need someone to watch the people and..."

"I'll take care of Spencer's body," Adam said.

Alex sighed.

"Thank you."

Cassidy volunteered to stay with the people in the barn and her, Alma and Alex split up and began gathering the bodies. She had to pull two of the corpses to the farm house. She was well trained and physically fit, but she simply wasn't a large person and moving the corpses was more difficult than she would have liked to admit.

Once they gathered the large arsenal of weapons and ammo, they found their food storage: an entire basement filled with canned food and military MRE's.

This was a comforting sight. She knew that without a society, winter was going to be difficult. Survival wasn't just a vague notion. It was now everyday business and always on her mind.

She didn't see Alex. Alma was writing down all the ammo types and numbers into a notebook. Lisa looked around until she found Alex in an upstairs bedroom that was free of bodies. He was sitting on the edge of the bed with his chin resting on his clasped hands.

She wanted to ask if he was 'okay,' but knew that he wasn't. She didn't know what to say and hated feeling that powerless to help him.

Wordlessly she walked in and sat down next to him.

"It wasn't your fault," she said.

"I know that. I keep telling myself that, but it's not helping."

She had never been a team leader and didn't know what it was like to lose somebody she was in charge of.

"He played guitar very well," she said.

He let out a short and desperate kind of laugh.

"That he did. He used to be in a band."

"That was the first thing I liked about coming to America: the music. I loved his playing."

"What was the second thing you liked?"

"Pizza."

He gave her a brief smile.

She suddenly felt like a very dishonest person. She had come to destroy the country and had ended up loving it. Now, in spite of her betrayal, she was stuck in America and trying to carve out a living. She was now dependant on the land that she had tried to conquer.

And worst of all, she could never tell Alex that. A part of her wanted to. She wanted to be nothing but honest with him. Yet, every time she opened her mouth she lied. She pretended to not speak English as well as she really did. She hated talking for that reason.

She had no more ideas of what to say so she remained silent and simply sat beside him as he lost himself in thought.

There had to be something normal people did at times like this. In her observations she saw that people touched other people's shoulders, though she didn't know what that was supposed to do.

She raised a hand and hesitated.

Did a touch on the shoulder signify something else? She had no idea but was willing to risk it if it helped.

She put her hand on his shoulder. A moment later he reached up and held her hand. It wasn't the death-grip of a desperate person, but a gentle grip of someone who was in control. His hand was warm and strong and she knew she was enjoying this moment far more than he was.

56

Rebekah

R EBEKAH DIDN'T SLEEP A WINK THAT NIGHT. HER NEW FAMILY was out there fighting and maybe dying and she was stuck here. It would have been better if she had gone. Then she wouldn't have to sit around here waiting.

She hated waiting.

She hated that they were treating her like a child. She wasn't.

Even more, she hated being useless. This entire past year she had tried to be useful. She had lived on her own for months while the world died around her. She could take care of herself.

Rebekah prayed that Alex wasn't hurt. Anyone but him. She hated thinking that way, but she couldn't help it.

It had been Alex that found her. It had been two months since her family died and she had been completely alone. She thought she was going insane. The entire world had died and for some reason she had been left alone in a way she had never thought possible.

He found her eating a bag of Oreo's in a grocery store. She hadn't even heard him approach.

"Got any milk to go with those?" He asked.

It startled her half to death and she was about to run when she saw a large man in armor and carrying a gun. But then she saw the smile on his face and knew that that smile would never hurt her.

She had broke down crying. She didn't remember how long it was, but she cried for what seemed hours and he held her the entire time. She must have seemed like a lunatic. He was her first family member in this new world.

Rebekah was sitting on the porch just after dawn when she saw four trucks coming slowly over the bridge in the distance. They'd go through some woods before reappearing in front of the farm.

She grabbed up her M4 and ran upstairs to wake up Jennifer.

"Jen! There are trucks coming!" Rebekah said.

Jen jumped out of bed and grabbed her rifle and they went downstairs.

Kierra, Ranbir and Rehka were still asleep so Jen went and woke them up.

Rebekah readied her rifle and pointed it out of the downstairs window. Jen came down and locked the front door and readied herself at another window. She had a shoulder bag full of loaded magazines.

She knew how to shoot. She trained with the others and could patrol if they let her. She wasn't made out to be a homemaker. She couldn't clean or cook or even farm. She wanted to fight.

"I really hope its Alex," Rebekah said.

"Rebekah, if it isn't Alex, don't let them take you alive," Jennifer said.

Rebekah knew exactly what she meant, but still the thought of killing herself was sickening. Even worse, was thinking of what those men would do to her.

She was a virgin and planed to remain that way until she fell in love. She had been hoping that Spencer would make a pass at her or flirt with her but so far she had been invisible to him. Maybe he thought she was still a little girl.

The world ended and she was in a group with a cute guy and he wouldn't even look at her. Figures.

Then the trucks rolled up in front of the house and stopped.

Lisa was the first person to step out of the truck and her icy, calmness showed that there was no danger.

Rebekah breathed out a sigh of relief and thumbed the safety back on and slung her rifle. Jen threw her a quick smile.

Her and Jen walked out onto the front porch to greet their family and meet the newcomers.

But then she saw Adam and Alex unload from the back of a truck a litter with Spencer lying on it.

Suddenly she stopped breathing. The looks on their faces told her everything. He was dead. She had seen that look hundreds of times as the world ended around her. She saw it first from her father when her mother died. Then she saw it from her sister, then her neighbors and then no one.

She ran over and looked down at Spencer's lifeless body.

He was dead. There was no mistaking it. He was gray and had a giant bloodstain on the bandages around his neck, just above the body armor. There was no life in that shell. It was some mannequin and not Spencer.

"What happened?" She heard Jen ask.

"Bad luck," Adam said.

Jen scowled for a second but it gave way to a slow nod.

"I'll prepare a funeral. Rebekah, come with me."

It wasn't the first grave she had ever dug. When no ambulance came for her parents and sister she had dug three shallow graves herself in their backyard. She saw Mr. Reynolds next door do the same.

She remembered how little she felt. She didn't cry or even feel sad. It was like she had suddenly turned into a robot. She felt nothing.

Now she felt similar but this time she knew the tears would come. She would cry later when she was alone and had time to think and remember.

As they gathered the shovels she saw the newcomers being unloaded from the trucks.

She saw a blond girl that looked her age and even a boy that looked like he was sixteen or maybe seventeen. That was young enough for her to catch their attention. Unless of course he was already attached to the blond.

How much did age really matter now? They were all people and had survived. That was it.

Maybe one of them was Jewish. If there was a rabbi in the group then she'd count that as a miracle. She didn't know what she'd do. She wasn't going to become a Christian, but she couldn't keep her religion alive without help.

She touched the Star of David she wore around her neck and told herself that she had to believe God was protecting His people. If He could deliver them out of Egypt then He could keep them at the end of the world.

"I think I'll learn to play the guitar," Rebekah said as they walked past the garden to a clear spot that would make a good cemetery. She didn't want to think about how fast it would fill up.

"Really?" Jen asked, only halfway paying attention.

"Yeah, I think Spencer would want someone to keep playing music for everyone."

"That's a good idea."

Rebekah looked up and saw that Jennifer was crying so she kept silent as they finished digging the grave.

Afterwards she went to find Kierra. She was already talking to the newcomers. There were four kids around her age. Not bad. She went from being the only teenager to being one of six. That wasn't all bad. She'd have friends again.

She saw that the boy that looked about seventeen was looking at her with a cute smile.

Later that day they buried Spencer near the edge of the woods. It was the first grave in what she knew would eventually become a graveyard: a graveyard that would one day hold her body and everyone else's.

Cassidy wrote down everything that happened and was quite as they sat around the table they had set outside and everyone had a long dinner. Her group mingled with the newcomers as they got to know one another.

"Just two days ago I was all by myself. Now I have a whole village," Kierra said as they ate fried chicken. It had been a year since she ate fried chicken.

It turned out none of the new people were military but they did have two mechanics, an amateur carpenter, and science teacher. There were six adult men, seven adult women, four teenagers and three kids.

Lots of new people to talk to. She wanted to hear all their stories.

Kierra had been wandering around the Lexington area for over a year. She had been alone this entire time. These others though, they'd have more stories. They'd seen more of the world.

Cassidy would probably write them all down. She said she was going to write a history book about the Apocalypse. Maybe she'd give her, her own chapter. That would be cool: having a chapter in a history book about her.

One day there'd be schools again and they'd have to do reports about her like she had about George Washington. That got her thinking about things.

"Are we going to fly the American flag or are we going to have our own? I mean, are we a new country or what are we?" Rebekah asked.

It must have been a good question because Alex stopped chewing and thought about it. She noticed how Lisa silently stopped eating as well. She was interested in the question too.

Jennifer and Spencer had thought Lisa was an unfeeling robot, but she really was anything but. She tried to hide her emotions, true, but anyone with half a brain could see the emotions rolling around behind her face. That was why she was so quiet, not because she lacked emotion, but because they affected her so much.

"I don't know, Rebekah, but that is a good question. We'll have to figure that one out."

Whatever flag they flew, she knew she wanted to fight for it. When she watched the news of the Russians, the EU and China invading her country, she grew furious. The history of her people was filled with wars and defeat. She didn't want to go down this time without a fight.

She mocked and cursed anyone that wouldn't join the military. She hated the Russians, the Europeans and the Chinese for starting this war. But especially the Chinese. They were the ones to start the war and turn everyone against the United States. All that happened was their fault.

She wouldn't sit on the sidelines forever. She would have gone out and fought.

If she had been there, maybe Spencer wouldn't have died. She wouldn't let that happen again.

57

ALEX AWOKE TO THE SOUND OF JEN'S CLASSICAL MUSIC DRIFTING up from downstairs. With the solar panels installed, the house was always full of music. Sometimes it was Alma's heavy metal and other times it was Adam's funk or old school blues. Whatever it was, it was always playing. As long as the music was playing he knew everything was alright.

Alex got up and readied himself for the day. He put on his boots and slid the 1911 into the holster on his hip. It was now his constant companion and he didn't feel complete without it. Not having it would be like going outside without his pants on.

He had found it in a house in Lexington and the handles were beautiful red wood. It was too gorgeous to pass up.

He found Alma and Cassidy looking over maps and discussing where they should go for their next long range patrol. Last month their patrol found a community of about twenty people living in Farmville. Out near Roanoke was another group of about ten survivors. A few more had trickled into Promised Land adding to their population.

He didn't like her going out on such dangerous patrols but once she had an idea it was impossible to get it out of her head. Her temper would change in an instant and she'd go from sweet as candy to mean as a harpy.

Alex walked outside and saw his growing little town. For now the people they had rescued from the Hunt Club were living in the guest house. Everyone had jobs and purpose. Nothing was wasted and new skills were being learned. One of the men had been in construction and was building a new house a little further out where the fields were going to be. It was being designed from the ground up for this new world.

The blacksmith's shop was a new addition. One of the refugees had been an artist that dug out and smelted his own ore. So, they had a primitive mine and were learning how to make replacement parts.

The two mechanics were working on making an engine that could run off the natural gas that a nearby well could produce.

Things were looking hopeful for the future. It would never be like it had been before but it could still be good.

One thing that hadn't changed for the positive was that Jen was no longer the cook. Adam and Kierra weren't nearly as good as she had been. Jen had many years of experience making organic vegetarian food into something edible. Adam was a wizard with barbeque but didn't know what to do with vegetables and Kierra was just learning.

Jen now taught their school. It wasn't just for kids either. Some adults went to learn new skills such as how to make a rope. Jen had slowly been moving much of the Washington and Lee library to her room.

Then he saw Lisa carrying two pails of fresh milk from the barn. She had her Glock on her hip, the one from the police station in Richmond. She had several pistols including a Tokarov and went back and forth between them. Today was a Glock day. Still, it wasn't as bad as Adam getting into large caliber revolvers. Didn't anyone have style anymore? Besides Cassidy, no one else had a 1911. But the 1911 was designed by a Mormon so it was only fitting that their resident Mormon used one as well.

"I hate cows," Lisa said as she approached.

"But they love you."

"I almost was kicked in the head."

"That's their way of telling you that they love you."

Lisa put down the two pails and stood beside him, looking out over their little settlement.

"It's growing," she said.

"It'll grow more when we get permanent trade routes going."

"We need to get ammo factory. We have mine, now we need factory."

"I know, Alma and Cassidy are working on that."

Lisa shifted her weight and looked down to the ground.

"I'm going to go on a long range patrol."

"When are we leaving?"

"No, just me."

They were partners. They never went anywhere solo. What was going on here?

"You know the rules. No one goes anywhere alone."

"Yes, I do know the rules."

"Why?" He asked.

"I want to do something by myself."

"Well, this shouldn't be it."

"I don't want you to go with me."

What the hell was with her? Did she not trust him anymore? Did she think that he'd hurt her now? He had thought that they were well beyond that point by now. Apparently not.

"Why are you going?"

"I can't say."

"Why can't you say?"

"You have to trust me."

"Fine. Go off by yourself. Don't trust me then."

He was angrier than he would have thought he'd be. He stormed away from her because he didn't want to say anything he'd regret.

After months of working as partners she was just taking off somewhere and leaving by herself with no backup or word about what she was doing. Apparently he had misinterpreted their relationship.

It wasn't that she was putting herself in needless danger that angered him. He was very worried about that to be sure, but the thing that pissed him off was that she didn't want to be with him.

He had been thinking about trying to start some kind of relationship with her now that everything had calmed down, but now she had made her feelings perfectly clear.

The trick was to make sure she didn't know what he'd felt or it would be too embarrassing. He didn't have time for unrequited love.

Lisa avoided him for the rest of the day. At their communal dinner Lisa sat on the far end of the table and never looked at him. She had been acting distant and cold for a few weeks now. This explained a great deal. She was so sick of this place that she had to get out for a while without anyone to bother her.

Well, if he was a bother then he'd be happy to stay out of her way.

Only, he didn't want her to leave. He wanted her by his side.

"What's wrong, *hermano*?" Alma asked.

She usually sat beside him at dinner with Cassidy on the other side of her.

"Nothing," he said.

"Something's up."

"Nothing."

He could tell by the look on her face that she didn't believe him but she didn't probe any further.

When he arose the next morning Lisa was gone. Adam said that she had taken a horse and left before sunrise.

This was a free country and he wasn't going to stop her.

Damn her. Did he mean that little to her that she could just take off without even a goodbye?

"Did she say anything?" He asked.

"She said she'd be back in a week," Adam said.

"That's all?"

"That's all."

"What did she take?"

"A silenced M4, side arm and a backpack."

That put him in a foul mood for the entire week.

He had plenty of things to do but none of them quite distracted him enough. The new survivors were busy working the garden and taking care of the animals. Some were out scouting the area for whatever else could come in handy. Everyone had something to do.

But it wasn't enough.

He needed her with him.

58

LISA HAD GOTTEN USED TO RIDING HORSES. ON SOME LEVEL SHE actually enjoyed it. They were beautiful animals and she loved the skill it took to ride them well. But she hated being in the saddle for too long. It wasn't exactly a cushioned, bucket seat.

She rode all day and only stopped when the sun started going low in the sky.

She had to do this but she regretted not being able to tell Alex about it. It hurt not telling him but he couldn't know what she was doing. She hoped that his trust was enough so he wouldn't ask questions.

It struck her as extremely hypocritical to demand such trust of him and not return it. Maybe she really was a bad person.

She missed Alex already. Even a day away was growing painful. She had gotten used to him being near. She enjoyed his company like no one else's. She missed his sense of humor that he kept buried but would emerge when she least expected it.

Everything she was doing now was for him. Why did her feelings have to be so complicated? Was it like this for everyone? She was doing to this to protect him, yet it was separating them. It didn't make sense.

When they made contact with Farmville, (Everyone always laughed when they said the name and said something about not sending Facebook requests. She didn't get it.) she heard the list of names and recognized one of them. Joe Chen, former Air Force pilot.

Joe was a member of Second East Coast Team. He was a plant just like her only he had been in the United States for much longer. She had met him when she first entered the country.

She had to meet him and find out his intentions. If they were peaceful, she would seal her mouth and keep their secret. If his intentions weren't peaceful, then things became more complicated.

The problem was, Joe Chen was an expert and had been at this a lot longer than she had. She didn't know if she could remove him if it became necessary.

It took all the next day to arrive at Farmville just before sunset. They probably would have greeted her with open arms but this mission didn't allow her presence to be known. If things went well then they'd never know that she was there.

She watched the old school building they were using for a home from the edge of the woods. They had started gardens and used the old playground as an animal pen.

It wasn't until near midnight that she spotted her target. Joe left the school to use their outhouse which was rigged to a system of pipes to collect what would probably become "fertilizer" for their gardens.

She had no idea how disgusting farming could be at times. Still, it was an idea she'd bring back to the others. If she made it back.

Every mission had its dangers and she tried not to think about it. She hoped Alex wouldn't be hurt. At the same time, she hoped he would miss her and think about her.

Lisa crept up to the outhouse with her silenced M4 and waited for him to emerge.

When he did come out he emerged with a pistol in his hand. He was good. When he saw her he lowered the pistol. She lowered her M4.

"Lisa, what are you doing here?" He whispered in Mandarin.

"I came to talk to you."

"Good. I know I'm still in shock from seeing you alive, but we do have business to discuss."

"I came to discuss our plans."

"Good. You still wish to continue on with the mission. I've been making plans. Only now our plans are in the long run."

"What do you mean?" She asked.

"Eventually America will get back on its feet. It might take a few decades or a few centuries. Either way, they'll pose a threat to China one day. If we cut this plant now before it has time to grow, they'll never threaten us again. Right now China has to have more survivors than America. It's just a matter of mathematics. We can ensure our dominance in the long run."

"How do you propose that?" She asked as she slung her rifle over her shoulder.

"By killing off the settlements we find. We poison their wells. Release toxic gas while they're sleeping."

He was mad. After everything that had happened he was still intent on destroying the Americans. He didn't realize that it was a completely different world now. Everything had changed and killing innocent people wouldn't help anyone. It never had.

Enough people had died. Yes, his plan had a cold, unfeeling logic to it that she recognized all too clearly, but it was just wrong.

But if she objected he'd kill her. One on one she was no match for him.

"Where do we start?" She asked.

"That's what I always liked about you, Lisa, you did your duty without question. You didn't have a heart and that's what you need for our line of business."

"Don't have a heart?"

"Yes, you were always the most cold blooded of any of your team."

She had no idea she had had such a reputation. Was she really such an animal?

"Surprised? I thought you acted that way on purpose."

"That's unimportant. What's your plan?"

He laughed.

"They have a well here. I thought I'd start there. Some poison will kill most of them and the ones left behind will be easy. I was going to contact you first before I started. We could time our attacks."

"We take out both groups at the same time so they couldn't warn the other," she said.

"Exactly."

He turned to face the school building and for just that moment she had an opening that she might not get again.

She pulled her Glock.

Almost at the same time he pulled his Sig.

She pointed her Glock at him as soon as it cleared the holster but his free hand came up and grabbed her arm, keeping her from aiming at him. Her free hand slapped the gun out of his hand and both their free hands went for their knives.

His knife was in his belt but hers was right on her tac-vest. She got to it first and managed to slice his arm before she had to block his upward knife thrust. She deflected the blow to the side and instantly his knee rammed up into her side. Pain shot through her body but nothing broke.

He was fast and well trained. She couldn't take him. This was a fight she was going to lose unless she thought of something very quick.

While locked together she kicked out to break his knee but he moved his leg out of the way, shifting their weight so he fell down on top of her. Her attack had turned into her disadvantage. Now she was pinned.

She tried to bring her knife up to his side to stab him in the kidney but his arm pinned her knife hand and her gun hand was also pinned to the side. They were now locked together and neither could move their arms without freeing the other.

He brought his knee up and used that to pin her gun hand. She tried to use her freed leg to kick him off but she couldn't get an angle on him. It was like a kid at school trying to fight off a bully. He had size and weight.

His free hand then clamped down on her neck and instantly her breathing stopped. She had very little time before she lost vision and then consciousness.

She had a gun in her boot, the Beretta PX4 subcompact. She had to get it or she would die right there in the grass in a town called Farmville. Alex would never know what happened to her. He'd never know how much she cared for him.

Life seemed silly then. As her vision started to blur she realized how stupid she was to not tell Alex. She cared for him. She should tell him. Why had she been afraid?

She had to get free.

Lisa tried to wiggle out from under him and managed to get the arm pinned beneath his knee free. Instantly she kicked her leg straight up and toward her head where she could reach the gun. Her fingertips brushed the butt of the gun.

Her vision blackened around the edges and soon she barely saw anything except exploding stars.

She had to kill this man or she'd never see Alex again.

With one last strain she stretched her arm and grabbed the pistol. Without seeing him, she rammed the pistol up into his armpit and fired. Red liquid sprayed across her face and Joe fell off.

She gasped for air and her vision slowly came back.

Lisa crawled away from Joe who was thrashing around. As her head cleared she heard voices from inside the school. They had heard the shot.

Joe tried to say something but blood gushed out from his mouth. Still, she couldn't have him even hinting at who had killed him.

She grabbed her knife from the ground and kneeling down beside him, rammed it into his throat.

With that done, she dashed back into the woods and didn't wait around. She hopped up into the saddle and rode as fast as she could.

It was a fast ride back home.

Yes, home was definitely the right word for it. She had never had a place she ever considered "home," but the farm in Lexington was it without a doubt.

Even more so, she was riding back to Alex.

59

Alma

ALMA RODE ALONGSIDE CASSIDY AT A LEISURELY PACE. THERE was no hurry. Today they were riding out of Roanoke with a pack horse carrying their loot.

"So, your brother and Lisa seem to get along," Cassidy said.

"She doesn't talk much."

Alma already didn't like the topic of this conversation.

"No, but sometimes you don't need to talk. They have a connection."

"Don't give me that mystical crap."

"They definitely do."

"You're making stuff up now. She's a heartless ice queen."

"Sure, she's...reserved, I'll grant you that, but she feels things as deeply as we do."

Alma thought Cass was seeing things she wanted to see because she was a hopeless romantic. Maybe she read too many romance novels.

She looked back and checked their cargo that was carefully strapped to the pack horse. Solar panels and other random things from a list of necessary items: mostly parts for their mechanic and medicine for their healers. The solar panels would go on the second house. They'd need heat during the winter.

"What do you think we'll look like in a hundred years?" Cass asked.

"We'll be dead, Cass."

"No, I mean civilization."

"A hundred years isn't a long time. Our little town will be bigger, but it'll still be small."

"You think we'll still be using these solar panels? Could we make more? I don't see how. We'll have to go back to using wood stoves I guess."

"We'll keep some things. Maybe wind turbines or something."

"It will depend on if we can organize with other towns. One town just can't do it. But if one town kept the power going, one did the mining and one did...I don't know, computer stuff, we could keep a lot of what we're losing."

"Sounds kinda hopeful to me. How you going to get all those towns to agree like that?"

"Because it's in all our best interest."

"Since when have countries worked together for the common interest? Look around you Cass. If that was the case, we wouldn't even be having this discussion."

"I know that, but this is a chance to make things right. We're starting over so let's fix things from the beginning."

"Okay, but people are still people. We'll find a way to mess things up. Maybe down in Florida a tyrant's making all the rules and two hundred years from now our Virginia's going to have to fight them for control of South Carolina. Or maybe a KKK or Black Panther controlled Alabama's going to start work camps. Even if things change, it'll always be the same."

She shook her head and unscrewed the lid. She hated water. She wanted a Coke.

"But that's what I'm saying," Cass said. "This is our one chance to fix it. I know we can't fix the whole world, but we can fix our little piece of it."

"Always the optimist. But I do wonder what it is we're making here. Is my brother going to be dictator for life or will there be elections? I don't think we really have enough people to be holding regular elections. Unless everyone gets a chance to be president. Can you imagine me as president?"

"No."

"Thanks for your vote of confidence."

"No problem."

Then Cassidy stopped her horse and tilted her head as if hearing something. Alma stopped as well and listened. After a while of listening she didn't hear anything out of the ordinary.

"What?" Alma asked.

Cass held up a finger.

"I heard it again," Cass said.

Then Alma heard it. It sounded like someone yelling.

Then she spotted it. A lone, small figure was running down the road toward them while waving their arms. The figure was coming from where they had already passed by.

They turned their horses around and began to ride toward the figure. Alma took out her binoculars and took a look. The figure was a girl, maybe sixteen or seventeen. She was wearing nothing but a dirty, ragged, long T-shirt. Her brown hair was a tangled mess.

The girl was still running and kept looking over her shoulder. Alma raised the binos and saw three men running after the girl. They were armed. Shotguns.

She unslung her rifle and turned on the red dot sight.

"We got trouble, Cass," Alma said.

Cass looked through her ACOG and frowned. She tipped her cowboy hat back and thumbed off the safety to her rifle.

They left the pack horse and galloped toward the girl. She was about fifty yards away and the men were about two hundred. The men saw them coming and raised their shotguns.

Without thinking both her and Cassidy raised their own rifles. Though the men were first on the draw, she was still faster. Years of competition taught her to be fast.

She remembered her father standing behind her with that damned stop watch. He'd time her down to the fraction of seconds. He was always pushing her to beat her own time. Every week it was the same drills. Reload, snap fire, multiple targets, moving targets. Honestly, sometimes she got sick of it and wanted to throw that stopwatch down the toilet.

Even now as she raised her rifle she could feel Dad behind her with his stop watch. She felt his pushing her to be faster and more accurate. Adrenaline instantly pumped through her veins and she held her breath.

She squeezed the trigger as smoothly and as quickly as she ever had and the gun gently kicked in her hands. Alma knew it would hit before she ever saw the man go down. The bullet struck him center of mass and he twisted to the side and fell down.

Cass fired her bigger and louder Broadsword and Alma felt the concussion. Her shot also struck home and one of the men's heads opened up like a melon.

The third man, clearly the sensible one of the three, fell to the ground and began scrambling toward the woods.

Alma had a split second to decide. Would it be better to let him go and show mercy or shoot him as he ran and end this danger? But when her eyes glanced over to the girl who was obviously terrified, she was shaking with tears running down her filthy face. Cuts, old and fresh ran up her legs and arms, Alma knew mercy was out the window.

Misericordia: Spanish for mercy. That was the name of her rifle now.

She fired and the man went limp.

Cass looked over to her as if about to object, but kept her mouth closed.

They jumped down from their horses to meet the girl. She slumped to the ground, sobbing. It looked like she had missed too many meals and her skin was pale, sickly and covered in filth.

The girl only cried as Cass wrapped her arms around her. The girl didn't need to say anything. Alma could guess the story.

"So much for doing it right this time," Alma said. "Humans are animals and always will be."

Yet, as she said it, she saw the angelic image of Cass, holding the weeping girl in her arms. Cass was not an animal. She was a figure of the Madonna brought to life in a scrawny, gangly red headed Mormon girl.

Maybe if Cass was in charge things could be better.

Alma looked back to the bodies of the three men and saw that one of them was still moving.

She pulled out her black combat knife.

"Cass, wait here. I'm going to go do something very uncivilized."

60

HE WAS AWAKE AND SITTING ON THE PORCH DRINKING COFFEE when Lisa finally rode back. It was a little after lights out and he had guard duty. Yeah, he was the unofficial leader but he still took his turn.

She wore her tac-vest, black baseball cap with her hair pulled through the back. She was strong, intelligent and utterly gorgeous.

She saw him but didn't wave or smile. She looked tired.

Lisa put her horse back in the barn and removed the saddle. Once she was finished with all that she carried her stuff up to the porch and stood there on the steps in front of him.

"You're back," he said.

She nodded. He saw dried blood on her sleeve and vest.

"Where'd you go?"

"I can't tell you."

So, she was still keeping secrets. He stopped himself from snapping at her.

"Have a seat. You look tired. Hungry?" He said instead.

He was going to get some answers but he wasn't going to force them out. That would defeat the whole purpose of trust and respect.

He cared about her wellbeing but he wasn't through with this conversation yet.

"Yes."

She dropped her stuff on the porch and sat down on the rocking chair beside him. She was home earlier than she said she'd be and she moved slower and clumsier than usual.

"Hold up here while I fix you something."

He went into the kitchen, sliced some of Jen's homemade bread and made Lisa a peanut butter and jelly sandwich. After getting a glass of milk (Because who can eat one without a glass of milk?) he walked back out and handed the food to her. She took it silently and instantly began eating.

Usually she ate very daintily, but not right now. She ate like a wolf tearing away at a deer carcass.

"Alma and Cass have gone off to Roanoke to get solar panels and whatever else they can find. Think you can hook up the other house?"

"Okay," she said between a bite and a drink.

"I don't like secrets, Lisa, but I am glad you're back."

She stopped eating for a second and she looked over to him with those dark, unreadable eyes. For a brief moment he thought he saw traces of a smile.

"I'm glad to be home," she said.

"I'm going to trust you on this, Lisa, but from now on, no more secrets. I trust you with my life but it's a damn shame you don't trust me. I thought I would have earned it by now."

Whatever smile had been on her face vanished in an instant. She looked down to the ground and kept eating.

Alex wasn't an idiot and knew she was keeping more secrets than this. He couldn't imagine what they were or how they could possibly be important now. The world ended and kind of made any little dark secret invalid. No one would care that someone cheated on their taxes or their final math test.

"Alex, I have to tell you something."

Was this going to be it? He tensed up, preparing himself for the worst. Because he had no idea what it would be, he expected something bad. If she was pregnant that would throw a lot of wrenches into his plans. It would mean she loved someone else and would also mean she'd be out of action for several months. Were they even ready to deal with something like that? They didn't exactly have a surgeon on hand.

The logical arguments were swept aside by the overwhelming feeling of potential loss. She hadn't said a word and already he was imagining losing her. He didn't know if he could take watching her with someone else every day.

If it meant losing her, would it be better if he didn't know?

She put down her saucer and glass and folded her hands in her lap.

"Alex, I have been less than honest with you. This is my home and you all are my people. Whatever you hear from me, remember that I love this place. It's my home and I'd do anything to protect it. You have to believe me."

Her accent was much less obvious and she was speaking in better English than he had ever heard her use before. It frightened him but he kept his mouth closed, waiting for the other shoe to drop. In this case, it'd be a combat boot.

"Your friends were right to distrust me," she whispered. "I was working for the Chinese government. I was a plant, sent to infiltrate and gather intelligence."

All the small bits of evidence streamed in his mind and he knew it was true. As insane as it sounded, he knew it and maybe had known for a while. It was almost obvious.

Sitting in front of him was someone who worked for the people that killed his mother. Out of all the good people that died, a Chinese spy was left alive.

But as he looked at her he didn't see the enemy. He saw Lisa Fang. She looked at him with those almond, dark eyes and for the first time he saw that she wasn't wearing a mask. She was no longer unreadable and he saw fear, loneliness and vulnerability.

It wasn't an act either. He could tell that she was struggling to maintain her composure. She was still trying to act tough and failing miserably.

He sat back in his rocking chair and thought. Rocking chairs were good for that. He had hundreds of questions for her. He wanted to ask if she had killed Americans but then he thought about the enemy he killed during the war. What if he had been sent into China to fight and kill and was stuck there?

Alex tried to put himself into her shoes. Would he have told him? Probably not.

She sat there, struggling to keep calm. She still had her hands folded in her lap and she was looking down at her feet. Her breathing was far more ragged than usual and her hands kept fidgeting.

"Where did you go?" He asked.

She took a deep breath before answering.

"Farmville. I heard one of my team was alive there. I went to see what he was doing. He wanted to continue the war by poisoning the wells. I killed him."

Alex nodded and kept on rocking as he thought. He didn't even know what he was thinking about anymore. When he looked at her he didn't see a spy, he saw a woman he trusted with his life.

This also explained why she hadn't fully joined the group as the others. She had been stand offish and no wonder. A year and a half ago she was trying to destroy their country.

But soldiers were soldiers and they didn't get to choose their fight.

"Damn. No wonder you're such a good shot. I thought I was just a really good teacher," he said.

She looked up at him with worried, confused eyes.

"Please say something. This is torture," she whispered.

"Lisa..."

Just what was he going to say? He had too many questions, some he didn't want the answers for. So, he decided to start with what he knew.

"Lisa, you're not my enemy. I know you're one of us. This is your home if you want it."

Then she took a deep breath and nodded. Her eyes watered up and even now she was struggling to control her breath.

He wished she didn't have to suffer. Right then, he would do anything to make her feel better.

"It must have been hard, being here with us," he said.

"Stop being nice to me. I lied to you."

"Yeah, but I would have done the same. What were you supposed to do? 'Hi! I'm Lisa. I was sent here to destroy you. Can I join your group?'"

"But you can't trust me."

"How many times have we fought side by side? How many times have you had my back?" He stopped rocking and leaned in towards her. "I trust you with my life. We're both soldiers Lisa. Believe me, I understand."

She gave a brief smile and looked back down to her feet.

"I gotta say, you are one hell of a shot though," he said.

She laughed a little.

"I am sorry, Alex."

"Don't be. Still, let's keep this between you and me."

She quickly nodded.

"And start improving your English. Slowly."

She smiled and nodded.

Well, that explains a lot, he thought to himself.

"I don't deserve this," she said.

"We're our harshest critics."

She wiped her nose and went back to eating her sandwich. He continued rocking in silence.

61

Lisa

Lisa awoke in the morning in her bed with the sun coming in through the window. She was stiff and tired but she felt better than she had in a long time.

It must have been momentary insanity that made her tell Alex, but now he knew and she felt as if a backpack full of rocks had been lifted off her shoulders.

Her trainers had made her run twenty kilometers with weighted packs many times and she knew what a great burden it was. Right now she felt as if she had just ended one of those painful runs.

She could breathe again and not always look over her shoulder and wonder what would happen. Alex knew who she really was and she was glad. Even if he had yelled and thrown her out, she still would have been glad she did it.

Lisa hurried over to a window and looked out at the river down the hill. It was a gorgeous, sunny day and the trees were turning all shades of reds, oranges and golds. It was the most beautiful sight ever.

And what made it even better was knowing that she belonged here now. She was no longer a pretender. Alex knew her past and accepted it.

He had been unexpectedly calm about the whole thing. He had accepted her and still trusted her. She thought she would be forced to leave at least and shot at worst. In China they would have had worse punishments for her which made her glad she wasn't back in China: a thought that had been occurring more regularly.

State Orphanage #23 was not a kind place and forgiveness had no room in their lessons. She made her first kill at age thirteen. A prisoner brought in just for that purpose. It wasn't until much later that she learned how abnormal that was.

Alex didn't like killing and often hesitated. But she had no problems with it. She'd gladly kill again if it meant protecting her new home and family.

Lisa got dressed and holstered a stainless 1911 she had found in Lexington. It was similar to what Alex carried. She normally carried the Glock but today she felt a little like dressing up. She tied her hair back in a tail and went downstairs to the kitchen. Jen was teaching Rebekah and Kierra how to cook bread.

"Good morning, Lisa. Glad you're back," Jen said.

"Good morning. Glad to be back. Seen Alex around?"

"He's sleeping in. He had guard duty last night."

"Oh, yeah."

"We got eggs in that basket over there and fresh milk. You'll have to wait on bread."

"Thanks Jen."

She made herself a quick Spam omelet, she was sick of spam, and ate it in a hurry. Then she went outside into the cool, fall morning and looked around her home as if for the first time.

Robert was working in the mechanic's shop on a car. He was trying to get it to run on natural gas or alcohol, she didn't know which they'd decided on, so she decided to walk over to see.

"Good morning, Robert," she said.

He was working under the hood and startled when he heard her voice.

"Oh, Lisa. Good morning. You're in a good mood."

The former leader of the Hunt Club's prisoners went back to his work. He had a long beard and a backwards cap that said "AC-DC."

"You think you can get this working?" She asked.

"Given enough time and trial and error, sure. Getting enough fuel might be tricky so we won't be able to use this for recreation if you know what I mean."

"Awesome!"

Then she heard horses coming down the road. She left the machine shop and walked outside. Alma and Cassidy were returning from their patrol and their packhorse was full of supplies.

She knew Alma didn't care for her and the feeling was mutual. Alma was an arrogant, hot tempered know it all.

But then Lisa saw the passenger riding behind Cassidy. It was a teenage girl that looked like she had been living in the wild. She was filthy with matted brown hair. She had on a pair of army uniform pants that looked several sizes too big and a camouflage jacket that belonged to Cassidy.

Lisa hurried over.

"Situation?" Lisa asked. The military way of speaking she learned from State Orphanage #23 was still the best and most efficient way of talking and she doubted she'd give it up any time soon.

"Situation is, we killed three men that needed killing and rescued this girl here," Alma said.

"What's her name?"

"Don't know," Cassidy said. "She hasn't said a word."

Alma dismounted and motioned with a jerk of her head to follow her. Lisa followed Alma a little ways off.

"The men had done things to the girl, so please don't say anything that could upset her," Alma whispered.

"Done things?"

"Do I have to spell it out for you?"

"Oh! No, no need."

She turned to look at the girl that Cassidy was helping down from the saddle. She couldn't imagine what horrors the men did to her. She had seen similar things during the chaos of the plague in Richmond and knew how depraved humans could be.

Lisa thought about her own situation. She had never even kissed a man before and had no idea what it was like, but to be brutalized like that...she shook her head to clear her thoughts.

"Poor girl," was all Lisa could say.

"Yeah, the world's a pretty craptastic place out there. We met another survivor in Roanoke, but he was an old man that just wanted to sit there and get a tan."

"He did not want to come?"

"Not really."

"Shame."

"I think we can find more people though. We're going to start leaving signs around."

Lisa only half listened to Alma. Her thoughts were on the girl that Cass was leading by the hand inside.

"Cassidy is a very kind person," Lisa said.

Alma turned to look.

"Unlike us, right?" Alma asked.

Lisa nodded.

"I'll go wake Alex," Lisa said.

"And I'll go get breakfast."

"Did you ride through the night?"

Alma raised an eyebrow and nodded.

"We did."

"You look tired."

Alma just shrugged and followed Cassidy into the house. Lisa then went inside and walked up to Alex's room. The door was closed.

She knocked.

"Huh?" Came Alex's muffled and drowsy voice.

"Alma and Cassidy are back. They brought a survivor."

"Alright, I'll be down in a minute."

She waited by the door until he came out. She wanted to see him.

When he finally emerged he saw her standing there and smiled. He was genuinely happy to see her despite their conversation from last night.

"Good morning," she said.

He chuckled.

"Good morning. Have you seen Lisa around? You know, the grouchy girl that never smiles."

"Was I smiling?"

"You were."

She tried and failed to suppress her smile.

What awaited them in the kitchen wiped their smiles from their faces. The girl looked even worse up close. Cassidy was sitting beside her and watching her eat an egg sandwich.

Alma took Alex off to the side and explained the situation. Lisa listened in and learned about their brief gunfight.

"You did good, Alma," Alex said at the end.

"Thanks."

"Now we have to look after our guest," Alex said.

"New family member," Lisa corrected.

62

ALEX WATCHED LISA PLAY TUG-O'-WAR WITH CAESAR. THEY were using an old piece of rope that the dog seemed to like above all other objects in the world. They were sitting in the living room by the fire and he was reading a good book, "The Stand" by Stephen King.

How had he not read this book before? His life had been incomplete.

Alma and Cassidy were over on a couch reading as well, though Alma was listening to her iPod too. She was reading Twilight.

"I gotta ask, why you reading that?" He asked.

"To see if I liked it or not. I figured millions did so there had to be something good about it."

"And your verdict?"

"I like it."

He had to let that go before he lost more respect for her literary tastes.

Cassidy was reading a fantasy book with a dragon on the cover called "The Golden Cord" and Lisa had been reading "Carnage and Culture" a history of how Western Culture shaped the way they fought. She seldom read novels but Cass was always pushing her in that direction: one of the many reasons he liked Cass. They were the only two people here who had read 'Dune.'

It was a pleasant Saturday evening. The daily chores were done and they had time to relax. No life or death crisis to deal with.

Lisa had been growing closer to the dog and though she insisted that she still didn't like the "mutt" she was always playing with it and rubbing its soft belly. She even let it lick her face on occasion which always got a grossed out, but delighted squeal, out of Lisa.

"Alex," Alma said without looking up from her book. "Last time we were in Roanoke, we saw a gun store that was locked up and still had all its stuff.

We didn't have time or the tools to get in, but I'd like to take Jen and Adam out with us and bring back as much stuff as we can."

"Take the truck then. We'll find the fuel," Alex said.

Alma nodded and went back to reading.

"Oh, go ahead and take Rebekah with you. I've been teaching her a few things. I'm not sure she's ready, but she'll kill me if I don't let her go," Alex said.

"She's as ready as any of us were," Cassidy said.

"That wasn't as ready as we should have been," Alma said.

"Yeah, right. You were born ready."

Then Bruce came in. He was one of the people they rescued from the Hunt Club and had a scoped Remmington ,308 in his hands. He wore the suit jacket he had worn as a lawyer and seemed to cling to it like it was his last connection to his past.

"We got three people coming down the road," Bruce said and pointed out with this thumb.

"We'll be right there," Alex said.

He looked to Lisa and didn't have to say a word. She knew what to do. They both hurried upstairs and got on their vests and guns.

Ever since Lisa told him her secret, the two of them had become closer. In a professional way of course. They were a team maybe even tighter than Alma and Cassidy. When things needed to be done they seldom had to say anything. A glance or a gesture was usually more than enough and sometimes it was like she could read his mind.

He grabbed his M14 because it was suitably intimidating.

Alex met Lisa in the hall. She was decked out in full kit and carried her FS2000. She had her sunglass and hat on. Lisa had been letting her hair grow out and her ponytail was now down to her shoulder blades. Overall it was a striking image and he had to keep himself from staring.

With a nod to each other they went down to the porch to meet with these three strangers. Alma and Cass came down a few seconds later, also in full kit.

"Bruce, go up into a second story window and don't do anything until you see shooting starting. Understood? I mean you keep that finger off the trigger."

"Got it," Bruce said and hurried upstairs.

Now all they had to do was wait. He had his game face on which he had been wearing for the past year and a half. Though lately it was starting to slip.

The three strangers entered their "piazza" as Jen liked to put it. It was the circular area that used to be the front lawn that was now surrounded by workshops and buildings.

Alex now got a good look at these strangers. One was a middle age woman with graying hair and still carried a bit of weight around the hips. She was tall and grim looking and had a hunting rifle on her back. She was holding the hand of a little boy that didn't look older than ten. He looked Philipino maybe.

But it was the third person that got his attention. He was wearing a suit with a white shirt and tie. He was clean cut with a shaved face and neat hair. The peculiar thing was the name tag he wore on his chest. Alex had seen that kind of nametag before. He was a Mormon missionary and he was carrying a shotgun. He also walked with a noticeable limp.

He glanced over to Cassidy and saw that she was wide eyed and holding her breath. Alma was trying not to laugh.

"Careful, everyone. People aren't always what they seem to be," Alex whispered.

Lisa cleared her throat and glared at him.

The three strangers came to a halt in front of the porch and the man held up his hands. Alex walked out onto the porch with his rifle down, but ready to swing up at a moment's notice. The others followed. He noticed that Lisa kept both hands on her weapon.

"I'm Elder Stevenson and this is Karen and Jacob. We saw signs telling us there's shelter and safety here," the young man said. His clothes were relatively clean and in good shape, though his shoes and pants cuffs were covered in dirt from the road.

"You look the part, but doesn't the end of the world kind of end your mission?" Alex said.

"I haven't been released, so I'm still on the clock. And I have to admit, I thought it would be safer if I continued on as is."

"How we know you're a real missionary?" Alma asked.

Elder Stevenson smiled a big, toothy smile.

"Just give me a half hour of your time," Stevenson said.

"Please," Karen said. "We've been walking down from New York trying to find a place to live. Winter's coming and we have no where else to go."

She said it matter-o'-factly, with no drama or theatrics. It was the voice of someone that was too tired to try.

Alex looked over to Lisa and Alma, his unofficial counselors. Lisa gave him a barely perceptible nod and Alma played at thinking about it until Cass elbowed her in the ribs.

"Alright, drop your weapons on the ground and come on in," Alex said.

He wasn't about to trust them until he learned a little bit more about them. Kindness didn't have to cancel out security.

They obeyed and dropped their weapons and their large backpacks on the ground. Alex slung his rifle and escorted them to the living room with the crackling fire. They sat the three strangers on one couch and he sat between Alma and Lisa.

It was a strange thing to notice but he realized that he had never sat this close to Lisa before. It was a small couch and the fit was tight. He couldn't help but notice how warm she was. And soft.

"So, tell us your stories," Alex said.

"I guess I'll go first," Stevenson said. "I was on my mission in New Jersey when the plague hit. See, I couldn't join the army cause of this."

Stevenson pulled up his pant cuff to reveal a metal leg.

"Car accident when I was fifteen," Stevenson said.

"Alright," Alex said. "It just so happens that we have an expert of sorts on Mormons. She'll ask you a few questions to make sure you are what you say you are."

Alex then pointed to Cassidy who was sitting in a chair off to the side. Was she trying not to be noticed? He hadn't pegged her as the type to be shy.

Cassidy looked up and gave the shyest smile he had ever seen. Yup, she was shy. At least around young, handsome Mormons.

"Oh, okay. I'll take you off to the side and ask a few questions," Cassidy said.

They went into the next room out of hearing range but still within his sight.

"He's real," Karen said.

"And what's your story?" Alex asked.

"I worked IT in New York City before the war. Lost my husband, my children and everything when the plague hit. I found Jacob here wandering around the streets on a new bike. He doesn't speak much."

"You can fix computers?" Alma asked.

"More like I made them," Karen said. "Kind of a useless skill now."

"Not as useless as you think," Alex said.

If they were going to get civilization back on its feet, they'd need people like her. He had heard that the internet was somewhat indestructible. If she panned out, they'd be able to put that theory to the test.

Then Cassidy walked in, barely containing a smile.

"He's legit," Cass said and sat back down in her corner.

"Alright then. Welcome to Promised Land. You can stay here as long as you like. We'll be more than glad to have you. There's plenty of work to be done. We'll find someplace for you to bunk down."

"I can show them around," Cassidy quickly said.

"Okay. Um...Cassidy, why don't you show our guests around?"

After Cass and Alma took the visitors out he noticed Lisa removing her hand from the butt of her pistol.

"It went well for us this time," Alex said.

"But might not next time. Sooner or later someone's going to do something that requires punishment."

"I know. We need to set up rules and government."

"So, why wait?"

"Because I don't want to be leader."

"Too bad. You are the leader."

"No one elected me."

She sighed.

"Then have an election if that will make you feel better. It won't matter because you'll still be the leader."

She was right about that. He would still end up in charge but at least it would put his mind at ease.

Now all he had to do was figure out how to run an election.

63

EVERYONE WAS GATHERED IN THE BARN. MOST PEOPLE WERE standing but a few had brought chairs. The kerosene lamps were lit and the bugs clouded around the light.

Alex looked around the room and saw every hand raised.

Just like that he was unanimously elected president, chief, dictator for life or whatever his job was called.

Alma was smirking at him with that "I told you so" look on her face.

Lisa stood just to the side and behind him. He could feel her warm, assuring presence.

He raised his hands to silence the crowd.

"Alright, listen up. As your newly elected leader I have some positions I'd like to fill."

He hadn't told anyone about this yet. This was payback for putting him in charge.

"As your leader, and we really should come up with a title, I propose to name Lisa Fang as head of internal security which is military and police. Also, I'd like to name Alma as head of our military training. Next I'd like to name Jennifer as head of education."

He enjoyed the looks of surprise on Lisa and Alma's faces. He knew he'd pay for it later, but it was worth it.

He went through his list of head mechanic, farming, construction and health. They were all elected without much fuss at all. No one challenged the positions and it was all unanimous. That would probably be the only time that ever happened.

With that over, he asked for any problems or grievances to be discussed. Most of the problems were mundane like sleeping space. With their growing population they needed more housing and no one wanted to live too far away.

But then someone brought up the question of ownership. Who owned the houses? The horses? The vehicles?

"For now, we have to share them. There's not enough horses for everyone so everyone gets to use them when they need them," he said.

Sure, he and his original group could lay claim to most everything, but then it would be another feudal society with him as king granting permission to use royal property and land.

Hell no.

This was still America and everyone was still equal. The problem was, no one really owned much anymore. They had things they all found but if everyone hoarded what they had, they wouldn't survive. This winter was going to have to be a team effort or their supply of canned food would run out.

He ended the meeting with a promise of sorting it all out as soon as he could.

After the first ever, official town council, he went to his living room and sat by the fire with his book to clear his mind of all the problems starting a town was causing. It wasn't just a town but a new society.

The others came in, talking in hushed conversations and sat around him.

"Well," Jen said. "Looks like we have a real brain teaser. We have to rebuild civilization but we can't afford to mess it up."

"Yeah, no pressure, right?" Alex said.

"If it was larger we could apply the old models," Cassidy said.

It was the first time he had seen her without Stevenson beside her in three days. He was on clean up duty and she wasn't about to stay away from the decision making.

"The ownership issue has to be dealt with. No one owns the horses. No one owns the farms," Jen said.

"I know. It's starting to look like some kind of autonomous, democratic collective," Alex said.

"Would that be so bad?" Lisa asked.

"So says the communist," Alma said.

"I'm not a communist," Lisa said.

"The fact of the matter is, this is about survival," Alex said. "Once we get things running and we don't have to worry about starving in the winter we can make things nicer and more civilized. But for now we have to realize that survival depends on sharing what we have."

"I don't like it," Cass said.

"If you have a better idea, let me know."

"What if we divide everything to everyone? Maybe some people own horses, others land and others shops?" Cass said.

"What about down the road?" Jen asked.

"What do you mean?"

"I mean, what about a few generations from now when our population's much bigger. If we divide it up like that, some people, like the ones in charge of horses or vehicles, will be much more powerful than the people who take care of the carrots," Jen said.

"I need a way where we share now, but will allow for the possibility of enterprising people getting ahead. Without that, there will be little to no incentive to grow and become the best."

"For one year we share. After that, we give them summer to become independent?" Lisa said.

"Sounds doable," he said.

It hurt just to think about it. He was tired and just wanted to get to bed.

"Meeting dismissed. Go sleep on it and maybe we'll have something more definite in the morning," he said.

Alex went up to his room and collapsed on his bed. His head hurt from thinking circles in his head.

This was why he didn't want to be a philosopher major.

He wanted a system where the government was weaker than the people and served them. The United States before it fell had started off like that but had become the opposite. The government had enough power to do pretty much whatever it wanted and the People had little, to no say, in what actually happened. He wasn't going to allow that to happen this time.

Alex began to imagine his resignation letter already.

When he woke in the morning he wasn't closer to having anymore answers than he was the night before. He lay there soaking up the early morning sun. He was perfectly willing to let it all just go away but then he heard a knock on his door.

Couldn't they just leave him alone for five minutes?

"Yeah?"

"Lisa," came her soft, strong voice.

He had time for her.

"Come in."

He was wearing his X-Men pajama bottoms and a T-shirt.

She came in with a tray of breakfast.

"Hey, I'm the chief now, but that doesn't mean you have to serve me breakfast," he said.

"This is a one time thing. I wanted to," she said.

She placed the tray down in front of him on the bed and took a seat on the opposite side of the bed.

"I don't have any answers," he said to her unasked question.

"There's no rush. Things have been working out well enough so far," she said.

"So far."

As he ate he looked at her as she sat there, as calm as a statue. With the first bite he could tell that it wasn't Jen's cooking but Lisa's. Even something as simple as an omelet had her signature.

"Thanks," he said.

This disrupted whatever train of thought was in her mind.

"What?"

"Thanks for breakfast."

"Of course," she said. "I'll leave you to it."

She got up and left, wearing that stone mask of hers again. Something was troubling her. He could see it but didn't know what to do about it. She wasn't the most open of people after all.

And why breakfast in bed?

64

Lisa, Thanksgiving

LISA LOOKED OUT OF HER WINDOW, HER FAVORITE VIEW FROM THE house, at the mist covered, rolling landscape. It was morning of the American holiday called Thanksgiving. It had something to do with turkeys and eating a lot, but other than that, she had no idea.

The sky was still red and gold from sunrise and down below she could see people walking out to the cow pasture and the chicken coup.

It would be a perfect day if it weren't for the fact that she was completely confused. All she could think about was Alex. She made up excuses to talk to him and stayed near him as much as possible.

She always kept her professional manner though. She didn't want him to think that she was going crazy. How would it look if his Head of Internal Security had to be the first patient in their insane asylum?

There had to be something she could do about this. She wanted her clear and rational head back.

As confused and crazy as she felt, she also never felt more sure about anything in her whole life.

This was now a more primitive world and Alex was the warlord here. If she wanted to secure her future and any children she would have, he would be the man to be with.

But it was more than that. Even if he got demoted to pig feeder she'd still want to be with him.

This was insane.

She put her hair up into two buns like she used to do as a child and went downstairs for breakfast. Jen, now with more important duties, had left the kitchen in the hands of Adam, Rebekah and Kierra. Rebekah was part time though because she often trained with their defense force that Alma and

Cassidy were setting up. She was just one of several recruits. She feared that they'd need them one day.

Alex was there. Of course. His distracting presence filled the room. She didn't need to think logically this morning apparently.

She felt a scowl cross her face and she went over to sit by him.

"We're having pancakes and waffles," Adam said.

"Waffles, please," Lisa said.

"Are you okay?" Alex asked.

"Of course. Why wouldn't I be?"

"That's why I'm asking. You look...upset."

"I'm not."

By the look on his face she saw that he wasn't buying it. As someone who had been trained in espionage, she'd think she would be a better liar by now.

"Happy Thanksgiving at any rate," he said.

"Oh, of course. Happy Thanksgiving. What do you do for this holiday?"

"We're going to have a huge, wasteful feast full of turkey, duck, corn, stuffing and anything else we can think of," Alex said.

"Oh, Lisa, Jen wanted me to ask you if you if you'd prepare the duck for this afternoon. She said no one does duck like the Chinese," Adam said.

"I can do that," Lisa said.

Then the door burst open and a group of kids ran screaming through the kitchen. Leading the way was a floppy eared Caesar and the biggest smile she had ever seen on a dog. She didn't know dogs could smile.

"Hey! Be careful!" Adam shouted.

The kids tore through, chasing Caesar on their way to the back yard.

"I guess he's getting all the attention he could hope for," Alex said.

"I don't know if there's enough attention in the world for that dog," Lisa said. "Okay, I understand that we'll be eating, but what are we celebrating?"

"We're celebrating everything we're thankful for. I think we have a lot of thanks to be giving."

"We're doing okay for the end of the world," she said.

"If we can have a place full of screaming, happy children, then we're doing alright."

She'd never thought of it like that. She didn't remember playing like that as a child. She remembered strict discipline and hard lessons from her masters. She remembered disciplinary beatings, days without food and no words but harsh reprimands.

"Tomorrow Alma, Cassidy, Adam, Jen and Rebekah are heading out to

Roanoke to that gun store. Make sure to step up patrols tomorrow," Alex said and left the kitchen.

He didn't even say goodbye.

The rest of the day she somehow got stuck in the kitchen. She didn't think it was traditional American Thanksgiving, but she made hand made, thick noodles in peanut sauce to go with the duck.

Their population was now so large that they had to set up several tables in the barn to fit everyone. The teenagers were in charge of cleaning the barn for the occasion.

As she worked in the kitchen she noticed something between Jen and Adam. The way they smiled at each other and touched each other showed an abnormal level of intimacy. They were in love. It must have been Adam she heard with Jen that one night.

They acted so casual about it, like it was the most natural and easy thing in the world.

For Lisa it felt like anything but easy or natural. She'd rather do more 20k marches with a backpack full of rocks than be in love.

Love. That was the word. There was no other possible explanation. She loved Alex and there was no denying it.

She sighed.

"Something wrong, Lisa?" Jen asked.

"Just thinking."

"About what?"

"Nothing important."

"When a girl gets that kind of sigh going, I'd say there's only one thing on her mind."

"It doesn't matter. We have work to do," Lisa said.

"Don't try to brush it off, missy. I know what's going through your mind."

"Please don't mock me."

"I'm not mocking you. I'm trying to help you. You really have no idea what you're doing, do you?"

She didn't know what to say. Somehow this woman was seeing right through her. Her esteem as an infiltrator was being damaged by the hour. If only her master trainer could see her now. Would it be a 20k or a beating? Probably both.

"Don't say anything then," Jen said. "But if you have feelings for someone, now's the time to make them known. The world's a different place and nobody can afford to procrastinate."

She didn't know what "procrastinate" meant and wondered if it was something dirty. Because if it was, she procrastinated while thinking of Alex just the other night.

"What is procrastinate?" Lisa asked.

"It's when you keep waiting and putting something off until it's too late," Jen said.

That made more sense.

She thought back to the night at Farmville.

"It's all silly," Lisa said.

"No it isn't, Lisa. It's even less silly now than before."

Before. That was a word that now held oceans full of meaning. Everyone always said "Before" and everyone always knew exactly what that meant.

"But...what do I do?" Lisa whispered.

"Tell him. Show him. Do something. It doesn't even matter what, just as long as you let him know. Even the smartest, sharpest man can be dumb in matters of love."

Lisa felt the familiar, fearful anticipation that occurred just before a battle. This was a battle she didn't know how to fight or if she'd get out of it alive.

65

<u>Alex, Thanksgiving.</u>

LISA HAD DEFINITELY BEEN ACTING STRANGE LATELY. IT WAS AS IF she got upset every time she saw him now, like she felt more comfortable without his presence. That wasn't very flattering for a man's ego.

Why was she doing small, trivial things to help him if she didn't even want to be around him?

He didn't understand women at all. Never had. And Lisa was the most un-understandable woman he had ever met.

Alex went to the barn and saw that it was as clean as any meeting hall. It had a dirt floor and smelled of animals, but it was clean and with the tables and chairs being set up it looked alright.

The smaller children had been put in charge of decorations and paper turkeys and streamers hung from the walls and ceiling. An iPod attached to speakers was set up for music. The year's first pumpkins were also set up on bales of hay along the sides of the walls giving the place a genuine rustic vibe.

It was downright festive.

In the distance he could hear the faint 'crack, crack crack' of Alma and Cassidy's target practice for the security force.

He had told her that it would be alright to take Thanksgiving off, but she refused. He was proud of his sister. She should be leader, not him. She was the one that crossed the United States to find him. She was the one that always seemed so sure of every decision she made. Surety was not a skill he was practiced in.

"Alex!" One of the little boys called out.

He ran up to him and hugged him around the waste. He had a huge smile on his face.

"What's up, Dan?"

"Are we going to open presents?" He asked.

"No, that's Christmas. This is Thanksgiving."

"Yeah, but I thought if we're doing everything over, why don't we have presents on Thanksgiving and Christmas?"

He had to laugh at the logic of a child. The kid did have a valid point.

"We'll keep it traditional for now. Maybe we'll change it later."

"Alright."

He ran off to catch up with the others that were still chasing Caesar around. One of the other kids said, "See? I told you it wouldn't work."

Finally the hour arrived and bowls and platters of food were arriving. Yeah, it was wasteful, but they had enough to last the winter if they managed it wisely. They'd just send search parties out even further and bring back more food if they started running out.

They'd be well fed until the canned food expired. By then they had to have their farming on a self sustaining level or they'd be in trouble. Maybe by then the deer population would be enough to help out.

He watched Lisa come in carrying her platter of roasted duck. She moved with such precision and grace. It was almost inhuman. Every mannerism or little gesture was like the most beautiful dance he'd ever seen.

Sure, there was a bit of lust in there. He couldn't deny that. But he also respected her. More than respected, really. He trusted her with his life and knew that she'd do anything it took to defend their home.

She was a remarkable, intelligent, brave woman.

"*Cera tu boca*," Alma said. It meant, "shut your mouth."

"Was I gawking?" He asked.

"Si."

"I thought you were out doing target practice."

"Just got back in."

"Holy darn!" Cassidy said from somewhere behind him. "We got a real spread today."

He looked back and saw that she was with Stevenson. He no longer wore the trappings of a missionary. Apparently he couldn't court Cassidy if he was a missionary.

"Your wing woman's awfully busy with her new boyfriend. That was quick."

"She said it was meant to be or some other bull crap."

"She'll get back to relative normality soon enough."

"They should hurry up and get married so they can start ignoring each other. Then I'd get my friend back."

"Marriage? They just met."

"It's a different world, Alex. Love is less refined now. Maybe that's for the better. A girl can't wait around forever anymore. Besides, where else is she going to find a young, single Mormon guy?"

Can't wait around forever. Did that mean Lisa would eventually seek a man out if he didn't make himself out as a possibility? Or someone else would see her and move in and sweep her off her feet.

He had to do something soon.

People began filtering in and taking seats. There were smiles and laughter and it felt like a real celebration. Someone turned on the music. Mostly Classic rock. It was probably Cassidy's iPod.

Once everyone was in and he'd given them enough time to mingle and relax, he called them to attention. They all took their seats at the giant table that was made form many different tables. Carved pumpkins and lanterns decorated the table and the children's paper decorations hung on strings over the festivities. He sat at the head of the table with Alma at his right and Lisa at his left.

He welcomed them out and officially opened the feast. Stevenson said the blessing on the food and then they began. Instantly plates, bowls and dishes were passed around and the talking increased to a roar.

It was a good sound.

Everyone here had lost something precious to them. They had all lost loved ones, wives, husbands, fathers, siblings. They lost their homes, their way of life, their dreams. But here they could find happiness. They could build new lives and new dreams.

They were safe and had a future, but he didn't have to say any of that. They all knew it.

He was thankful for the literal miracle that brought Alma back to him. She came despite all hope and odds. He had his sister again.

He looked over to Lisa. She was eating quietly and looking around the room. He wondered if she was thinking the same thing he was.

She had a life here now: a place to call home.

She looked over and saw that he was looking at her. He suddenly felt stupid for staring at her but he saw that she returned his smile.

"Enjoying your first Thanksgiving?" He asked.

She nodded.

"Your roast duck is excellent. I don't usually like duck, too gamey, but this is delicious."

"Thanks. I made it for you," she said and quickly went back to eating.

Made it for him?

He looked at her and for the first time saw...what was this? Shyness. The female terminator was shy?

All the little things she had done for him began adding up in his head. He had confused the tough exterior for her real self. Now he saw an awkward, shy, girl that didn't know how to express herself.

It became so obvious that he stopped eating and sat back in his chair to think about it.

Alma noticed and leaned in to him.

"Not hungry? Better eat up, *hermano*. This stuff is good and we don't have refrigerators. Maybe next year I'll fix carne asada to go with this."

"Oh, I'll keep eating. Don't worry about that. I'm just thinking about something."

As he sat back he noticed for the first time the glances Lisa kept stealing at him. She would reach for her glass and use it as an excuse to look at him.

He had never felt this...high before. He had never taken drugs but he imagined it had to feel something like this.

Euphoria was a good word.

As the dinner wound down, people began dancing. Alma and a few others broke out instruments and played live music as well. She had been practicing on an upright bass and was actually getting good at it. Rebekah was on guitar. She had started learning after Spencer's funeral.

It was Lisa and him sitting together now, watching the people have a good time. They were his people now.

The key to any battle was knowing when to make the right move at the right time. So, he decided to strike. It was now or he'd lose his courage and retreat.

Alex moved his hand over and took Lisa's, thin but strong hand in his. She stiffened up and gasped a little, but when she turned to face him he saw that she was smiling.

It was a faint smile but it was written all over her face as if she had been shouting.

She squeezed back.

They sat there in silence, holding hands and enjoying the evening and good company.

The celebration went well on into the night and he doubted that it would stop before sunrise.

"Would you walk with me to the house?" He asked.

She quickly nodded.

They didn't really walk to the house. Instead they walked around the house and the fields. They didn't say much. They didn't need to.

At the end of their walk they finally made it back to the house. They stopped at the porch steps and he turned to look at the glowing barn where laughter and music spilled out of.

"You make me very happy," she said after a while.

"I want to make you happy."

Then he drew her close and kissed her.

66

Alma

ALMA WAITED FOR THE OTHERS TO FINISH MOUNTING UP. CASS was helping Rebekah with her saddle and Adam was double checking everything on a notebook. Being meticulous was fine but they had to leave soon.

She tapped her fingers on the pommel of her saddle while she waited for the slowpokes.

Adam and a new guy were driving the Humvee. Cass and her were on horses. Derrick, the new guy, was former Air Force and was top of the training class she led. He'd probably be their first officer as soon as she got around to organizing their force a little more. If he wasn't already with a girl from the group they liberated from the Hunt Club she might have considered him.

"Okay, we're ready to go," Cass said.

"Finally."

She watched as Adam said goodbye to Jen and Cass said goodbye to Chris, the former Elder Stevenson.

Where was her goodbye? Didn't she have anyone to see her off?

She had a good guess where Alex was. He had left the party early with Lisa. She hadn't checked but she imagined that they were curled up in bed next to each other.

Damn him. How could he just let her go without saying goodbye?

"Right! Let's move out!" She said.

Then the front door to the house opened and Alex came running out. He was still putting on his coat. He looked around and when he saw her he smiled.

Damn him again. That smile always had the power to make her forget why she was angry.

"There you are. I was afraid I missed saying goodbye," Alex said.

He came up and began checking her saddle.

"I'm good to go. I checked everything."

"Can't blame me for worrying."

"Have a pleasant night with Lisa?"

He looked up at her and raised an eyebrow.

"I didn't sleep with her."

"Oh, really?"

"I swear."

"Why you up so late?"

"Because we were up talking."

"Talking? Her? I assume you did most of the talking then."

"Just because you don't get along with her doesn't mean she doesn't talk."

"Fine. We gotta go."

"Alma, don't be like this."

"We'll be back in three days."

She road out and left him standing there with his arms folded and an upset look on his face

It wasn't till she was a few miles out that she decided that she wanted to leave him with a happier goodbye but it was too late.

Her quick temper got her in more trouble than she would have liked. She didn't want to argue with her brother. He was the most important person in her life.

She just wished the feeling was mutual.

"You okay?" Cass said.

She had ridden up beside her without her noticing.

"Yeah."

"You angry that him and Lisa are together?"

"No."

"Yeah you are."

"It doesn't matter what I think."

"Of course it does."

Cass reached a hand out but she pretended not to see it and spurred her horse to go on ahead of the others.

• • • •

They arrived in the ghost city of Roanoke and found the roads jammed with cars that would never move again. They shut the Humvee off while the riders went off to find passable roads. It took the rest of the afternoon to get to the downtown gun store. Things had been easier last time when it had just been her and Cass on horses.

They dismounted and spread out to watch for signs of trouble as the Humvee pulled up in front of the barred up store. Metal grates covered the windows and the door was thick metal.

"Got a regular Fort Knox here," Cass said.

"It won't be a problem," Derrick said.

He pulled out a large metal box from the back of the Humvee and strolled up to the door.

"What you got there?" Alma asked.

"C4."

"Awesome."

She didn't look because she was scanning the empty streets of the city for movement. There was the occasional wind blown piece of garbage or a cat slinking around, but no people. If there was a survivor nearby they were probably watching them and trying to judge how big of a threat they were.

It wasn't easy to look non-threatening when they had a bunch of guns and were breaking into a gun store.

Cass had her cowboy hat on and a jacket with a fur lined collar. It was getting cold. She hated the cold. Back in Mexico she didn't remember ever being cold. She wore shorts year round.

She had her black biker jacket on and a scarf. She hadn't had much opportunity to wear scarves back in Vegas, but had always thought they were cool. Instead of adding bulk to her body she wore tactical thigh rigs for her magazines and pistol. Cass and Rebekah did the same.

Derrick finished rigging the door and went behind the Humvee.

"Everyone take cover. It won't be big but there might be flying bits of death," Derrick said.

Alma took cover with Rebekah behind the building's corner. The alleyway was filled with garbage and a long dead body that was barely recognizable as human. She wondered if it smelled. She had become so used to the horrible smell of rot from countless corpses baking in the Vegas sun that she didn't notice it anymore.

At first the smell of the rotting Las Vegas had been so bad that she had wanted to find a gas mask, but after two weeks of bad appetite she had gotten used to it. Maybe the smell was gone now.

"Cover your ears!" Derrick shouted out.

She let her rifle fall on its single point sling and used both hands to cover her ears. A few seconds later she heard the sharp 'bang' and felt the sudden change in air pressure.

She hurried back around the corner and saw that the lock on the door was gone. The metal was burnt and blasted inward.

"It worked?" She asked.

"About to find out," Derrick said."

Adam, Rebekah and Cass covered them while she went with him to the door.

It opened easily.

"Excellent job," she said.

"I do take pride in my work."

She took out her flashlight and went inside. The windows in front let in some light but not enough for details.

The store was filled with bulk cases of ammo, magazines of every type and lots of guns. She walked over to the glass counter where all the handguns were and looked over to the wall behind it. Tactical rifles of all kinds were there.

"Cass! Get in here!"

Cass walked in and turned on her flashlight.

"Whoa! Nice selection. I told you this was a good store. This isn't no sportsman, outdoors store. This is a fighting guns kinda store," Cass said.

"I call first dibs."

"Look, an FS2000. We can get Lisa a backup in case she breaks hers."

"That wasn't top of my list."

"You should get something nice for Alex."

She had a good point there.

She looked around and thought. Adam and Derrick began hauling cases of ammo into the Humvee while her and Cass began loading up the guns. Rebekah remained on over watch.

Then she saw a black 1911 with gold filigree designs and ivory handles and instantly knew it was meant for Alex. She even found a cool shoulder rig for it. He might not use it but she figured he didn't have one and might get a kick out of it.

Cassidy came out from the back room where the entrance to the indoor range was. She was carrying a large RPK.

"Alma, check it out. It's full auto."

"Waste of ammo."

"I know, but it's pretty cool."

But then again, it could be good for stopping vehicles and perimeter defense.

"Bring it," Alma said.

Cass just smiled and hurried out to the Humvee with her prize.

Then she looked up at the FS2000 hanging on the wall. Like it or not, Lisa was here to stay. She had to deal with that. Maybe a peace offering would do some good.

She sighed and reached for the black, rounded bullpup rifle.

67

Rebekah

REBEKAH KEPT HER EYE ON THE BUILDINGS ACROSS THE STREET because she wasn't going to be caught relaxing on the job. Not a chance. This was her first time out with the big dogs and she wasn't going to ruin it by doing something stupid.

She wasn't no noob and she had to prove it.

The butt of her AK was tight against her shoulder and held down low, ready to spring up in case of trouble.

Alex had trained her on the M4, but it took too long to take apart and clean and all that so she switched over to the AK which took almost no time. She had better things to do than sit around cleaning all day.

After making sure her red dot sight was turned on to the right setting, she kept scanning the street in front of her. She was in an ally and kept her eyes moving.

Alma, Cassidy and Adam were inside grabbing what they could and throwing it into the back of the Humvee.

"See anything?" Derrick called out.

"Nothing."

This looked like it could have been a nice city, but now it was just another ghost town. Some of the buildings looked kinda old and some looked new and artsy. The streets were cracking and weeds were growing in the cracks. The abandoned cars had grass growing around the tires.

Just a block away she saw a Volvo wagon just like her dad used to have. That was one of the last memories she had of him. Her parents, her brother and her had driven down to Virginia Beach for vacation. She had spent hours in that Volvo wagon eating cheap fast food burgers and listening to her iPod so she wouldn't have to listen to Rob talking on and on about football practice.

She didn't care about football. Football players were meatheaded, book hating, dumb jocks. She had wanted to marry an artist, writer or poet. Someone who was smart but also creative and passionate.

Her requirements were very different now.

By the time their Volvo wagon got to Virginia Beach, whole cities were being quarantined. It had happened so suddenly. The day before all the news guys were saying that the reports of massive deaths were gross exaggerations by the liberal or conservative media. (It depended on who was talking.)

Mom and Dad had some audio book playing while they drove so all day they didn't hear a word about the news after that. She doubted that it would have made a difference.

They all died anyways and there was nothing she could have done to stop it.

"We'll be alright," Dad kept saying.

Liar.

She looked at the car through her sight and imagined shooting it to pieces.

Suddenly she saw something dart from behind the car into an ally.

"Hey! I saw something!" She yelled.

Derrick hurried over with his SCAR and silently looked around. She pointed to the car where she saw it.

"Could have been a cat or dog," he said and shrugged.

"It wasn't a cat or dog, moron. It was a person."

"What kind of person? Man? Woman?"

"I...I couldn't tell."

"What were they wearing?"

"I don't know."

"Obviously not an animal."

She flipped him off as he went back to his corner of the building.

The Star of David pendant beneath her body armor had shifted to her armpit. Seriously? So she reached in and straightened it back out.

As she did she saw the running figure again. It was definitely a man and he definitely had a rifle in his hands.

She quickly pulled her hand out and raised her rifle but the man was already behind a line of parked cars.

"I saw him again! It's a guy with a gun!"

This time Alma walked over. She was chewing on a Slim Jim.

"What's going on?" Alma asked.

"I saw a man with a gun. He's hiding behind those cars over there."

She pointed at the car with her gun.

"You sure?" Alma asked.

"Absolutely."

Alma nodded and squinted at the parked cars.

"Hey! We see you, *pendejo*!" Alma shouted out.

Alma's voice had a supernatural way of being ten times louder than it should be.

The man poked his head up and a second later the rifle came into view.

"Duck!" Alma said and tackled her to the ground as a shot rang out.

Rebekah heard the bullet impact on the brick wall behind where she had been.

"Cass! Get your scrawny butt out here!" Alma shouted.

Rebekah looked through her sight but didn't see anything. Where was he hiding?

At least she had been right. She saw the man first. That had to count for something.

Cassidy came out of the store and hid behind the Humvee. Alma told her where to look and Cass nodded. She crawled over to them and lay down next to Rebekah. She looked through the ACOG on her fancy, big gun.

"I see his feet," Cass said.

"Take him," Alma said.

Rebekah had just enough time to cover her ears before her Broadsword fired. She felt the concussion bounce around in her head.

A half second later she heard a man cry out.

"Got him," Cass said.

How did they get so good? She wouldn't have been able to make that shot in a hundred years.

"Hey! Psycho boy! You wanna talk nice now? We don't like getting shot at!" Alma shouted out.

Cursing was the shooter's only reply.

"Wish we had a grenade launcher or something," Cass said.

"Warmongering fascists!" Came the man's only intelligible reply.

"Warmonger....what?" Alma said.

"He called us warmongering fascists," Rebekah said.

"What the heck you talking about?" Alma yelled.

"You're looting guns to perpetuate the carcass of the military industrial complex! You just want to continue waging war on the unfortunates of the world!" The man called out from behind the car.

"Hold on, you have a gun! You shot at us first!" Alma shouted.

"I'm here to stop the new world from being poisoned by the old one! I'm going to stop the hatred and the killing by the elite!"

"But you wanted to kill us!"

"Stop talking to this goober," Rebekah said.

"Should I shoot him again?" Cass asked. "I can see where he's sitting. I'll hit his butt or shoot through the car and kill him."

"He might be a danger to other survivors," Rebekah said.

Alma looked at her.

"You say we should take him out? It's your call," Alma said.

Rebekah was about to answer but Cass interrupted her.

"Think about it. This is a man's life. Are you willing to take it?"

Rebekah paused and thought it through. Could she really be responsible for a man's life?

"Let's see what he does."

"Very well. Rebekah, wait here and watch. If he so much as looks up at us, shoot him," Alma said.

Alma and Cass got back up and continued loading the Humvee. She kept watch on the man. She could see where he was and if he tried to move to make another shot she'd shoot him right in the head.

She kind of hoped that he'd try to fight back. That would take the judgment out of her hands.

Rebekah didn't lose focus once and kept track of every little movement the weirdo made.

Once the Humvee was filled they mounted up and pulled away from the store.

"Adios hippie!" Alma shouted out one last time.

Then the man raised up and pointed his gun.

Cass was already prepared for it and aimed her rifle.

68

<u>Lisa</u>

LISA WALKED TO ALEX'S DOOR AND TRIED TO DISCERN IF HE WAS awake or not. Last night had been the best night of her life. Nothing else had ever compared. It wasn't just the kiss, her first one ever, it was what was behind the kiss.

Alex loved her.

Her trainers would deride her as acting like a little girl, but right now she didn't care what they'd say.

She gently knocked on the door.

"Hello?" Came Alex's voice.

"It's me."

"Come in."

She opened the door and peeked in. He was at his desk looking over maps and books of some kind. She walked over and stood behind him.

"Homework?" She asked.

"Just trying to decide the best way to expand. We need to divide our people up even more, one family unit per house." Then he turned around and faced her. "But I suddenly find myself very distracted."

She couldn't help but smile.

"You should focus your mind to free yourself of distractions."

"I don't want to be."

He reached an arm around her hip and pulled her in. She wasn't used to it but she liked it and let herself be drawn in. She sat on his lap and she looked into his eyes before kissing him.

She had never guessed how pleasurable a kiss could be. She didn't want to do anything else.

Alex was very bad for her inner calm.

"I think the others had fun last night," he said.

"I believe so. Good food."

"Good company."

"Very good company."

She still couldn't believe it all.

"Hungry?" He asked.

"Yes."

He took her by the hand and they went downstairs. When Jen saw them she tried to conceal her smile but failed miserably.

"Looky what we have here," Jen said.

"Go ahead and get your fun out of the way," Alex said.

"It's about time, you two. I was wondering when you'd stop all this nonsense and just get to it," Jen said.

Lisa felt her cheeks redden but didn't feel ashamed. Not ashamed of this. Never.

"I make you breakfast," Lisa said.

She sat him down and went to the pantry. She was very tired of Spam and found some cheese and peppers instead. So she made them omelets with apple juice and toast.

They ate in silence. They didn't have to fill the space with empty words. She knew what he thought and he knew what she thought. Words were sometimes a waste of time.

Adam rushed into the house, banging the front door open. He held his rifle in his hands.

"Over here," Alex said.

Adam hurried into the kitchen.

"Got a truck coming our way. Black SVU," Adam said.

"Just the one?"

"No sign of anything else."

"Perfect."

Without saying anything they both rushed up to their rooms, threw on their gear and came back downstairs with their weapons and ammo. This time she carried her AK-SU. The short AK was small and handy and she liked it for close-in situations.

The SVU was coming around the bend in the woods by the time they made it out onto the porch.

"We got overwatch?" Alex asked.

"Yeah, Sam's up in the attic with is .338," Adam said.

Alex nodded.

Lisa readied herself and got her mind focused again. She made sure her red dot was on and checked the safety.

The shiny black SVU pulled up into their "town square" and came to a halt. All four doors slowly opened and men in khakis, bullet proof vests and M4's stepped out. They had American flag patches on their chests and shoulders.

They looked like mercenaries or special forces of some kind. She'd seen the type before. They had beards and dark sunglasses.

Her grip on her AK-SU tightened.

"Who's in charge here?" One of the men asked.

"Who are you?" Alex asked.

She wished he had let someone else do the talking. She did not trust these men.

"We are representatives of the Provisional Government of the United States," the man said.

These men were ruining her good morning. She just wanted to bask in Alex's glow and here these men were. Her inner calm was almost non-existent.

"What do you want?" Alex asked.

"We are here to make an assessment of your personal, supplies and situation," the man said.

"We don't accept solicitors. Kindly leave," Alex said.

The man laughed.

"Do you know someone named Alma Attaway?" the man asked.

She noticed from the corner of her eye that Alex froze. It probably wasn't noticeable to anyone but her.

"Maybe," Alex said.

"We're looking for a fugitive calling himself David Ganges. He claims to be following a woman named Alma. If you see either of them, please let us know. Here's our contact information."

He held out a card that neither she nor Alex reached for.

"Very well. You said your message, now leave."

"Sir, we're official representatives of the United States Government."

"The United States Government doesn't exist. Whatever pieces of paper or cute badges you have don't mean anything anymore."

Lisa was having a hard time understanding this. Yes, she understood these men in suits' point of view, but she also understood Alex's view. Before she would have thought Alex was being destructively selfish. But now she understood it. Her teachers back in China were rolling in their graves or coming out of them as hopping ghosts to seek revenge on her.

"The government is reforming at Ft. Knox, Kentucky. We have the Secretary of Finance and two senators. By the rules of succession –"

"I don't care."

"Pardon?"

"I don't care. You have a few old guys in suits that are probably hiding in a bunker somewhere. They don't mean crap to us."

She knew Alex but was still shocked at this disrespect to authority. She steeled her face and kept it professional.

"We have to work together, share resources and bring our country out of this crisis."

"You're not rolling in here, taking what you want and telling us what to do. Lisa?"

Lisa snapped her AK-SU and put the sights on the man's forehead.

The man didn't flinch.

"I don't recommend this course of action," the man said.

"Good day," Alex said and turned to walk back inside.

She didn't budge but kept her AK trained on the man.

"We'll be back," the man said under his breath.

"I wouldn't recommend it," Lisa said.

She didn't lower her gun until the SUV was out of site.

Alex came back out to the porch.

"When will Alma be back?" Lisa asked.

"Tonight."

"Think they were lying?"

"No."

"I meant about being from the government."

"It doesn't matter. They have no power and all they want to do is take. We're starting over." He looked out at the woods. "I hope Alma gets back soon."

"We're going to need her trigger finger."

That was the only part of Alma that she did like.

69

Alma

THEIR CONVOY PULLED UP TO THE "TOWN SQUARE" OF PROMISED Land and Alma dismounted: glad to finally be off that horse. She wasn't meant to be a cowboy like Cass was. She looked like she was born in the saddle.

Chris came jogging out the door and helped Cass off of her horse. That wasn't necessary. Cass was quite capable of getting off a horse all by herself.

Alma led her horse to the stable where they took it from her and led it to a stall. She was glad they had enough people to work in the stable because after a two day patrol, she just wanted to lay down.

"Where's Alex?" Alma asked the freckled stableboy.

"Not sure. Think he's out on patrol or at the training grounds."

"Figures. He's doing my job while I'm out. He needs to learn to relax."

She looked over and saw Cass and her man kissing.

Sure, the apocalypse happened, but what kind of world was this where Cass got a boyfriend first?

Alma wondered what it was like to have a boyfriend. All her life she had put those kind of things to the side. She had spent her life training to be the best. Granted, it turned out extremely useful, but she wondered if the cost had been too high.

Maybe she should have had more fun. There certainly wasn't a lot of opportunity for fun nowadays. Work, work, work. Or more like, survival, survival, survival.

"Hey, don't unsaddle her just yet," Alma said to the two boys working the stable.

She needed time to just be by herself for a while.

Alma saddled up and rode out, heading toward Lexington. If she was going to wander around and think, she might as well do some scavenging.

"Where you going?" Cass called out.

"I'm going for a ride."

"You shouldn't go out alone!"

"I know."

She ignored them and continued down the road and across the bridge. VMI loomed over her as it sat on top its rocky hill. It was a fortress in a well protected area. They'd have to preserve it in case they'd ever have to use it. Just because the Hunt Club was gone didn't mean they were completely safe.

The sun was getting low and she judged that she had about two good hours of light left.

There were a few places she wanted to check out back in Buena Vista, so she spurred her horse and picked up the pace.

Lexington had been searched for the most part, but Buena Vista was bound to have some more useful stuff.

It was foolish to run off by herself. She knew it was, but she had to do it anyways. Being constantly surrounded by people grated on her nerves.

The red towers of Southern Virginia's main building loomed over the trees as she rode parallel by the river and entered the town. The paper mill marked the real start of the town and she wondered if they'd be able to get it up and running again. It would be nice to have an inexhaustible supply of paper again.

Alex would probably like to write a book. She'd bring it up with him when she got back...after he was done yelling at her for going off on her own.

Books. That would soften Alex's inevitable chewing out. So, she rode up the hill towards SVU's library. She'd get him a nice history book.

In the orange light of dusk the Main Hall of SVU looked downright ominous. The bright red now looked like blood and all the overhangs and porches created dark, impenetrable shadows.

Maybe she should have taken Rebekah. She would have jumped at the chance.

Alma tied her horse to a tree beside the library and walked in.

The whole campus was covered and surrounded by old buildings: buildings that needed maintenance or they wouldn't last much longer. Already the Main Hall was in bad shape and didn't have much time life. A few years at most.

She doubted that they'd be able to spare the manpower to keep it up. Looking around the school reminded her of all the things they'd lost. She'd never see Times Square again. She'd never see London or Venice. It was all gone.

Alma turned on her flashlight and began looking around for the history section. Sure, libraries had some kind of code system that would tell her right where to find things, but she had never been able to make sense of it. Maybe librarians did that on purpose so they could keep their job necessary.

Fortunately it wasn't a huge library like Washington and Lee and she found the history section in a few minutes.

There was a book about the Napoleonic wars, the Civil War and the Fourth Crusade. She began to put the Fourth Crusade one back, but then stuffed it into her backpack along with the other two. He preferred more modern stuff. He could stand to learn something a bit older now and then.

She was about to keep looking when she heard the library's front door open. She turned the flashlight off and whipped out her Glock. She paused and listened before she crept to the front.

The wooden door was swaying in the breeze. She must not have secured it tight enough. She went over and closed it again, making sure the lock caught.

Alma holstered her pistol and walked back to the history section.

Then she heard some movement, like the scuff of a shoe.

Someone was there.

Unslinging her AR, she crept through the shelves of books. It could be just noise from an old building but she wasn't going to take the risk.

Suddenly something flashed out of the dark and knocked the rifle out of her hands. A red crowbar with chipped paint. Funny how she'd notice such useless details.

Before she could draw her pistol someone crashed into her, knocking her to the ground. Whoever it was, was on top of her and struggling to pin her arms. If she let that happen it would be over.

Whoever this guy was, he was hairy and filthy and smelled like a dead skunk. The stench stung her nostrils with the worst case of B.O. she'd ever encountered.

Then something else flashed in the fading light. Alma saw it a moment too late.

The man's knife stabbed into her side sending a shock of the worst pain she had ever felt.

She gasped out and punched the man in the face. She had hit him hard but he barely moved.

"I finally caught up with you girly," he said.

As punctuation he twisted the knife. She screamed and for a second all she could do was clench her fist and arch her back.

Alma tried to kick him off but couldn't get her legs in position. He was sitting on her stomach and holding the knife with one hand while holding one of her arms with the other.

She tried but couldn't reach the Glock on her right hip with her left hand.

"Thought you could get away from me. I followed you across the whole country."

Then she recognized him. He was the freak from Nevada.

"Get off me you pervert!"

"I was alone for a year and when I finally see another human being, she tosses me aside like a used diaper!"

"Because you're crazy and smell bad."

She tried to move her foot up. Tucked in her boot was a tiny Glock 30. If she could reach it she could blow this madman away.

"I won't kill you quickly. I'm going to stab many times and watch the life drain from your whore face."

She had to keep him talking.

"How'd you even find me?"

"The people of Salt Lake and Colorado were very helpful. Then when I got to Virginia I saw your little fliers telling me right where to find you."

He smiled, showing rotted teeth.

"I'm going to kill you. I hope you know that, right?" Alma said.

"Of course."

Then in one swift motion he yanked the knife free and stabbed her again. This time the blade of what looked like a kitchen knife sunk deep into the spot just below the collar bone.

She felt herself cry out but didn't hear it.

When the crazy withdrew the knife it was covered in thick blood. A lot of it. His hands were covered in the splatter.

She could see the maniacal intensity in his eyes. His face was twisted up in the middle and all she saw were his yellow teeth and yellow eyes.

She couldn't get to the pistol. But she did have a knife in her boot. She grabbed that but found her hand too weak to do much with it. Her fingers barely gripped the handle. The wound to her shoulder didn't hurt, yet, but it was having its effect.

Her left hand was pinned far out to the side. She'd never get the knife to it. She had to use her weak hand. She took a few deep breaths and then with whatever strength she had in that arm, she stabbed upward.

She didn't let go and the blade slide halfway into his side near his kidney.

He screamed out like a child and fell off of her.

Alma scrambled out from under him and got to her feet. Her head was swimming and she had to brace herself on the nearby bookcase.

Without waiting she reached over to her right side with her left hand and grabbed the gun. As the man struggled to pull the knife out, she shot him square in the chest. For a brief moment the muzzle flash illuminated the filthy madman. He was wearing a ragged t-shirt that was covered in several layers of stains.

The man was bleeding all over the place. He was gasping for air and trying to stop the blood flow. He had a punctured lung and she could hear the wheezing of the hole.

An unintelligible stream of curses poured out of her mouth as she shot the man several more times until he stopped moving.

Then the dizziness overcame her and she found herself suddenly on the ground. She was losing a lot of blood which decreased her blood pressure and would cause her to pass out.

Strange how she could be so analytical about it. She had read all about it in case there was ever an accident at the range. But now she was living it.

She had to stop the blood flow. At least she remembered that.

Her pack was over by the history section and had a first aid kit.

The ground was slick with her own blood and she had trouble getting traction.

This was bad.

How did this crap happen? Some psycho followed her from Nevada? It seemed almost freaking poetic.

Alma looked down and saw a lake of blood. It was everywhere and she was covered in it.

All that came out of her? No, some had to be from psycho.

She crawled to her pack and opened the first aid kit on the side. She would thank Alex for insisted the first aid kits be on the outside instead of buried somewhere in the pack.

The blood was still coming out and unless she did something quick she would die.

The thought of death tightened her chest so she couldn't breathe. She was too young to die. She had too many things she wanted to do.

She had to kiss a guy, fall in love, see Alex again.

She couldn't die alone. That was too pathetic. Where were her parents? Weren't they supposed to be here to help her? Wasn't that a parent's job. They had abandoned her to this hellish world. They just left her here alone. She swore at them but it came out as pain filled grunts.

She really wished Mom was there. She'd take care of this. Where was she? There was an awful lot of blood.

70

<u>Alex</u>

ALEX PACED BACK AND FORTH AND WATCHED THE SUN GO DOWN over the trees.

"She's only been gone for a few hours. She'll be back," Cass said.

"It's getting dark," he said.

"She's ridden in the dark before," Cass said, but this time he saw the worry on her face as well.

Lisa stood up from her chair across the fireplace and checked her pistol.

"You're worried? Then let's move," Lisa said.

He took a deep breath and stood up.

"Cass, go grab one or two more people for our search party," he said.

"Right."

She jumped up off the couch and dragged her limping boyfriend with her.

"She can take care of herself," Lisa said.

"I know, but this feels different."

She put a hand on his cheek and looked at him. Her eyes showed calmness and reason.

"You say we go look for her; we go look for her," she said.

He kissed her hand and she closed her eyes as he did so. She smiled. It was the smile she reserved just for him.

Then they went to their separate rooms. He knew that would change eventually, but not when. So far all they had done was kiss. That was no small thing though. A kiss with her was better than a thousand kisses from any other woman. Hers meant something. Each kiss was a flood of meaning and love.

As he strapped on his IBA body armor Adam ran into his room.

"Dude, there are three SUV's heading down the road toward us."

The Provisional Government of the United States. They said they'd be back but he didn't think this soon. This was not what he needed right now. Alma was out there alone and now he had these idiots rolling up on him.

"Go grab everyone. Tell them to bring their guns and get ready for a fight. And I mean everyone."

Adam nodded and bolted off.

He grabbed his M-14. It had more punch in case these jackwagons got cute and were wearing armor.

Lisa was in the hall with a PSL of all things.

"Armor piercing rounds," she said when she noticed him eyeing it.

"I didn't say anything."

"You looked."

"The PSL is a fine weapon. Just sort of heavy, inaccurate and clumsy."

"You'll see."

When she turned to go down the stairs he saw that she also had her AK-SU slung on her back and a Sig on her hip.

She was ready for anything and that was one of the many reasons he loved her.

By the time he got to the living room he could see the headlights of the SUV's pulling up into Town Square.

"Everyone, go to a window and pick your targets. Don't shoot unless I give an order or they start shooting. Understood? Pass it along."

He went to the door and Lisa got on the other side. He opened it and peeked out.

Men were getting out of the trucks. They looked almost like mercenaries but they were too clean cut. Amazing how clean they looked considering a year and a half of apocalypse. Maybe they really did have a bunker.

It didn't matter. They were here to take what they wanted and take control. Neither of those would happen.

"We came to talk," a man in a white shirt and black bullet proof vest said.

The sun was almost down and the sky was a navy blue. The "government" men were becoming little more than silhouettes in the growing dark.

Some of the men were putting on night vision goggles.

"They didn't come to talk," Lisa said.

"I gathered."

To the right of the town square he could see his people moving into position. They were hiding beside and inside the barn, behind vehicles and behind trees. They outnumbered the government men a good five to one, but most of his people weren't properly trained and these guys looked like professional killers.

"Be reasonable, Mr. Attaway. We're on your side. You're hoarding resources and skilled people that we all need to put this country back on its feet."

"We barely have enough for ourselves," he shouted through the cracked door.

"That's what they all say. You'll have to learn to ration a little better but it's better than having some others starve."

"Maybe you're with the government and maybe you're not. It doesn't matter because you have no authority here. We're taking care of ourselves and don't need your help."

The white shirted man shook his head.

Cassidy came up beside him and scrunched up her face as she peeked out the crack.

"I count fifteen," Cass said.

"Fifteen men that know what they're doing. Maybe if we had a AT-4 or something."

Then Cass perked up.

"Hold on here and don't do anything crazy until I get back!"

Cass then ran upstairs without further explanation. He looked to her boyfriend who gave a confused shrug.

"Let's break it down, Mr. Attaway," the white shirted man said. "Yes, you have more men than us. Yes, you have more guns at the moment. But don't think for a second that a fight with us will go well for you. Let me play devil's advocate and assume you somehow win in a gun battle with us, which I assure you, will not happen. Even if you win, you'll still lose people. People close to you will die. That little Chinese girl might get a bullet to the chest. Then who'll keep your bed warm?"

He saw Lisa tense up but she kept her cool.

"You want to risk that, Mr. Attaway? You want to risk your pretty house getting full of holes? Do as we say and nobody will be hurt. You'll have plenty of food to last the winter."

"And we'll have to live under your rule, right?"

"Under the U.S. government. Besides, we'll leave you alone mostly. It'll be like old times."

Then Cass came running back downstairs with an M4 with a 203 grenade launcher on it.

"Where'd you get that?" Alex asked.

"Thought it might come in useful."

Then he remembered that he had one as well.

"Hold on and let me talk to my people," he called out.

Then he dashed upstairs and grabbed his 203. He loaded it, snatched the bandolier of grenades and hurried back downstairs.

Adam came up to him with his shotgun ready.

"We're not listening to these fools, are we?" Adam asked.

"Hell no. This is what we're going to do. Me and Cass will fire the grenades at the same time. Then I want everyone else to open up. Don't spare anyone. If one gets away, he'll go back and tell his bosses."

They passed the word around and then they all got into position. Cass took the window right of the door and he took left.

"I'll take the rear truck and you take the front one. On the count of three," he said.

Cass nodded. He looked around to make sure everyone else was ready. Hopefully his people near the barn would know what to do.

"You have five minutes," White Shirt said.

"Three...two...one."

They fired at the same time. The "blooop" of the grenade launcher pushed his shoulder and his grenade sailed in a lazy arc toward the last black SUV.

Both trucks erupted in explosions that were as sudden as they were brutal. The trucks they were using for cover became flying shards of shrapnel death. Most were knocked over, either dead or wounded. The few near the middle that managed to stay upright quickly took cover as bullets began to pour down on their position.

Lisa fired the PSL and one of the armored men jerked back and fell to the ground. More bullets tore through the SUV's and hit the men hiding behind them. A few managed to fire back but with so many bullets flying toward them, they didn't last long.

Alex put down the M4 and picked up his M-14. It was dark out and he had a hard time seeing any distinct target.

He heard the remaining SUV's doors slam close and before he realized it, the black four door was peeling out in a cloud of dust. He took aim but his red dot was still set to a day time setting and was far too bright. All he could see was the glaring red light. He fired at where he guessed was the truck.

The others must have been having trouble picking targets as well because the truck tore out of there with a few bullets pinging its side.

Them getting away was not a good thing.

"How many?" He asked.

"Two, maybe three," Lisa said.

"I think we just declared war," he said.

"Wouldn't be the first time," Lisa said as she rested the butt of the PSL on her hip and raised the muzzle to the ceiling.

As much as a war with a fake U.S. government worried him, the thought of Alma out there in danger worried him more. Now his search party will have to stay in larger groups and go slower to watch out for vengeful PGUSA men.

A delay was not something he wanted right now.

71

Alma

ALMA LAY ON THE FLOOR OF THE LIBRARY IN A GROWING PUDDLE of her own blood. Her hands and arms were covered in the sticky stuff that in the darkness reminded her of maple syrup.

She was no medical expert but she knew this was bad. Really bad.

Now she was feeling light headed and the pain was fading away to a dull roar in the back of her mind.

She felt like laughing for some reason.

It was kind of funny in a pathetic, wasteful sort of way. She had traveled through a destroyed United States all the way from Nevada to Virginia to find a brother that mathematically should have been dead a thousand times over. She fought *cholos* in Salt Lake, FEMA troops in Colorado and fascist survivalists in the Shenandoah.

And then she ended up getting shanked by some lone freak who followed her across country.

What was the point?

Really, what was the point of anything? God had decided to end the world and now all he had to do was mop up the few stragglers. Why do anything with everything you do God takes as a joke? He was up in heaven looking down on her and laughing.

Of course she hadn't told anyone where she was going. That would have been the responsible, level headed thing to do. Alex always said her impetuousness would get her into trouble. She didn't know 'trouble' was a shank in a dark library.

She took a deep breath and tried to get up into a crawling position. There was a first aid kit on her saddle.

Her legs felt like jelly and she could barely get them under her.

But then her feet slipped in her own blood and she fell on her face. She would have screamed out curses if she had had the strength.

Then she heard the library door open. She looked around for her gun but it was gone in the darkness somewhere.

It didn't matter. She was done. She was going to die here in this stupid place. Damn. She was still a virgin. That sucked. Maybe that'd give her a few bonus points in heaven: make up for all her cursing.

A dark figure came around the corner and looked down at her. A second later a painfully bright light blinded her and she turned away.

Then the light swooped right down on top of her and a face appeared. It was a man's face she didn't recognize. He was large with a shaved head and wore a serious expression. He had a tac-vest covered in pouches and had a scar running down the side of his face.

"Hold still," he said in a deep voice.

"No problem. I'll be still enough pretty soon."

"Shut up and lay down."

A hand pushed her head down. Normally she wouldn't stand for that kind of crap but once her head was down she didn't have the strength to raise it. She felt him doing something down there, like he was massaging her side where she got stabbed. She heard some ripping cloth and then her mid section was lifted off the ground.

Maybe it just didn't matter what this stranger was doing. At least she got the guy that killed her.

"At least I killed the guy that got me," she said.

"I said shut up. Save your energy and don't move."

Something tightened up around her waist like an uncomfortable belt and a sharp pain shot through her side.

The man's face came into view.

"I'm going to put an I.V. into you, okay? Don't move."

"I won't."

He didn't have to worry about that.

She barely felt the needle. He placed the bag on a nearby shelf propped between books.

"Stay still and you'll be alright," the man said.

That's what they always said when there was a big problem.

"What's your name?" He asked.

"Alma Attaway."

"You live near here?"

"Out by Lexington, behind the Walmart on the other side of the river."

"How far is that?"

"I don't know, man. Two hours by horse?"

"Okay. I patched you best I could for now. Once the bleeding stops I'll try to sew you up. I won't lie. It looks bad but you can live."

He said it all in a calm, level tone.

"Who are you?" She asked.

"I'm Jason."

She remembered him saying other things but it all faded out into total darkness.

• • • •

When she opened her eyes next, bright sunlight poured through the dusty, library windows. The big man from the library was sitting down beside her on the floor and was leaning up against a book case. Looked like he fell asleep watching over her.

Alma looked down and saw that her clothes were covered in dark brown blood. She pulled up her shirt and saw several layers of bandages covering her midsection and chest.

It hurt but she was alive. She tried to sit up but sharp pain from her wound shot through her like electricity and she had to snap her mouth shut to keep from crying out.

Jason had a huge gun in his lap, a SAIGA 12 gauge with a EOT Tech holo sight, quad rails, drum and foregrip. It was a beast of a weapon. Well, at least her mind was clear again.

"Hey, big guy," she said.

What was his name again?

The man's head jerked up and he was instantly alert.

"You're still alive," he said.

"I'll thank you if I live. How long was I out?"

He checked his watch.

"Eight hours. I was expecting more."

"I'm full of surprises."

He looked at her bandages and checked her IV. Everything he did he did with precise, well practiced moves.

"I don't have anymore IV's." He dug through his backpack. "I have salt crackers and canned chili. You need to eat this."

"Sure thing."

He opened the can for her with some kind of survivalist multi tool that happened to have a can opener.

She wasn't hungry but started eating anyway.

What was his name? Jack? Johnson? No... Then she remembered it.

"Where you from, Jason?"

"Does it matter anymore?"

"Still does."

"Baltimore. Joined the Marines eight years ago and haven't been back."

"Why?"

"It was always a graveyard, but now it's actually full of dead people."

"Not a fan, huh?"

"No, not really. What are you doing out here alone?"

"Pretty stupid of me, huh?"

"Very."

Jackass. He didn't have to agree in such a hurry.

"Don't you ever just want to be by yourself?" She asked.

"Not lately. You're the first living person I've seen that hasn't tried to kill me long enough to hold a conversation."

"Where have you been?"

"I was up in New York when it all went down."

"Fighting?"

"No, serving ice cream."

Yes, this guy was a jackass.

Before the news stopped she had heard the fighting in New York was terrible.

"Can you draw me a map to your friends and then I'll need to know the best way to not get shot when I approach them."

He handed her a pad and pen and she drew a rough map of where they were.

"Just approach with your hands up in the air."

"Right. I'm going to go find them. Finish eating. I left some water right there and your gun."

"I'll just stay here then," she said.

He didn't even smile.

Jason stood up and lifted his pack to his shoulders. He paused and looked down at her.

"You'll be fine," he said but the tone of his voice told her that she wasn't as "fine" as she needed to be.

And then like that, he was gone out the library door and she was alone.

72

ALEX THREW EVERYTHING INTO THE BACK OF THE TRUCK AND looked around for Lisa. He had food, medical supplies and ammo. Alma was out there when enemies were around and he was going to find her. They had enough natural gas for their converted truck to get them to Roanoke and back if they needed to.

It had taken all night to clean the mess from the battle and secure the surrounding area to make sure there weren't anymore of them. The whole time he kept thinking about where Alma was.

He had a bad feeling and he had learned not to ignore his gut.

Adam was organizing home defense and Jen was moving the children into the house. They knew what to do so he didn't have to babysit them. He had to go look for her. She drove across the United States to find him, after all.

Lisa came running out of the house with her FS2000 and a portable spotlight. It was dark out there and there were a lot of places to hide.

"I think we're ready," Lisa said.

"Alright, let's go."

Without further discussion they jumped in the truck and started it up. It didn't have the horse power it used to have when it ran on gas, but it worked.

He pulled out of Promised Land and stopped at the highway in front of Walmart. To the left went off into the country with scattered rich people's houses and a truckstop. To the right was Lexington and Buena Vista.

Alex hadn't slept and the sun was coming up. Something had to be wrong if she was gone all night. She would not willingly make him worry like this.

"VMI," Lisa said.

He agreed and drove up the steep hill to the top where the VMI barracks and main campus were. He didn't see Alma's horse or any sign of a disturbance. Still, he had to check.

They got out and shouted out for Alma. After a half hour of searching they moved on to Washington and Lee University next door and searched all through those buildings.

"Now Lexington," Lisa said.

She was thinking logically and clearly. He wasn't. She led him block by block, shouting out her name and checking inside the windows of each building. If it were him he'd just run through the town in a frantic dash.

As he was looking through the glass doors of a movie theater he heard the distant sound of a whining engine. Lisa looked up as she heard it as well.

Their truck was parked two blocks away. Whoever was coming would see it. No chance in hiding that but they could still set up an ambush. The sun was now fully up so whoever it was, he'd be able to asses any potential trouble.

They took positions behind the corners of buildings on opposite sides of the building. He watched Lisa take her position and give him a thumbs up.

She was gorgeous. She was more than he ever deserved in a woman.

Then a single light came into view. It was coming from the direction of Buena Vista. It came up over the hill and stopped. It must have seen their truck. It was a man on a yellow dirt bike. A large man with a large gun strapped across his back.

The rider then started back up, riding slow down the street toward the truck. This man might know something about Alma but just because he wasn't in an SUV didn't mean he wasn't with the "Provisional Government of the United States."

If whoever this was caused a problem, he'd just shoot him and hurry on with finding Alma.

Across the street, Lisa shouldered her FS and readied herself.

As the rider came closer Alex stepped out and aimed his M-14.

"Don't come any closer," Alex called out.

The dirt bike came to a slow stop and the man put his hands in the air without rushing.

"I'm looking for a man named Alex," the man called back in a deep voice.

"You're speaking with him. You better make this quick."

"You have a sister named Alma?"

His chest tightened and suddenly he couldn't breathe. He knew something bad had happened or this stranger wouldn't be here. Every horrible scenario played out in his head.

"Yes," he managed to get out.

"I found her in a town down the road. She's hurt and needs a doctor."

Almost all his worst fears were coming true. But she was alive at least.

"How badly?" Lisa called out when he didn't say anything.

"She was stabbed. Lost a lot of blood. We need to hurry."

Lisa ran across the street to him and whispered.

"I hate to say this, but this could be a trap," Lisa said.

"Right now, I don't care. I'm going."

Lisa opened her mouth to say something but quickly closed it and nodded. That meant she was coming with him.

Alex approached the man. He was large and looked like he could hunt bears with his hands. And it was all muscle. He had a shaved head, a pistol on his thigh and a rifle strapped to his back.

"Where is she?" Alex asked.

"A library in Buena Vista."

"What happened?"

"She was stabbed. She shot the guy but she's hurt. We need to hurry."

Lisa ran back and brought the truck up.

"We'll follow you," Alex said.

"If you're less than honest with us, I'll shoot you first," Lisa said.

"Of course," the man said.

They followed the large man on the dirt bike back to Buena Vista and up the hill to Southern Virginia University. The whole time he kept wanting the man to drive faster.

When they pulled up to the library he threw the truck into park and jumped out. He ran up the stairs and into the library.

Lying in the middle of the floor was Alma. There was blood everywhere. She was lying on her back with her hands over a mass of tightly bound bandages on her belly.

She looked over and relief spread across her face.

Alex ran over and kneeled down.

"You alright?" He asked.

"No, idiot. I've been stabbed by a psycho."

Her voice was shaky and weak.

"How bad?"

"Pretty bad."

Then Lisa came in behind the large man. She had her pistol drawn on him.

"Its okay, Lisa. He helped me," Alma said.

Lisa frowned but holstered the pistol.

With the stranger's help they got Alma into the rear seat of the truck.

They threw the dirt bike and the man's backpack into the bed of the truck and tore asphalt back home.

They got the doc, a former male nurse, and they got to working on Alma right away. A blood transfusion was needed and they didn't waste time in asking Alex. They weren't related but he did have the same blood type.

As he sat there with a tube in his arm he saw the large man come in. He carried a 12-guage AK-47 on his back but it looked like a small carbine to him.

"How is she?" The man asked.

"She'll make it," Alex said.

"She don't look like your sister."

"Step sister. I want to thank you."

The man shrugged.

"Just helping out," he said.

"What's your name?" Alex asked.

"Jason."

"Well, Jason, I owe you. You may stay here as long as you want. If you do leave, take whatever you can carry with you."

Jason nodded but didn't say anything. Alex could tell that his mind was churning. Whoever this man was, he saved Alma and that was a debt he could never repay.

73

Lisa

LISA WATCHED AS ALEX SUFFERED. HE PACED AROUND THE HALL as the doctor continued to work on Alma. It was a blood transfusion and Alma was mostly out of danger, but still Alex worried.

She wondered if he'd worry like that for her. Or did Alma hold more of his heart than she ever could?

Lisa shook her head and cleared away those thoughts. Of course Alex loved her. There were different kinds of love. At least that's what she had heard. She had never had a family like that so didn't understand how it felt.

"Hungry?" She asked.

They had skipped breakfast hours ago and it was time for lunch now.

Alex just shook his head.

She didn't know what to say. What would normal people say in a situation like this? All her life she had been taught that death was just a part of the job. It was inevitable. The few people she had known that died she hadn't known well enough to mourn.

Lisa, unable to come up with anything to say or do to help Alex, went downstairs to the kitchen.

The large man, Jason was sitting at the table talking to Jen. Jen looked over her shoulder to her.

"You hungry, dear?" Jen asked.

Lisa nodded.

"All the kitchen help are out guarding against those Provisional Fascists. It's just me today," Jen said as she got up.

Jen fixed her an egg sandwich and let her have the seat at the small table across from Jason. Jen excused herself to go off and find her helpers.

She took a bite and knew she had to say something to the stranger. The man saved the life of Alex's sister. Someone needed to thank him.

"Thank you for helping Alma," Lisa said.

The man just shrugged.

"Where are you from?" Lisa asked.

"I'm from nowhere."

Either he was being secretive or obtrusive. She didn't like either choice.

"Where's that?" She asked.

"All over."

Lisa looked the man up and down. He wore all his gear as if he knew what to do with it. Everything was in the right places, tightened or loosened in the right places and the way he moved was with controlled power. This man was a dangerous person.

"You from Kentucky?" She asked.

"I'm not from the Provisional Government. I passed through and saw how they rolled. Didn't want any part of it so kept riding."

"And how do you roll?"

As she asked her hand slipped down to the butt of her Beretta. It was habit.

His eyes went down to where her hand would be.

"I'm not a threat," he said.

"You are."

"And so are you. Do they know what you are?"

He had read her better than she had read him.

"Some of them do," she said. By "some," she meant Alex.

"And if they find out?"

"I don't imagine it would go well for me."

"I fought people like you."

"Women?"

"Chinese operators."

She knew she was scowling but no longer cared. This man saw through her.

"Are we going to have a problem with that?" She asked.

"Not from me. But are we going to have a problem down the road?"

"I'm trapped here. Same as everyone. This is my home. This is my family."

"You're hardly the same as everyone. Neither of us should pretend that."

"A few months ago I might have agreed."

She took a moment to look him over. He was definitely trained by the best. She saw the calluses and scars on his hands from training and putting that training to use. The only question was, who was he? Ranger? Force Recon? Green Berrets? Delta?

"Army?" She asked.

"Used to be. Rangers."

"And then?"

"Black Thorn."

He was a mercenary. That explained it. He was former special forces and then went to the private sector. Chances were, he saw much more action as a mercenary than a soldier.

"Jason, I have a new life here. I love Alex and they are my family. Alma is my family. If you do anything to damage my life..."

"Relax, I'm not going to do anything. I don't care where you're from. That war's over."

"What are your plans?"

"I was looking for someplace quiet that could use an individual with my talents."

"We're going to have problems with this Provisional Government."

"I've met them before. They didn't like what I had to say."

"Are you willing to talk to them again?"

"If I can have food, shelter and polite society, I'll talk to anyone."

He patted the giant AK shotgun in his lap.

Lisa nodded. She didn't trust him and she knew mercenaries were greedy. If he tried to blackmail her down the road, she'd shoot him in the head.

But the truth was, they needed every fighter they could get. If this Provisional Government had the resources they suspected they did, then they could definitely use Jason's help.

"As Alex said, you're welcome to stay. In fact, we'd like it if you did."

Jason nodded and took a drink of coffee.

"I think I'd like that as well," he said.

Lisa then grabbed an apple and went back upstairs. She handed the apple to Alex.

"Eat it," she said.

Without thinking he took a bite.

"She's going to be okay," Lisa said.

"So they say."

Not knowing what else to do she put her hand on his shoulder. It felt awkward until he took her hand in his and pulled her in for an embrace. There was nothing she loved better than being close to him.

"I don't know what I'd do if I lost you," he said.

She smiled and rested her head on his shoulder.

"Don't think about that," she said.

Then she reached up and kissed him. They kissed for a long while. When she would normally stop and break away, she didn't. She didn't want to.

Then he picked her up and held her in his arms. Her legs dangled out to the side but she felt comfortable as he cradled her.

"I love you," he said.

"Will you always be there for me?" She asked.

"Always."

He then carried her to his room and her heart pounded through her chest as he did. She wanted this more than she had ever realized. Alex wasn't just someone she loved or someone that she helped. He was her partner: her other half. And after the door closed she was going to share everything she had with him.

74

Alma

ALMA WOKE UP IN HER BED WITH THE SUN COMING THROUGH closed curtains. There was no telling how long she'd been out. She wasn't certain but it felt like a long time. She had foggy memories of coming in and out of consciousness.

When she tried to sit up pain shot through her midsection, but it was bearable. She sat up and swung her legs to the side of the bed and looked down at the bandages on her side. She was wearing a sports bra and boxer shorts.

She really hoped Cass had changed her and not one of the guys. Especially not Alex. That would have been extremely awkward.

She saw a pair of fuzzy slippers (not hers) but didn't see a robe or any other clothes within arms reach.

After painfully standing up, she shuffled to her closet and rummaged through her things. Most of it was cargo pants and t-shirts. She didn't want anything as tight as a t-shirt so she found an AC-DC hoodie and slipped it on and then a loose, cotton dress over sweatpants. Then, for added style points she pulled Cass's Voltron blanket over her shoulders. The mornings were cold.

She wasn't out to win any awards. She wanted comfort and warmth.

And food.

She was starving.

Alma made her way down the stairs one step at a time. Each step caused fire to burn through her abdomen.

Where the hell was everyone?

"Hello?" She called out in a voice that sounded weaker than she would've liked.

When no one answered she continued her descent, swearing with each step.

No one was downstairs but she heard people talking outside. She stumbled to the front door and opened it.

The "Town Square" was full of vehicles and armed people going around. She didn't see Cass, Alex or Lisa anywhere. But she did see Rebekah standing on the porch with her arms folded and a Remmington 700 slung across her back.

"Rebekah, what's going on?" Alma said.

Rebekah turned around and gave her a wide eyed, huge smile.

"You're awake!"

"I noticed that already. What's going on?"

Rebekah hurried over and helped her down into a rocking chair. Great. She was turning into an old woman now.

"We're fueling up all our vehicles. That Humvee there is going to go on a patrol to find these Provisional Government jackwagons and the other three trucks are heading to Farmville for the meeting."

"Meeting?"

"Yeah, the big council of the towns."

"Start from the beginning. What's this council?"

"Well, last week we got an invitation from Farmville to go to this council of all the surviving towns. We're taking fifteen people in three trucks."

"Who's going?"

"Well, Alex and Lisa are going. Cass and Jason are staying."

"Jason?"

"The big fellow that saved your life."

"Oh."

She remembered now. The past week had been a little confusing.

"What's this meeting about?" Alma asked.

"Trade, mutual defense, borders."

"Sounds fun."

"You bet it will be! I can't wait to see other survivors. I hope there'll be a cute Jewish guy...or at least rabbi."

"When you heading out?"

"In an hour or so. Want me to go get Alex?"

"Sure."

Rebekah hurried off and ran over to where Alex was organizing supplies for the trip. She saw Alex's head shoot up and him and Lisa quickly walked over to the porch. Alex walked up the steps and leaned up against a pillar. Lisa was right beside him.

"How you feeling, Sis?"

"Peachy. You heading out to some post apocalyptic United Nations?"

"It's a start. We need to trade for things we can't get or make."

"Like what?"

"Glass, medicine, ammo."

"And the Provisional guys?"

"We're going to talk about them too. Jason mapped out their location and strength."

"Where is this Jason guy?" Alma asked.

"He's over with the recruits," Lisa said.

"What's he doing there?" Alma asked.

"Training them. He's very good," Lisa said.

"Sis, you mind being in charge while we're gone?" Alex asked.

"I think so. Cass is staying, right?"

"Yeah, she'll be here."

Alex walked over and sat down on the porch swing next to her.

"You had me worried," Alex said.

"That's what I get for being introspective and crap and wandering on my own, right?"

"Something like that."

"Won't do it again."

"Good."

Lisa turned around and started to walk off but then stopped.

"Cassidy will want to know that you're awake," Lisa said.

"Thanks, hun," Alex said.

"Now it's my turn to tell you to be careful," Alma said.

"I will be. Lisa and Rebekah are coming with me. Adam is as well but Jen's staying here. Keep your eyes open. I don't want the Provisional Fascists sneaking up on you."

"We'll keep lookouts and send out patrols," she said.

Then Cassidy came running into view. She was holding down her cowboy hat as she approached the house. She stomped up onto the porch and threw her arms around Alma.

"Bout time you woke up, girl!" Cass said, almost smothering her.

"Easy there, Cass. I just came back from the dead."

"Right. How you feeling?"

"Like I was shanked by a psychopath."

"Oh, yeah. Makes sense."

Then she looked back to Alex.

"How big a threat are these Provisional guys?" Alma asked.

"Big enough. They have military vehicles and lots of big guns. That's why we're having this conference, to discuss a mutual defense treaty. We can't take them by ourselves."

"The world's just ended and we're talking about war already. I was hoping for a generation or two before it started up again," Alma said.

"We'll talk about that as well."

"Sounds like you got a lot of work to do," Alma said.

"We're building new countries. It's not as easy as it sounds," Alex said.

Lisa walked up and slipped her arm under Alex's. A public display of affection from Lisa? How long had she been out?

"You're going to help me out, right Cass?" Alma asked.

"No, more like I'll be doing all the work for you," Cass said.

Alex turned to look at the vehicles and the assembling people.

"We got to hit the road soon," he said.

"Fine, go do what you gotta do. I'll be here," Alma said.

He leaned over and kissed her on the forehead.

"Take care, Sis."

"Take care, Bro."

Alex got up and walked over to the trucks with Lisa in his arm.

"They're buddy buddy," Alma said.

"They're engaged," Cass said.

"I feel like that Hand Solo guy from Star Wars."

"Han Solo. See? My nerd education is rubbing off on you."

She watched as Alex and his crew drove off to their conference in Farmville. That had to be the most unfortunate name for a town. Eventually the memory of Facebook will die out though and Farmville could take some of its pride back.

She knew she'd see him soon so she wasn't worried.

Cass relaxed in the porch swing and flung her hat on a nearby chair.

"This aint so bad," Cass said.

"At the moment, I guess it aint," Alma said.

They were building a confederacy of towns to stop the progress of a bunch of uptight politicians that thought they were still in charge. They had to form trade routes and find other survivors. Farms had to become self sustaining and civilization had to get back on its feet.

She knew it'd be a long time before they got close to what they had, but at least they were on their way.

Things could have been worse. At least they didn't have zombies, mutants or Cthulhu running around. (Cass had made her read about Cthulhu.) No. The biggest threat had been other people and always would be.

Alex was happy. Lisa was a soulless ice queen, but Alex seemed to love her so she couldn't wish Lisa harm. Nobody was perfect.

She looked over and saw that Cass was smiling as she looked out over "Town Square." Cass saw the good side of things and right now she was happy. That was something else of Cass's that was rubbing off. If only she could get Cass to swear then things would be even.

Life at Promised Land wasn't bad at all. It wouldn't always be rosy, but it could be good. They had a home. They had a family. And they had a future.

About the Author

Zachary Hill has written stories as long as he can remember. In high school he filled up notebooks full of stories. In army basic training, after lights out, he wrote using his flashlight and notebook. During his two deployments to Iraq he wrote stories in his down time.

Zachary Hill graduated from Southern Virginia University with degrees in History and Art. He taught English in Italy and fell in love with Rome and Venice. He has done illustration for Larry Correia's *Grimnoir Chronicles*. He loves pizza and Mountain Dew.

You can find him at his blogs at *Broken World* and *Minimum Wage Historian*.

Here's a list of other great
White Feather Press Titles !

Uprising USA by George Hill

Uprising UK by George Hill

Uprising Italia by Zachary Hill

Blood and Tequila by Colin Webster

Blood on the Mississippi by Colin Webster

Available on amazon
and anywhere books are sold.